THE STONE KNIFE

By Anna Stephens

Godblind
Darksoul
Bloodchild

THE STONE KNIFE

ANNA STEPHENS

HARPER
Voyager

Harper*Voyager*
An imprint of HarperCollins*Publishers* Ltd
1 London Bridge Street
London SE1 9GF

www.harpercollins.co.uk

First published by HarperCollins*Publishers* 2020
1

A catalogue record for this book is available from the British Library

ISBN: 978-0-00-840400-0 (HB)
ISBN: 978-0-00-840401-7 (TPB)

This novel is entirely a work of fiction.
The names, characters and incidents portrayed in it are
the work of the author's imagination. Any resemblance to
actual persons, living or dead, events or localities is
entirely coincidental.

Set in Sabon LT Std by Palimpsest Book Production Ltd, Falkirk, Stirlingshire

Printed and bound in the UK by CPI Group (UK) Ltd, Croydon CR0 4YY

MIX
Paper from
responsible sources
FSC
www.fsc.org
FSC™ C007454

This book is produced from independently certified FSC™ paper
to ensure responsible forest management.

For more information visit: www.harpercollins.co.uk/green

For Lisa,
who asked the question when we were fourteen
– and who always believed the answer

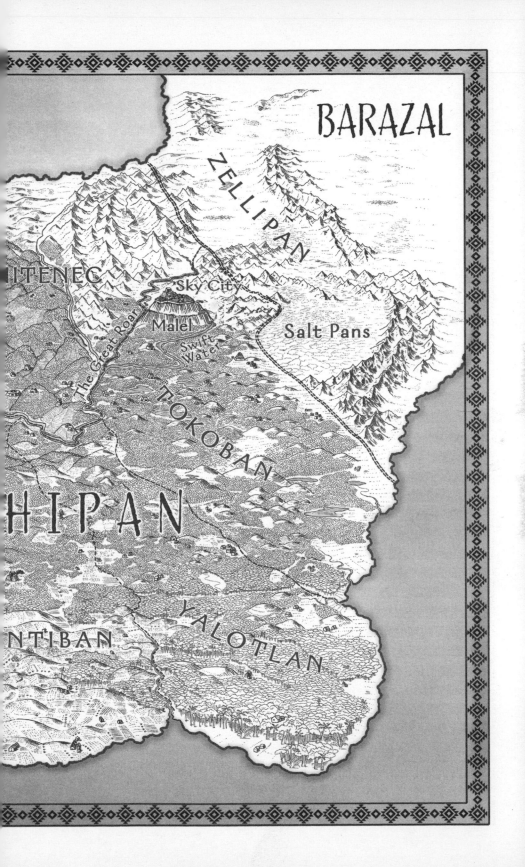

THE SINGER

The source, Singing City, Pechacan, Empire of Songs

The song is life and wealth and bounty from the earth. The song is courage in childbirth, strength in war, cleverness in creation.

The song lifts us and binds us, as beautiful and inevitable as my brother, the Great Star, in his endless cycle of appearances at dawn and dusk, and his regular absences to do battle with the lords of the Underworld.

As the Great Star always returns on the appointed place in the calendar, victorious as he rises from the depths to watch over us once more, so the song cannot, does not, falter. For the song is mine and I am its Singer. I take strength from my brother, and I give strength to him. Between us, we bring the earth into harmony.

And today, on the Great Star's 118th appearance at dawn, I enter the eleventh year of my reign. All you Singers who have gone before, you holy Setatmeh who send the rains that bring the crops to fruition, see me wax into my power and know that you are honoured. My song is but

1

an extension of yours, my glory but a shadow of the glories you achieved.

Soon, all Ixachipan will be ours.
Soon, it will be time to awaken the world spirit.
For I am the Singer, and this is my will.

XESSA

They said that the Drowned were the souls of the dead, angry that the living still walked beneath the sun, still breathed the air and ate the good food of the land. They said that this anger made them vicious and desperate, and that they sang to lure the living into death with them.

They said the Drowned were the ancient spirits of the land displaced by the Tokob people, who were the first children brought into being by Malel, and that the Drowned were slowly reclaiming the world for themselves, one life at a time.

They said the Drowned were those who had died of grief or betrayal, that their hurt was so great they clung to life in another form, their bodies as twisted and ruined as their hearts had been. That they would stop taking people if only they were loved. That their songs were laments.

And they said the Drowned were another branch of life, like the great jaguar and the tiny chulul – the same but different. That they were trying to communicate, and meant no harm, but their songs were irresistible. That they ate what they caught because it was in their nature to do so.

So many tales. Xessa had grown up with the myths and legends of the Drowned, the theories of Tokob historians and shamans and storytellers. She thought the stories were the biggest pile of steaming monkey shit she'd ever read.

Whatever they were or might be, one thing was certain: the Drowned were somehow linked to the vast, sprawling Empire of Songs that these days covered almost all of Ixachipan. To the Pechaqueh of the Empire, the Drowned were sacred, and that said all Xessa needed to know about that people and the lies they told of peace under one Empire, one ruler.

She cleared her mind of thoughts of the war against the Empire to focus on the battle to come. She'd left Toxte, another eja and her duty partner, in the water temple further uphill, ready to begin turning the water screw once she had the pipe in the river and connected the turning rods. The pipe's hard rubber coating bore fresh claw marks; a Drowned had tried to destroy it during the night. When they succeeded, they smashed the wooden scoops of the screw that lifted water uphill, forcing ejab like Xessa to risk proximity to the water to fix them.

Xessa squatted on her heels, bare toes dug into rich loam, her spear in the crook of an elbow, and studied the river's edge. A warm breeze tickled beneath her salt-cotton armour and the bamboo scales stitched over it; she ignored it, ignored too the flash of a bright bird whirring from the trees on the slope below, ignored everything but the water before her and the earth beneath her.

Her dog, Ossa, hadn't signalled; there was no other danger she needed to be aware of. Just the Drowned, then. Xessa's smile was grim. That was still more than enough for one eja and her spear.

Xessa ran her tongue around her gums and eased forward, dropping her knee into the soil and releasing a spike of scent – rich rotting things, moist earth, life. She ignored it the way she'd ignored the bird. The spear slipped from her elbow down her forearm to slap comfortably into her palm, warm and ready and lethal. Her movement didn't cause movement in response; there was no explosion of water, of snapping teeth and clawing fingers and long, black talons. The edge of the river was six strides away and seemed serene, innocent. Xessa knew better. She'd known better all her life; all the life she'd lived for this moment, all the training, the hardships.

Water was life and breath and plenty, and water was death and pain and fear, held in a balance like day and night, sun and moon. Xessa was a thief, stealing from the balance without offering anything in return except her sweat, her fear, her blood. One day, perhaps, her life. It was a fair trade for the lives of her people and the refugees from Yalotlan, fleeing the Empire's endless ravening.

Eja, the ancient Tokob word for snake: patient, cunning, and resourceful. Her brothers and sisters; her kin. Ejab walked the snake path, winding and oblique, stillness into movement without hesitation. The strike and recoil, faster than blinking. The life-and-death dance of sacred harmony, the balance made flesh.

With a snake's patience, Xessa eased herself onto her feet to approach the river when a double thump like a heartbeat shivered up through the soles of her bare feet and something black flashed in the corner of her eye.

Ossa. She took four rapid steps away from the river before looking. The dog jumped again, landing back feet, front feet, the impact on the hard earth easily missed were it not for her acute focus. She raised her arm, palm forward, requesting information. If she hadn't seen him, his next action would have been to race towards her and grab her by one padded sleeve, but now he merely pointed his nose and Xessa followed his gaze to the burnt-back ground on the other side of the river.

A spotted cat, its ears back, padding slowly down to the river's edge, wariness in every smooth, lethal line of its beautiful body. It paid her no attention, its gaze fixed unwaveringly on the water, as alert to its danger as she was. Xessa clicked her tongue twice and Ossa raced to her side. She scratched behind his big ears, tapped his nose once so he looked up at her, and then gestured in a wide circle. The dog bounded away, on the alert again for more danger.

The cat knew she was there, so it was unlikely it would attempt to skirt the edge of the river to get into the fields and orchards and lie in wait. They'd lost four farmers this planting already and there were more cats than ever coming to drink, coming to stare at the fields and livestock and people, their eyes hungry and patient and so very dangerous as they tracked the crowds of hollow-cheeked Yaloh who'd fled the warriors of the Empire of Songs.

Nerves pinched Xessa's belly as she moved slowly back to the water's edge, scanning its surface, the spear ready and the net hanging from the back of her belt. The Drowned had two targets now, both armed, both dangerous. Even as she thought it, one's head broke the surface. Mottled brown and green like the riverbed, thin ribbons of hair on its head like weed, it stretched a clawed hand towards Xessa and opened its mouth.

Xessa knew it was singing; all the Drowned sang and all their songs were lethal, an irresistible lure to any human who heard it. Like nectar to a hummingbird, the Drowned's song was the sound of life itself, or so those with hearing said. When they sang, people walked straight into their embrace, going to death like a lover to their partner's bed, and with less regret.

The cat leapt backwards and bared its teeth, but the Drowned had eyes only for Xessa, its arms yearning towards her, its webbed fingers and long black talons beckoning.

But Xessa was eja – water-thief, snake-cunning. Deaf to its song as all ejab were, whether through Malel's blessing or the shamans' magic. Its eyes darkened and it slapped at the water in frustration; then it moved closer to the bank. She might not be able to hear it, but the creatures were fast; it could still drag her into the river if she wasn't careful.

The cat had approached the opposite bank again to drink and Xessa saw the path of still water in the current, how it drifted in that direction. Still water in a swift current: a sure sign of Drowned. A second infesting this stretch of river.

The jaguar didn't know that still water meant Drowned. The one in front of Xessa sank below the surface, perhaps deciding the cat was the easier target. Meat was meat, to a Drowned.

Using the distraction, Xessa bent and grabbed the handle on the wide-mouthed ceramic pipe. She straightened, the spear in her left hand and up by her jaw, pointing at the water, and walked in an arc, pivoted by the joint in the pipe until it straightened and locked in position at the water's edge. The most dangerous moment. The pipe was between Xessa and the water, her body twisted side-on and the spear ready to lunge down over it in case of attack.

She began to crouch, lowering the pipe towards the river ready to open the lid, when the water exploded in front of the jaguar and a Drowned leapt for it, hands slashing the air where its head had been. The cat sprang away, up and back, ears flat as a single talon scored a line through the fur of its muzzle. It vanished, leaving the Drowned empty-handed and hungry.

Xessa jumped at the sudden attack and her arm came back in reflex as she straightened up, ready to throw or lunge with her spear. The surface of the river in front of her boiled apart and green-brown hands tipped with wicked claws reached for her as the second Drowned attacked.

Xessa had a glimpse of the round black eyes, the mouth open and filled with teeth like a piranha's, and then a hand grasped her shin. She screamed and dropped the pipe, the thick rubber-coated ceramic slamming into the Drowned's arm and breaking its grip, its claws tearing out of her doeskin leggings and flesh, and then her spear was plunging deep into its shoulder and its mouth twisted, opening wider, green blood gouting from its body. It twisted on the end of her spear and Xessa wrenched it free, whipped the shaft through the air and clubbed the creature with the butt end, freeing it from beneath the pipe and sending it splashing back. She dropped to one knee and thumbed open the lid to allow water into the pipe even as it righted itself.

A mistake.

The eja stumbled back to her feet, bloodied, her leg beginning to burn and throb and her arms and armour soaked with spray. She managed a single limping step before the Drowned launched itself off the riverbed again and grabbed the shaft of her spear in both hands, just behind the obsidian head. Xessa yanked backwards. The Drowned didn't let go and fear flared high in her chest as she pulled the creature half out of the water towards her. It was bigger than she was and, although its stringy limbs didn't look it, far stronger. One of the rare and even more dangerous Greater Drowned.

It pulled on the spear, jerking it perilously close to its own chest, and Xessa could've angled up and punched it through its throat and killed it, but she was off balance, her leg trembling beneath her, her toes bashing into the pipe and most of all shocked, confused that it had recognised the weapon as separate from her body, had *understood* what it faced. She teetered for a second, mouth open and screaming, at the very edge of the water, and then she threw herself backwards, pulling with all her strength.

The Drowned came out of the river amid a spray of crystal droplets. It flopped onto the soil like a landed fish and flipped onto its hands and feet, skittering towards her. A Drowned could survive on land for almost an hour, the lungs that fed its song sustaining it as it moved between water sources. And an hour was more than enough time for it to eat her alive.

It was on her leg now, its talons punching through leggings and skin, gouging into her again. Same shin, widening the wounds. Even the combination of snake-scale bamboo and salt-cotton padding wouldn't be enough to save her if she couldn't fight back; its claws would shred her armour and its teeth would open her belly in seconds.

They're clumsy on land, her teachers had told her, but this one didn't seem clumsy. Not clumsy at all. Xessa thrashed and squirmed, but it was anchored to her legs by claws and sinewy muscle. Its skin was slippery and she didn't dare push at it anyway: its bite would take her fingers off with a single snap. Instead, she stabbed clumsily with the spear, missed, stabbed again and caught it another raking slice down its shoulder, opening up pale flesh and green veins.

The Drowned reared up in agony and Xessa stabbed a third time, not deeply; the point stuck in the hardened plates that protected its chest, barely penetrating. Its hands closed on the haft again and it stared at her with its fish eyes, and Xessa would have sworn there was intelligence there, intelligence and calculation. A plan, even. As though it had allowed itself to be wounded to learn something about her. And then Ossa barrelled into the creature and sent them both into the water, a talon left standing proud in Xessa's shinbone.

No!

Xessa moved faster than she ever had, faster than she'd known was possible, flipping onto her feet and jumping knee-deep into the river, seizing Ossa by the scruff of his neck and flinging the big dog bodily onto the bank. He landed on his side, leapt to his feet and pranced at the water's edge, his throat rippling as he barked and barked.

The two Drowned rose on either side of Xessa like spirits come for vengeance. Their hands tangled about her legs, but one was weakening; Ossa's teeth had opened its throat. Still. She drove her spear tip at the uninjured Drowned and forced it back; a flap of her leg skin tore free in its teeth and she screamed some more, stabbing for it again. Red blood and green mingled in the current and fled downriver.

Even as it righted itself she jumped backwards, up and out. Her right foot came down on the pipe and she felt it crack beneath her weight, lost her balance and fell again. The Drowned came for her and her heels were still in the water, but Ossa seized the padding on her right forearm and dragged her, five strides, ten strides, out of danger while she jabbed with the spear and the monster held its place by the water's edge. She could feel Ossa's growls in his throat, in his teeth, as he pulled, straining every sinew to save her as she dug in her heels and shoved back from the river with ugly, desperate haste.

Another dog, Ekka, skidded to a halt on her left side and barked at the water, her legs stiff and her hackles raised.

Toxte would have sent her, and he'd be sprinting after her, coming to Xessa's aid.

The dogs stood over her, silhouetted against the bright sky, barking their warning and their challenge. Xessa forced herself to stand again, to brandish her spear at the water and unhook the net from her belt. One Drowned watched her, eyes just above the surface, and she whirled the net ready to cast. It sank, vanished, gone.

She waited another thirty heartbeats before dropping the net and pulling Ossa to her side to check for wounds – four shallow gouges along his right haunch, bleeding lightly. The Drowned venom coursed in Xessa's veins, but Toxte would have the medicine already prepared and kept warm over a brazier in the water temple, ready to pour into their wounds and down their throats.

Vision sparking sun-bright with venom and adrenaline, Xessa checked over the pipe – she'd felt the crack, but the rubber coating might have protected it and with Malel's blessing, they might not lose too much precious water before it was fixed. She was shaking now, badly, but she opened it at the joint and connected the long wooden turning rods to the thicker one leading uphill. Her hands were barely under her control. She closed the pipe and waved her spear overhead. She kept her eyes on the water, trusting that whoever Toxte had left in the temple would see the signal and begin turning the massive handle that drew water uphill. The Sky City would live another day, safe from thirst and from the Drowned.

Xessa wondered if she would. She vomited, Drowned venom snaking up her body from the wounds in her leg and into her chest, her neck, her head, itching-burning like the stings of warrior wasps, hotter than coals. She rubbed her face and mouth, smearing the symbols of protection and strength painted on her cheeks into jumbled incoherence.

Suddenly Toxte was there and the world tilted, jerking out from under her as he wrapped her arm around his neck and hauled her onto his hip and then, gracelessly, over his shoulder. She dropped her spear and tried to tell him, but vomited down his back instead. She had a glimpse of the dogs guarding their retreat, and then the venom drew her into the dark.

LILLA

When they were a few days away from the border into Tokoban, Lilla had told the refugees they would be safe, that no Empire warriors would have penetrated so far into their land.

He'd been wrong.

Now, ten days and what felt like a thousand regrets and recriminations later, he led the shattered remnant of his warriors uphill through lush, cultivated jungle towards the Sky City. Behind them, trudging in silence broken only by the intermittent complaints of exhausted youngsters, more than three hundred Yaloh came with them. They'd set out with twice that. They'd come with rations and blankets and ceramics, with medicines and seeds for planting. They'd come with hope as well as desperation, responding to the Tokob promise of shelter and protection. Tokob and Yaloh, the last two free tribes, standing together, living together, against the Empire of Songs. A dream that faded a little more with each morning until it left only bitterness on the tongue.

13

They'd passed a dozen small Tokob villages scattered through the jungle during their flight, each struggling to accommodate the hundreds of Yaloh who had crossed into Tokoban as the war penetrated ever closer to their homes. The Sky City was the only place that still had capacity, and every Tokob Paw that ventured into Yalotlan to aid its warriors returned with more refugees. Most came with tales of ambush or loss. Voices quiet, their mouths turned down, they spoke of kidnapped kin as if they were already dead. As captives of the Empire of Songs, they would be either slave or sacrifice, traded or slaughtered in Pechacan, the Empire's heartland and home of its song-magic.

Lilla shivered. He had never yet heard the song and had vowed he never would. He would rather die than live as a slave, his life and will held in the hands of another and the song his constant, unavoidable companion. Lilla would fight to free Yalotlan and keep it and Tokoban independent. If it was Malel's decree that he should die, he would go to the mother goddess without regret to await his rebirth. But he would not surrender his body and mind into the power of another. Not for anything or anyone.

It was a vow thousands of Tokob had taken in the preceding months, some even going so far as to tattoo their promise into their flesh. Lilla's promise was carved into his heart, and that was enough.

His surviving warriors led the way, for they knew the game trails and the safest route up the slopes to avoid the Swift Water that twisted and tumbled across the hill. The Yaloh warriors came last, turning often to stare down the trails for the tell-tale twitch of leaf or sudden silence in the usual clamour of the jungle.

Lilla's thoughts circled memories of the ambush like a cat returning to its kill, worrying at the meat of events, clawing at his decisions and picking them apart. Lilla was Fang, the leader of his Paw: the fault was his, and so were the deaths, but now, at last, they were in familiar terrain. The humidity had risen steadily until the air was thick as resin and just breathing was a labour. The Wet would come soon, months of rain and storm, deluge and flood, that would wash the Empire of Songs back into its own lands and swell the crops for harvest.

It would bring much-needed respite from the war, but not from death and watchfulness. The Wet carried dangers of its own, ones that ordinary warriors couldn't fight. But both the Wet and the war slipped from Lilla's mind, just for a moment, when they finally climbed out of the jungle and onto Malel's bare skin. Malel, who was at once the mother goddess, the world, and the hill itself upon which the Tokob, her first children, had built their greatest city. Up and to their right, still a few sticks away, the Sky City itself gleamed pale and majestic against the darker rock and splashes of green of the hill. The sun was high, picking out the glyphs and paintings adorning the city's perimeter wall. Within, a maze of houses and markets, great plazas and temples to Malel and her first creations, the Snake and the Jaguar, kin to the Tokob.

Outside the walls grew widely spaced orchards of fig, mango, palm and nut, and small stands of rubber and pom for practical and ritual purposes, and then rows of terraced fields below, seedlings just showing green against rich, black soil. Most of the Yaloh gathered here now had never seen the Sky City. Their voices were low with awe and wonder, and not a little relief. The Sky City's walls protected against more than predators; they were sturdy enough to protect its inhabitants from the Empire, too. Perhaps. Lilla heard their relief and felt it loosen something dark and hard in his chest. He was home. Safe. For a little while.

To their right the great bend of the Swift Water glittered and rushed, twisting towards them and then looping back on itself, following the contours of the land and its own channel, carved out of Malel's belly since the world began.

'What's that?' a child asked, pointing at a series of small, squat stone buildings running across the hill below the lowest fields.

Lilla followed her gaze. 'Those are the water temples,' he said. 'See those long pipes coming out of them? Every morning, they're put into the river so that up in the temples, we can turn the handles that draw the water up the pipes. That way, the people get the water they need and only the ejab have to face the Drowned.'

Her little face was round and her eyes were even rounder. Her finger wobbled as it pointed again, this time at the river. 'They . . . go down there?'

Lilla nodded. 'Every day. But you must never, ever, *ever* go to the river,' he added when the girl's mother scowled at him. 'And you see these markers,' he added, raising his voice for the Yaloh nearest. 'These mark safe distance from the river. Never cross them.'

They nodded and he waved them on, waiting for the last Yaloh warriors to make their way out of the jungle, led by Kux. 'We came the slow and safe way,' Lilla said as soon as the woman reached him. He gestured right, to where the jungle grew to within a hundred strides of the river and the two solitary trees that stood opposite each other, one on each bank. There was a rope bridge stretched between them. 'If we're running, we take the bridge and pray the Drowned don't spot us. Through the Wet, we'll build pits and traps and fortifications across here and cut down the bridge to slow the Empire's advance. It'll buy us time.'

'Why waste time digging ditches?' Kux demanded. 'We

should be in Yalotlan. We will make the enemy pay for every stick of land in blood, and that price will be too much.'

Her voice had risen as she spoke, and her Paw were responding, fire in their eyes and murmurs of agreement on their lips as they crowded close, knuckles yellow through brown skin.

'Too much?' Lilla demanded, his own anger matching hers, quick to flare these days. His warriors fought and died by the side of the Yaloh, and for what? For this slow, creeping retreat as they gave and the Empire took, stick after stick, inexorable as encroaching night. 'There is no such thing as too much blood to them. How many eagle warriors of the Pechaqueh have you fought? Barely any, because they're sending slave warriors and dog warriors from a dozen conquered tribes against us, making us spend our strength against fighters who are owned and have been corrupted by the Empire and its song. Only after they have broken us will the Pechaqueh themselves come, sweeping through Yalotlan like—'

'Let them fucking come,' Kux snarled. 'I will taste their deaths on my tongue and I will pull their Empire down around their ears. I will shatter their song so its foul magic can no longer hold the other tribes in thrall.' Her Paw whooped and shouted, silencing the jungle cacophony below them.

'Then you are free to go,' Lilla said, sharper than he meant to. He took a breath and lowered his voice, clinging to his temper by his fingernails. 'The decision is not mine, Kux, and nor is it yours. Our councils will discuss the matter; if they find merit in sending warriors into occupied Yalotlan through the Wet, then that is what we will do. And the Tokob will go with you, I swear by my ancestors. Until that decision is made, at least rest. Eat. Dance the death rites for those we lost, and for yourself as much as them.'

Kux stared at him, her dark eyes unreadable. 'You seek to delay me?'

'I did not drag you all the way up Malel's flank against your will, did I? No, I'm not delaying you; I just want to know you have grieved and rested, so that if we are to fight, I can rely on you.'

Kux snarled. 'I am the one fighting for my land; you need not concern yourself with me.' She paused then, and some of the fire went out of her. 'But I will dance for my dead, Fang Lilla. I will do that. And I will see you at the council meeting at dusk.'

She pushed past him before he could say any more, and the rest of her Paw followed her in silence. In an effort to calm his temper, Lilla stared into the depths of the jungle, lush and green and vibrant, living and dying in the eternal dance, the eternal balance. Was it Malel's will that her children fall to the Empire's magic and the Empire's warriors? Was it time for the first children to pass from the world and be reborn anew?

'No,' he whispered fiercely to the sun and the trees and the bright splash of parrots that broke from the canopy above his head, red against the aching blue of the sky. The breeze kissed the sweat on his brow as if in agreement and lifted the heavy curtain of his hair, tugging playfully and stealing cool fingers across the back of his neck. His heart twisted with an almost violent love for his home and his land, this place where his feet rested upon Malel's skin, where she breathed within him and he within her. 'No. She cannot want an end to all this. She cannot.'

If the Yaloh and Tokob fell, then all the peoples of Ixachipan would belong to the Pechaqueh of the Empire. And their song would infect them all.

* * *

The room was crowded by the councils of two tribes, sitting in a double circle. There was one space free, between Kux and . . . Lilla came to an abrupt halt, joy swiftly subsumed by a sense of dread. *It can't be him. He shouldn't be back this soon.* Perhaps feeling the weight of his gaze, the man twisted and looked up, confirming what Lilla's heart was already telling him from a single glance at those slender shoulders.

'Tayan?' His voice was hoarse.

Tayan scrambled to his feet and rushed into his arms, his expression complicated by too many emotions, before High Elder Vaqix rapped the smooth, polished stone on the floor in front of him. 'Sit, please. There is much to talk over.'

'Are you well, my heart?' Lilla asked and Tayan nodded quickly, his eyes running over him with worried intensity, looking for fresh wounds or hurts. 'I'm fine,' he added soothingly, 'but you weren't at home. Have you only just now returned?'

'I had to go straight to the shamans' conclave to report; there wasn't time to—'

Vaqix rapped the stone again.

Lilla tore his gaze from Tayan's face and looked over his head at the high elder. Vaqix was tall and stooped, his beaked nose adding to the impression he gave of an angry vulture as he hunched on his cushion, glaring. Flanking him was Apok, the warriors' elder, and Tika, the ejab elder, both sleek and powerful beside his gnarled frame. Lilla glanced back at Tayan again, at the formal blue band painted across his brow, and the second, slender line that ran from his bottom lip down the middle of his chin. The unfamiliar kilt was blue too – he had dressed in borrowed shaman's finery for this meeting and Lilla's heart ached to see him. He'd been gone for too long and, despite Vaqix's glare, which had physical weight now – they were the only two still standing – he stole a soft, chaste kiss from his husband's mouth and heard the tiny hitch in Tayan's breathing, a sound he knew as well as he knew his own voice. It spoke of relief, and love, and want.

Lilla had so many questions, but instead they stepped into the circle and sat. Tayan squeezed Lilla's hand and they held tight through the welcome of councillors, warriors, and travellers, and the formal invitation for Malel to witness the meeting.

'Peace-weaver Betsu, Peace-weaver Tayan. Your return is swifter than expected. Have the Zellih agreed to our request?' Vaqix's tone was formal, his voice neutral, but there was tension in his shoulders.

Tayan's hand became damp in Lilla's grip as the silence grew heavy. 'The Zellih say no, High Elder,' he croaked, the usual music stolen from his voice. 'They will not aid us against the Empire of Songs.'

'They say more than no!' Peace-weaver Betsu shouted as mutters rose among the elders. She was a short, stocky woman who'd come to council in her armour. She knelt on Tayan's far side like an angry toad. 'They say they have no quarrel with the Empire of Songs and no love for the peoples of Ixachipan. They reminded us that three generations ago, when the Pechaqueh suddenly began their conquest of the world, they urged us to stand with the other tribes and grind Pechacan to dust. To stamp the Singing City back into the mud. They know we look outside of Ixachipan for aid now because all the other tribes have fallen and we have nowhere else to turn.'

Her words had silenced the room and into that silence she laughed, bitter as venom. 'And they're right. We did ignore the pleas of the Chitenecah when their land was threatened, and the Zellih, even so far away as they are, did urge us to fight. While we cowered in our cities and villages and prayed for the Pechaqueh to look elsewhere, the Zellih called for war. And we said no.'

'You blame us for this?' High Elder Vaqix demanded, fury weaving through his voice. An echo of it stirred in Lilla.

'Yes,' Betsu said, 'but no more than I blame my own people and every tribe that walks Ixachipan. Pechacan, its people and its song are a curse upon the world and they have stolen the lives and lands of too many – of almost everyone – but still, not all the obsidian and jade we could offer will make the Zellih fight the Empire now. They believe them too strong; they believe them unstoppable. They trust in their hills and the salt pans to protect them.' She took a deep breath. 'We are alone.'

'You are not.' Vaqix's voice was strong as mahogany despite Betsu's scorn and the shaken expression flickering across his gaunt features. 'Tokoban stands with you.'

Betsu laughed again, its edges jagged. Lilla leant away from her sharpness. 'Then perhaps we will survive one season longer as a result. I am sure that will comfort the new parents among both our peoples. They can spend it deciding whether slavery or death is the future they want for their children and themselves.'

The council chamber descended into hostile silence.

'The Zellih also warned us that refugees will not be welcomed,' Tayan said. 'They are stationing warriors on the edge of the salt pans at the border of Ixachipan and Barazal, and they will kill any who attempt to cross.'

Lilla had thought the news couldn't get any worse, but at Tayan's pronouncement he felt the blood drain from his face and blinked, suddenly dizzy. At some point he'd let go of the shaman's hand and now he stared down into his lap, focusing on his fingers with unblinking intensity.

'*What?*' Vaqix shouted, all his composure fleeing. The old man lurched to his feet, the council stone skittering across the floor as he kicked it. Under normal circumstances, it would have been a gross violation of protocol; now no one even glanced at it as it bounced to a stop. 'If we have nowhere to retreat to, we'll be massacred. They must help us!'

'The Zellih elders advise us to either win or surrender,' Tayan said in a monotone. 'We will find no succour with them.'

'Then we fight.' Kux's voice was strident with anger. 'We fight to the very end and we make the Pechaqueh rue the day they sent their Talons against us. Once the Wet is fully upon us, if not before, they will send their warriors home and leave only enough to occupy those parts of Yalotlan they have already stolen. We'll outnumber them, and I say we show no mercy and we leave none alive. Retake Yalotlan so that when they return after the rains they must begin their conquest all over again. And again, and again, until they give up.'

Every eye turned to Eja Tika at the pronouncement. The woman's face was hard, her smile bitter. 'If we fight through the Wet, we will be facing both the Empire and the Drowned at their most active. It would be foolish in the extreme.'

Kux started to protest, but Tika glared her effortlessly into silence. 'But . . . we Tokob know our land, and we trust our Yaloh allies to know theirs. We can stay away from the rivers and ponds, and those areas that we know flood through the Wet. It would certainly take the invaders by surprise. It shouldn't be dismissed out of hand.'

Kux was wild-eyed and grinning, savage in her small triumph, and Lilla realised he should say something, either for and against her proposal, but if he opened his mouth he was likely to throw up. So he sat in stricken silence as the argument raged back and forth for war through the Wet, for no break from the stress and terror and eternal vigilance.

His chest was hollow with grief and fear, and at his side Tayan, peace-weaver and shaman, his husband and his heart, had no words of comfort.

Because Kux was right. Fight or die. Win or surrender. They had no allies and they were out of options.

TAYAN

Sky City, Malel, Tokoban
120th day of the Great Star at morning

It was deep night when the council meeting finally broke up. No consensus had been reached, and so Tayan had offered to journey to the ancestors and ask them and Malel for guidance. The councils had agreed, though he'd been able to feel Lilla's disapproval coming off him in waves.

Now, as they left the council house, his husband seized his hand and dragged him along the side of the building into the deepest shadow. The night was intermittently lit with braziers and moonlight, diffuse through building cloud, though Tayan wouldn't have cared if they'd been standing on the council-house steps at noon. He let Lilla push him back against the wall and slid his arms around his husband's waist as his face was seized in a gentle, calloused grip. This kiss was not chaste, not in any possible way, but neither could it go where they both wanted it to. Lilla's body was firm and warm against his and Tayan stretched up onto his toes to wind his arms around his neck.

It was a kiss of promise and welcome and more promise, heating until Tayan could feel his cheeks flushing under Lilla's palms, and his husband felt it too, one of those hands sliding down his chest and around to his back in a long, languid caress that drew a shiver from his skin and a low whimper from his throat. Lilla smiled against his mouth and kissed him deeper, pressing him closer, and after so many weeks apart and despite his exhaustion, he wanted nothing more than to bury himself in Lilla's hair and body and never come out. Instead, he broke the kiss.

'And you're really unhurt,' he demanded when Lilla sighed and opened his eyes. Tayan had to swallow at all the promises they contained, but the shaman stroked his back and flanks, searching for a hint of pain in his expression or a flinch.

'I'm really unhurt, my heart.' He winced as Tayan's hands slid along his chest. 'Ah, except for a small – love, it's fine.' He laughed softly and batted away Tayan's hands as he tried to lift his tunic and examine him. 'I promise it's not serious. I promise you can treat it when we get home,' he added.

Tayan huffed. Neither of them would be going home for hours. Vaqix had made it clear they needed answers tonight.

'There are other shamans, Tayan. Ones who aren't newly returned across the salt pans.'

'I am the one who failed,' Tayan snapped. He took a breath and stretched up onto his toes again to kiss Lilla's cheek in unspoken apology. 'This journey must be mine. We need greater wisdom than the living can provide. I am the peace-weaver; it wouldn't be fair to ask another to make the attempt for me.'

'Then I'll journey with you,' Lilla said, fingers tingling down his flanks.

Tayan smiled and kissed him again and had a deep, powerful urge to just keep kissing him until the world changed for the better. As if the force of his love alone was enough. Lilla seemed happy to try, too, and it was long moments before they came up for air. 'I need you here in the flesh world, love. I need you to watch over me and bring me out if . . . You know how this works.'

'I know I don't like it,' Lilla grumbled and pressed himself back against Tayan and Tayan back against the wall. 'I like this.'

Tayan arched an eyebrow. 'I like it, too.'

'It's dangerous.'

Tayan pressed his hips forward. 'This? Are you scared of me, warrior?' he asked in an attempt at sultry spoilt by a giggle. Lilla just shook his head, but the corner of his mouth turned up.

'You know what I mean. A journey now, when you're already exhausted . . .'

'Ah. So you stop fighting when you're tired, do you?' he asked and Lilla blushed and stood back up. Tayan didn't blame him for worrying, but that sounded suspiciously like he didn't trust him. 'You walk the jaguar path with honour, my love, but mine is a spiral and I must journey it. Tonight. Please.'

Lilla let out a noisy, resigned sigh and kissed Tayan's knuckles in silent apology. 'The womb?' he asked.

'The womb,' Tayan confirmed.

They'd stopped back at home to collect Tayan's ritual tools before making the long climb uphill out of the city to the womb. Unlike the two large healing caves dug into the bones of the city, this system was different: tunnels of dark rock leading to a small cavern made from a paler stone and flecked with tiny crystals. Malel's womb. The birthplace of the world and all the creatures within it, and the place from where the Tokob first children had sprung.

The birthplace of the shamanic magic, the shamanic ritual.

Tayan knelt on a square blue mat facing the rows of spirit carvings, representations of ancestors and the gods in their many guises. Carefully, he mixed the dried herbs and fungus into the small clay vessel containing the drops of diluted frog-venom, adding a little water before grinding them into a thick paste. He breathed deeply and set out the drum, the idols of his spirit guides and ancestors, and his paints. In the wavering candlelight, Lilla used a thin feather to draw vision symbols on Tayan's brow, black against the blue.

'Ready?' he asked.

Tayan nodded and licked his lips, then began the drumbeat that would bind heart and mind and spirit to the realm of the ancestors. Lilla nodded in his turn, made sure the gourd of water was at hand, and then rose to stand behind him, a familiar, beloved pillar of strength and protection who would guard his flesh. The warding of his spirit, Tayan would have to see to himself.

The drum was the rhythm of life itself, of Malel the mother, who was at once the world, its goddess, and the hill inside which he knelt. She was home and judge and the route to rebirth. She was ancient and new, mother of gods and all the creatures that lived upon her skin. She was life and death, the bringer of disease and its cure. She was all things, and Tayan strove to connect the tiny wisp of his being, brought to life through Malel's magic, to her immensity.

His spirit vibrated to the drum's rhythm and the walls of the womb seemed to take the sound and double it and feed it back to him, as if the stone itself breathed. When his spirit was prepared, he swallowed the paste that would spark the journey-magic. It was bitter, sucking the moisture from his mouth and clinging to the insides of his throat, but he fought it down, fingers never faltering as they tapped the beat.

It didn't take long for the magic to pull him into its grip; the flesh world began to glow and then disappear, the spirit realm, over and within and around it, fading into view. At his feet lay a wide trail, spiralling gently upwards. Innumerable others twisted around, above and even through it. Only one path was true: the others would take him to the Underworld, even as they seemed to lead upwards. If he concentrated, Tayan could see the flesh world too, his hand on the drum and the idols laid on the mat before him. But the flesh world could not answer his questions and so he let it sink and vanish.

Tayan changed the beat, calling on his spirit guides for aid. Something brushed his senses: a presence hot and volatile, a barely contained volcano. A huge black cat appeared on the path before him, tail lashing and fangs bared. Tayan allowed himself no unease, despite the fact that, of all his usual guides, this was the least predictable. Young Jaguar was often filled with caprice and sometimes with malice. More than once he had sought to trick Tayan's spirit onto the wrong path for his own amusement. And yet his power was undoubted, and if he chose to stand with Tayan's spirit and defend him, none could harm him.

'Young Jaguar, I honour your presence here and offer you my thanks. I seek wisdom from the ancestors on the spiral path. Perhaps even from Malel herself. Will you show me the way to them as you have before?'

The spirit guide crouched lower, as if to spring, his eyes glowing with inner fire. Then his lips covered his teeth and he spun on his haunches and bounded away. Tayan spared a single glance down at himself: the golden thread connecting spirit to flesh was strong and anchored within him. It would lead him back to his body. He set out after Young Jaguar, hurrying in the giant cat's pawprints. The spirit guide leapt onto a particular path and didn't bother glancing back; Tayan ran after him, stepping off one trail onto another, questing outwards with his senses and his magic to see whether he had been led false. He had not.

When they reached the Gate of the Ancestors, tall and imposing, blocking their advance, Young Jaguar let out a roar that knocked Tayan back a step and then vanished, not waiting for the shaman's thanks or offering. He provided them anyway, his empty body picking up the carved stone idol of the jaguar from the mat and spitting on it. 'My body and breath, Young Jaguar,' he murmured in both the flesh and spirit worlds. 'My thanks and adoration.'

The Gate of the Ancestors swung open and the path continued on through it. A single path now, the true path, for the lords of the Underworld had no power to confuse here. Tayan checked the golden thread of his life again and stepped forward. From the mists, ancestors began to coalesce, drifting towards him, their translucent outlines shimmering and ragged, motes of light swirling deep within their forms.

The shaman strove for calm as dozens and then scores pressed in around the bright, life-filled shape of his spirit with its golden thread leading back to his body. The ancestors lusted to live again, even though only spirit could animate flesh and the ancestors were what remained when a spirit ascended to rebirth.

Still, if one of them could rip the thread from Tayan and follow it back to his flesh, it would possess the shaman's body, leaving him formless on the spiral path, neither living nor dead and unable to ascend to Malel for rebirth or return to his form. Eventually, his wanderings would lead him to the Underworld and eternal torment. He would not be the first shaman lost in the spirit world.

And while he was lost, the ancestor would do its best to

live again, even though it was but a memory. A half-life in a hollow shell, Tayan's body stumbling around unable to communicate, food sickening in his belly until he fell down in the dirt and the ancestor was expelled with his flesh's final breath.

Malel, guide my steps and my words. Malel, watch over me.

'Ancestors, I honour you. I am Tayan, shaman of the Tokob, called the stargazer,' he called, drumming faster now, louder, to better tie his spirit to his flesh. Young Jaguar had been one potential danger; the confusion of trails another; but this was the greatest. 'I come for wisdom about the war, about the Empire of Songs. I come to ask what we must do for peace. Will any advise me?'

Anit, Tayan's two-times distant father, drifted closer, the shape and feel of him familiar to the shaman. While Anit's spirit had been reborn more than once since his death, the memory of him, the shape made of light and shadow, remained as an ancestor able to impart wisdom to his people.

Yet Tayan hesitated. Anit was one of the Tokob elders who had rejected the Chitenecah call for aid fifty sun-years before. He had been there when the Pechaqueh began their insatiable expansion and he had let Chitenec fall and its people be taken into slavery.

A low, disturbing chuckle rose from Anit's form and Tayan realised he'd been lost in thought for too long – and that the ancestors could read strong emotion. 'You wonder what help I can be, yes? And yet, how are we unalike, stargazer? You let Xentiban fall four sun-years past. You let Quitoban be overrun eleven years before that. Time's circle turns and old mistakes are made anew. How Malel must grieve for us.'

Tayan let himself hear the beat of the drum in the flesh world. His way home. 'Then your advice remains the same as it did when you lived: to abandon all others until the might of all Ixachipan is arrayed against us?'

The ancestor chuckled again. 'Perhaps it is time for the first children to end,' it said. 'What have the Tokob ever done with such a gift anyway? Shouldn't the first children have educated those who came after? Shouldn't we have shown them the balance so that they might live within it? No, perhaps falling to the Pechaqueh is best.'

Tayan's spirit shuddered at the words. 'Malel has a plan for us,' he began, more harshly than anyone should ever address an ancestor.

'And who is to say that that plan is not for us to end? For the Tokob to return to her womb and be reborn as a new tribe? Quitoban and Xentiban have both fallen during your lifetime – what have the Tokob done about that?'

The words sawed at the golden thread connecting Tayan's spirit to his flesh, filling him with shame and regret. He had argued they help the Xentib, had begged the council of elders to listen, but his had been one of few voices. Now their selfishness was returning to haunt them. The Tokob had thought themselves so noble, so secure as the goddess's firstborn, that they had ignored the plight of others. Anit was right; they should have been teachers and shamans and advisers. Perhaps the people of Pechacan would never have started down this bloodstained road if they'd taught them Malel's wisdom from the beginning.

'What of the Zellih, honoured ancestor?' Tayan persisted, vaguely aware of the sting in his palm as he drummed, hard and relentless, its cadence showing none of the alarm he felt.

'It is Ixachipan the Pechaqueh want, not mountainous Barazal and its scattered tribes. The Zellih know this and they have already refused you. Do not tempt them to anger by begging them again.'

'They offered aid during the days you walked Malel's skin,' Tayan tried and Anit's form swirled and blew apart, then coalesced a little darker, the motes within agitated.

'They did. They do not now. Not even Malel can turn back the sun and make it those days again.'

'And yet without Zellih aid, we will fall.'

Anit's shade dissipated again, and this time re-formed directly in front of Tayan, close enough to touch. Its hands rose, clawlike, towards the golden thread of the shaman's life. Tayan stepped hurriedly backwards. 'Revered ancestor, how may we survive the storm to come?' he tried for what he knew was the last time.

Anit was growing in size and density, preparing to fight for possession of Tayan's flesh. Even more were gathering, drawn by the golden light of life until he was surrounded by swirling blackness. '*How do we defeat the Empire of Songs?*' he shouted even as he backed further towards the gate. Ancestors blocked his advance up the spiral path – the way to Malel was closed to him.

'Only a Pecha can defeat the Pechaqueh.'

Anit made a final lunge through the closing gate and Tayan turned and fled, racing back along the golden thread of his own being. In the flesh world, he raised the ancestor idol to his lips and licked it, not having enough saliva for more. 'Honoured ancestor, I thank you for your guidance. Rest in your realm in peace and seek not to return to life.' His voice was a croak but it held none of the bitter disappointment – or curdling fear – in his heart.

The thread of connection grew thicker as Tayan drummed the recall beat and his flesh urged him home. He fell into his body and was lost inside it for a time, overwhelmed with sensation, with everything pressing in on him, the weight of his flesh and the rush of blood in his ears. He panicked as he felt his chest move, ragged and too fast, before remembering what breathing was. He concentrated on his hands, one drumming, the other still clutching the idol, observing the sensations from a distance before making cautious contact with them.

Gradually, reluctantly, the spirit world sank back beneath the surface. Sound and sight and smell returned, the weight and presence and solidity of his flesh cocooning him, holding him safe. Smothering the great expanse of his spirit and crushing it down small and tight inside until it flowed into every line and curve and corner of his body. His spirit; not Anit's. The drumbeat stuttered to a stop and Tayan placed the idol back on the blanket with a shaking hand, focusing in order to make his fingers unclench.

A figure appeared in the corner of his vision and although their movements were slow, Tayan flinched hard and then recognised Lilla. Familiar. Beloved. *Husband*. Lilla didn't touch him, instead waiting for him to settle and reconnect with his body.

Thirst was a predator chewing at Tayan's throat and he fumbled for the gourd; Lilla snatched it up and handed it to him. The shock of their fingers touching rocked Tayan, a contact he struggled to understand and one that wrenched a gasp and then a whimper from his throat. Still, he brought the gourd to his lips. The water was warm and washed the residue of the journey-magic from his mouth and throat, and by the time it was empty, he was almost himself again.

Lilla watched him with forced calm so as not to startle the spirit back out of him. The magic was weakening, but he could still feel his husband's emotions as if they were his own. He rode them, focused on his breathing.

'Only a Pecha can defeat the Pechaqueh,' he said when he had remembered how to speak.

'What does that mean?'

Tayan shrugged, his spirit sloshing within him, and then packed away his ritual tools with shaking hands. 'It means I take the peace-weaving to Pechacan and try to convince them to end the war.'

Lilla argued hard once Tayan was able to think and move again, but even he couldn't deny the logic and the truth of it. There were simply no other options. Someone had to go, and Tayan and Betsu had been appointed by their respective councils.

Tayan was stumbling by the time they got back downhill and into the city, twitches from the aftermath of the journey-magic in his eyelids and fingertips. Lilla wrapped an arm around his waist and supported him through the streets and home. Tayan glanced once at Xessa's house, which was next to theirs, but there was no candlelight this late and as much as he wanted to see the friend of his heart, he was too exhausted to even think about waking her.

So they unpinned the door curtain and took off their sandals and slipped inside and Tayan headed straight for the long, low wooden-framed bed at the far end, stripping off his kilt and tunic as he went. It was lazy, but he didn't even have the energy to wash the paint from his face or kneel to take a stoppered jar of water from the storage chamber beneath the floorboards.

Instead, he folded himself onto the bed with a long, heart-felt groan that had Lilla chuckling. The warrior padded around for a while without bothering to light a candle, swearing mildly as he tripped over Tayan's discarded clothes. Floor mats rustled as they were dragged aside. The shaman smelt cool earth and heard the thump of the jar being lifted out and set down. He needed food and lots of water, but his eyelids were already heavy.

'Come here, love,' he breathed, holding out a hand to the darkness, and Lilla took it. Lilla would always take it. His husband forced Tayan to drink, more than he wanted but likely not as much as he needed, and then wrapped him in his arms and pressed kisses lighter than butterfly wings against his temple and hairline.

Tayan slept, smiling.

Dawn had broken before they woke, and mid-morning threatened to be upon them before they extricated themselves from each other's hands and mouths and bodies, sticky with sweat and sweetly exhausted all over again. The council would be waiting for the results of Tayan's journey, but he stubbornly refused to contemplate dragging himself out of bed. What he'd learnt was important, but in the golden light of morning it didn't seem as urgent as it had last night. On balance, he was glad he'd got the journey out of the way and could spend a few more hours in bed. Or so he thought.

'Ossa! Ossa, here, boy. Come on, dog.' Lilla whistled, but the sound broke off as Tayan thumped him on the chest. 'Ow!'

'I want to sleep.'

'No, you don't. You want all the latest Xessa gossip, including whether she and Toxte have fucked yet. I don't know which of them I want to hit harder for stringing it out this long.'

'They won't have.'

'Bet?'

'You buy me snake on a skewer when you lose.'

Lilla shrugged: 'Fair enough,' and Tayan knew that although it would be expensive, his husband wouldn't begrudge him such a meal on their first day back.

Lilla stood and found their kilts, threw Tayan's at his head and slipped into his own.

Tayan huffed and dressed, but his expectant grin faded as no prancing dog and smiling eja burst into their small, neat home. He padded to the door and pulled back the curtain. 'Firepit's not lit,' he said, frowning.

'Really? Maybe she spent the night at Toxte's.'

Tayan chewed his lip. 'And didn't hear that we'd both returned home on the same day? No. I don't like this.'

Lilla's hand was gentle on his arm, and when he turned, he passed him the half-empty jar and then his tunic. 'Then let's go and find her,' Lilla said and drank the last of the water Tayan had left for him. Together, they stepped out into a morning patched with cloud, the humidity already stifling, and strapped on their sandals. 'Water temple?'

'Makes sense.'

They were halfway down through the city, hurrying through the plazas and markets and sidestepping shrieking children and squabbling dogs when they heard a piercing whistle behind them and stopped to look. A grin was already breaking across Tayan's face, but it faded when he saw the woman behind them wasn't Xessa.

Eja Elder Tika strode towards them, her dog Yalla prancing at her side. 'What wisdom from the ancestors, shaman?' she demanded, without even any pleasantries. Tayan wasn't surprised; Tika was elder because she was tough and well respected and an exceptional eja, though the spirit-magic did not ride her senses today. And at least this way, he could tell an elder what needed to happen and then go and find Xessa without feeling guilty.

'The ancestors left me with little, elder. They say that only a Pecha can defeat the Pechaqueh. As such, it is clear to me that I must go to Pechacan, to the Singing City itself. There, I must convince a high-ranking Pecha that the war must end, that Yalotlan and Tokoban remain free.'

Tika was silent, tapping a fingertip against her pursed lips as she thought. 'It is not what I had hoped, but then again neither was the outcome with the Zellih. Perhaps it is the only way, and I admire your courage. That is a long journey and a dangerous one. And I suspect the Singing City itself will be even more lethal. When will you set out?'

Tayan swallowed against the nerves fluttering in his belly. 'That will be for the council to decide, elder. I would hope for at least some days here, to rest and prepare. And . . . now that you are here, elder, can you tell me where Eja Xessa is? Her house is empty and—'

'The little fool tried to take on a pair of Drowned at the Swift Water three days ago. Toxte and the dogs had to drag her to safety and Ossa is hurt too. They're both in the upper healing caves, under Shaman Beztil's care. Your friend's good, but she's reckless. It will get her killed young.'

Worry filled Tayan's belly, along with anger at Tika's casual dismissal of Xessa's abilities. She was one of the best of the thousand or so ejab in the Sky City, despite having seen fewer than twenty-five sun-years, though he had to admit that this wasn't the first time she'd been injured.

'How bad?' he demanded as Lilla's hand came to rest on the back of his neck in wordless comfort.

'Poisoned, lost some leg skin. She'll have a pretty new scar to remind her.' Tika stroked the four pale lines that extended from her cheek down the side of her neck, reminder of her own tangle with a Drowned two decades before. 'But she'll make a full recovery. The dog too.'

'Thank Malel,' Tayan breathed. 'Please, will you take the ancestors' answer to the council? I need to see her.'

Tika nodded and then twitched, her eyelid flickering rapidly. She rubbed at it. The elder had been consuming spirit-magic for years to deaden her to the songs of the

Drowned, and the prolonged exposure was beginning to take its toll.

The pair hurried back uphill towards the upper healing cave dug into Malel's bones, inwards to the heart of creation, where the goddess's power was most potent and the shamans' treatments and spells most effective.

They skipped over the deep, narrow drainage channels carved in the centre of the limestone road that would carry rain downhill to the terraced fields during the Wet. They'd been designed to prevent a Drowned getting so much as one gill beneath water to aid its survival so far from the Swift Water and its many tributaries.

'Lilla! You're back!' a voice called and Tayan would have ignored it if not for his husband's answering shout.

'Ilandeh, hello.' The woman waved and hurried over, Dakto at her side.

'Blessings on you,' Ilandeh said, as she always did. 'And welcome back to the city.'

'I am glad to see you unhurt, Fang Lilla,' Dakto added. 'And you, shaman. I pray your journey to the Zellih was a success.'

Tayan was already hurrying on, leaving Lilla to make their excuses. It didn't matter that Tika had said she'd live; he had first-hand experience of Drowned venom and knew exactly how awful it was. He had no time to spare for Xentib refugees, no matter how likeable the pair was.

They had arrived before the last Wet, fleeing the Pechaqueh advance that had swallowed their lands and their people in the conquest four sun-years before. They joined the few hundred other Xentib who already lived here, the lucky escapees from slavery. Together, they'd taken over the dusk-side lower quadrant of the city, now known as Xentibec.

Ilandeh and Dakto were the last to make it so far north;

they'd kept to themselves in the jungles, living hand-to-mouth, until the Empire's push towards Yalotlan forced them to beg for refuge in the Sky City and there discover the last free remnants of their people.

But in the months since the Yaloh refugees had begun arriving, tensions had risen in the city. The two tribes had shared a border and there were generations of bad blood between them, and despite the fact they were all refugees together, and guests in Tokoban, insults and brawls had been becoming more common before Tayan had left to try to weave an alliance with the Zellih.

Tayan cared for none of it as he pushed his way around the edges of the busy market and up the wide avenue leading to the healing cave before darting in through the wide mouth gaping from the hillside. 'Eja Xessa,' he barked and an apprentice pointed the way.

Three days ago. Three days without me. Beztil was a talented shaman, but when it came to healing and medicine for his loved ones, Tayan wouldn't let anyone else touch them. 'I heard what happened. Are you all right?' Tayan demanded as he burst through the curtain into Xessa's room, and then signed the question after he'd touched her arm. Sometimes she would feel the change in the air when someone entered her presence. The scent of rain, or just the awareness of another person nearby would alert her, even if Ossa didn't. This time she hadn't noticed him pushing into the tiny underground cell.

The curtain moved again and Lilla and then the two Xentib crowded around her low cot. Tayan spared an instant to glare at Lilla before fixing his gaze back on the eja and sitting carefully next to her. He stared into her face, sickly grey with venom even now. The smile she managed was alarming rather than reassuring, and by her side Ossa lay in twitching, whimpering misery. Her gaze roamed over the three behind Tayan and she managed a grin and a raise of the eyebrows towards Lilla. The warrior nodded that he was healthy, which Tayan had at least managed to ascertain for himself that morning, and then flickered over the Xentib. She smiled again, but looked quickly away. Neither had learnt more than a few signs for the most basic communication, and Tayan knew their incomprehension made Xessa uncomfortable. He put his hand on her shoulder and squeezed.

A ripple of twitches ran from her scalp to her toes and he peeled back the edge of the cotton bandage swathing her from ankle to knee and sucked his bottom lip as he examined the wounds. While Drowned venom was rarely fatal in an adult, the medicine was slow-acting and it'd be a week before the burning in her bones faded and she stopped praying for death. Xessa's fingers clenched at a spasm of pain and then she laid her hand on the dog's head; he flopped onto his side against her flank, curled so his triangular skull was on her hip bone, tail thumping weakly into her armpit. Another shudder racked her and Ossa whined.

Tayan squinted down his nose at them both. 'You look like shit,' he said. 'Want to tell me about it? Tika says you nearly died.'

'Didn't though,' Xessa signed.

Tayan rubbed the back of his neck. 'Only because your duty partner has more common sense than you do. Two Drowned? You tried to draw water when there were two of the fuckers circling you?' He sat back and resisted the urge to shake her. She hadn't followed everything he'd said, but she understood enough.

'What other choice was there? We share the city with two thousand Yaloh now, plus our old Xentib friends. We need the water.' She signed it simply, with the fatalistic calm common to ejab, and one that made him clench his teeth every time he witnessed it.

'We've had early rain, in case you hadn't noticed. People are already hanging gourds from the eaves. We'll manage. And you're too important to lose.'

Xessa rolled her head on the mattress. 'Not enough rain yet. You know that. And it's not like it was in our ancestors' time. There are too many Drowned now; we have to cull their numbers where we can. That's just how it is.' She paused to cough. Ossa whined again, his pink tongue licking her belly beneath her tunic.

'Have any more Yaloh agreed to be tested for the snake path while I was gone?' Lilla asked, signing as he spoke. 'It would be so useful, even if they just did it for a year or two. Once the Wet is here, all the ejab will have to work harder to keep so many of us safe and the spirit-magic . . . well, we cannot ask them to use it more often than they do. The toll is already too great.'

'A hundred have,' Xessa signed and Lilla repeated it in a low voice for the Xentib. 'Tika's taking charge of their training and is giving them the magic one at a time. Sixteen failures so far. Two successes. And another eight who are deaf or partially deaf have joined. They only need a weaker type of spirit-magic or none at all, like me. It might eventually make up for the four we lost this last sun-year when the magic faded during their duty.'

She didn't need to elaborate. Those ejab, knowing all they did of the Drowned, knowing *everything*, would have walked into the river with open arms to embrace the teeth and claws of their enemy. Tayan shivered and the rock walls seemed to grow colder and tighter around them.

Ten thousand Tokob kept safe by the efforts of one thousand ejab. *And now two thousand Yaloh to add to the burden.*

Every problem seemed bigger than the last. *We're losing two wars, not just one. We're losing everything.*

Still, a hundred Yaloh volunteers showed a huge shift in their guests' thinking. Before fleeing to Tokoban, the Yaloh had lived in small, independent villages of no more than a hundred or so. They had gathered water exclusively from bamboo and water vines, which they cultivated in dense stands around their homes. They dug fire breaks and burnt back the forest half a stick from the edge of any water source, a warning not to approach within hearing distance. It was rare for a Yalotl to come to the Sky City and ask to take the snake path. If a drought came, they had always preferred to trade with the Tokob for the services of an eja – and to pay a stiff price in meat and jewellery – rather than take the risk themselves. Until now, anyway.

'What did Eja Elder Tika have to say about what happened to you?' Tayan asked.

Xessa grimaced. 'That I'm going to get myself killed sooner rather than later if I'm not more careful. Not that there's anything more I can do. Too many people, too many Drowned, not enough ejab. And it's getting worse. Tika wants us doubling up whenever we can, but . . .' Her hands fell still.

'But there simply aren't enough of you, and it takes time to recover from the spirit-magic.'

Xessa shrugged and nodded as a grimace twisted her lips. Sweat popped out on her brow; she'd need to rest soon. *And she doesn't need me making her more worried,* Tayan reminded himself. He started to stand up.

'Why don't more of your people become ejab?' Ilandeh asked. 'Your warriors, at least, who already know how to fight? Why not ask them?'

'Our people choose their own paths and there's no shame

42

in that,' Lilla said, his voice sharp. 'We won't start forcing them to take on one of the most dangerous tasks in our society. If we were like that, we'd have asked you to try the spirit-magic by now and sent you off to the river with a spear and a net.'

The Xentib looked away hastily and Tayan tried to feel some sympathy for them, but it was hard. They were good people and good friends, but they'd arrived with nothing and while Dakto was a decent fighter and Ilandeh could weave, neither had made a huge contribution to the city that had fed, housed and clothed them for most of a year.

'That said, a lot of our people take the test, myself included. I spent my childhood convinced Malel had put me in the world to walk the snake path. When I was old enough, a shaman gave me and the other candidates the spirit-magic. I was so excited at the prospect of the spirits deadening me to the Drowned's call. And it worked – at first.'

Lilla fell silent and Tayan realised Xessa was watching the warrior. 'Can you see his lips?' he signed and she nodded.

'What happened then?' she asked, even though she knew the story. It was important the Xentib understood why the snake path was not stepped upon lightly. Tayan shifted on the bed so he could see the rest of the room's occupants. Lilla gave him a wan smile. Ilandeh and Dakto were silent, rapt.

Lilla signed as he spoke. 'I heard the spirits. A sort of high, ululating whine. It was all I could hear, just that, and I was so happy, because it was working. I was going to be eja.' He paused and bitterness chased regret across a face too gentle to be a warrior's. 'But then it changed. I could see the spirits too, not just hear them, and they weren't friendly. They were angry.'

'What did they look like?' Ilandeh asked and Tayan translated for Xessa.

Lilla shuddered and met the shaman's eyes. 'Awful,' he whispered and Tayan nodded. While his journeys were mostly spent with ancestors and familiar guides, he'd encountered enough wild spirits in his time to have a healthy respect for both their abilities and the terror and awe they inspired.

'What happened then?' Dakto demanded, an ugly sort of fascination in his face.

'The spirit-magic lasts most of a day, and I spent those hours screaming and fighting things that existed only in the spirit world instead of being able to think and fight and draw water or kill Drowned in this world. And that was the end of my dream.'

'It takes some like that, love, and there is no shame in it,' Tayan said and signed at the same time. 'And now look at you, one of the finest Tokob warriors, your feet firm upon the jaguar path instead. Now the monsters you fight come from Pechacan and its dominions, and that is a fight of just as much importance.'

Lilla mustered a smile for them all, but Tayan knew him and knew it was an old pain and an old shame that he wouldn't let go.

Xessa snapped her fingers, drawing their attention. 'Besides, how would I have won any glory if you'd been eja?' she signed and the Tokob laughed, the Xentib looking on in polite incomprehension.

'So no,' Lilla finished, 'our warriors can't also become ejab, even if just for the duration of a Wet. It's too much to ask, even if not for the different fighting styles each employs. Stabbing a Pecha and defeating a Drowned . . . they're completely different. We can't – we won't – ask our people to face a threat they're not trained for, or to risk the spirit-magic failing or killing them or making them . . . different for the rest of their lives. And so we manage, as we have always done.'

'And if we're to continue managing, this eja needs her sleep,' Tayan said, turning back and signing to Xessa. He bent to kiss her cheek.

'But the Zellih?' she signed.

'I'll come back tonight,' he promised. 'I'll tell you everything then. Sleep now.'

Xessa scowled, but her eyelids were already drooping and Ossa was deeply asleep, paws twitching. Tayan stood and ushered the others out and they were silent until they were back under the open sky.

'Forgive us,' Ilandeh said with a grimace. 'The Sky City . . . well, it's beginning to feel like the first proper home we've had since Xentiban fell. We have friends here and . . . we're afraid. Of the Drowned, of the Empire, of what's going to happen. If we offended you, any of you, we are sorry.'

The Tokob exchanged looks, but what was there to say? They were all afraid.

'What about your retired ejab?' Dakto asked after a decent pause. 'They couldn't resume the duty?'

'No,' Tayan said and there was an edge in his voice. He was tired, he was worried, and the Xentib endless curiosity scraped at him. He was self-aware enough to know he had the same effect on others, but today he didn't feel like being charitable.

'For most, the magic eventually opens a permanent channel between the eja and the spirit world. They give up the duty only when the spirits force them to, when they can't stand the magic any more and their hearts and thoughts are permanently changed. We honour them and care for them, for they are living testimonies to sacrifice – their lives for ours – but to welcome the spirits now would likely kill them before they even reached the Swift Water. After a lifetime of sacrifice, who would ask them to give even more?'

Tayan's heart was hurting as they reached the breeze and sunlight and bustle of the upper market again. 'It was nice to see you both,' Lilla said, as ever reading his husband's mood perfectly, 'but I'm afraid we are both still tired from our travels.'

When the Xentib had said their farewells and vanished into the market, Lilla wrapped big arms around Tayan's shoulders and pressed a kiss to his hair. 'Let's go back to bed,' he murmured. 'I just want to forget about the world for a while.'

'Mm. Don't forget my snake on a skewer, though,' Tayan said into his neck.

'What? You didn't even ask her about Toxte,' Lilla grumbled. 'That bet is—'

'You really think if they'd started fucking in the last few weeks that he'd be anywhere but at her sickbed? You've just propositioned your innocent, unworldly husband in the middle of the day, after all. Which is scandalous, by the way. I am shocked. Really very shocked.'

'Yes, I can tell,' Lilla muttered as Tayan's hands stroked down his hips. Tayan smiled and stretched up for a kiss, and then took his hand and led him home through the market and past the food vendors until Lilla laughingly gave in and bought them both snake on a skewer.

They ate it in bed.

ENET

The source, Singing City, Pechacan, Empire of Songs
122nd day of the Great Star at morning

The song was a brassy, contented rumble today, stroking along the nerves of every citizen who heard it, its ceaseless melody rippling through hearts and minds and bones and uniting them all in glory. Purpose. Triumph.

The song was their magic, their strength, never ending; it whispered its harmonies into the spirits of every person within the Empire's bounds, from full-blood Pecha to the lowest slave. It was a sound that Enet had heard every day since her first breath, that made her not only who she was but part of a greater whole. For the song was eternal and soon would be heard across all Ixachipan to the Singer's glory and the Empire's triumph. And then, finally, they would have peace in which to attempt the great work – the waking of the world spirit.

Enet lay among pillows with the Singer, her smooth skin lightly sheened with sweat. Beside her, the faintly iridescent glow in the Singer's own skin was fading as satiation took

47

over from urgency. Enet smiled to herself, a small and secret smile, and trailed her fingers over his lower belly; he twitched and growled, and she laughed. Laughed, but stopped the caress. Best not to rouse his ire so soon after his lust.

'Eleven years, holy lord, since the magic passed into you and raised you to greatness,' she murmured. 'How much you have accomplished in that time. And how your strength yet waxes. Surely you will be remembered as one of our might-iest Singers.' The Singer didn't respond. '*The* greatest,' Enet whispered and caught the hitch in his breath. Ah.

'Because of you, Tokoban and Yalotlan will be brought under the song. Because of you, Ixachipan will know peace.' She leant forward to kiss his ear and breathed the next words. 'Because of you, the world spirit will awaken.'

'And I will be its eternal consort,' the Singer murmured. He stared at the bright murals painted on the ceiling, seeming to speak only to himself. 'The god at its side, the vessel for its will. Forever.'

'Yes,' Enet said. 'Forever.' Awe and fidelity filled her to the brim. She had a child with this man; her place, too, was guaranteed. She would make sure of it.

'You are thinking,' the Singer began, scowling at her. 'I can't quite . . . tell me your thoughts.'

She leant up on her elbow and gave him a lazy smile. 'Holy lord, it is not easy to think of anything when you have brought me such pleasure.' His scowl remained, but it was tempered with a smirk. Still, he waited for an answer. 'I was thinking of the stories my body slave told me when I was a girl. She said the earliest Singers didn't ascend to godhood, holy lord. She said that, before we truly understood the magic of the songstone and the world spirit's will, they remained mortal and died as mortals. It saddened me, to think of their great sacrifices going unrewarded.'

'Heresy,' the Singer grunted. 'We have always ascended. We always will. We become the highest expression of our nature. Instead of controlling the song, we go deeper, further, into it. We become song. To say otherwise is to court disaster.'

The Singer rolled towards her and examined her from beneath heavy lids. His eyes, though, were sharp. Sharper than most gave him credit for. He was tall and broad, heavy in the shoulders and arms and sculpted by the song-magic that suffused his ordinary features and strong jaw with divinity, until he was as far above mortals as the pyramid's songstone cap was above the earth.

The magic didn't glow in him now that his desires, as ever heightened by the song itself, were sated. Still, Enet allowed herself to be overcome by the power of him lying beside her, by her proximity to glory. 'To wonder such things as a child is barely acceptable,' he said, bringing her thoughts back to the conversation. 'To raise them now is blasphemy, and to do so here, in the very source of the song itself, in my presence . . . Should I have you punished, Enet, Spear of the City?'

Enet smiled wickedly. 'As the great Singer desires,' she murmured. 'And such desires he has. Of course, I but make idle conversation. Our son asked me for some old tales this morning and those sprang to mind. I think I first heard them when I was about his age. But of course, holy lord, I shall accept your punishment with due humility.' There was another layer to the story she'd been told as a child, but she didn't so much as acknowledge it in the depths of her mind, let alone speak it aloud.

Singer Xac grunted again. 'You've never been humble in your life,' he said, but there was the tiniest smile at the corner of his mouth. Enet let out a silent breath that her gamble had paid off. The Singer's moods changed faster than a hawk's stoop and there'd been a chance, just a breath of a chance, that he would have ordered her punished for her arrogance. *Despite the truth of it.* 'I hope you at least killed the slave.'

'Not quite,' Enet said and pointed to the old woman who knelt at the far wall in the shadow of Nara, leader of the Singer's personal bodyguards – the Chorus. 'We removed her tongue though, so that she could not repeat such foulness.' She made a noose from the Singer's long hair and looped it around her own throat; then she leant in for a lingering kiss that would stir his song-given desires again.

'They are strange stories though, are they not?' she breathed against his mouth as his hand grabbed her shoulder with bruising force.

'Enough,' the Singer snarled. 'Enough talk. It is impossible. Singers are gods and ascend as gods. Those they take with them become divine, too.'

'Impossible,' Enet agreed, the word blurred against her mouth as the Singer kissed her again, intent once more upon her body.

'Perhaps I will put a child in you this time,' he muttered against her throat.

Enet's insides clenched. 'We already have Pikte, holy lord. A finer son you could not hope for. And your first song-born.' He had other children, at least four that she knew of from before he became Singer, and more since, but Pikte occupied that special, sacred space of the first born from his divinity.

The Singer paused, leaning over her. His expression was hard now. Disappointed. 'One child. One.'

Enet affected a careless laugh and put her hands on his hips, coaxing him forwards. He resisted. 'I am Spear of the City, holy lord. I administrate your councils, run the Choosers and the flesh markets and oversee the provision of songstone and erection of new pyramids. My days are full of work on the Empire's behalf and for your glory. You have fifty other courtesans, great Singer,' she added when he seemed unmoved. 'Any of the women among them can and do give you children, and I know of at least five of the men who are actively seeking promising youngsters you might wish to adopt with them. Our time here together is for pleasure, not for—'

'You are a courtesan,' the Singer interrupted. 'My courtesan.'

'Spear of the City,' Enet corrected him with a smile. 'And so much more than a mere vessel for your seed.'

The Singer went very still and too late the words echoed in Enet's head, the tone of them misjudged and faintly repulsed, curdling with the choir singing softly in another room. Their teasing, faintly barbed banter was a spice to their relationship, but she knew that this time she'd gone too far.

Singer Xac reared up, lurching off her as if she were a week-dead corpse. 'What?' His tone was deadly.

Enet scrambled onto her knees and put her forehead to the mats. The quick patter of feet behind her and then the cold, lethal point of Nara's spear was pressed against the side of her neck. Heartbeats later the soft weight of her body slave crashed onto her back, shielding her from harm.

'Holy lord?' Nara's voice was colder than the obsidian. Just as deadly. The Singer was quiet for far too long and Enet began to sweat again. The slave was little more than wrinkled skin stretched over bird-hollow bones, but her elbow was jammed in the crook of Enet's neck and shoulder as she sought to protect her, though the absurdity of their tangle was more painful than the pressure. It was also deeply humiliating.

And then the Singer began to laugh. 'I do love Chitenecah

slaves,' he said. 'Loyalty is bred so deep in their bones they can't help themselves. Either that or she wants to fuck you, eh, Enet?'

Enet blushed but was silent. The Singer waved and Nara stepped away and hauled the slave off her back. She still didn't move. Around them, the song grumbled and then settled, and the Singer's emotions were palpable, swirling through the source like the breeze through the colonnaded wall out to the gardens.

The slave scurried away and Nara retreated to the wall, slow and wary. Enet still didn't move.

'Dancers,' the Singer called and she heard the slap of bare feet running into the room. A drum began, and then a reed flute. The Singer settled back in the pillows. Enet still didn't move.

The Spear of the City let none of the scalding humiliation she felt show on her face or in her manners. She refused to think of it, of how the Singer had left her kneeling there through seven dances, before finally dismissing her like a whore, not a courtesan. Like a no-blood slave.

Her own slave had a red handprint slapped into the side of her face and a bead of blood at the corner of her mouth. It was deserved; Enet's humiliation was not. With ruthless precision, she excised that thought from her mind.

She'd ordered the litter's curtains left open so that she could be seen as her slaves bore her and Pikte back towards her estate. The old woman laboured behind them where Enet didn't have to look at her. She let the Pechaqueh awe and excitement at seeing their Spear soothe her until the memory of what the Singer had done . . . She did not complete the thought, bending her mind to adoration of the holy lord. If Singer Xac or one of his Listeners was reading her through the song, they would find nothing in her heart and mind but love.

The slaves trotted across the plaza in front of the great pyramid which held the source, the Singer's temple-home and the heart of his power. They moved onto the Way of Prayer, travelling past temples to the holy Setatmeh and former Singers, and out into the city. The wide roads here were built of limestone and swept daily to keep them bright. They contrasted with darker stone of the temples and the councillors' great palaces. Enet had a palace here herself, owing to her position as Spear, but she preferred her family estate on the outskirts of the city. The air was sweeter, and there were fewer beggars.

Her bearers were swift and smooth, and soon enough they passed from the temple district into the markets. This close to the great pyramid and palaces, only the finest pottery and textiles and carvings were sold, only the freshest and sweetest fruits and meats. Choosers patrolled in pairs, armed with stone-headed clubs, their presence scaring off the cast-out and abandoned who tried to steal from the shops and stalls. There were few enough about this afternoon; the monthly offering to the holy Setatmeh was only a few days away, and those with no status or protection knew better than to fall beneath the gazes of the Choosers so close to new moon.

It both pleased and irritated Enet. Pleased, because she did not have to smell their stench or see their filth. Irritated, because the Choosers would have to hunt them down, searching the whole city and the surrounding fields for offerings.

The Spear put it from her mind and instead allowed Pikte to climb into her lap so that he could point out the market's finer items. The boy had seen one Star cycle since his birth – eight sun-years – and was as lively and clever as she had prayed for. She revelled in the simple joy of his presence, of his warm wriggling in her lap. She had no need of more children – another thought she cut off before it could form.

Pikte's status as offspring of the Singer made him both someone for the ambitious to befriend, particularly as he grew older, and a target for disaffected councillors or those ruined by the latest purge. In addition to the four litter-bearers, four warriors surrounded them, clearing the way and ensuring no one came too close.

Everywhere in this district, Pechaqueh in brightly dyed and woven kilts and tunics hurried, glancing up at the darkening sky and the coming rain. Among them were slaves in undyed maguey cloth, holding purchases or carrying messages, their eyes down and brands visible on their upper arms.

'Look!' Pikte exclaimed, pointing. 'Axib.'

Enet gave him an indulgent smile. 'And how do you know that?'

'Because they shave one side of their heads. See? And they're free, too.'

'So they are,' Enet murmured, distracted. Free Axib in the most exclusive market in the Singing City. It was . . . unusual. 'Guard,' she called and the warrior leading them looked back. 'Tell the next Chooser you see to find out what those free are doing in here and move them on. They're unsightly.'

'As the Spear commands,' the man said.

'They weren't born free, though,' Pikte added as they passed the trio. He pointed again. 'Look, their slave brands have been cut through.' He was quiet for a while, craning his neck to keep them in view as the litter passed. 'How horrible to be a slave.'

'And yet now they are happy and productive members of the Empire,' Enet said, making him look at her. 'Why?'

'Because they have embraced the song and become

Pechaqueh in their hearts,' the boy said obediently. Enet smiled at him and he grinned back, delighted at her approval. 'Have you ever been outside the Empire? Have you ever not heard the song?'

She shifted him in her lap again. 'I have, yes.' His eyes were round. 'Many years ago. The silence is . . . unpleasant.' The Spear changed what she'd been about to say at the last moment. She had no desire to terrify her son. 'You may hear it too, one day, when you are older. If you join the Melody and become a great warrior, it may be your destiny to travel outside of the Empire and hear the quiet.'

The awful, clanging, emptiness in the blood and body. The disconnection from people and duty and honour. The violent absence of purpose.

Pikte was watching her and she pushed away the memories and found another smile for him. 'There now, it is not so terrible. All our warriors have done it at least once, even the lowliest dog warriors. But before you are old enough, all Ixachipan will have been brought under the song. We are already close, are we not?'

'Yes, Mother. And my father the holy lord will wake the world spirit and put an end to hunger and disease and death.'

The Spear smiled. 'Almost,' she said indulgently, but the boy was no longer listening. He gave an excited squeal.

'Oh, look, look at it!' He scrambled out of her lap and slid off the litter; the slaves stopped immediately and the nearest slave warrior wrapped a long arm around him to hold him close and safe. Pikte didn't struggle; he peered around the guard's waist into the shade beneath a bright awning. In a cage of thin bamboo slats sat a spider monkey, young and small and depressed, one tiny paw curled around a bar. 'I'm going to look closer,' he said, with the unconscious authority of someone who had never been refused a request by a slave and never would be. The guard looked to Enet and she flicked her fingers at them. Pikte wriggled with impatience, and the warrior released him, following closely as the boy scampered into the shade.

The merchant approached, a Pecha of course, and well enough dressed. 'Under the song, high one.'

'Under the song,' Enet said. 'My son likes the monkey.'

'Ah, a fine specimen, brought from the forests in Quitoban only a moon ago. Young enough to tame. Healthy too – a young male. They make good pets, high one.'

'It comes with the cage?'

'Of course, and a fine deerskin collar and tether. Already I have trained him to sit on my shoulder. May I demonstrate for the honoured child?'

'If it bites my son, I will take everything you own and cast you onto the streets for the Choosers and flesh-merchants to fight over.'

The vendor blanched but managed a low, bobbing bow. He sweated as he eased open the cage. The monkey came to him readily enough and he threaded a thin cord through its collar and then coaxed it onto his shoulder. From there it leapt to Pikte's head and Enet's guards tensed, fingering weapons, but the boy laughed in delight, standing immobile and rolling his eyes up as if to see through the top of his own skull. He glanced at Enet; she said nothing. Waiting. Testing.

'He is a fine little beast,' Pikte said eventually, nearly masking his regret, 'but we must go. Thank you for letting me look at him.'

Enet's heart swelled with pleasure. He'd been polite and courteous and restrained, honouring the Pechaqueh status without forgetting his own. 'We'll take him,' she said and the merchant jumped. Pikte gasped and whirled to face her and the monkey screeched, paws clinging to his hair and its long tail tightening around his throat. 'My slave back there will pay you. I am sure the price will be fair. You, carry the cage. And you, boy, will keep it under control on the journey home, do you hear me?'

'Truly?' Pikte breathed, and his joy wiped away the dregs of sourness arising from Enet's humiliation. She nodded and the vendor passed the tether to him and this time his thanks were effusive and accompanied by a blinding smile he shared equally between the Pecha and his mother. Enet gave Pikte the long, slow cat-blink of affection that was their secret expression of love and he would have run to her if the monkey hadn't been tangling them both in its tether.

They hadn't even cleared the markets before Enet began to regret her decision; the monkey stank and, despite his promises, Pikte couldn't keep it from climbing all over the litter and himself, or from chattering and screaming and tugging at the collar on its neck. Eventually, she made him put the animal back in the small cage the slave woman carried at the rear of their little procession. Pikte knew better than to sulk, though he flirted with the idea for a few moments before subsiding into polite silence. He was learning.

They passed through the merchants' living district and into the flesh markets. A crop of fresh Yaloh had come in and Enet had the bearers pause to inspect them. Many were still wan from the wounds they'd sustained in their misguided resistance to the will of the Singer and the glory of the song. It would have taken them three weeks to reach the Singing City, heart of Empire, source of magic. Three weeks in which they would have discovered the song and become immersed in it, saturated in its harmony and community.

She climbed out of the litter and approached the nearest, a woman whose eyes were dulled with captivity and hopelessness, who had not yet understood that within the song lay her freedom. The Spear walked up to her, two of her guards flanking her. 'Listen,' Enet breathed to the woman. 'Listen with your skin and your blood. Hear with your heart and your bones. Accept the song into your very spirit, proud woman of Yalotlan. Your freedom – spiritual and physical – lies within its ever-changing, never-changing melody. Listen, and understand how you will one day walk free among us, a proud and noble member of the Empire of Songs.'

The woman was silent, watching her, and for a moment Enet thought she might have got through to her, might have saved her from months or even years of fruitless disobedience or the protracted death of one who would not conform. But then the woman lunged, her bound hands reaching for Enet even though she was tied on a line to the captives on either side of her. There was a mass jerk and stumble and the Spear's guards leapt between her and the Yalotl. The woman was screaming insults and threats, meaningless babble as grating as the monkey's screeching.

Enet's warriors hustled her out of range, one clubbing the Yalotl in the face as he retreated, breaking skin and chipping teeth, but not causing enough damage that the flesh-trader could demand payment for her. The trader flung himself onto his knees and put his head in the dirt, for the insult had been done by his stock and was therefore his responsibility.

'The song is in you now, all of you,' Enet said, her voice loud as Pikte ran to her side, concern twisting the delicacy of his features. 'Its glory can be your glory; its fame your fame. Cast off the superstitions and traditions of your past, honour your ancestors one last time and then sever your link to them, for they cannot help and have only held you back all this time. Embrace the song, embrace the Empire, and be reborn in its image. I promise you will not only live, but you will thrive, if you but see our values for what they are: the future. Your future.'

'Fuck you, Pecha whore!' shouted the woman Enet had spoken to. Blood sprayed from her mouth along with the poison of her words. Her guards rushed back in to exact justice, the flesh-trader uttering a horrified little squeak, but Enet held up her hand and stopped them.

'This one is destined for the Melody, I presume?' she asked.

The flesh-trader grovelled even deeper. 'She is, high one, yes. All this line are warriors and will fight for the Empire soon enough. Unless . . . I could offer her to you for a good price if—'

'Holy Setatmeh, no,' the Spear said, waving off his words with mock horror. 'That one needs the discipline of the Melody and the kinship of warriors. The only thing she would do on my estate is destroy its harmony. Send them off at dawn; there's too much fire in them. Another week on the road on half water rations should cool them down.'

'As the Spear commands,' the flesh-trader said. 'And I beg your forgiveness for the insult done you.' Enet said nothing, waiting. The flesh-trader squirmed some more. 'May I offer you first pick of this stock or the next to make up for the insult?' he said eventually, as he must. He raised his head just far enough to see her nod, and relief washed over his features.

'I will take him.' Enet pointed to the man's scribe, a youth of perhaps twenty who had been writing the slaves' names and details in the record that would accompany them to the Melody.

The trader gaped, but it was too late. He could not tell the Spear of the City that she was mistaken, that the boy was not a part of his stock. He could not shame her like that, or bear the risk that such words could provoke.

'As, as the Spear commands,' he mumbled. He stood and the youth rose with him, fear and bewilderment smeared across his face. 'Serve with honour and do everything you are asked. Do not shame me, understand? Do not shame yourself.'

'High one?' the scribe whispered, and the flesh-trader's face twisted.

'Go.'

'Un-under the song, high one.' The youth walked in a daze to the rear of the litter, next to the tongueless body slave. Wordlessly, he took the cage and its tiny, stinking occupant from the old woman. Enet pursed her lips; the boy had initiative, kindness. Perhaps she should . . . but no. She climbed back into the litter with Pikte and the bearers lifted her smoothly and broke into a trot. The sky was a riot of pink and orange and gold, the sunset wearing its finest plumage, it seemed, just for her. She watched it as they exited the flesh market and approached the wide, lazy loop of the Blessed River and the wooden bridge spanning it. Her estate lay only a stick away on the other side.

'Here,' she said and the bearers halted again. She nodded to her guards and they surrounded the youth and began to drag him forward. Enet let Pikte lead the way to the gap in the stone wall bounding the river. The scribe began to struggle and then to scream.

'It is not time, it is not the appointed day!' he shouted. 'It is not new moon; you mustn't. *Please!*'

Enet raised her arms and Pikte copied her. 'Holy Setatmeh, you gods who bring life and plenty to our world, accept this offering from your humble servants.'

A single holy Setat raised its head above the water, watching them out of those wide, black eyes. A claw-tipped hand broke the surface and it flicked its fingers in a way so very human, a simple beckoning. A thrill of fear fluttered through Enet's stomach as it opened its mouth. Would it sing for her, for all of them? Would it call them to their glorious deaths?

'Wise Setatmeh, gods of water and of life, take this one in thanks for the bounty and the glory you bring us. Know that we revere you eternally, and pray that one day we will be joined with you forever in the awakened world spirit.'

She gestured and her warriors braced themselves; then they flung the youth into the river. He spluttered and surfaced, striking out for shore with flailing arms, choking and shrieking in an ecstasy of terror. The water god glided forward and snagged his ankle, dragging him back. The holy Setatmeh mouth opened again and this time it did sing, a liquid stream of notes that spoke directly to Enet's legs and heart. Everyone on the bank stepped forward into the shallows, her son included, all of them yearning towards the perfection of the Setatmeh voice, song within the greater song.

Hearing it, its promise, the scribe turned in the Setatmeh arms and embraced it and it wrapped him up and buried its face in his throat, its song falling silent and releasing those who listened. Blood arced across the sunset, crimson against gold, the very essence of life ending against the ending of the light, and Enet stood in the shallows and watched her god feed, her spirit yearning to hear again its perfect voice.

'For the glory of the Empire of Songs. For the world spirit. For the Singer,' she breathed, and under the words – which she meant with every bone and muscle in her – other words drifted, unsaid and unthought. *Glory. Influence. The right person to wield the song-magic as it is meant to be wielded.*

When it was done, Enet and her attendants returned to the road and the litter. The body slave picked up the cage holding the monkey, the bearers picked up the litter, and, in awestruck, contemplative silence, the party crossed the bridge and made their way past the wide, walled palaces of nobles under a bloody sky and within a triumphant song.

Whatever had happened up to this point, the day had ended in song-given glory, and Enet would not forget it. The Empire was all. And all would live within its bounds.

THE SINGER

The source, Singing City, Pechacan, Empire of Songs

The song and the Empire that lives within its embrace are mine. It is my will that shapes the song and so it is my will that shapes the Empire. And my will cannot be denied.

The song is brought into being by my flesh and mind, my spirit and intentions. It is my duty to the people of the Empire, my greatest gift, my deepest honour. And the honouring of the song and its Singer is the Empire's own duty. It is my right and the Empire's truth. Inviolable.

Reverence is my due.

The song sings in their blood and bones as it does in mine, drawing us together into one nation. The song binds us in joy and harmony, restoring the balance when it falters, bringing peace where there is strife. The song is the question and the answer, the bringer of life and the bringer of death – of balance. Harmony.

The song guides and supports all who hear it. It can never be undone, unsung, unheard. My will cannot be denied. Will not be denied.

The song beats in the blood of a million people, lulling them to sleep and rousing them to the defence of their homes, succouring the fearful and strengthening the weak. When all the world is brought beneath its harmony, there will be peace.

When all the world shows the Singer and the song the reverence we are due, there will be glory.

The song is all. The song is good.

And I am its Singer.

XESSA

The Swift Water, below Sky City, Malel, Tokoban
125th day of the Great Star at morning

She was scared, but she was ready and the other ejab needed her. The *city* needed her. They'd let her leave the healing caves for home four days after her injury, and she'd walked painfully out into a day grey as an eagle's back and thick with rain. The Wet had come harder and faster than in previous years. It would put an end to the skirmishing in southern Yalotlan – unless the councils decided to fight on through the season, a path they were still debating – but the rain gave the Drowned an advantage, and so despite the lingering burn in her joints and the pull of stitches in her lower leg, she had a duty to perform, and so she would.

And Tayan leaves tomorrow.

The thought brought an almost physical pain. Her lifelong friend, so bright and curious and interested in everything, a skilled shaman and healer, was not suited to long travel along dangerous trails. His eyes couldn't see far into the distance and while he could bring down small, nearby game with a sling or blowpipe, he was no warrior. And they were walking, not just out of Tokoban, but into the Empire of Songs, into its very heart. Tayan's ancestor had told him that it would be a Pecha who ended the Pechaqueh thirst for conquest, and so the shaman and the councils were convinced that this weaving would work. Xessa prayed that he was right, but it didn't help the cold, hard ball of anxiety that grew in her stomach whenever she thought of her friend walking into that Empire and placing himself in its power.

Focus, Xessa reminded herself. The thoughts were a distraction from the fear tickling the edges of her mind as she stared at the river, but distractions were deadly. She frowned, skin tugging with the familiar and yet strange tightness where the paint had dried in swirls and loops that brought her strength and protection. Eja Elder Tika herself had painted the red and blue symbols on Xessa's brow at dawn, arriving at her house unannounced to do her this honour, to welcome her back onto the snake path.

Ossa was off to her right, a streak of black fur as he raced parallel to the twisting of the Swift Water, his paws kicking up stones and mud and sprays of water. She whistled and he gave her the head-down-rump-up all-clear. Xessa shook out her shoulders and wiped sweat from her eyes. The river was flowing fast, full of the previous day's rain, brown with silt from the thin soil on the uplands above the Sky City. The murk made it harder than ever to see the skin or shape of a Drowned, and the wounds in her leg throbbed in urgent reminder of the last time she'd been down here.

She glanced left and right along the length of the river. Three other ejab were approaching the water below their own water temples. Four targets. A one-in-four chance of attack – usually.

The hairs on her arms stood up and Xessa raised her spear,

trusting the warning of danger at her back. She leapt sideways, parallel to the water – not getting any closer – and spun to face the Drowned bearing down on her, poised to stab.

It wasn't a Drowned.

Ossa hadn't given the danger signal because there was no danger. It was Ilandeh. The Xenti wasn't blank-faced and answering the call of the Drowned; she was standing there with an anxious smile, halfway through an apology Xessa was far too enraged to read. She wasted a second, just gaping at the other woman, and then seized Ilandeh's wrist and began dragging her back up towards the fields and orchards and city, her heart thudding in her chest.

They got all of three steps before Ilandeh twisted out of her grip and faced the river. Xessa whirled again, bringing her spear up to her jaw, but again there was no danger, again Ilandeh didn't run for the water. The Xenti tapped her on the arm. 'I just want to see,' she said slowly. 'I'm perfectly safe with you here – I just want to see one.'

Xessa shook her head so hard the rings and charms in her ears and hair slapped against her cheeks, refusing to rest her spear long enough to sign a response – not that Ilandeh would understand anyway. Instead she pointed it uphill and jerked her chin in the same direction.

Ilandeh's face fell. 'But I want—'

Xessa click-whistled the guard command and Ossa leapt at the woman, snapping and snarling. Ilandeh stumbled back, face slack with sudden fear as the dog harried her, driving her up the slope. Eja Toxte was in the water temple: why hadn't he stopped her? The woman never should have got this close.

Xessa made sure Ossa and Ilandeh were well on their way before facing the Swift Water again; best just get it over with now that her stealthy approach had been ruined. She ran forward, scanning the water, scooped up the pipe and pivoted it, dropped to one knee and let it fall into the river with a splash. No time for subtleties. She thumbed open the cap and made it to her feet just as a Drowned struck, launching itself out of the water in a spray of foam.

Xessa leapt away from its slashing claws, twisted and struck back, but it had moved, its powerful froglike legs and wide, webbed feet propelling it further upriver and then out onto the bank. It was another Greater Drowned, taller than she was if it stood upright, its arms and legs sinewy with muscle and its chest, belly and lower back protected by overlapping plates of toughened skin. Its throat sac bulged with air, its mouth of needle teeth opening wide as it began to sing.

Ilandeh!

Xessa went for it again, vaulting the pipe, right hand throwing the net she'd pulled from the back of her belt. The Drowned skittered to its right, plunging into the shallows so that the net flared and fell wide, the edge sliding off a mottled green shoulder. And then it leapt.

Xessa planted both feet and set her spear, watching it come; it was in flight, unable to change its direction, would impale itself through the belly, armour or not. All she had to do was to brace and duck the claws as it died.

Ilandeh slammed into her, sending them both stumbling ankle-deep into the river, and then the Drowned hit them, mouth wide, hands and feet extended like a cat dropping from a tree. The three of them went down in a tangle of thrashing limbs and great sheets of water crystal-bright against the cloud. Xessa's senses were filled with the stink of it, the cool wet skin of it, the scrabbling, wiry strength as it struggled for purchase. She was fighting two monsters – one on top of her trying to rip her open, and Ilandeh beneath her, desperate to give the Drowned her throat.

By now, Toxte would be on his way, sprinting from the water temple with a net and spear of his own. She hoped he was on his way. She prayed he was.

Xessa got her right hand around the Drowned's neck and squeezed, shoving it away, but its claws were caught in the snake-scale bamboo sewn into her salt-cotton, anchoring it to her torso. It tightened its grip and pulled, yanking her up off Ilandeh while the claws on its feet dug into the padding stitched into the front of her leggings. Padding that wasn't going to be enough.

The grip she had on the Drowned's throat must be preventing it from singing, because Ilandeh was thrashing to get away now, not to give herself to it, but her movements threw off Xessa's aim and every jab of her spear missed, awkward at such close range. She dropped it and snatched the obsidian knife from her belt instead, rammed into the creature's side and sawed. Its hide was like wood.

She had a terrifying view of all its teeth as its mouth opened and it strained towards her; its breath, cold as the river, blew across her cheek. Xessa stabbed again, missed. And then Ossa, her brave, brave Ossa, sank his teeth into the Drowned's leg and began to pull, ripping the claws out of her padding and savaging its limb. The Drowned twisted to face the dog and Xessa tore its face open with her knife.

It turned back and swiped at her, green blood spraying, and she jerked her head away hard, fast, cracking the back of her skull into Ilandeh's face. The claws cut through the air just above Xessa's cheek and then the Drowned twisted again and lunged for Ossa. The dog released his grip on its leg and bounded out of reach; the eja kicked it off her, snatched up her spear and scrambled to her feet to stab it through the lung.

Ilandeh, panicked beyond reason, lurched up and yanked on Xessa's arm, spoiling her aim and dragging her away before she could kill it. By the time Xessa had broken her nose to free herself, it was too late. With a slither and a splash, the Drowned was gone.

Xessa pivoted side-on so she could see both uphill and towards the Swift Water from her periphery. Toxte was pounding down the trail, Ekka streaking ahead. The fight had lasted seconds, though it had felt like hours in that peculiar, stretched way common to moments of terror. To left and right, the other ejab had already placed their pipes. Water would flow uphill to the city and no one was dead. This time, no one was hurt. *Except her.* Xessa stared at Ilandeh with vicious, all-consuming satisfaction.

The Xenti stood with both hands pressed to her face and blood leaking between her fingers. Her shoulders shook as she cried and Xessa whirled her spear around and smacked it hard into the woman's flank. Ilandeh stumbled sideways, mouth a rictus of pain as she dropped a bloody hand to her side. Xessa pointed uphill; the woman fled. This time she neither slowed nor looked back.

About fucking time too.

Xessa turned back to the Swift Water and sucked in air as she stilled Ossa, smoothing his hackles with a shaking hand. She tried to contain her anger and failed; she roared at the water in defiance and rage and fear, sparking Ossa into a frenzy of motion. Ekka appeared in her vision and she sent both dogs out on a run to calm their jitters.

She opened the pipe joint and connected the mechanism, and then Toxte was there, his usual calm competence fled. His eyes when he reached her were spirit-haunted and wild; the magic was strong in him and a shock like this could send him into a spirit-daze – or even a rage. Xessa calmed herself – outwardly at least – and checked for the tell-tale hints of a spirit-borne fury building within him.

'Are you hurt?' he signed, propping his spear against his chest.

'No. Take some deep breaths, Toxte. No one's dead; the pipe is ready. Be calm.' She squeezed his hand until it unclenched and he laced their fingers together. A little haunting left his face, a little colour returned to his cheeks. He nodded that he had the magic and the spirits under control and she breathed more easily.

Together they backed up the hill as Ossa and Ekka stood guard near the pipe. 'Stupid bitch said she wanted to see the river,' Xessa told Toxte when she was sure he was in control – and she was herself. 'Drowned came up and sang and she nearly got us both killed. She slip past you somehow?'

The colour in his face changed rapidly again, this time flushing with embarrassment. 'I didn't see her pass the temple,' he signed. 'I'd never have let her distract you, I swear. She must've come the long way round.'

'But why?' Xessa demanded, her anger heating her again. 'The fuck did she think she was doing?'

'Xentib are all moon-mad,' Toxte signed. 'No wonder the Empire conquered them.'

Spite surged in Xessa's heart – she understood now why the Yaloh held their former neighbours in such low esteem. Even so, it didn't explain how the woman had got to the river's edge undetected. She watched Toxte watching Ekka. He'd never let anyone approach an eja on duty, but maybe the magic was beginning to slow him. It took some ejab that way, even young ones, furring their decisions, slowing their reactions and capacity for clear thought. Perhaps Toxte's time on the snake path was coming to an end.

'Any news from Tika on when the Yaloh ejab will be

ready?' she asked. Toxte chewed the inside of his cheek and it was Xessa's turn to blush – he could clearly see the path of her thoughts. His mouth thinned and she put her hand on his arm and squeezed an apology. 'I didn't mean it like—' she began but he was already replying.

'They've begun learning to control the spirit-magic,' he signed, the gestures cold and precise. 'Some have said they'll do it only until the crisis is passed, but the others seem to be embracing the life. They won't be ready before the start of the next Wet, so we'll just have to manage this one as best we can.'

Toxte gestured and they walked back up towards the water temple, the dogs following. He didn't look at her as they ducked inside, just loosened his armour and then began to turn the massive handle. Xessa felt the vibration through her soles and moved to the end of the pipe and the stone trough beneath. Twelve revolutions of the handle and the first splash of water spurted from the mouth and she caught a palmful and lifted it to her lips to drink. *Thank you, Malel.*

She touched the tears in her armour and the places where the bamboo was missing, but she wasn't even scratched, not this time. Still alive, despite how close it had been. That was one way to come back to the duty after an absence, she supposed.

Xessa watched the muscles in Toxte's arms flex as he turned the handle, a smooth, tireless motion. He'd braided half his hair back and she watched the pulse in his throat, steady and slow despite the effort. She tapped his arm. 'Beer later?' she signed, though ejab weren't supposed to drink when the spirit-magic was in them. Most of them did anyway – the magic lasted a day and usually by the time night fell, they were starting to get the shakes and beer or honeypot was the only thing that could stop it.

'You buy it, I'll drink it,' Toxte paused long enough to sign, recognising her offer for the apology it was. They were all worried about the increase in their duties, after all; Xessa just wished she hadn't been so thoughtless. But Toxte was fine; what had happened was bad luck, nothing more. The spirit-magic wasn't harming him. 'And lots of it,' he added with a grin. They were still alive and so was the Sky City and Xessa planned on celebrating that by getting disgustingly drunk. Then he gestured over her shoulder and she turned to see the first Tokob with their gourds and pitchers and buckets, waiting patiently for their day's ration.

Xessa moved out of their way. 'You all right here?' she asked Toxte. He nodded. 'I'm going to find Tayan and then the Xenti,' she went on. 'I want to be sure she's absolutely clear on what I'm going to tell her. In detail.'

Toxte winced and grinned again, but he waved her off. The water sputtered in fits and splashes from the end of the pipe and into the trough as he worked the mechanism. The city lived, though the Xenti would soon wish she didn't.

Lilla had insisted on coming along as well, and belatedly Xessa realised that she had interrupted them when they only had today together before Tayan left for Pechacan. Her narrow escape at the river had upset her more than she'd realised, especially being her first duty since her injury, and she was ruining the day for everyone else as a result.

Xessa told them she'd handle it herself, but by then Tayan was angry on her behalf. He and Lilla were closer friends with the Xenti than she was, who had to rely on others to translate for her, but that meant nothing to him in the light of Ilandeh's incomprehensible actions at the river. Now the three of them stood ranged against Ilandeh, with Dakto just behind looking wary and defensive. Ilandeh was stroking her left thumb over the inside of her right wrist and the small tattoo of a chulul it bore. It was a nervous habit and the eja was disproportionately pleased to see it. Dakto had the same tattoo, on the inside of his bicep, though his didn't seem to have the same power to soothe.

'Eja Xessa would like to be very clear that you understand what you have been told.'

Xessa switched her gaze from Tayan's face to Ilandeh's. The woman pressed a fingertip to the swollen, bloody mess of her broken nose. A shaman had reset it, but it was swelling up nicely and blackening both her eyes, too. Xessa felt a twinge of savage pleasure. Ilandeh's nod was a jerk and a stuttering inhalation. She cupped her nose again and said something Xessa missed.

'She said she is very sorry and it won't happen again,' Tayan translated for her. 'She didn't mean to put you or herself in danger.'

'And tell her to stop covering her mouth when she talks,' Xessa signed. 'Has she learnt nothing since coming here? Is she deliberately insulting me?'

Xessa clenched her fists as the shaman translated. She was too inexperienced to have been loaned out to the Yaloh during a drought but the thought of that now, of living with people who couldn't understand her, made her guts watery and her chest tight. She realised suddenly that she might never be sent into Yalotlan – supposing the war ever ended – for that very reason and the tightness grew thorns and pricked at her heart. This was her home and the duty was her life, yet she felt . . . outcast, even unwelcome.

All Tokob signed, because without it, those ejab who used the spirit-magic would be unable to communicate while it rode their senses and so their sacrifice would also be a punishment, an exclusion from the very life and society they fought to protect.

But the Xentib didn't know how to speak with signs and neither did the Yaloh, despite the tribes' close relationship, and they looked at Xessa as if she was different, making her uncomfortable in her own skin as she'd never been before.

'You nearly killed me,' Xessa signed so angrily that Lilla took a step sideways and then came back to pat her back. 'Never, *never* go near the river again. If you do, I will let them eat you.'

Tayan hesitated, but then he repeated her words aloud and Xessa watched with deep satisfaction as both Xentib nodded frantically. They signed 'sorry' to her, but somehow their attempt caused even more anger to burn beneath her skin, and so she squeezed Tayan's arm in thanks and strode out of the house, straining for calm.

It was nearly time to remove the pipe from the water so the Drowned couldn't damage it. Any distraction on her part and the encounter from earlier could be repeated – and this time with lethal consequence. It was enough – just – for Xessa to swallow the rest of her anger. Watching Ossa prance ahead of her and concentrating on the grain of her spear shaft against her palm, she stormed out of Xentibec and began the long walk back to the Swift Water.

Xessa's house was a single room, like most houses in the Sky City, with storage in the rafters and in cool pits dug into a corner beneath the floor and mats. She and Toxte sat cross-legged inside, Xessa's foot resting on the wooden rocker that moved when trodden on, alerting her to guests.

Ossa and Ekka lounged next to each other, big triangular ears twitching in lazy contentment. The jug of beer was cool and frothy and Xessa was laughing helplessly at one of

Toxte's jokes when Ossa raised his head and looked at the doorway a moment before the rocker jolted under her heel.

Xessa clapped twice and Tayan poked his head through the door curtain. 'Are we interrupting?' he signed with a sly smile and Xessa's gesture needed no translation. Tayan and Lilla came in, and, after a pause, Dakto and then Ilandeh. Xessa's good humour vanished as fast as the temperature in the room dropped.

'What is she doing here?' the eja demanded even as Toxte put his hand on her knee and gave her a crooked, encouraging smile.

Ilandeh knelt opposite her, carefully in the torchlight but not backlit so Xessa and Toxte could see her face and hands. 'I'm sorry,' she signed and Xessa huffed out a breath. This again. 'It was wrong to distract you,' she continued, 'and it was wrong to visit the Swift Water. It won't happen again.'

Her hands were slow and she bore a look of concentration rather than contrition, but Xessa understood. She flashed a glance at Tayan – ever the peace-weaver, it seemed, for of course it was he who'd taught her.

'I would . . .' Ilandeh tried and then paused. She swallowed hard and Xessa narrowed her eyes in suspicion. 'I would like to learn. If you would teach.'

'Learn what? To be eja?' she signed, though she thought she knew the answer.

Ilandeh looked horrified at the suggestion when Tayan translated and Xessa's chest warmed at it. 'To sign.'

Everyone was watching her. 'I'll be gone soon and for who knows how long?' Tayan signed when her gaze reached him. 'You need another friend. You do,' he interrupted before she could respond.

Ilandeh tapped the wood under Xessa's foot. 'Gift for you,' she signed, clumsier now. Dakto handed her a basket woven from palm and she pulled from it a long cord threaded with tiny, red-dyed bones. A charm. 'Bat,' she signed. 'For . . .' She looked to Tayan. 'Sight,' she finished.

It was as if they were all holding their breaths waiting for her to respond. Ossa rose to his feet, ears up and ready for her command. Toxte put his hand on her leg again and this time left it there, warm and rough.

Sight. So I can see fucking idiots creeping up on me and trying to get me killed?

'Thank you,' she signed instead, and only because Tayan wanted her to. 'It's lovely.' She held out her hand but Ilandeh smiled with delighted relief and scrambled across the mats.

'. . . braid it for you,' Xessa just saw before the Xentib fingers were at her temple. She sat stiff and stony until the charm hung in the mass of her hair with the others. Ilandeh surprised her again, pulling her into a quick hug and kissing the side of her face, before she hurried back across the room to Dakto's side. Together, they unpacked a stoppered jar and some leaf-wrapped meat and cornbread. Tayan appropriated her spare cups and they filled them with beer and portioned out the food.

'Please enjoy,' Dakto signed, and despite Tayan's protests – Xessa said nothing – the Xentib left them to it.

Xessa realised Toxte's hand was still on the bare skin of her leg. She put her own over it and squeezed and the look he gave her was hot and questioning. It spoke directly to the part of her mind that watched the way he moved, graceful as a dancer, as a killer, that watched the crinkle around his eyes when he laughed and how comfortable he was in his own skin. She swallowed and then managed an embarrassed smile, wondering if the heat in her cheeks was visible to everyone else.

Tayan flicked the foam off his beer at her. 'It's me you're

supposed to be paying attention to tonight,' he complained. 'Seeing as Betsu and I leave tomorrow.'

'That's why we're celebrating,' Lilla told him with mock solemnity and Tayan flicked beer at him, too, but they smiled at each other with such mutual adoration that it made Xessa warm. She had long since outgrown her jealousy at sharing space in Tayan's heart.

But tomorrow. Her childhood friend was leaving tomorrow, on a journey infinitely more dangerous than his meeting with the Zellih had been. She raised her cup to him in salute and together they downed the contents.

'. . . you'll be gone?' Toxte was asking.

'Three moons, perhaps,' Tayan said, signing at the same time. 'Depending on how fast we can move through their Empire. Thirty days in the Singing City to find someone senior enough we can negotiate with and get them to understand why it's in everyone's best interests they remain content with what they have. The Yaloh have reluctantly agreed to cede the portion of land that the Empire has already stolen in return for peace. And we can offer tithes of meat and gems, skins and obsidian.'

His body language was confident, even excited, though Lilla's jaw was tense as he watched his husband. The warrior shifted closer until his thigh pressed against Tayan's and the shaman broke off long enough to look up at him and rest his head on the taller man's chest for a second. Lilla reached out and ran his finger along the pale yellow marriage cord resting on Tayan's collarbones, its twin tied around his own throat. The cords were knotted with promises and some were hung with tiny charms that meant those promises were fulfilled. A life mapped out; a life shared.

The gesture was so strangely intimate that Xessa blushed and looked away, and was caught by the lovely planes of

Toxte's face as he watched her in turn, the broad sweep of his cheekbones and the heat of his expression. Toxte stroked her hair back from her cheek and refilled her cup, leaning close as he did. He smelt of sunlight and fresh sweat and smoke, the faint sweetness of honeyed beer.

A sudden twitch as the spirit-magic left his system and the beer slopped over the side of her cup. Xessa steadied his hand, her fingers lingering on his. When she looked up, Tayan was laughing at her again. She repeated the gesture from earlier and drank to hide a foolish grin. A knot loosened in her chest even as another tied in her gut. She was losing Tayan, for a while, but she knew with sudden certainty as her gaze returned, without volition, to Toxte, that she'd gained something – someone – else.

Warrior and shaman left earlier than usual for their own home and bed and privacy before they were separated again. The way their eyes had lingered on each other again and again sparked longing in her belly, and when Toxte, tipsy and laughing, said goodbye later that night, she surprised him with a kiss, the first against his cheek, the second grazing the corner of his mouth.

He blinked at her, hope and caution blurring in his eyes, and Xessa's belly filled with butterflies. 'Get some sleep, drunk eja,' she signed, her cheeks warm, 'and we'll see if you remember that in the morning.'

Toxte's lips parted and she couldn't prevent her gaze flickering down to watch. They curved in another smile. 'Believe me, I'll remember,' he signed. 'Though I'm not sure I'll get much sleep thinking about it.' And he touched her cheek with his knuckles, light as feathers, and then he was gone.

TAYAN

The Neck, Xentiban, Empire of Songs
140th day of the Great Star at morning

'We wear the peace feathers; we mean no ill intent or violence, but seek passage to the Singing City to begin a peace-weaving that will end the war on Yalotlan. We would speak with your Singer himself if that is possible; if not, then one of his representatives.'

The warriors surrounding them wore the tattoos, paints and hairstyles of three different tribes. 'You'll be lucky,' one scoffed from the rear of the group that barred the trail. 'Peace-weaving? May as well turn around now, little shaman, and scurry back home. We'll be along to take it soon enough.'

'Enough,' snapped another. This speaker, a woman, wore a long scarlet feather in her shoulder-length, tightly braided black hair. A frog tattoo was visible at the base of her throat, just above her salt-cotton. She turned back to Tayan and Betsu. 'Though the Coyote leader speaks true. The Pechaqueh have no need for nor interest in peace-weavings, and you would never be granted so much as to look upon the source, let alone meet the Singer.' There was a bark of mockery in her tone. 'No one meets the holy lord, and certainly not a no-blood, frog-licking, god-killing Tokob.'

'I am Yaloh,' Betsu said heatedly and was ignored.

Tayan blinked at the raw hostility in the faces of the warriors. 'One of his council then. You . . . you do have a council?'

The warrior sneered at him. 'Even they are too far above you,' she said.

'And yet that is our destination,' Betsu said, her tone even and far calmer than Tayan had expected after her last comment. Her mood had been increasingly unpredictable in the two days they'd been under the song, not that he could blame her. The song didn't stop, not ever. Worse, they couldn't even drown it out through music or song of their own, or through plugging their ears or shouting at the tops of their lungs. It was there, a constant, nagging presence, a slow insidious poison. And it was beautiful. Oh, ancestors, it was beautiful. It was what frightened Tayan most about it. The disdain in the Coyote's voice, and that of the woman, resonated within him. Who was he, after all, to think to negotiate with so mighty an Empire?

Betsu, it seemed, had no such insecurities. 'Stand aside. You are not even Pechaqueh. Our business is with your owners.'

As one, the group of warriors, at least fifty in number from what Tayan could see under the low branches and heavy rain, brandished weapons. The woman with the scarlet feather lunged forward; Betsu's spear came up in defence and Tayan bellowed and knocked it down. The Empire warrior's spear raked across his ribs, and unlike the rest, he wore no salt-cotton. He was a shaman. Fire erupted in his chest and he gasped, his knees suddenly weak, but he planted himself between Betsu and the enemy.

'Peace,' he screeched, 'fucking peace!' Hot blood ran freely down his side. Tayan tried to ignore it and the churning nausea and the sickening pain. He was fairly sure the woman had sliced off his nipple.

Either his words or the blood had had an effect, for the warriors drew back, their weapons pointing at the ground. Tayan shoved one hand behind him blindly, hoping Betsu wouldn't be so fucking stupid as to do, well, anything.

'We wear the peace feathers, and you have broken that sanctity.' The woman paled a little at his words. 'You may not believe in our peace-weaving, but you understand peace feathers, I see that in your faces.' He paused to catch his breath. 'Yet there was . . . hastiness on both sides. Please, we must continue our journey to the Singing City. If you will not aid us, then at least do not hinder us.'

'Already our journey will be slower while the shaman heals,' Betsu added, and this time the woman with the scarlet feather blushed.

'I will escort you,' she said, 'with seven of my warriors. As for the rest, continue as ordered. Report my whereabouts when you reach your destination.'

Deliberately vague, Tayan thought, but he didn't question her. Tokob and Yaloh warriors would do the same.

'I am Beyt of the macaws, of the Fourth Talon of the Melody. I – your wound, it—'

'I am Tayan, shaman and peace-weaver of the Tokob. This is Betsu, warrior and peace-weaver of the Yaloh. The wound is, I hope, no more than a scratch.'

'Then tend to it.' She went into a huddle with a couple of other warriors and Tayan finally allowed himself to sag against a tree. He winced and pulled his shirt away from the wound, and then Betsu was there, yanking up the material. He hissed a curse.

'You're right. Little more than a scratch. Won't need stitching. Straighten up and I'll bandage it.' The shaman complied, gritting his teeth at her less-than-gentle touch. 'Well done on getting them to split up; it'll be much easier to get rid of this lot now, then we can circle back and pick up the trail of that coyote-fucker with the yapping mouth.'

Tayan gripped Betsu's wrists, stilling her. 'We are peace-weavers,' he hissed. 'And we now have an escort to guarantee us safe passage to the Singing City. That means they – and we – get to stay alive and that is my only concern at this time. No, listen,' he continued when she tried to pull away. 'You are a peace-weaver. Whatever else you are, while we are in the Empire, you are a peace-weaver. And I could do without any more scars when I get home to my husband. *When* I get home. Understand?'

Betsu's expression was mutinous and hard as flint, but then she nodded once, a single reluctant jerk of the head. 'You are right,' she said at last, and finished bandaging his chest in silence.

'Are you ready, peace-weavers?' Beyt called and the pair exchanged a last look before nodding. 'Then stay close. We'll reach a proper road in a couple of days and our progress will be swift then. I hope you can keep up.'

That last seemed like a challenge, warrior to warrior, and Betsu took it as such. Tayan sighed and then winced. The bandaging had done absolutely nothing to stem the burning agony in his chest, even if it did stop the bleeding. Beyt and three of her warriors took the lead, and the other four followed the peace-weavers. He had been two days under the song, and had had his flesh torn and was in the hands of enemies. He prayed neither were an omen.

* * *

The Neck was so named because it was the narrowest part of Xentiban, a thin corridor of jungle and farmland separating Yalotlan from Pechacan. All too soon they were across it; all too soon they were into Pechacan itself, the song's heartland.

Tayan hadn't been sure what to expect – would the song change again, become more powerful, or purer, or have more meaning for him? Would it sweep him up so that he was lost in its promise? They crossed the border marked not with a pyramid but a tall, carved finger of rock, an ancient marker that had once formed a symbolic barrier between two lands and two tribes. The warriors escorting them passed it without a flicker of hesitation, but just as when they had finally come under the song, Tayan and Betsu paused and slowed their steps. The shaman held his breath as he walked through the shadow of the stone.

Nothing.

Sighing and slightly embarrassed, he hurried after the others. The jungle disappeared a little more each day they walked, becoming tamer, shrinking into strips and wedges of trees and shrubs and tumbling vines only a few sticks across between wide tracts of brown and green farmland. Huts were gathered at each end and entire families toiled between the small shoots of beans and maize. Only the bamboo and water vine and wide-leaved plants were allowed to grow wild and lush to provide Pechaqueh and their slaves a safe water supply.

Children ran, arms flapping to scare away the birds pecking at the crops. It took Tayan a couple of days to realise why it made him uncomfortable. Tokob children did the same thing, but they laughed and squealed and chased each other as they did so. Here it was silent, without joy. They were too young to learn such lessons, but the wide leather collars on the children's necks were eloquent teachers.

Over everything loomed the pyramids, more and more of them, some old and crumbling, liana-covered, others newer and shining in the sun, their paint vibrant, the murals almost alive.

The sky was too open for Tayan's liking, despite the fact he lived on the sparsely treed slopes of Malel. He was used to the confines of the Sky City, the comforting press of building and plaza and steep, walled streets. This was different, an artificial emptiness, and every horizon was bounded with smoke from burning jungle, acrid, the taste of ash and defeat ever on his lips.

The trail they followed was wide enough for ten people to walk abreast and made of finely carved blocks of limestone and sandstone. 'This is how they move their warriors so fast,' Betsu hissed, gesturing at the trail. 'This is how they conquer so easily, by moving thousands at once to the edge of the territory and then invading in huge numbers, unstoppable. This is what they're doing to us. The resources to quarry so much stone . . .' She paused, both wondering and worried. 'Are their numbers as vast as the stars at night?'

The steep slopes and narrow trails of hilly Tokoban would slow them when they came, but as the horizon widened day by day and he saw the multitude of slaves toiling in fields too wide for him to see across, and they passed cities greater than the Sky City and stepped off the road to let free people, not only Pechaqueh, pass them, he knew the hills wouldn't stop them. He began to suspect nothing would. Were they still on a peace mission, or just a negotiation to delay the inevitable? Could trade and tithes stave off their endless numbers? Or would they be forced to accept the song before they were allowed to live in peace? Would even that concession be enough to sate Pechaqueh lust? Would anything?

PILOS

It was good to be home. Better than good, it was cleansing to the soul to be back in the Empire, to be back under the song that had been absent his blood for so many months. It coursed both around him and inside him, through his veins, beneath his skin and within his bones, the comforting endless music of divinity, of glory. Of home.

High Feather Pilos, commander of the Melody and all its Talons, wore a fresh tunic and kilt in alternating bands of red and black, new sandals laced up at his ankles, and a cloak of feathers denoting his rank, brushed of dirt and freshly oiled against the rain. More feathers were braided into his hair, war feathers and honour feathers, and the single stiff tail feather of a turkey sticking up over his ear to announce his peaceful intent.

At his side marched Atu; the young warrior was his second in command, not that it was apparent from his gleeful, grinning appearance. He'd been away from his home and

86

wife here in the Singing City for a year, and she'd been one of the first waiting beneath the ceremonial arch to welcome the Melody home in victory. Pilos smirked at the heat of her welcome for him – he knew what Atu would be doing within an hour of being dismissed.

Behind them in a long snake marched the Melody, slave warriors at the rear, dog warriors in the middle and the elite, full-blood Pechaqueh eagle warriors immediately behind the High Feather. The macaws, wearing their scarlet feathers, patrolled to either side of the long lines of captives – they were half-blood Pechaqueh, a step below elite, a step above the no-blood slaves and dogs. Scattered among them were the secretive, anonymous Whispers, more rumour than fact, more legend than living.

Every warrior wore a peace feather above one ear, and that covenant was sacred.

In the Melody's midst, long lines of Yaloh and even some of their Tokob allies walked, hands bound to their waists, roped at the neck. Men and women brought under the song to learn its glory, to serve its majesty, to understand its power, all taken before the Wet forced Pilos to abandon the offensive for the season. The fighters would be inducted into the Melody as slave warriors, the rest sent to the flesh markets and from there to every corner of the Empire that needed their labours so they might learn of the song and the Singer's mercy. Not as many as he'd have liked to have brought under the song by now, but enough to give advantage to the Melody and, with the Singer's blessing, a swift end to the annexation after the rains. Another year and it would be done and then, perhaps, a time of peace.

The Street of Fighters was crowded with cheering Pechaqueh in their brightly coloured kilts, as well as clumps and spatters of house slaves in the dun of undyed maguey, holding palm-leaf rain shields and bowls of fruit and meat for their owners. Pilos was impressed that so many had turned out despite the weather – citizens of the Singing City weren't known for their enthusiasm for inconveniencing themselves. He acknowledged faces in the crowd with the occasional wave, indulging Atu's more enthusiastic responses and those of his subordinates behind them.

They reached the first loop of the Blessed River and Pilos and his Feathers came to a halt. The offering was fine – a young, healthy Yalotl with clear skin and wide, dazed eyes. Pilos had ordered her bathed and her clothes washed and now she stood dumb, not understanding why she wasn't bound with the rest of her people. The long walk had dampened her fire to embers and the holy Setatmeh would be pleased with her quality.

Feather Atu gave her the traditional cup of liquor and she choked it down, and then they approached the edge of the river with the girl gripped between them. She began to squirm and then to yell, digging in her heels as those embers sparked into the raging fire of terror. Behind them, the Melody processed over the wide wooden bridge, the captives in their midst panicking and screeching like monkeys and even some of the slave warriors still skittish. It was the same with every new batch until they understood the way of the world and the Singer's divine will.

'Holy Setatmeh, gods of rivers and lakes, you who bring life and plenty to our world, accept this offering as your just due,' Pilos said, tugging the girl forward. She struggled harder, bound hands clubbing at him. He transferred his grip to the back of her neck, his long fingers compressing the big veins on either side. He squeezed until her face filled with blood and her screams became wheezed whimpers.

'Wise Setatmeh, gods of streams and waterfalls, you who

control the crops and the rain and bring the barren to ripeness, accept this offering as your holy reward,' he prayed, and scooped her into his arms. Pilos walked forward until he was thigh-deep in the river, a thrill of religious fear raising the hairs on his arms. She was fighting hard as he lowered her into the water and held her head down while she thrashed.

The offering was accepted.

A form glided through the water to Pilos's side and he suffered the exquisite terror of looking it in the eye. 'I honour you, god,' he said. It wrapped webbed hands around the girl's waist and Pilos let go and stepped back. 'Take your prize, sacred spirit,' he added and the offering shrieked again as the black claws bit into her back. The holy Setat dragged her away from shore, and then it tore open her belly and vanished with her beneath the water, trailing bubbles and thick streams of blood.

'Blessed are the Setatmeh, and glory to the Singer,' Atu murmured from the bank.

Pilos echoed his words and saw the shadow of awe in Atu's face as he exited the river. He managed a grimace, making no effort to hide the trembling of his hands. To be so close to one of the gods was to know fear and rapture in their purest forms – there was no shame in shaking afterwards. Besides, there was another loop of river to cross before they reached the heart of the city and the great pyramid, and an offering would be required there too, in thanks for a victorious return to the Empire.

'To finally meet the Singer himself,' Atu muttered as they resumed their march. 'The thought of it frightens me more than facing the enemy ever has,' he admitted as the next offering was passed forward. This one began struggling straight away, knowing what awaited him.

'We come to report victory,' Pilos assured him. 'The Singer

will be pleased with us.' Despite his words, he felt a flicker of unease. The council was a nest of vipers. The High Feather needed to be on his guard.

As always, the palace never failed to exact its toll in awe. A great tiered pyramid of seven pale stone levels and a grand central staircase that led all the way to the summit, with its precious songstone cap. There was one entrance off the main staircase, halfway up, that led into the pyramid's interior and then to the very source. Brightly coloured images were carved and painted on its sides, and each level was green with cultivated gardens.

The pyramid crouched at the end of the Way of Prayer, surrounded by the smaller, lesser palaces of the council and of the Singer's family and confidants. The wide plaza before the pyramid was thronged with more citizens, and it was soon full to capacity as the Melody marched in to accept their cheers. The slave and dog warriors gaped up at the pyramid and their wonder was a tonic to Pilos's nerves. *This is why we do what we do. This is glory. This is Empire.*

In a rare show of support, the Singer himself appeared on the flat platform at the pinnacle of the pyramid, surrounded by four tall columns carved with images of the first Singers and Setatmeh. Above the Singer reared the songstone cap, through which his magic and his song poured, spreading across the Empire in a slow, rich tide, like golden honey.

Pilos knelt, the Melody and crowd following suit. Silence, but for the tap of rain on the limestone road and the song, brassy with triumph and loud with power, ringing through them all. Pilos breathed in stone and rain and home and song and triumph. He could have longed for bright sun to show his warriors in their finery, the glint of obsidian and the rich flashes of their feathers and the paint on their arms, but this was somehow more suitable. Within the dull greyness of rain, under a moody, malevolent sky, the Melody was a dark force, ripe with power, rich with violence. No one seeing them could doubt their strength.

The High Feather waited until the song's pitch changed before looking up; the Singer was gone but in the pyramid's entrance waited members of the council. Another honour he hadn't expected. But not just councillors, he noted as he and Atu began the long climb towards them. Singer Xac was surrounding himself with his faithful, men and women who supported him in all things, sycophants who would hang from his every utterance and who would deny him nothing in the hopes of securing his blessing when the time of his ascension was upon him.

Pilos was three years into the eight-year cycle of his other role as Spear of the Singer, the second of the holy lord's closest advisers, and these days he was increasingly tasked with working for the glory of the Empire and holding together the fractious council, while the Singer's favourites worked only for the glory of their future selves. As for Enet, the Spear of the City, she was cunning enough to not only appear diligent in her administration while in reality shifting many of her duties to others, but had risen to be the Singer's primary courtesan. The combination had secured her place in the very heart of the Empire of Songs, and, according to Pilos's latest information, her power was said to be second only to the Singer's.

It all fell to Pilos; whether or not he was fighting the Singer's wars, the reports and messages and pleas found their way to him, and though it was an honour to be so trusted by the holy lord, it was a burden he sometimes longed to put down. Carefully, he turned his thoughts away from criticism.

The Singer was wise and powerful beyond human understanding, a living god, but he had once been a man. And even Pechaqueh were fallible. Singer Het, his predecessor, had been only twelve when she was chosen and had relied so heavily on the counsel of her family that when it was her time to ascend – a mere three years after the magic entered her – it had surprised no one that she chose Xac, her older brother, as her heir. She'd taken thirty members of her family with her when she ascended, but had left behind her council to aid him. They had missed their chance at glory and immortality as a result. It was clear they weren't prepared to do so again.

And yet Xac still waxes, a full eleven sun-years into his reign. He is strong where Singer Het was not, not in the way the people needed. The holy burden was too much for her. But Xac's song rings across every stick of Empire. With honest guidance, he will be a Singer remembered through the ages.

With honest guidance.

Pilos cleared his mind as he and Atu bowed to the councillors at the entrance, thighs warm from the climb. They removed their sandals, cloaks, and weapons and entered, all of them bent at the waist and scuttling along the corridors like wading birds looking for food.

The cheering of the Melody and the Pechaqueh faded away, replaced by the sounds and scents of the Singer's palace: citrus and incense, the trickle of water and soft hush of leaves in a breeze, a child laughing, the crackle of fire. Sounds and scents of life and strength, which the Singer in his power and his magic wove into the song that kept them all safe and united. Pilos had no idea how he did it. In his darker moments, on the front line, when battle was joined and his warriors were dying all around him, he wondered if the *Singer* knew how he did it.

Pilos shut away the thought and filled his mind with awe and wonder. It wasn't difficult, even when staring at the floor in front of him, the bright murals painted on the walls only visible from his peripheral vision. He'd be at leisure to examine them on the way out: the stories of war and glory and expansion, the legends of the earliest Singers, and everywhere, repeated, depictions of the holy Setatmeh and the world spirit itself. All of them painted by the best and most famous artists of Pechacan throughout the years and Star cycles since the discovery of the song-magic.

The song hummed and grew in volume and strength as they wove their way through the palace corridors. Choosers and courtesans, body slaves and the elite eagle warriors of the Singer's Chorus all watching them pass with curiosity and not a little suspicion.

Eventually – and yet too soon – the smooth cool stone beneath their feet changed to thickly woven mats in azure blue and they paused until the council had entered and sat, then stepped into the Singer's inner sanctum, the very source of the song itself. Atu's breathing roughened just a little as he took in the huge oval room, the colonnaded wall opening onto vibrant gardens alive with finches and parrots and hummingbirds flitting among the palms and bamboo and small trees. Green life and incense mingled on the gentle breeze. The other walls were covered in murals even more exquisite than those of the corridors, including one that depicted the whole of the Ixachipan peninsula. There was space left to paint in Yalotlan and Tokoban when those lands and tribes were brought under the song. Pilos vowed to be the one to achieve that for the Singer's glory. Atu had halted, overcome, and Pilos flicked his arm lightly with his fingers.

'Spear of the Singer and High Feather Pilos, and Feather Atu, second in command of the Melody, request entrance to this council,' Pilos said. The other councillors had already taken the cushions closest to the holy lord, leaving them on the outside of the circle. It didn't matter; Pilos was Spear and his voice would still be heard. Should the Singer so wish it.

The song was a living thing here in the source, with weight and substance that sat not just on their skin but in their bones. The Singer's will, inviolable anywhere in the Empire, was in this room as immovable as the pyramid itself. Everyone inside these walls could do nothing but obey the Singer and the dictates of his song.

As always, the holy lord sat behind a rippling curtain of pale pink cotton, the weave so fine that his bulk was visible through the translucent material, enhanced by the tall head-dress of feathers and jade that crowned him. Here, in the innermost of his chambers, the music from which he made his song was constant – the liquid trilling of captive birds, the happy chatter of a small streamlet over carefully placed pebbles, the thumping of a dog's tail on the rugs. In the distance, children shrieked with laughter as they played.

A woman sang in a sweet, high voice, a hymn of praise for the Empire that listed all 174 Singers from the founder, Tenaca, all the way to Xac. Pilos remembered the hours he'd spent as a boy learning those names, the slaps when he got the order wrong. He rubbed his neck and brought his mind into harmony.

'High Feather, you are welcome back in the Singing City,' the holy lord rumbled, the strange harmonics of his voice sending flutters of anxiety and reverence through Pilos's gut. The councillors fell silent. 'You have had some recent successes in the war against the Yaloh, and you have had some failures. The first I applaud, but not the second. You will explain.'

The council turned flat, blank gazes on him, calculating, weighing, assessing.

'Great Singer, the Yaloh are a wily and courageous people and as you know they have convinced the Tokob to join them, swelling their numbers. They fought long and hard, and pushed us back several times, it is true. Their lack of civilisation means they have no great cities we can take and so win a decisive victory, and there are no limestone roads to speed our movement. They conducted small, fast raids on our camps or as we marched and then faded into the jungle again. We have not yet brought sufficient numbers of them to bay to force a decisive reckoning.'

He paused, but there was only attentive silence from behind the curtain.

'So determined were they to withstand us that when they knew they had lost the southern half of Yalotlan, they burnt their stands of bamboo and water vine, to make it useless to us. Our shamans advised against fighting through the Wet, since the rains have come heavy and early. I brought back the bulk of the Melody to rest, though I have left a Talon of three thousand warriors in Yalotlan. They will protect the builders I have sent there, who will construct pyramids to carry your song through the land. We have taken three and a half thousand prisoners. It is perhaps a fifth of the Yaloh population, and consists mostly of warriors or other adults. So far.'

Pilos took a breath. 'The war has had one other outcome. The holy Setatmeh of Yalotlan have begun taking offerings again in the old manner. Some of my warriors have been lost.'

There was a rising babble of noise at the revelation; usually the only Pechaqueh taken by the gods were those who'd been cast onto the streets for their crimes, and among whom the Choosers walked like lords of the Underworld when selecting the new moon offerings.

'This is Yaloh magic, and yet you bring them to the Singing

95

City?' a councillor squeaked. 'Who knows what havoc they will wreak in our sacred waters here? You should have offered them all to the holy Setatmeh in their own land.'

'The Yaloh slaves do not belong to the High Feather,' Councillor Yana said mildly, though his voice carried over the murmuring. 'It was not his place to decide what should be done with them.'

Pilos breathed a silent sigh of relief. Yana was as honest and unbending as his back, despite his years. He had been an eagle warrior and Feather and still trained daily with the spear, and Pilos knew he had a warrior's integrity, a warrior's commitment to duty and to Empire. He also showed little ambition to supplant the other councillors or any of the Singer's favourites, which sat well with the others.

'The holy Setatmeh are righteously angry,' a woman cut in. 'Perhaps this is their response to your cowardly retreat from the fight! Why is the Melody here if there is work still to be done? We must do all we can to honour the gods.'

'You are correct, Councillor Chel,' Yana said smoothly and with a smile as cold as a snake's, 'we must all play our part. A gift of jade or slaves from each councillor will help speed the construction of new pyramids. The Melody is made up of warriors, when what they need are engineers and builders, and the slaves to both carry out the work and present to the holy Setatmeh to prevent . . . unnecessary offerings from among Pechaqueh. Do not forget the Melody are also there to protect the holy Setatmeh and the workers from Yaloh and Tokob. They cannot do everything.'

'Then the rest of the Melody should go back and finish what it started,' Chel snapped. 'Not come here in triumph and demand reward when the conquest remains unfinished.'

'Or, as I said, we can assist them in their work. High Feather, I will buy a hundred slaves and send them to Yalotlan to work and be offered as necessary. And I will purchase enough stone for one full pyramid.'

Even Pilos blinked at the size of Yana's promise. The man must have risen far to afford such a generous gift. *And he is planting himself firmly on my side in the struggle to come.* Pilos didn't know whether to be worried or delighted, but Yana was an old friend and an old comrade; his offer was one of support for Pilos personally as well as for the Melody, and the warrior would honour his generosity. He inclined his head to Yana with gratitude.

'Who expects us to pay for the High Feather's failure?' queried a voice and Spear Enet's head snaked from behind the hanging to stare at him. Pilos's heart clenched at her sudden appearance. Years before, during the reign of Singer Het, their families had negotiated an alliance the pair had been expected to fulfil through marriage. Yet when it came to it, Enet had refused. Pilos had been a boy and desperately in love with her – or so he'd thought. He'd believed himself shamed in front of the court and council and for years he'd been bitter at the rejection. These days he knew better, and thanked whichever holy Setat had spared him the fate of marrying her.

Now she was the Singer's chief courtesan as well as his Spear and, despite sharing the status with Pilos, he knew that what she whispered in the pillows carried more weight than the council's words or the Melody's needs.

'Councillor Yana merely proposes a course of action and offers a gift of aid, Enet,' he said evenly, his voice and face serene, refusing to be goaded. 'The decision rests with the Singer.'

Her beautiful black eyes narrowed. 'You will address me correctly.'

Pilos pursed his lips. 'I have been at war for some time, Enet,' he said, deliberately using her name again as his gut roiled with unease. 'I am unaware of any change in your status. Please, how should you be addressed?'

Enet glanced back at the Singer behind the curtain and her face softened, lips curving in a smile that set Pilos's balls to aching. She'd smiled at him like that, once. 'I have the honour of being known as Great Octave now,' she said sweetly, her head on one side to better study his reaction.

Pilos's balls stopped aching and tried to crawl into his belly. Great Octave? Chief adviser to the Singer, above even the Spears, head of his household, master of wealth, and senior Chooser? The title had not been granted in a hundred sun-years, it was so dangerous to the harmony of the Empire. Between them, Xac and Enet ruled the world – and no one could gainsay them.

Enet was beautiful and powerful and rich, and the Singer, their living god, was in thrall to her, and he either didn't realise it or, worse, he knew and didn't care. She would ascend with him, of that there was no doubt. Pilos didn't care about that – he cared about the amount of damage she would do to the Empire beforehand. And now she had the reach and power to accomplish it.

He stared around the advisers and noted the discomfort in some faces, the pleasure gleaming from others'. The Singer's cronies had split the council neatly down the middle and as the Singer began to wane, bloodshed would increase as all vied for a position close to his heart and the chance to ascend with him. What damage they did the Empire of Songs during that mad scramble would mean nothing to them. Only those who were left behind would face it. *Whatever danger I have been in before, whether in the council or in battle, is as nothing compared with this.*

'We are awaiting your answer, Spear,' Enet snapped and Pilos dragged his scattered thoughts back together.

'Singer,' Pilos said, addressing his lord instead of the Great Octave, 'you are right: the war is not yet won. We have taken half their territory and expect to complete the conquest after the rains have stopped and the land has firmed enough for battle. If it is *your* will,' he placed the tiniest emphasis on the pronoun, 'I will of course turn the Melody around and march them straight back to war. As Spear and High Feather, by your grace, my advice would be to wait until after the Wet. We have fought through it before, in Quitoban. We lost more than half our warriors and the Empire's expansion was delayed as a result.'

'The Singer does not need reminding of your past failures,' Enet hissed, her face appearing again.

Pilos raised both hands, not even bothering to remind her that he had been been promoted to High Feather only a few days before Quitoban finally fell and that the length of the campaign had been neither his fault nor unexpected. 'The Quitob were brought under the song, Great Octave. Where is the failure? I mention it only because once we have brought the Yaloh into the Empire, we will still have to face the Tokob – unless we take both tribes at once.' Atu huffed at that. 'We cannot afford to wait for our full-blood youngsters to mature and replace any needless losses. And the Yaloh slave warriors will not be fully integrated under the song for years. We won't be able to trust them.'

There was a rumble from the Singer, as of thunder, that stole Enet's reply. The council paused, waiting for the lightning to accompany that threat. It didn't come, or at least it wasn't aimed at them. 'High Feather, the shamans were right; the war is over for this season. Rest your warriors, break in the new slaves, and be ready to march after the Wet. I will give you the exact date when I have consulted the stars.'

Pilos bowed his forehead to the floor, hearing the rustle

as the council did likewise at the Singer's rising. Their lord padded from the council room without another word, his favourites scurrying behind. The High Feather stood and beckoned; Atu jumped up and together they strode out of the source without a backward glance, though Pilos could feel eyes on him all the way. Slaves waited at the exit with their sandals, weapons, and cloaks, and they dressed and stepped back out into impending dusk and a city shining with moisture.

They descended the pyramid in silence – the Melody had long since dispersed to barracks and the homes of families, brothels, and drinking huts. The slaves would be penned in the flesh markets for onward transportation.

'That was . . . not what I expected,' Atu said eventually.

Pilos grunted and clapped him on the back. 'The council meetings rarely are. Go and fuck your wife and get drunk, Feather. There will be many people who seek my favour now they know I'm back. I'll send the new slaves on to the Melody compound, but depending on how things play here, we might be leaving soon. Make the most of the time you have.'

Atu grinned and touched belly and throat in salute. 'Under the song, High Feather.'

'Under the song.' The young warrior practically sprinted through the plaza towards the litter-bearers for hire at the far end. Pilos smiled again. 'All right, Elaq, out you come,' he said and his bodyguard, a retired eagle warrior and the head of his estate here in the Singing City, emerged from the shadows at the edge of the pyramid.

'Spear,' he said, touching belly and throat and using the title Pilos preferred when in the Singing City. 'Under the song.'

'Under the song, my friend. How are you?' He clasped Elaq's wrist and clapped the big man on the arm. Retired a decade and still with shoulders wider than the bole of a mahogany tree.

'I am well, Spear, thank you, and your estate and the fighting pit too. Your wealth increases.'

'And much of it is down to you and the others,' Pilos said as they began to walk. 'I know it and I will not forget it.' The look on Elaq's face reminded him why he preferred paid Pechaqueh to slaves, no matter the cost. All his guards had partners and children who lived on the estate with them and who Pilos educated and cared for at his own expense. It wasn't entirely altruistic, of course – most of the children entered the Melody when they were old enough and all were fiercely loyal to him. Still, he could afford it and it meant that his estate was secure and his employees virtually incorruptible.

They strode into the temple complex that spiralled out from the great pyramid, and had made it less than half a stick when Elaq paused to kick a babbling, yelling wreck of a woman out of their path. She shrieked and clawed for him, and he clubbed her in the face and dragged her to the side of the street. Pilos trod through blood as he tried to work out whether he'd once known her, back before she was disgraced. There was something familiar about her. Or maybe she was no one, just a slave who'd displeased her owners and wasn't good enough to offer to the holy Setatmeh. He'd forgotten how commonplace such sights were here in the heart of the Empire, but the woman's situation sparked a question.

'I take it there's been another purge since last I was home?' he asked.

Elaq grunted his disgust as he wiped the head of his club on the hem of his kilt. 'There has, Spear, a large one. The properties and wealth of the traitors and dissidents flow ever to where it is most needed, but the . . . human waste that is left behind causes issues of its own. We have had to throw them off your estate several times; the offal were trying to rob you.'

'I've a proposal to clear this mess from our streets and help the Melody at the same time. It wasn't something to mention to the Singer on my first day back, but now I see this' – he gestured at the shacks of pole uprights and leaking thatch roofs tilted drunkenly against the sides of temples – 'I can see something must be done.'

Elaq gave him an approving nod. 'I pray your words find the Singer's ear.'

'As do I,' Pilos said. 'I see Enet has been elevated again.'

'I only found out myself this morning, Spear, or I would have warned you,' Elaq said in apology. 'And the last I'd heard, the Singer had punished her in the very source itself, though why, I couldn't find out. But as ever, the snake wriggles its way free and flashes its pretty scales to best advantage.'

Pilos punched his arm lightly but there was unspoken warning in his eyes that Elaq noted. Such words were dangerous and Enet was wealthy enough to have her own personal Listener. Pilos, on the other hand, was wary enough to assume that he was always being listened to.

'She thinks to put me on edge,' he said and shrugged. 'But she is not the one who has brought back slaves and taken land.' He almost hoped her Listener might pick up on that; how it would bite at her, like ants on her skin.

'No,' he added with a feral grin, 'I remain secure in the Singer's favour, at least for now. But anything you can find out, of course, please do so. Enet's games are nothing if not long and complex and I would prefer to concentrate on honing the Melody through the Wet rather than avoiding the knives aimed at my throat.'

Elaq scowled. 'That's what you have me for,' he said. 'I've knives of my own and the will to use them.'

'All in good time, my friend,' Pilos said. 'All in good time.'

LILLA

Southern Tokoban, near Yalotlan border
150th day of the Great Star at morning

Lilla sat with his back against the bole of a fig tree and rubbed a handful of water over his face and chest, licking it from his lips and chin and fingertips and palm. It was warm, kissed with salt where it had mixed with the sweat on his skin. There wasn't much left in the gourd, but the nearby tangle of water vine was full, so he enjoyed the small extravagance, closing his eyes as the liquid momentarily cooled his face.

The rest of his Paw sprawled around him, with the game they'd hunted smoking over wide, low fires. The scent carried on the still air, not just to predators but potentially to enemy warriors; they were only three days' walk from Yalotlan's border, and although scouting Paws had confirmed the bulk of the enemy had left when the rains started in earnest, the threat of skirmish or ambush was ever-present – even within Tokoban itself these days. Still, they were too far from home to transport the meat before it spoilt and with so many refugees to feed, the jungle closest to the Sky City was increasingly bare of game. Descending Malel and passing the villages scattered at its base for wilder land was their only option to keep the city fed.

Around them, a Yaloh Paw under Kux's command was concealed in the trees in a wide perimeter, half a stick out, on the alert.

'I heard people in the lower market before we headed out,' Tiamoko was saying. He was young, barely an adult, but big and strong and keen. Perhaps too keen; Lilla needed to watch him. 'They were saying that if we send the Yaloh back into their own land, Malel would accept that sacrifice and she would ensure the Pechaqueh left us in peace.'

'And would you live in peace, big man?' asked Lutek, one of Lilla's best warriors. She was sitting cross-legged, knapping a new blade for her knife, and although her tone was mild, Tiamoko flushed like the boy he mostly still was. 'Knowing you'd left your neighbours – our friends – to become the slaves of those bastards? That'd sit easy with you, would it?'

'Wasn't me saying it, Lutek. I just heard it.'

'I heard what Malel wants is a proper sacrifice,' someone else said and they all went quiet at that. Many faces turned towards Lilla and he sighed. Being married to a shaman had its downsides.

'Before Tayan left, the subject had been raised in conclave, but the shamans want to see what happens with the peace-weaving first. If Malel demands blood, she will get it. Until then, the councils will continue to debate our next steps and await the outcome of the peace-weaving.'

He was stern enough that the conversation died away and Tiamoko checked the meat on the smoke racks, eager to be of use. Not that Lilla blamed him for his words; he'd heard the same rumours. They all had. That's what happened when fear gripped a city by its throat and began to squeeze. Next would come the voices urging surrender, that living under the song wouldn't be so bad. When those arguments began, the Sky City would fall into chaos.

And although he should focus on that, Tayan's name had fallen from his lips easily, conjuring images and memories of his husband, of their life together that seemed so distant sometimes, almost unreal. Would they have that again, those days spent hunting for game and foraging for medicine, content in each other's silences and laughter, present and close and warm as sunlight? Or would the shadow of war forever stretch dark and cold around them?

Tayan had already been gone almost a moon and Lilla missed him, the pain a thorn pressed high up behind his lungs when he thought of him walking through conquered land and giving himself into the power of their enemies.

He tried to put it from his mind and concentrate instead on the latest information from Yalotlan. Pyramids were being built in the south, and once those tall, unmissable sentinels of the Empire of Songs marched across the land, they would claim it more fully than Pechaqueh words or spears – or even Yaloh lives and ancestors – could. When the magic in the pyramids came to life, the song would choke the land like a strangler fig, entering the bones and bellies of those who heard it, never to be forgotten.

The song would permeate the soil, the trees and plants and animals. The song would enter all who heard it and bring them under its sway. And the Empire of Songs would grow, its borders marked not by the gold stone and bright paint of the pyramids themselves but by the limits of the song that breathed inside the air and lived inside the living. The eternal presence. The Singer's will.

Parasite. Master. God.

A single howler monkey screeched an alarm and Lilla's Paw leapt to their feet and fanned out, ducking behind the smoke racks or into the shadow of trees. The sound of fighting erupted a short distance away as part of Kux's Paw engaged an enemy and Lutek looked to Lilla. He nodded and signed 'five' and she led four warriors at a run towards the noise.

The rest waited, alert, straining every sense. Another of Kux's Paw called the alarm, from the east this time. 'Snake's tongue attack,' Lilla bellowed. He sent a piercing whistle into the jungle, calling back all those who could extricate themselves so they could stand together in the clearing.

A heavy javelin whined through the trees, and then a dozen more, flying hard and fast, before any of their allies made it back. Another skimmed past Lilla so close it stirred the hair by the side of his face. He jerked sideways, tripping on a root and sprawling to one knee. The javelin buried itself in the tree behind him.

'Empire!' Lilla shouted as he recognised the distinctive pattern on the bannerstone halfway along its length. Though of course it was the Empire; they were still in Tokoban and their own people wouldn't be attacking them. There was a screech as a woman was caught on the thigh, a javelin's point ripping into and then out of her doeskin leggings, leaving a bright slash of blood and torn flesh behind.

A third volley and the enemy hard after it, sprinting along the game trails from two, then three directions. Impossible to tell their numbers as they lunged out of the jungle or loosed arrows and darts from its shelter. The clearing erupted into motion – the stabbing whirl of spear fights, lightning fast, the hard clack of haft on haft, grunts of impact, screams of pain.

Lilla wrenched the Empire spear out of the tree and flung it at a man racing towards Tiamoko. It clipped a branch overhead and dipped early, landing between his feet so that he tripped, sprawling headlong into the leaf-litter but unhurt. Not for long. Lutek burst from the trees and rammed her own spear into his back, punching him down onto the earth just as he rose to his hands and knees.

Lilla was halfway to her side when a warrior a head taller than him barred his path. The man bared his teeth, the front two filed into points – one of the Tlaloxqueh people from the far southwest. He jabbed and Lilla blocked with his hatchet, thrusting back with his spear. The Tlalox was fast, but so was Lilla, the weapons spinning around them in a blur as they parried and blocked. Lilla split the man's knuckle with a hard swipe and pain flashed in his eyes, though his hands never faltered.

Screams and roars all around them, cries for help, shrieks for mercy ungiven, and then the Tlalox fell for a feint and Lilla skipped sideways, shearing the hatchet into his throat. It came back out with a puff of blood and a strangled attempt at a scream. The man dropped his spear and slapped both hands against the wound, his eyes so wide Lilla could see himself reflected in them. He didn't care to look too closely, just stepped around the dying man and back-swung the hatchet into the nape of his neck.

Kux and her Yaloh poured out of the trees and now the Empire's warriors were trapped between the two forces. Even so, they fought for longer than Lilla expected, neither surrendering nor fleeing. And they took a bloody toll on his forces. Another Toko fell, her salt-cotton armour no match for the stone-headed club that crushed her sternum. She dropped without a sound, her lungs and ribs smashed to ruin and bright blood vomiting from her mouth. Roaring, Lilla leapt at her killer, a man wearing a cap of coyote skin, the animal's eyeteeth strung in his hair.

Lutek had Lilla's flank and together they cut him onto his knees, bleeding from a dozen wounds but none of them fatal. Yet. Around them the clearing was falling still, bodies scattered like dead branches after a storm. The Paws had the victory, and those few enemy who fled into the jungle weren't pursued; the chances of another ambush were too great.

'Who are you?' Lilla spat at the man, his chest heaving as he fought for breath. There was a long, freely bleeding slice in his right forearm he couldn't remember getting, but the hurt of it mingled with adrenaline and anger and shock and twisted his voice into something savage, though the kneeling man didn't react to it.

'Aez, Coyote leader of a hundred dog warriors of the Second Talon,' he said, as calm as though he were chatting among friends. His breath came easily despite the exertion, despite the blood. 'And you are trespassing in the Empire of Songs.'

Lilla's lips peeled back from his teeth.

'You mistake,' Kux said as she strode over, surprise and anger vying for supremacy in her voice. She held a strip of material to her head and blood leaked from beneath it.

'The Singer has decided Yalotlan will be brought under the song,' Aez said, in that same calm and condescending tone. 'And so this land now belongs to him.'

'Monkey shit,' Lilla snarled. 'And you're in Tokoban, anyway.'

Aez looked around. 'Am I?' he asked mildly. 'All looks the same to me.'

Lilla itched to hurt him. 'You understand nothing and your words mean less than nothing. Our land will always be our land.'

'Of course it always will be,' Aez said and Lilla paused. 'I am from Axiban and I will always be a member of the Axib, even as I am also of the Empire.' He laughed at their confusion. 'It is you who understands nothing. When you are part of the Empire, you will learn. You will know glory then. And life.'

'We will never be part of the Empire. We will never be slaves like you,' Kux snarled.

Aez's eyes narrowed. 'I am no slave. I am a Coyote leader of dog warriors. I serve willingly.'

'Dogs that bark at their master's command but are too cowed to tear his throat out,' Kux sneered and Lilla snorted. 'But you press far north without reinforcements, little barking coyote. Why is that?' Aez was silent. 'Are there reinforcements coming?' Still nothing. The Yalotl spat in his face.

Aez inhaled through flared nostrils as he wiped her saliva from his cheek. But then he settled back on his heels, his gaze fixed somewhere beyond them all. He was looking pale now, though with blood loss and pain rather than fear. 'Holy Setatmeh and great Singer, judge me by my deeds and not my words, my devotion and not my fears. Sacred spirits, may my death secure your glory, and my name live in your mouths forever. I commend my family into your care, that they too may honour you.'

'*You're not even a Pecha!*' Kux yelled. Aez paid no attention.

Rage built in Lilla's chest and he chuckled, low and nasty, a sound that until the war he hadn't known it was possible to make. A sound that threatened like the low rumbling growl of a jaguar. 'No need for prayers, slave,' he said. 'We're not killing you. At least, not yet.' He tore the coyote-skin cap from Aez's head and stamped on it.

Shock and fury twisted the man's face. 'I am no slave! I am a free Axi, a Coyote commander and—'

Lilla punched him in the jaw and he fell, boneless. 'Bring him and any meat that's ready that we can haul alongside the wounded,' Lilla said.

'What about the dead?' someone muttered. 'We drag his carcass with us but not our kin?'

'We're at war,' Kux said, though her jaw was trembling with suppressed emotion. 'Strip them of talismans, honour them, and then leave them. There's no time for more.'

'Besides,' Lilla added, searching out Tiamoko in the press and relieved to find him alive. 'There's been talk Malel might demand a sacrifice.' He jabbed the unconscious Axi in the ribs with his sandal. 'Looks like we've found one.'

There was a pause, and then they set to work, taking jewellery and hanks of hair from Tokob and Yaloh dead and placing jade beads on their tongues, payment to see them safely through the Gate of the Ancestors. The dead feeding the jungle that fed the living.

'Be at peace in the harmony of living and dying. We sustain what sustains us, in the endless circle.' The same whisper, over and over as each corpse was honoured. 'We will drum for you. We will dance your spirits through the spiral to rebirth. Rest now.'

'Let's go,' Lilla said softly when it was done and the wounded were on their feet or being supported. The Axi dangled like a dead deer from a long carrying pole slung between two warriors.

Lilla took the tail and Kux the head of the group and they set off with many bitter glances back at the clearing and their dead. The mood was blacker than the clouds and guilt filled Lilla's chest until he thought he would choke.

They encountered no further ambushes during the march back to the Sky City. A march in which two of the wounded died from the brutal pace they set.

Lilla sent the Paws to rest and then he and Kux dragged Aez up through the city to the council chamber, intermittent sun lightening the limestone streets beneath their feet. He tried to coax the embers of his anger back into flame, but he was too tired.

Both councils were there, seated in a double ring on thin mats, spaces left free for the Fangs. Other warriors took possession of Aez and forced him to kneel at the rear of the chamber, spears poised. Even so, Lilla didn't much like turning his back on him.

High Elder Vaqix called the meeting to order before they were even properly seated. 'Kux, Lilla, you return from scouting and from hunting – and from battle. How many warriors have stepped onto the spiral path under your command?'

Lilla winced. 'Seventeen bodies have returned to the earth, High Elder.'

'What were you doing so far south?' Vaqix demanded.

'We weren't,' Kux said before Lilla could. 'We were inside Tokoban. They should not have been within a hundred sticks of us.'

'This is not the first time,' Elder Apok said. 'Other lowland villages have reported sightings and missing hunting parties, bodies discovered on game trails. They haven't yet reached the towns below Malel's slopes, but it seems there are Melody warriors at large in Tokoban now, too. It is no longer just in Yalotlan that we are fighting. Although their main strength has retreated, there seems to be a pattern emerging of skirmishes where we least expect them.'

'Why?' High Elder Zasso of the Yaloh demanded, her voice a thin croak.

'Many reasons,' Lilla found himself saying. 'To put us on edge; to make us fearful to leave our villages or towns; to cut off communication between settlements. Perhaps they want us sending out double-strength Paws when hunting in order to weaken the defences of villages. Perhaps it's all a distraction so they can continue building pyramids to bring the song ever closer.'

Behind him, Lilla heard a snort of what might have been laughter from the Axib prisoner. His back prickled.

Kux leant forward, her eyes fixed on Zasso. 'Whatever they have planned, however many their numbers roaming Tokoban, they seek to keep us off balance and penned in up here while they consolidate their hold on *our homes*.' She flung a hand passionately towards Aez. 'He admitted it when we captured him. He said Yalotlan belongs to the Empire already. He called us *trespassers*.' Her voice was a sibilant whisper on the last word and it lingered in the sudden, disbelieving silence. And then, uproar.

Lilla sat within it like a leaf on the current, helplessly buffeted this way and that. He ached for Tayan, for his husband's pragmatism and unquestioning faith in him, but also for his sense of the absurd. The slender shaman had a knack for dispelling tension and they needed it now, needed it desperately before they worked themselves into a frenzy and made a rash decision. Unless . . .

'Stop. *Stop!*' Lilla bellowed and the council chamber rang with echoes. 'The Empire wants unthinking, angry responses; it wants us to mount a poorly planned invasion; it wants us to leave ourselves exposed. None of us know how much of their Melody they marched back to Pechacan. Did they even go that far? Who's to say they're not five sticks into Xentiban, just waiting for us to over-extend ourselves trying to regain lost land?'

'Stolen land,' Kux grated.

'Stolen land,' Lilla amended. 'But we have to give the peace-weavers a chance. We can't go on the offensive while Tayan and Betsu argue for peace.'

113

'So we just let them keep on stealing land and lives? Stealing people to make into slaves? No!' Kux was loud, vibrating with anger.

'They're building pyramids in southern Yalotlan,' Lilla said. 'That we can do something about. It's not an act of open aggression but one of resistance – and we won't kill unless we must – but we could prevent their construction. Delay them, smash the stone so they can't be built while we wait for the peace-weaving to conclude.'

'And you think they'll let us do that?' High Elder Zasso scoffed. 'Of course not. They'll defend themselves and their cursed pyramids. When the peace-weavers left, it appeared that the Melody had retreated. Now it seems they are advancing again, perhaps only in small numbers, but we cannot allow them to roam Yalotlan and Tokoban unanswered. We simply cannot. You were ambushed, Fang Lilla, and you lost seventeen warriors between the two Paws and that is a tragedy, but the reports from the market administrators say that you also came back with only a third of the meat you'd hoped to hunt, and – dare I say it – that is a greater tragedy. And one that may well be a shadow of things to come. What happens if we can't hunt at all? What happens when we are trapped between the Melody and the Drowned, when we are starving, because you want us to delay?'

'But the peace-weaving—' Lilla tried.

'Fuck the peace-weaving,' Kux yelled. 'Yours isn't the land and people stolen.'

'We fight alongside you,' Lilla said and his voice was no longer quiet, no longer even. 'We die alongside you. Do not—'

'Enough.' Vaqix's voice was implacable. 'Enough. The peace-weavers must be given the time to work.' He held up a finger to still them. 'But I agree that having enemies wandering our land is unacceptable. We will send out combined Paws – a show of strength. They will be large and obvious. They will sweep the game trails and ensure our towns are safe. They will show the Melody that we are aware of their presence and not afraid to engage. But we will not attack. We will defend ourselves if we must, but our forces will deter, not provoke.'

'And what about him?' Zasso demanded, pointing. She wanted blood; she wanted vengeance and Lilla couldn't blame her.

The Axi put his head on one side and even dared a smile, as if among friends.

'The shamanic conclave spoke of the potential for an offering to Malel,' Vaqix said quietly. Apok was signing for those ejab under the influence of spirit-magic and their heads swivelled between his explanatory hands and the prisoner. 'We will continue to consult the goddess and the ancestors and spirits. We will continue to show our strength to our enemies. And if Malel demands it, she will have his life.'

TAYAN

'There it is.' Beyt had halted at the top of a small, flat rise amid muddy fields. The rain out here, without the cover of the canopy, was relentless, and all of them were muddy to the knees, tunics and kilts and hair plastered to their skins. Tayan's paint had long since washed off and he'd decided not to bother reapplying it until they were dry and able to meet with someone who would respect it.

He squinted, but the Singing City was too far away for him to make out in any detail. One thing he could see, far too close, was the wide, lazy curl of a river below them. He let out an involuntary yelp and leapt backwards from the lip of the hill, Betsu following. The four warriors who always marched at their backs caught them roughly, pinning their arms.

'We wear the feathers, the peace feathers!' Tayan shouted.

Beyt was frowning, but it melted into a delighted laugh. She shook her head, clapping. 'You poor, misguided fools.

116

Another reason why you'd be better off under the song. Bring them.' She vanished down the other side of the hill and her warriors wrestled Tayan and Betsu forward. Helpless and sliding in the mud, Tayan strained to pull himself free. If this had all been some elaborate joke, some drawn-out murder, he would make them earn their laughter.

The river twisted around the base of the hill, a monstrous, sluggish, lethal snake of brown water, straining its banks with runoff from the Wet. Spanning it was a bridge, wooden and as wide as the limestone road. It wasn't strung high between the trees like at home, only to be used as a last resort. Instead, it sat solid and stable and only an arm's length above the water.

Betsu was shouting curses, wrenching at the grips of the men holding her, her muscles bulging. Beyt sent a third warrior back to help and he pulled her into a headlock while the other two dragged her arms up behind her back. She let out a strangled screech of pain. Beyt and the pair of warriors flanking her walked onto the bridge without hesitation.

'Holy Setatmeh, gods of rivers and lakes, of the rain and the crops, revered spirits, we worship at your feet,' Beyt said. 'Know that you live within the song with us, that you live in our hearts with the song, and that the song lives within us all. If it be your will, let us pass.'

Sweat blinded Tayan but he blinked desperately as he was dragged onto the bridge, the planks loud under his scuffling sandals. He squinted right and then left, looking for the mottled skin, the dead black eyes, the reaching hands. He'd only ever seen one up close, and he had the scars from mid-thigh to ankle and a dead eja on his conscience to prove it. His heart was pounding hard enough to burst.

And then they were over, thumping down into waterlogged soil, the river behind them. They were dragged a little further and then released, and Tayan slumped to his knees, barely resisting the urge to embrace the ground and kiss it.

When he looked up, Beyt had her hands on her hips. 'You're learning many lessons of the Empire's greatness on this journey, aren't you?' she asked, the mocking edge to her voice sharper than obsidian. 'You see how proper reverence, proper understanding, shows your childish fears for what they are?'

Humiliation flashed through Tayan, followed by the first unwilling stirrings of awe. The song was right: the Pechaqueh were truly blessed, truly special. They had even tamed the Drowned. But then he saw it, a lucky break in the clouds casting just enough brightness onto the woman's face. Sweat at her hairline and glistening in the lines on her palm as she wiped casually at her upper lip. She'd been afraid. Terrified. Only bravado was giving strength to her voice now, when in truth crossing that bridge had been as hard for her as it had for them. Tayan deliberately crushed his awe and replaced it with contempt.

'Admitting fear makes a person stronger than pretending they don't feel it at all,' he said and forced himself to his feet. 'The Drowned are an abomination sent by the lords of the Underworld. They—'

'You should stop talking before we take you back and throw you in,' Beyt said, and the edge in her voice had hardened. She jerked her head and the seven warriors spread out around them again. The woman took the lead, striding along the road towards the city.

'That was well said,' Betsu murmured as they followed her. The nod of respect was unexpected, but it poured strength and courage into Tayan. He nodded back and set his sights on the Singing City, straining to make out the details and wondering what other tests and horrors lay in wait.

There were horrors, but they were far more mundane – and so all the worse for it. The peace-weavers had become uneasily used to the presence of slaves. On the occasions they'd stopped in a city or village during the trek, slaves had been everywhere, obvious in their undyed maguey and bare of jewellery, charms and feathers. Many still bore tattoos, but without the honour that would have once accompanied them.

Here, too, around the scattered dwellings and in the vast fields lining either side of the road, were slaves. And worse. Tayan hadn't thought there could be anything below the class of slave. He had been wrong. As they walked towards the most opulent, populous city he had ever seen, the shaman had to force himself not to stare. Starving, filthy, naked beggars, calling out in a dozen accents, the tattoos of their tribes barely visible beneath the grime. Men and women, even children, offering their flesh in return for food. Some had made badly woven baskets or crude pots that hadn't even been fired, their eyes dull with hopelessness.

'Why?' Tayan asked, but his voice broke and he had to repeat it. 'Why are they here?'

Beyt glanced around as if only just noticing them. 'The Singing City is the centre of the world and the source of the song. It attracts both the highest and the lowest of society. These have probably displeased their owners and been cast out, or didn't sell in the flesh markets. Ignore them; the Choosers chip away at their number each new moon.' She paused in thought. 'And let me know if one of them touches you,' she added eventually. 'It is death for them to touch a free, and while I don't quite understand your status here in the Empire, I won't be responsible for your honour being fouled by them.'

'There would be no dishonour,' Tayan said quietly, but

119

Beyt had already turned her back and increased her pace. She was as eager to reach the Singing City as Tayan was suddenly reluctant.

'No wall,' Betsu murmured. 'Your Sky City has a wall to protect it from Drowned and to deter cats. This place has no wall. They don't count either of those as a threat.'

She was right. More and more buildings began springing up to either side of the road, like mushrooms growing in cool shade. There was no clear entrance into the city; rather, it grew around the road – and grew big. Each building was easily the size of the council house back home, surrounded by high stone walls and tree-filled gardens.

'These have walls,' Tayan pointed out.

Betsu snorted. 'That's because rich Pechaqueh live here and they don't want their fine senses ruined by having to see or smell these poor broken creatures.' She gestured at the beggars. 'Still, it would make taking this city more difficult. Every single estate becomes its own defensive position, and while that means those inside are isolated, it also means scaling walls and knocking down gates every single time. It would slow down any offensive, break it up into hundreds of individual skirmishes. Each estate would fall, but it would take time, and those surrounding it could launch attacks of their own, with multiple places to retreat to.' Her footsteps slowed. 'If they have a network of tunnels running between these estates, they could reinforce when necessary, move non-fighters, replenish supplies . . .'

Tayan let her mutter away to herself. Her warrior instincts had changed from dismissive to intrigued. It would be vital information to take back to the tribes, and he didn't want to interrupt her as she analysed their surroundings. They might not get another chance to see the city from this angle.

Not that we're going to need to know the defensive capabilities of the Singing City anyway, he reminded himself, but the words were weak. He shook himself; they were here to negotiate a lasting peace. He brushed at the turkey feathers again, the action instinctive after so many weeks' travel.

Beyt and the warriors in front turned off the road and padded along a packed dirt track between two tall stone walls. They stopped in front of a thick gate set into the stone and Beyt knocked the butt of her spear against it.

'Wait, where are we?' Tayan asked in some alarm. He had expected to stay in the traders' quarter, if there was such a thing, where rooms could be hired by the night or the week.

'Spear of the City Enet lives here,' Beyt said impatiently. 'I'd brush some of the mud off your sandals if I were you.'

Twelve days they had travelled together, and not once had Beyt alluded to the fact she would bring them directly to someone of power. The idea was so absurd it hadn't even occurred to them to ask. Tayan exchanged a horrified look with Betsu; they were filthy and he wore no paint. The gate swung open.

ENET

Great Octave's estate, Singing City,
Pechacan, Empire of Songs
152nd day of the Great Star at morning

The holy lord has my complete devotion. The holy Setatmeh have my worship. And the world spirit holds my hope of rebirth.

Enet centred herself with the prayer, clearing her mind and inhaling the song into the very depths of her body. Only when she was sure that she held the Singer foremost in her thoughts, wrapped with the pure love of devotion, did she return to the old, painted fig-bark book one of the traders in her employ had uncovered. A book of prophecies made by the 142nd Singer forty cycles of the Great Star before. Three hundred and twenty sun-years. An eternity and yet the blink of an eye in the grand round of histories and prophecies, ancestors and futures. The space of a single dream during the world spirit's slumber.

Many of the pages were illegible now, the glyphs faded or stained, and the last fourth of the book itself was missing. Still, Singer Tecotl had lived closer to the time of those first

Singers who were said to not have ascended upon death – the stories that had been the cause of her humiliation in front of the Singer a month before. Though he appeared to have forgotten it, even confirming her in the position of Great Octave in the intervening days, Enet hadn't forgotten it. Enet would never forget it.

But the legends Singer Tecotl knew and had written down in these pages might, to him, have been histories rather than stories. Might have been fact. Enet sat in the small, concealed room within her estate palace. Only two other people knew of the room's existence. Both were slaves. Both were sworn to her. One still had a tongue and could speak what he knew, but he'd been with her since he was a child. Enet trusted few, but she trusted them.

The room was cramped with shelves of books and loose pages and artefacts and transcribed tales from every land the Empire had brought under the song. Relics from those lands: sacred objects, charms, idols of false gods. Anything that might bring her closer to the truth that even here, in her most secret heart, she could barely bring herself to contemplate. The truth of the Singers who did not die, but nor did they ascend; the Singers who remained themselves and yet undying, and who still walked, she knew, *she knew*, somewhere in this world.

This truth that was Enet's path to immortality. *For the good of the Empire of Songs. For the waking of the world spirit. For peace.*

Her ancestry and wealth guaranteed her a place on the Singer's council, but it was her mind that had seen her elevated to Spear of the City and then Great Octave. And still there was so much more that she could do for the Empire. This was but a means to achieve stability for Ixachipan and beyond.

Enet wasn't like the Singer's other courtesans. She didn't just rely on the delights of her body to charm him. Instead, she studied the histories and the prophecies, the old tales and those yet to come. She cast fortunes with dice and bones until she was the most sought-after diviner in the source. She learnt, she thought, she spoke, until Singer Xac was as enamoured of her mind as he was of the warm hollow between her thighs. Enet intended to keep it that way until she had all the pieces and had cast all the possible futures and was ready to act.

There was a knock at the door. Enet flinched, the book dropping from her hands. No one knocked at this door; no one would dare. Heart lurching, she darted a glance at the massive chunk of rock, flecked with tiny crystal until it almost seemed to glow, that dominated the centre of the room. The other item that made this place both secret and sacred. She stood, brushing off her kilt. 'What?' Her voice was harsh.

'High one, there are . . . there are peace-weavers at the gate,' her estate slave murmured. 'From Tokoban and Yalotlan.'

'Peace-weavers?'

'Yes, high one. They say they are here to negotiate a truce and a lasting peace between their peoples and the Empire.'

A high, disbelieving laugh broke from Enet's lips. She put the book back on the shelf and then faced the stone and touched her belly and throat in salute, before licking her finger and running it across the section she'd been working on with the chisel. Her fingertip gathered a fine white coating and Enet sucked it clean, relishing the way the dust had the slightest roughness against her gums and tongue. Then she crossed to the door and pulled it open. The slave stood back against the tall painted screen that normally concealed the entrance.

'They've travelled all the way from Tokoban?'

The slave nodded. 'Yes, high one. They wear . . . full heads of turkey feathers.' Enet's eyebrows rose. 'I have sent a boy to fetch what he can, should you wish to see them and be likewise attired. Eight Melody macaws led by Second Flight Beyt brought them. They await your pleasure at the door. The peace-weavers' – he stumbled over the unfamiliar phrase – 'I have shown to the small room.'

Irritation took over from amusement. 'I will see this half-blood macaw and learn their intent in disturbing me. Make sure Pikte is kept away from the northerners.'

'As the high one commands,' the slave said. He stood aside and then wrestled the screen back into place so the door was invisible. Enet didn't wait for him, striding along the brightly painted corridor towards the main door.

The Second Flight stood just inside the entrance, her mouth slightly open as she gazed at the murals and woven hangings adorning the walls and corridors leading to the public and private parts of the palace. Four of Enet's slave warriors surrounded the woman, while the other macaws waited out in the gardens.

'What is the meaning of this?' Enet demanded and the macaw shut her mouth and dropped to her knees.

'We found them in Xentiban two weeks ago, Spear,' the woman said. 'A Tokob shaman and a Yaloh warrior. Peace-weavers. They wanted to come to the Singing City and negotiate. I thought it was best to escort them so they couldn't get up to any mischief. I . . . thought you might be prepared to speak with them.'

'You should have killed them.'

The macaw flinched. 'High one,' she said, adding the honorific though her half-Pecha blood didn't strictly require her to, 'they wear a multitude of peace feathers. My place is not to determine whether such as they might be harmed.'

'So you brought them all the way here, into our very heart, instead of to the nearest eagle who could make that decision for you?' Enet's voice dripped with scorn, but they were here and, worse, they'd been invited in. The Great Octave's own honour and status demanded she at least see them.

'Forgive me, high one,' the macaw said.

'No,' Enet snapped. 'You will leave your name with my estate slave and you will get out of my house. Now.' She already knew the warrior's name, and there was only one macaw Talon in the whole Melody, but the woman needed to understand the consequences of what she'd done.

The warrior pressed her blushing face to the floor and then rose and fled, pausing to whisper to the estate slave who waited at the door. Enet watched her go, sorely tempted to give her guard the nod, but didn't. She'd have to end all eight of them, and it would be loud and messy before it was done. A boy came in with a basket of turkey feathers soon after, while she was putting on a fresh tunic and kilt and reapplying her cosmetics. She allowed him to bind one into her hair, over her right ear, as the warriors wore it. She would be interested to see what these peace-weavers made of that. She found she was interested to see what they made of everything – and what she made of them.

Peace-weavers. What a novel concept. She smiled to herself as she patted the feather again and then made her way to the small room with the view of the gardens. She paused in the doorway for just the briefest moment, seeking to gain whatever advantage she could. Her mouth thinned and then she smiled to herself. They were filthy. They were exhausted. They'd been brought straight here, judging by the packs her slaves had taken from them and the dampness of their clothes and hair. That, at least, the macaw had done well.

The man was slender and fidgety, hastily rubbing blue

paint onto his brow from a small pot, while the woman stood with her arms folded across her chest and looking like she'd just bitten into rotten meat. She was older than Enet, heavyset, shoulders thick with muscle and hands and wrists hatched with scars. There were bands of grey in her hair and lines around her eyes and mouth, but violence sat lightly within her, ever ready to be tapped. The Great Octave didn't let it bother her.

'Welcome to the Singing City and the deep magic of the song, honoured guests. I am Spear of the City Enet. I am also Great Octave, though you need not concern yourself with that. Under the song.'

They'd whirled at her first words and Enet recognised the wide-eyed blink from the man as he got his first look at her. She took it as her due. 'Thank you, Spear, I mean Great Octave. I am Tayan, called the stargazer, shaman of the Tokob and peace-weaver. This is my friend and colleague, the warrior Betsu of Yalotlan. We are honoured that you have agreed to speak with us. And . . . under the song. Or as we would say, may the ancestors guide your steps.'

He rubbed the last of the paint in a hasty, slightly crooked line from the middle of his lower lip to the point of his chin.

'Betsu,' the woman said, as if she needed to imprint her authority on the meeting. Or as if she didn't like this Tayan speaking for her.

'And do you offer me the grace of your ancestors, Betsu of Yalotlan?' Enet asked, her head on one side and her hands clasped before her. The woman grunted. 'Ah, well. I am sure the Tokob ancestors will watch over me, even if yours do not.'

'Hundreds more of my people are now ancestors because of you, because of Pechacan and the Empire and your—'

'Peace, Betsu,' Tayan barked and then, astoundingly, blushed. 'Forgive me, Great Octave, I should not have raised my voice in your house. It was impolite and goes against the protocol of the peace-weaving. May we begin?'

Enet suppressed a sigh and sat; then she gestured for them to do the same. She clapped once. 'Refreshments for my guests, and arrange clean clothes for them. And some cloths so that they may remove the worst of the mud,' she added. They'd removed their sandals in the entrance, but their feet appeared just as filthy and there were already marks on her mats.

Tayan grimaced and looked down. 'The Wet is heavy already, is it not?' he asked. 'I apologise for the mess we have made. We were, ah, unaware we would be meeting you immediately upon our arrival or we would have ensured we were more presentable. Thank you,' he added to the slave handing him the square of cotton. He scrubbed at the mud coating his feet and legs, then used a clean corner to squeeze the water from his hair. It was long, coming halfway down his back, threaded with strings of dyed-blue bird bones and painted clay beads. His kilt was patterned with blue squares, as was his sleeveless tunic. Four long, pale scars marred the side of his left leg; that would have been a nasty injury.

'Would you like to bathe?' she asked before they were settled and was gratified to see them both recoil.

'Thank you, no. Unless that is a requirement of your society? We do not wish to cause offence and this is only our first meeting.'

Enet met Betsu's eyes and an understanding as to the nature of these meetings passed between them.

'You cause no offence,' the Great Octave said softly.

The shaman retrieved his bag and knelt opposite Enet. Betsu joined them, impassive, as he began to lay out items on the low table between them. One of Enet's guards shifted away from the wall and she raised her hand to still them, curious. There was a small clay jar, tightly stoppered, a series of well-carved statues, and a soft deerskin pouch. 'Do you have a bowl and grinding stone for us to prepare the magic?' he asked.

'The . . . magic?' Enet asked. The man indicated the vial and the pouch. 'Oh yes, your frog-magic. It is true you lick them? Is there one in there?' She leant forward and prodded the pouch with a long fingernail; it was disappointingly soft.

The shaman coughed. 'See how we already learn about each other?' he said with forced cheer. 'When we journey to the realm of the ancestors, or to speak with Malel, our goddess, or those spirits not yet reborn, the path is arduous, and to speak with the dead is a difficult task. Our magic eases that passage. Does your song-magic require the same?'

'It does not.'

The Toko waited for more, but Enet was silent. Her estate slave knelt behind the peace-weavers, alert to her smallest gesture or requirement. It clearly made the pair nervous to have his silent presence behind them.

'I hope that over the coming days we will continue to learn about each other, the better to reach an agreement that pleases all parties. For now, shall we begin? The grinding bowl?'

'Begin what?' Enet was losing patience. She had been called from her books and her research for this, these childish overtures of friendship, this babbling nonsense of ancestors and herb-magic.

'At the commencement of a peace-weaving, it is customary to visit the ancestors, so that all know we hold the same purpose and that our hearts are pure. It creates trust. The ancestors will know if anyone has evil intent.' He picked up the pouch and gave her a bright smile.

Enet ran a considering finger across her lower lip. Betsu rolled her eyes, but Enet's performance wasn't for the Yalotl.

'Forgive me, Tayan – or should I call you Peace-weaver? – but our dead rest within the world spirit, and we access that through the song. The song is the voice of the world, you see. Do you see? We are constantly, endlessly connected with our dead. We need no frog-juice to show us our past. Or our future.'

Tayan lowered his head. All Enet could see was the tension in his shoulders and the rather tatty crown of turkey feathers. Betsu was blank-faced next to him, as if she didn't even speak the same language. Enet waited, the patient, smiling host, until Tayan's shoulders dropped and he raised his head. He smiled again.

'You are right, of course. We have come to your land to request a peace-weaving. It is your traditions we should honour here, not ours.' He packed away his instruments and tucked the bag behind him. 'Tell me then, Great Octave, how should we begin the peace-weaving?'

'Ah, my honoured guests, that is where there is a small problem,' Enet said, holding up her palms. 'We have no such thing.'

The silence was dumbfounded – until it was broken by ugly, wheezing laughter. Betsu's face was red and tears filled her eyes as she laughed, her face twisted into a horrible grimace that was part humour, part despair.

'Betsu? Betsu, peace,' Tayan hissed. 'Great Octave, you have no protocol for establishing peace with others?'

'We already have peace,' Enet said, pointedly not looking at the Yalotl as she struggled to contain herself. 'All the Empire is at peace. When you are brought under the song you, too, will know it.'

'Then the peace-weaving can proceed,' Tayan said with clear relief. Enet arched an eyebrow. 'Your position is that we will only know peace if we join your Empire. Our position is that we wish to retain our autonomy and end the war. The negotiation now will lead to a compromise satisfactory to all parties.'

'Yes, indeed you can end the war here and now,' Enet said and she let irritation trickle into her voice. 'Join the Empire and not one more of your people will be lost to our weapons. Look around you, look at our wealth, feel the song's might in your hearts. You walked through hundreds of sticks of farmland: imagine the amount of crops they grow. Your warriors can join our Melody and serve with honour. Your artists will find new subjects and new markets. Your shamans can learn about the song and our magic, our ways. The whole world will open up to you.'

'We do not wish to join your Empire,' Tayan said when she paused for breath, and his voice was as smooth as polished jade. 'But let us not try to solve everything in one day. A peace-weaving traditionally lasts for thirty days, so we have plenty of time to—'

Enet threw back her head and laughed, genuinely amused. 'Thirty days?' she gasped, one hand pressed to her chest. 'You expect me to sit here and listen to such nonsense for thirty days? Only because you arrived unexpected and unasked-for at my home have I done you the courtesy of listening so far. But do not forget: you *are* in my home, and you *are* here unannounced. You come in spouting traditions and waving around herbs and you demand my attention and time – and then you demand thirty days of it? No, honoured guests, no. I am curious, and so I will grant you seven days of my valuable time. You will stay in my home and I will show you the city and Pechaqueh ways and all that might be yours upon joining the Empire of Songs.'

She stood and they stared up at her, dumbstruck. Enet

snapped her fingers and the slave kneeling behind the peace-weavers rose, collecting their bags.

'I'm sure that by the end of our time together you will be eager to return home to tell your people of the virtues of laying down their weapons and surrendering. We will speak again tomorrow. You, show them to a room and feed them.'

'You subjugate your neighbours and keep them as property,' Betsu said, her voice heavy with scorn as she rose. 'You worship the Drowned. You steal from the balance and the Ixachipan you profess to love suffers as a result. Ancestors' bones are disturbed, spirits forced from their resting places in tree and rock. That is not balance; it is sacrilege against Malel – against the world. And you say we will beg to join you in this wholesale slaughter?'

'Betsu, peace,' the shaman snapped, his eyes flashing with an uneasy mix of anger and pleading. 'This is not how to begin a peace-weaving.'

'How much land is enough land?' Betsu demanded, strident.

Enet put her head on one side and gave them a quizzical smile that masked her seething outrage. 'That is for the Singer to decide. The song is a glory to all who hear it – as you know. We wish only for as many peoples as possible to live within the joy of the song. We do not steal; we bring a gift of immeasurable bounty to those who join our Empire. This is something you will come to understand.'

'*Join* your Empire?' Betsu mocked. 'You mean be enslaved by it. Stolen from our homes and our ancestors. Turned into *things*.'

Enet shrugged. 'What better way to learn how our society works than from the bottom? With faithful service, slaves are made servants who receive compensation. Servants save up enough to pay off their debt and become free. The free live and farm and make babies and raise livestock under the glory of the song. Peace, peace-weavers,' she added with another smile. 'That is what we offer the world.'

Betsu's face reddened, veins standing out in her throat.

'Betsu,' the shaman warned in a low voice. 'We are guests—'

'Your Singer has ordered you to flood over the land like locusts, conquering all in your path and forcing them to serve you like dogs, but it was not always so. This noise you call a song is poison and it has poisoned you all. We will never—'

Enet's polite mask fell from her face. Her slave knelt and pressed his forehead to the floor. The guards rushed forward from their places around the walls. 'The Singer is a living god and the song is his grace spread across us,' the Great Octave said in a soft, deadly voice. 'It unites us in one great, glorious purpose, a purpose every Pecha believes in. And our free, our servants and our slaves all hold that purpose in their hearts alongside the glory of the song.' She gestured to the slave. 'You. You're happy, aren't you?'

The man bobbed his head and raised it just enough to speak. 'Of course, high one.'

'Do you even know his name?' Betsu demanded.

Enet didn't so much as glance at her. She wouldn't be able to convince Betsu, but the shaman. Oh, the shaman was promising. 'The song would light up your lives,' she said, soft and coaxing now. 'It would take your small, sad world and polish it like jade. Like pearls from the ocean. It would enhance everything you did and saw and ate and smelt, every feeling, every decision. The song is the world, Tayan.'

She stepped between her guards and put her hand on the shaman's chest, felt his heart thudding against his ribs, and looked deep enough to see his spirit burning in his eyes. 'It has been inside you for weeks now, brightening you, glorifying you; I see its light in your face. When you reach the border you will no longer hear it. You will be lost. Bereft. Don't throw it away. Don't discard the glory inside you and condemn your thousands of brave warriors to pointless death.'

'She is a scorpion, Tayan. Her words are venom.'

'Betsu, peace,' the shaman said, but he neither looked at her nor moved away from the pressure of Enet's hand on his chest. They stared into each other and she felt him waver, she felt him teeter on the edge of surrender. And step back. 'May we speak again tomorrow, Great Octave?' he asked formally.

'I have duties in the source, with the Singer,' Enet said. 'But I will find some time to show you the city.' She walked to the door and looked back over her shoulder. 'You are lucky you arrived when you did,' she added as if it was an afterthought. 'The new moon will come before you leave. You can take part in our ritual offerings to the holy Setatmeh.'

'Is that a threat?' Betsu demanded, clenching her fists.

Enet only smiled. 'Under the song.'

THE SINGER

The source, Singing City, Pechacan, Empire of Songs

The song is eternal. My song shall be eternal, spreading across Ixachipan and then the world until all know my strength and the Pechaqueh power.

I, Xac, 174th Singer of Pechacan, wielder of the magic that binds the Empire, will be the once, last, and only Singer, walking at the world spirit's side for eternity.

I honour my ancestors, who have brought the Empire so close to its final glory. Because of them and the grand work of expansion they began, I shall wake the world spirit.

Because of myself and all the reverence I am owed, I shall achieve greatness so radiant it will reflect back through the years to burnish their legacy brighter.

Through me Ixachipan will be brought to harmonious glory. Through me will be an end to war and division. Through me will the Pechaqueh rule supreme and the Empire be prosperous. Through me the world spirit will awaken.

And with that awakening, I shall wax into my full power. None shall withstand us. None shall want to withstand

135

us. The world spirit and I will make a garden of the world, and a music of living. All shall know my name. All shall know me.

For I am the Singer, and my will is stone.

TAYAN

Great Octave's estate, Singing City,
Pechacan, Empire of Songs
153rd day of the Great Star at morning

'I mean it, Betsu. Yesterday was a disaster – already she has refused us the full length of the peace-weaving. We must make progress in the days we have, which means that if you cannot charm her, then you must hold your tongue.'

Betsu paced their room like a jaguar on a riverbank debating whether it was safe to drink. 'Who do you think you speak to?' she spat. 'I am a Yalotl – it is my people dying, my people fleeing Pechaqueh spears. And you ask me to charm her?' This time she did spit, accurately, out of the window.

'And it is our warriors dying alongside yours, our cities feeding and housing those refugees who flee. We are in this war, standing shoulder to shoulder with you. We have been all season.' Tayan fought for calm, fidgeting with the peace feathers woven into his hair. They were old now, shabby. Much like the prospects of the peace-weaving itself. 'We're

137

running out of time and we've been stuck in this room all morning waiting for her to agree to see us.' The shaman took a deep breath. 'I think if we haven't made progress in three days, we have to make the land and trade offer.'

Betsu stopped and faced him. 'That's the offer of last resort,' she said, incredulity colouring her tone. 'That's the end of Yalotlan. We said we'd let them keep what they've already stolen only if there was no other choice.'

'There already is no other choice.' He bit off the words that wanted to tumble from his mouth, that Betsu had practically assured there would be no other choice through her behaviour. She hadn't been like this with the Zellih, but something about Pechacan, or the song – or Enet herself, maybe – had stripped the diplomacy from her tongue.

'If you make that offer, you condemn us to death. If they know we will give them half our land, they will know they can take it all. I cannot allow it.' Betsu's voice was very cold.

'And yet your council of elders agreed it. And you would be welcome in our lands,' Tayan tried, sick at heart, for he was not at all sure that they would be. 'You would have farms, homes, as you do now. You—'

'We would live on your charity because you gave away our homes? Gave up on us, on the fight? No.'

Tayan whirled from the window, acid burning in his throat. 'Let us at least begin the weaving,' he said. 'I am merely suggesting that we agree in advance which concessions we are happy to make and when.'

'You talk of selling us, as if you are Pechaqueh yourself.' There was violence in the air, but it was Betsu's words that made Tayan take a step away from her. The breath caught in his throat. How could she *say* that?

She crossed the room and held up a clenched fist. 'There is no peace we can weave that will preserve Yaloh and Tokob autonomy – only violence can do that. So that's what we give, side by side, offering violence for freedom. As your council promised us.'

Tayan didn't answer her. Instead he stared out at the Spear's estate, filled with people and gardens and small plots of crops. It seemed so normal, if you discounted that every person was a slave and the estate had been built with, and was maintained by, their blood. Not even the most fevered journeying had ever shown him something like this, so subtly, nauseatingly wrong.

The Pechaqueh sat in these grand stone houses and ate food they hadn't planted, tended, harvested or killed. They wore clothes they hadn't made themselves or traded their own skill for, ate from plates they hadn't created, took medicine they didn't know how to gather and prepare. They did nothing but accumulate wealth and enemies and buy people to tend to them, as though they were helpless newborns.

Their actions tilted the world beneath their feet, destroyed the harmony of nature, the delicate pause between plenty and poverty, life and death. The ancestors cried out at the indignity, at the brands of ownership, the bowed heads, the fearful silence. Surely the lords of the Underworld stirred, restless and secretly pleased with the turmoil – as if the Pechaqueh were calling to them through their monstrous intermediaries, the Drowned.

The Empire was sick, Tayan realised, feasting on its own flesh and bones for sustenance, unable to see the poison for what it was. There were *rivers* out there, rivers curling through the city. Infested with Drowned so bloated and gorged on human flesh that they did not sing, did not need to. Slaves were thrown into those rivers every new moon.

And we are going to see it.

Hundreds of sacrifices to placate the so-called gods –

though really just to feed their bellies. In an Empire that prided itself on its song-magic, the Pechaqueh lived in terror of theirs. The irony was so thick Tayan could taste it.

Under the song. The blessing and valediction, words that were both a promise and a threat. And the song itself, a low, voiceless melody filled with emotion and power and yearning and comfort, pulling at his spirit, bleeding into his ears, his mind, never to be expelled. He'd miss it when they returned to Tokoban, just as Enet had promised. *It's poison. But so sweet, so gloriously sweet that my skin drinks it like nectar.*

'This weaving is done,' Betsu said, interrupting his reverie. 'We leave, and we kill this fucking Enet before we go, kill as many as we can on our way out of the city, maybe see if we can rouse the slaves in the flesh markets Beyt told us of. Spark a rebellion. Either way, we go home and we tell our people to prepare for war.'

'The weaving is not even begun,' Tayan said, genuinely shocked. 'We have been here a single day.'

'We can't negotiate with people who sacrifice others to monsters to ensure their own safety, who are so deluded they think the Drowned are gods. And if they ever run out of *inferior people* to feed to them, it will be fine, upstanding Pechaqueh who get eaten instead. And that is something they will not allow. It has to be us.'

It churned Tayan's gut to hear the words said out loud. He'd known, of course, somewhere deep inside, in a place he hadn't wanted to examine too clearly, but Betsu had dragged it screaming into the light, monstrous and deformed and very, very real. It felt as though spiders were crawling over his skin.

She gestured at the slaves in the garden. 'That will be us within a sun-year, toiling over crops we'll never get to eat, this bastard music forever in our heads. Our slightest infraction putting us one step closer to being a meal for a Drowned. Unless we win. I don't know about you, shaman, but I'd rather die fighting than die at the teeth of one of those things after years on my knees for these arrogant shits.'

The door to their room opened and Enet strode in, her kilt dyed blood-red – an omen that made Tayan's breath stutter. How much had she heard? His hand fluttered to the peace feathers again, then further back to the frog-bone charm hanging amid the dense black mass of his hair. He bowed. 'Under the song, Great Octave.'

Behind her, the corridor led to the main entrance. The door was open, slaves and slave warriors hurrying in and out. 'I thought perhaps you would like to see the city today and learn more about our way of life here. Shall we?' Her voice was bright and friendly, but there was no polite way to refuse – and the small lift at the corner of her mouth made it clear she was aware of that.

'It would be our pleasure. We saw very little on our arrival,' Tayan said with an effort.

She made a gesture as graceful as a dancer's, and they followed her through the corridor and out into the gardens. A single large litter sat on the ground, six burly slaves waiting to lift it. Tayan felt sick, and Betsu looked murderous.

'We would enjoy the walk, with your permission, Great Octave,' Tayan said.

Enet raised an eyebrow. 'Really? But you have walked such a very long way to be here. No, no, sit with me so that we may talk without being overheard.'

Betsu balked at the edge of the litter and Tayan poked her in the back. A burst of air blew from her flared nostrils, but then she bent and clambered in, sitting as far from Enet as it was possible to get. Tayan had no choice but to take the centre of the litter, huddled cross-legged and mortified as Enet lounged beside him. They were lifted smoothly and the gates swung open. The morning was bright and the road they had come in on led deeper through the estates, more and more buildings crowding its edges the further they travelled.

Slaves in plain maguey hurried out of the way; even Pechaqueh moved to the sides of the street, many touching their bellies and then their throats as they spotted Enet in the litter. She left the peace-weavers in silence awhile, perhaps hoping to awe them with grandeur. All Tayan saw were slaves, his eyes dragged again and again through the press to their plain clothes and blank faces. They were everywhere. Some clean and well cared for, their clothes neat and well made. Others ragged and filthy, barefoot but not through choice, unlike Xessa. All bore brands on both upper arms – a triangle marked into their flesh. Those free they passed had their scars amended, another line cut through to show their status.

'Why don't slaves just run away and then cut through their brands?' Betsu asked, her tone anything but courteous.

Enet sighed. 'Do you know why when we bring a tribe under the song we remove them from their ancestral lands for a time and have them work for us?'

Betsu snorted at her choice of language.

'I do not. It is something we have wondered about,' Tayan said hurriedly. He didn't dare look at Betsu in case the fragile dam holding back her anger should burst under the weight of his gaze.

'Because severing the links to ancestors and the magic of your soil is the surest way for the song to find its way into your hearts, for a people to fully understand its power and majesty. How could we ever trust you so close to the source of your magic until you had proven yourselves to be Pechaqueh in your hearts?'

142

Pechaqueh in our hearts? 'Great Octave, forgive me, but we—'

Enet cut him off. 'Even as allies, you could plot against us with the aid of your goddess and the spirits. We guard against that by bringing people to other parts of the Empire until they have seen the strength that lies in unity. Here and elsewhere they can work within our households and with our farmers and artisans. They can mine the songstone and see how the Pechaqueh way of life brings peace and plenty and contentment. They learn from us, are educated by us, understand how we trade and sell and buy, how we live, how we worship. They come to understand the glory of the song, the glory of the Empire. Why then would they run away?'

'You're honestly telling us that slaves do not escape and carve through their brands?' Betsu demanded and Tayan was too shocked to caution her.

Enet spread her hands. 'Some,' she admitted. 'But you speak as if we are monsters, not teachers. The vast majority of new citizens come under the song and embrace it. It is of benefit to all. The system works. Peace works. You are fond of that word, are you not?' She grinned so disarmingly that Tayan blinked, and then she leant forward and squeezed his knee and, like a youngster on the cusp of his first relationship, he blushed. His hand went automatically to the wedding cord around his neck, but if she noticed, she gave no sign.

'You speak of songstone,' he said, floundering for a topic. 'We do not know of this. Is it . . .' He paused as something suddenly made sense. 'I see. This is how the song travels across your land, yes? You build your pyramids out of songstone and your Singer's magic is channelled through them somehow so the song is heard all the way to your borders?'

Enet laughed. 'Songstone is far too rare and precious. No,

the pyramids are built from any stone, whatever is local and to hand, but each is capped with songstone. Other than that, yes, you guess correctly. You are clever, aren't you, shaman?'

Tayan didn't answer that. 'Fascinating. May I see a sample of this stone? Perhaps we know it by another name, other properties. How does the magic work, exactly?'

Enet's smile was enigmatic. 'Ah, we are here,' she said, gesturing. 'This is our craft district. Most of our textiles and ceramics are made here. All the people with dyed hems to their kilts are servants. They are working – for jade – to buy their freedom. And see how many wear the traditional and fully dyed clothes of their homelands? They are all free. All of them, working alongside us. Where is the subjugation you are so fond of imagining? Where are the punishments? No, my friends, a slave class might be necessary, but it is neither cruel nor permanent. You have been sadly misinformed by the wildness of your own rumours. Stop,' she added and the litter-bearers paused.

Enet beckoned to a free making balls of clay outside a shop. He rose and approached, bowing his head and touching belly and throat. 'Under the song, high one. Are you looking for something special today?'

'My friends here are from the north. They are curious about society within the Empire. Would you be good enough to explain the story of your life here?'

The man bowed again and then smiled, showing filed front teeth. 'I am Oata from Tlalotlan. The Tlaloxqueh were brought under the song thirty years ago and many have worked their way free. I was born free and then apprenticed as a servant, as is the way with all non-Pechaqueh born in the Empire. I was—'

'You were born free and then made a slave?' Betsu asked, almost springing from the litter.

Oata's face went hard and cold. 'I was not,' he said with stiff formality. 'I was born free and I was apprenticed; I paid to learn but I was paid for my work in return. When those two payments equalled, I could stay with my teacher or set up on my own. I chose the latter. I was free and remain free.'

'Only because your parents worked themselves probably to death to afford a freedom that was theirs to begin with.'

'Peace, Betsu,' Tayan said. 'Forgive my friend, Oata. Forgive her, Great Octave. We seek to understand, that is all.'

Enet waved away the comments as if Betsu's outrage meant nothing, but the Tlalox was not so easily calmed. 'Did your parents not work to make you happy and healthy, northerner? Do you not do the same for your own children? You know nothing of what you speak.' He seemed to remember Enet then and bowed again. 'Forgive me, high one.'

'There is nothing to forgive except, perhaps, this pair's prejudice.'

'Then why does he call you "high one" as if you are some great being?' Betsu demanded, raising her voice. People in the market were beginning to stare, and Enet's face had lost its easy indulgence. Tayan was reminded of her position as one of the most powerful people in the Empire.

'Betsu,' he hissed, pinching her leg hard. She batted away his hand.

Oata scoffed. 'Don't you know whose litter you sit in? Don't you have terms of respect for your councillors? Truly you are in need of the civilising ways of Empire. I will pray for your people, that you are swiftly brought into the Singer's grace and under the magic of the song.'

'You are a wise man, Oata of Tlalotlan,' Enet said and flipped him a jade bead. 'With my thanks for your trouble.'

'Under the song, high one.' He touched belly and throat and vanished.

Enet gestured languidly and the litter began to move once more. She didn't speak; nor did she look at her guests, not for a long time. They moved through the markets and bustling buildings and yards where pots, plates, cups, and statues were being made, or kilts and blankets and tunics were being woven in a variety of colours and patterns. Everything was exquisite, finished or not, the cotton weave so fine it was translucent despite the cloudy morning. Tayan even recognised Xentib patterns, though those people had been conquered less than a Star cycle before.

Enet laughed when he tentatively asked her about it. 'No, tribes do not become free quite so quickly as all that, I'm afraid. But some of our children like to adopt the fashions of others. As the Xentib are the most recent to join in the glory of the song, you can imagine they are quite popular at the moment. And as any people do, we enjoy indulging our youngsters.'

'Their patterns are sacred to them, as I expect yours are to you,' Tayan blurted.

Enet was quizzical. 'They are children; they mean nothing by it.'

'Tell that to the Xentib,' Tayan muttered, but too quietly for her to hear, he hoped. Either way, she didn't respond.

Enet ordered the litter stopped again a few stalls further on. She beckoned, and the merchant scurried forward with an armful of lavish, bright shawls. With his free hand he touched his belly and throat, his head bowed. 'Under the song, high one. Your beauty outshines my wares, as ever.'

The corner of the Great Octave's mouth ticked up. 'And one day your tongue will rot, covered in so much sweet flattery.' The merchant laughed and spread the shawls between them on the litter, even draping them over their knees where they sat. 'I'll take two today,' she said, and although there was easy familiarity in her voice, Tayan noticed how she didn't speak the merchant's name. He bit the tip of his tongue to still his laughter, convinced that she didn't even know it and was trying to hide that fact.

Betsu was staring over the merchant's head, refusing to be drawn into conversation, but Tayan couldn't help examining the shawls. They were beautiful, edged with red and green beads of clay and dyed bone. Each had its own distinct pattern, though he didn't recognise which tribe it belonged to.

Enet made her selection and one of her slave warriors paid, removing three jade beads from the long cord that hung around his neck and down inside his salt-cotton. Tayan blinked at the cost, though Enet didn't seem to notice. *Why would she? Her palace is more luxuriously decorated than our temples.*

The merchant collected up the rest of his wares and retreated with another bow and the litter-bearers began moving again. 'Here,' Enet said, handing them each one of the shawls.

'No,' Betsu said immediately, trying to give it back.

Enet narrowed her eyes, just a little. 'Do the Yaloh have no rules of guest friendship?' she asked, in such a way that told Tayan she knew perfectly well that there were, and that to refuse a host's generosity was to offer insult.

'We have no gifts in return,' Betsu said, but Tayan cut her off.

'You do us much honour, Great Octave,' the shaman said, breathing a swift prayer of thanks to Malel for his foresight and a second to his spirit guides for their forgiveness. He slipped his fingers into the neck of his tunic and found the right string hanging around his neck and pulled a small deerskin pouch free. He licked his lips but passed it over without hesitation. 'Please accept this as a small token of our humble thanks.'

Enet opened the pouch and tipped three small statues into her palm – Young Jaguar, Old Woman Frog, and Swift Hawk – carved from jet, greenstone and pom wood respectively. 'How lovely,' the Pecha murmured, though Tayan thought more because she had to than anything else. He could tell her how sacred they were, but she wouldn't care. Their value was clear, however, and he hoped it would be enough.

She looked up and gave him a smile and another squeeze of his knee. 'I shall treasure them,' she said, and he had no idea whether or not she was lying.

Soon enough the buildings fell away, and even the limestone of the road itself, and there was a wide, empty expanse of packed dirt. In the middle, twisting lazily beneath the building clouds, a wide, slow loop of moving water.

'This is the same river as the one you will have crossed yesterday,' Enet said conversationally as the slaves carried them towards the bridge. 'Back in the north – in fact, Peaceweaver Tayan, I believe it even borders your land? – it is called the Great Roar, but here its might is lessened, and it is known simply as the Blessed Water. Much of the city is built around it. And there, can you see, over in the distance? That is the great pyramid. In there is the source, and in the source is the Singer, our holy lord.'

Tayan and Betsu both leant out of the litter and the slaves grunted and staggered as the balance shifted. The shaman hurriedly withdrew, gripping the padded seat. 'Sorry,' he gasped when he saw Enet clinging to the woven handle hanging above her head. 'I would not be able to see it anyway; my vision is not strong when things are far away.'

'It is . . . impressive,' Betsu said with clear reluctance, but he noticed the tinge of awe in her voice and a slight shine of sweat on her upper lip. Not just impressive, then, but intimidating.

'The peace-weaving,' Tayan began, but Enet cut him off with a wave of her hand.

'Do you like to gamble, honoured guests?' she asked. 'There is a fighting pit just ahead and I do so enjoy an entertainment. Come, let us visit. You can use my jade, bet on whoever you like. It's only to first blood today, but it can still be exciting.'

'First blood?' Tayan asked. 'What do you mean?'

'She means that they force slaves to fight to the death for their entertainment. Don't you?' Betsu said. She was running her fingers over and over the fine beadwork on the gifted shawl and didn't look up as she spoke. 'Blood,' she whispered, as if to herself, 'this entire society is built on it, one way or the other.'

Enet laughed and raised an eyebrow at Tayan, inviting him to share her mirth. 'Oh, my friends,' she said expansively. 'Every society is, and anyone that tells you different is lying. Come on, let's place some bets. I promise it will be fun.'

XESSA

Xessa sat on the step of her house, looking over the city and down across Malel, hazy with mist and the coming dawn, just a splash of blue and the tiniest hint of red at the lip of the world. The rest of the land lay shrouded in darkness, only pinpricks of firelight below indicating the earliest risers.

The air smelt of growth and green, the heavy stink of rich soil from the garden and the sharpness of wet stone. Xessa sucked it in and let it soothe her. Rain beaded on her hair and face; it sat proud like stars on the blanket wrapped around her shoulders.

She bit into a guava and let the juice flood her mouth as she watched the dawn blossom. Smoke tickled her nostrils as someone lit their morning fire just below and she felt the city begin to wake, a tingle through her nerves, a taste on her skin. She grinned at a memory of Tayan telling her she was more shaman than he would ever be. It was magic, he'd said, and there was an end to it.

Her smile faded and her appetite with it. He'd be in Pechacan by now, meeting with their elders and doing all he could to persuade them to end their aggression. Persuade them that what they already had was enough. Too much. Xessa made herself eat the rest of the guava and then a thick piece of pepper-stuffed cornbread. She was due at the water temple in an hour, to work the handle and keep the peace among the citizens coming to collect their ration while Toxte braved the Swift Water.

Xessa tugged on her earlobe, pierced and cuffed with a dozen rings, beads, feathers and dyed bird bones. The sun cleared the horizon and flooded across the world and she threw off her blanket and let the rain patter against the skin of her arms and legs, into the open neck of her tunic.

Unbidden came the memory of Ossa leaping into the river to save her life, of the water swirling up to her thighs as she went in after him, that impatient, cold, and dangerous tug of current right before the Drowned rose and came for her again . . .

She shook her head hard, hair and ear cuffs slapping her cheeks, and then wrapped the blanket tight around herself once more. This wasn't the morning to be remembering such things. Better to think of Toxte, not risking his life at the river, but the feel and taste of his skin and the deep steady throb of his heart when she pressed her face to his chest. A smile pulled at her mouth.

Movement, as Lilla pulled back the door curtain of the house he shared with Tayan. He waved and then pointed at the communal fire-pit. Xessa scowled, but he was right: it was her turn. Ossa shoved his head under her elbow and she paused on the step a while longer, scratching the dog's neck and ears, pressing kisses to his muzzle. Ossa's ears pricked and Xessa looked up; Lilla had his hands on his hips and a look of melodramatic outrage on his face.

The eja sighed and dropped her damp blanket before crossing to the pit to lay the kindling. The rain stopped as the sun rose higher. Steam would be rising from the stone soon, filtering the morning through its haze until it was as if the spirit world had overlaid the flesh world and magic was in everything.

She found the bow-drill and set to coaxing a flame into life, the exertion warming her arms and shoulder and back. She blew on the embers and then built the fire, enjoying the increasing heat against her face. Lilla squatted opposite to rest three small leaf-wrapped parcels around the edges. Xessa perked up, watching him until he felt her gaze and looked up.

'Not a chance,' he signed. She batted her eyes at him and put her head on one side, the way Ossa did whenever she had turkey or lizard. Lilla poked at a piece of wood with a stick. Xessa kept watching him and moved slowly, stealthily, around the fire and then shoved her head under his elbow, as the dog had done to her. Lilla burst out laughing even as he fell onto his arse and then Ossa added to the confusion, leaping into the tangle and seemingly managing to lick both of them at once.

Lilla scrambled away, Ossa prancing around him, and made a show of wiping dog drool and dust from his face and clothes. Xessa lay on the floor, laughing and feeling closer and yet farther from Tayan than ever. They'd been friends all their lives, though she liked to think the first few years he'd existed before she was born had been terrible for him. Her friendship with Lilla now was deep and genuine compared with the brittle, jealous thing it had been when he'd first come into Tayan's life and stolen him from her.

She checked the cooking parcels of bean, nut, and ground

turkey and flipped them over with two sticks. Lilla bent down to wave in her eyeline and then pointed, and Xessa felt a ridiculous and unstoppable blush creep up her neck when she recognised Toxte ambling up the plaza towards them. She looked over to Lilla instead and bared her teeth at his malicious glee. 'Justice for stealing my breakfast,' he signed solemnly.

'I haven't stolen it yet,' Xessa pointed out, but they both knew that one of the parcels was hers – and that that was why he'd made three in the first place.

The spirit-magic was beginning to work in Toxte and his pupils were dilated as he squatted next to the fire, his dog, Ekka, tussling with Ossa. 'Elder Tika told me two more Yaloh were taken at dusk,' he signed without preamble. Xessa stilled and Lilla came to her side. 'They were in the fields. The irrigation ditch was just deep enough.'

Grief and rage and frustration, at herself and the world. At Malel, even. And at the Drowned. Always at the Drowned. 'We should kill them all,' she signed. 'Take the fight to them, every eja at once. No more trying to steal water, no more hiding from them. Just kill them.'

'Tayan would say they're part of the balance, as much as we dislike it,' Lilla signed.

'Well, Tayan isn't fucking here,' Xessa signed angrily and jumped up. 'Even the Lesser Drowned sing for us and they can't even eat an adult. They can barely finish a child! Yet they take us and gorge themselves and leave our bloody remains to the scavengers.'

She was shaking, racked with guilt that was as insidious as it was irrational. She hadn't been on field duty last night; the fault wasn't hers. Except it was, somehow. Every loss, every death or sudden disappearance that was presumed to be a Drowned attack was her fault. Ossa came to her side and pressed against her leg. His tail was low and his big eyes worried. She dropped back to her knees and wrapped her arms around him, burying her face in his short black fur.

Hands on her back and shoulders and a warm flank pressed against hers. Toxte cupped her face in his hands and made her look at him. He shook his head, denying the emotions he knew she was gripped by and then he kissed her, gently, almost chaste. Almost. It sent a spear of sudden want through her, and it stopped dead the treacherous whirl of her thoughts. Toxte twitched as the spirit-magic pulled him further under, and she put her hand over his on her cheek and kissed him back, fixing his spirit in his flesh by running her other hand down his chest.

Toxte sighed against her mouth and leant back and she grinned at his obvious delight. Movement opposite them and she saw Lilla sitting cross-legged and eating his breakfast. He winked and she blushed again – seemingly the only thing her face could do this morning. Which was ridiculous after the last two weeks, during which she'd spent more time kissing Toxte than she had signing with him.

'Let me guess,' Lilla signed with his mouth full of food, 'you're going to bring up yours and Tayan's stupid plan again.'

Xessa stuck out her tongue at him. 'It's a good plan.'

'It's the stupidest thing either of you have ever come up with. And that's saying something.'

'This sounds promising,' Toxte interrupted. 'Let's do it.'

'You don't even know what it is,' Lilla protested.

Toxte waved his hand in airy dismissal. 'Mere details,' he signed and grinned at Xessa and there were hummingbirds charging around in her stomach. She smiled back, but then Lilla threw a stick at them and forced them to pay attention.

'The idiot in front of you and the idiot wandering around

Pechacan want to catch a Drowned for study,' he signed. 'They've got it all planned out, with just one problem: the council won't allow it because of what happened last time it was attempted. Which shows they're not idiots,' he added pointedly.

'That was ten Star cycles ago,' Xessa protested.

'Sixty-three people died,' Lilla signed.

Xessa shifted, uncomfortable and suddenly aware that Toxte's opinion of her could be about to plummet. She watched him from the corner of her eye: his mouth had dropped open and a profusion of twitches rippled through his cheek. Then he sucked his lower lip into his mouth and stared into the distance. He was thinking about it. That was his thinking face; she knew it well.

Xessa raised her eyebrows at Lilla and now it was his mouth hanging open in shock.

'It's past time we tried again,' Toxte signed. 'Every eja I've spoken to wants to try it. What happened in our ancestors' time wouldn't happen again. We've learnt from those mistakes.'

Lilla threw up his hands at the pair of them. 'You're supposed to talk sense into her,' he signed. Toxte shrugged an apology and the warrior muttered something Xessa didn't catch and stomped off into his house in disgust.

'I mean, he's right. It's moon-madness. But tell me anyway. Because there are around twice as many Drowned now as there were fifty sun-years ago.'

'When the Empire of Songs started expanding.'

They stared at each other. That correlation, whether co-incidence or not, never failed to send a shiver through Xessa's spine. The last capture attempt had been a generation before that, but now every Wet seemed to bring more Drowned to the Swift Water, more death to their people. They couldn't afford to wait any longer, surely.

'The numbers we see at the Swift Water each day now . . . they frighten me,' Xessa signed in the end.

'And nothing frightens you,' he signed and she couldn't tell whether he was teasing or mocking. It must have shown, because Toxte reached out and cupped the side of her face for a moment. 'I'm not being cruel. I mean it: I've never seen you frightened.'

'Then your eyes are as bad as Tayan's,' she signed, 'because I'm close to pissing my leggings every day I have the duty.' *And when you look at me like that,* she wanted to add, but didn't.

Xessa shifted to sit opposite him on the damp stone so they could sign freely, but her belly warmed when Toxte casually extended one leg and pressed it along the length of hers – maintaining contact as naturally as if they were married. The line of her thoughts broke for a moment and she couldn't suppress a smile, nudging at his leg with hers.

'You'd need at least three ejab,' he continued as if he, too, had whiled away hours wondering how to capture a Drowned. Perhaps he had. Xessa fell a tiny bit in love with him just at the idea. 'But the question the council will ask is why now, in the middle of the Wet? In the middle of a war?'

Xessa swallowed the anxiety of her next words. 'Because if we're fighting Drowned *and* fighting Pechaqueh, we *will* lose. We're already losing. We will die or be enslaved, every last one of us. The council won't say it, but we all know that if it gets bad enough, they'll have ejab lining up to fight the Empire. Do you want to be killing men and women one day and fighting Drowned the next? Do you think we could? Say we lost a fifth of our ejab in the fighting but prevailed over the Melody. Could the city survive those losses, especially with all the refugees we have here?'

Toxte pursed his lips and then shook his head and Xessa

noticed Lilla watching her side of the conversation from his doorway. She pretended she couldn't see him, but her words were for him as much as Toxte now. 'I don't want to start killing Empire soldiers, but I will if I have to. What I do want to do is understand the enemy I've trained my whole life to fight. I know I don't have years of experience like some. But being younger doesn't mean I'm being reckless with this. I'm not trying to get anyone killed and if it goes wrong, even if we're a heartbeat away from getting one, we back away and run. It's a risk, but I won't add unnecessary risks on top of that. Contrary to popular belief' – and she waved towards Lilla – 'I'm not stupid. I just want to know my enemy so I can kill it.'

'Yes,' Toxte interrupted, excited. 'Its armour, for instance. What exactly is it? What can penetrate it? They breed – we think – but we've never found an infant. Capturing one probably wouldn't answer that question, but are there, I don't know, particularly deep stretches of river crawling with dozens of baby Drowned?'

His hands stopped at that and Xessa felt nausea rise into her throat. Toxte looked just as horrified at the image he'd conjured. He shivered.

'So, lots to learn,' Xessa signed briskly. 'We have a responsibility to protect the city, not just now, but the next generations, and if catching a Drowned allows us to do that . . . besides, I don't want to be eja the rest of my life. I have other things I want to do.' She blushed *again*.

'Like what?' Toxte asked, willing to be distracted.

'She's an artist,' Lilla signed as he wandered back over. 'And a fine one.'

Xessa winced and held up a hand before Toxte could ask anything else. 'The point is, there are a thousand of us who took on the duty without regret, but also because someone has to. What if we didn't have to? What if they were gone? I don't want ejab like you to risk your lives with the spirit-magic day after day. I don't want any more to end up broken like my father Otek. And besides, if Tayan weaves a peace, we won't be at war. Then they can't argue, can they?'

Toxte reached forward and took her hand, grazed a kiss across her knuckles and another to her palm that made her shiver. 'All right, we're due at the water temple soon. Let's talk it over after that, yes?' Toxte signed and Xessa nodded. 'And then we'll talk to Tika.' Xessa's eyes bulged. 'I don't know what she'll say, but you've got a plan. Most of us have a plan. I say we put them all to the elder and see if one stands out as workable. I say we know our enemy.'

In the end, it had been an easy duty at the water, which seemed unfairly at odds with their earlier discussion and conviction that the Drowned's numbers had increased to critical levels. The queue for water had begun to gather before Toxte had even reached the river, but he hadn't let anyone's impatience distract him and she'd watched him move, swift and smooth and strong, a lethal dancer. When she was certain he was out of danger and on his way back uphill, she'd begun turning the water screw's handle.

Lutek was lurking by the stone trough. She was relating some outrageous tale about a Yalotl she'd slept with the previous week and Xessa was laughing as she drew water into the trough while Lutek ensured everyone took only their daily ration. The warrior's head jerked around and her hands stopped moving. Xessa looked in the same direction and saw a scuffle in the queue. People pulled them apart and she saw one was Ilandeh and the other three were Yaloh.

Lutek snatched up her spear and hurried out to intercept them. The civilians who'd hauled them apart had started shouting now, too, and Xessa strained to see. Since the incident at the Swift Water, Ilandeh had been cloyingly friendly, but she had also made a determined effort to learn more sign language, and not just from Xessa. The former merchant had little aptitude for it, but the eja allowed herself to be mollified anyway. She liked the woman well enough, despite everything, and felt sorry for her, too. She and Dakto had fled the conquest of their land with family, but they'd been the only two to reach the Sky City alive and if it made them a little strange, quick to anger and overly friendly, well, they didn't have anyone else, did they?

Xessa wondered what Ilandeh had argued about this time, but then the queue was melting away from the trough and Otek shambled towards her. Xessa smiled at her father and paused the water screw just long enough to move around to the front of the trough and take Otek's face in her hands. She kissed the old man on the cheek, but when she pulled back there was no recognition in his face. She smiled again, through the spike of hurt. A string of gourds hung forgotten from his hand and she took them from him gently.

'Let me fill these, Father,' she signed. Still nothing. Otek had been eja for most of his adult life, until the spirit-magic had broken him. The shamans said he was spirit-haunted and unlikely to ever return, but he never seemed that way to Xessa. He was just . . . empty. Somewhere else.

The Tokob at the front of the queue spoke to him with voice and sign, their hands coming to rest on his arms and shoulders again and again, gentle as butterflies. Honouring his sacrifice, though he paid them no heed. None of them begrudged his place in the line, or Xessa stopping the handle to tend to him. Otek's eyes were empty, as blank and dead as the spaces between the stars. Eyes that had seen too much, a mind that had been invaded by the spirits over and over until it was devoured by them, or until it resided permanently in the spirit world. Until Otek was as hollow as the gourds he had carried.

'If you wait, I will be finished here soon and we can talk,' she signed after she'd passed back the string of gourds. There wasn't enough in them to last, but people dropped by old ejab houses every day to top up their rations and see they had food. 'We could eat together.'

Otek's eyes watched her hands and face and then he shuffled around and wandered back out into the sunlight. Xessa watched him go with fierce pride and aching sadness. *I'll make you proud. I'll catch a Drowned for you and we'll learn how to beat them, how to prevent them singing or breeding, or which poisons will kill them. I'll make you so proud.*

When she turned back to her duty, Toxte had arrived. He was reaching for the handle but she resumed possession of it; his fingers trailed over the backs of hers and up to her elbow before he looked away to signal the next person forward to the trough. Xessa was confronted with a sudden image of him, spirit-haunted and empty, and shoved it roughly away. Otek had chosen duty over his future and his family and remained eja until the spirits stole him. Tika was doing the same. Many ejab did, and it was their right to do so, as it was their right to give up the duty before they became too damaged. If Toxte chose to give his life to the spirits, she would respect that decision. It was his to make, not hers.

But by my hope of rebirth, I pray he does not.

She was distracted from her gloom by Lutek and Ilandeh's return. The Xenti had a bruised cheek and was tight-jawed with anger, but Lutek's warning glare stopped her from speaking. 'Trouble in Xentibec,' she signed briskly. 'Water rations going missing in the night. The Xentib blame Yaloh, who deny it.'

'Well, it won't be Tokob,' Toxte signed as if he could read Xessa's thoughts. 'No one would dishonour our work with such pettiness. Xentib, Yaloh – you're more alike than you'll admit. We risk our lives every day so that you can steal from your neighbours?'

Lutek was translating and Ilandeh was getting angrier by the word. 'We? We are the ones stolen from!' she said, clearly enough the ejab could read her lips. 'We are the ones wronged, and again you side with your neighbours over us.'

Lutek took one look at the ejab faces and dragged Ilandeh out of the water temple. Xessa closed her eyes, shutting out the world, and concentrated on the strain in her muscles as she turned the handle and drew water up the pipe. She timed her breathing to the turns and focused on it to the exclusion of all else for a hundred heartbeats. It was that or chase Ilandeh out of the temple and break her nose again.

Xessa wrapped a thin skin of calm over the heat of her anger and opened her eyes. Toxte was watching her with concern and she gave him a swift smile to say she was all right. He went back to his post at the other side of the temple, watching downhill in case the pipe came under attack from Drowned. As he went, he trailed his fingers down her spine. A shiver went through her, taking her bad mood with it.

Tika hadn't just agreed; she'd spoken to as many ejab as she could find and then she'd requested a special meeting of the council – just the Tokob council this time.

Every excited thought Xessa had ever had, every evening of outlandish speculation she'd spent with Tayan, had come back to haunt her.

We're going to die. We're going to die badly.

'You've poked a stick into a wasps' nest this time and no mistake,' signed Kime, her second father. She flashed him a look full of guilt and regret and his lined face lit up with his habitual sly humour. 'You pissed your kilt yet?' he asked and flicked a finger at the material. Xessa punched his shoulder and then swooped in for a hug, wrapping his chest in her arms and squeezing hard.

He slapped her back until she loosened her grip and then kissed the top of her head. 'The plan's good,' he signed when they stepped apart. 'And it's the right time to do it. Well done.'

Xessa flushed with pleasure and they entered the council chamber behind Tika and Toxte. The elders watched them with hooded eyes. *Like a flock of vultures waiting to pick our bones.*

She took a deep breath and pushed away the image, bitterly resenting Tayan's absence. She'd spent two days blaming Lilla for bringing up the subject and Toxte for his enthusiasm, but she knew the problem was her own fear. The fear they all thought she didn't feel. Licking dry lips, she sat between Toxte and Kime. Sweat glistened in the creases of her palms and trickled down the hollow of her spine. How had this all happened so fast?

Vaqix didn't waste time. He waved a feathered fan in the air to attract attention and then rapped the council stone on the floor. 'The threats against the Tokob way of life, and against Malel herself both as goddess and as our land, are many and grievous. Some here have already argued that this is not the time for us to consider Eja Elder Tika's proposal, but the truth is that the Drowned are growing in number, faster than we have ever seen before. It used to be that if they were in the river they weren't in the ponds; now they are in both, in all. Ejab patrols have confirmed the Drowned are in every clean water source on every slope of Malel.'

Xessa shuddered and Kime gave her hand a brief squeeze.

'Last night, Eja Elder Tika counted fourteen Drowned in the river between water temples one and four. Fourteen. This is more than unprecedented; it is an infestation. A plague. And despite the ejab best efforts, people are dying. Instead of the fifty or so in a season we have historically lost, it is almost that many from one new moon to the next. Children and greyhairs, shamans and potters, elders and warriors. The very life of the Sky City, bleeding out one drop at a time, weakening us death by death when we should be preparing for war.

'The ejab are water-bringers, life-givers and life-takers. This Wet, the lives being taken belong to Tokob and Yaloh. Innocents are dying and the ejab cannot stop it. They are failing.'

The statement was a blow to Xessa's chest. Shame and rage filled her in equal measure. How dare the old shaman say such things about them? They were doing all they could, making sacrifices he could never even begin to understand—

Tika waved and turned slightly to face the ejab flanking her. 'It's true.' Another punch to Xessa's chest and ego, bruising her heart. 'We are losing. It doesn't matter that only the Greater Drowned can breed, or that they breed slowly. Whatever the reasons, whether they are fleeing the Empire of Songs or something else, the salt pans between Ixachipan and Barazal are a barrier not even they can breach. And so it seems that they migrate this far but then can go no further. And here they stay, their numbers increasing.

'We must act now,' Tika continued. 'We must capture a Drowned and we must study it. We must not just rely on our histories and books but make our own extensive examinations. We must not let the failure of the past stop us in the present. What we face now is different, is so much worse, than what our ancestors have lived through.' Tika stopped abruptly and twitched, a violent spasm of the face that made her eyelid and lip writhe. She shook her head furiously.

Kime squeezed Tika's hand; then he began to sign. 'We must learn whether the voice strings can be cut and if they can be poisoned. We need to know what happens to people who hear the song but cannot respond to it – yes, even that. We propose that ejab who have not taken the spirit-magic be restrained and then exposed to the song. Xessa and I, and the other deaf ejab, well, we can of course be with the creature without fear of its song; we can do . . . whatever the council deems needful. And we must do it now, before the rains end and the war returns.' He cast an apologetic glance at Xessa; he had never believed in the peace-weaving.

'What we must do is train more warriors and more ejab,' Elder Apok signed angrily. 'Eja Tika, you have recruited a hundred Yaloh to the snake path. Why then—'

'Of those hundred, elder, only forty-six have mastered the spirit-magic and agreed to become eja. None of them will be ready to take on the duty for a sun-year; most are warriors and need to unlearn many of their ingrained skills. I have ejab paired with them, fighting the way Drowned fight, and they are brought down within moments every single time. We cannot rely on them and suggesting otherwise is irresponsible.'

Xessa winced.

'Sixty-three people were torn apart by one escaped Drowned,' Apok signed.

'That plan was poorly thought out,' Kime interrupted. 'Ours is not. If it was, the high elder would not even have let us get as far as this meeting.' He leant forward. 'Think of what we can accomplish. What if they truly are a product of the Empire of Songs? What if we learn how to destroy them? Think how this could affect the war, elders. Think how it would be to no longer fear the water, to be able to move and outflank our enemies, to travel concealed by riverbanks or attack out of the cover of swamps. To be able to move hundreds of warriors at a time without worrying about depleting the water vine or bamboo along the trail.'

'This isn't just for the ejab,' Tika added when Kime fell still. 'This isn't about glory. It's about living through the war and then, perhaps, living without fear.'

Xessa's heart was a wild bird fluttering against the cage of her ribs when the pair finally stopped signing. She'd never thought Tika could be so eloquent, though she knew her father's spirit was that of a poet. All her own doubts had been burnt away, despite the fact he'd volunteered the pair of them as the captive Drowned's keepers. She looked at each elder in turn, trying to gauge which way they'd go. She found Toxte's hand and squeezed it tight.

There were fifteen elders. Nine voted aye, including Vaqix. And as simple as that, it was done, and nothing would ever be the same again.

PILOS

High Feather's estate, Singing City, Pechacan, Empire of Songs
158th day of the Great Star at morning

Pilos loved being at the estate, among his eagles and their families as they reminisced over campaigns past and watched the youngsters practise their weapons, but he could not deny that after only ten days he was ready to leave and head back to the simpler ways of the Melody's great fortress in the south. To be out of the jaguar's den. To be free from prying eyes.

Councillor Yana, of course, would back his proposal when the Singer deigned to hear it, and he'd been gratified that most of the others he'd met so far had also seen both the sense and the opportunity of it. Enet would oppose him as a general principle, but that was to be expected. She might be Great Octave, but the decision rested with the Singer, not her. Still, from what he could gather, the council was split and more than half of them would wipe their arses with poisonwood leaves if she asked them to. And then there were the Singer's favourites.

166

Much had changed in the half-year he'd been gone, and most of it he didn't like. The Singer's vices were well known, his distractions too. Many of the protocols governing behaviour in the source had been allowed to slip, endangering the Singer's harmony and so, in turn, the song. The Singer's wellbeing, his happiness, was of the highest importance: negative emotions bled into the song and darkened it, and all who lived within its magic would be affected. It was why the council meetings were little more than rituals conducted to obtain the holy lord's approval or rejection of a scheme, while the real debates were held out of his earshot beforehand. It was why he was surrounded only with beauty in all its forms.

Pilos had spent an afternoon with Chorus Leader Nara as the man told him about the usual courtesans' fights and the over-indulgences of the Singer's favourites. What they did in private was up to them; what they did in the Singer's presence could have far-reaching effects.

There wasn't a Pecha alive who didn't know the histories of those Singers who had lost control of themselves or the song and the consequences for those who lived within its sacred bounds. What he'd seen and learnt had been enough to convince him that discipline was lax among the members of the council, among the courtesans, and definitely among the Singer's favourites, those nobles who held no official position in the governing of the Empire but instead danced and diced and drank and fucked in the Singer's company. Pilos had spent the last week finding those favourites and pointing out their errors in soft, respectful, and compelling tones. The Singer's health and wellbeing were paramount.

Pilos thought over the plan again. It was born out of duty and loyalty, without room for any to insist it was a path to glory for himself. There should be no sidelong glances of the sort the other councillors exchanged when a member brought up some new scheme. His proposal benefited the Empire, and it benefited the Singing City. All he had to do was pray the holy lord in his wisdom agreed.

It's the right plan. More than that, it's the only plan. The only option if we're to bring the last tribes under the song with swiftness and mercy.

The Xentib slave warriors were still too unreliable to risk in open battle so close to their homeland, and the Melody had been depleted by the intensity of that people's resistance. They needed more warriors.

Pilos's thoughts were interrupted by a messenger from the Great Octave. He read Enet's note with increasing disbelief – 'peace-weavers' from Yalotlan and Tokoban were in the city, staying at the Great Octave's own estate. Would Pilos join them for duskmeal? Not for the first time, he wished there was a way to insert a Whisper into her household to relay such news to him in a timely fashion. The peace-weavers might have been here for months for all he knew; she was probably only inviting him because it suited her purposes, not because she wanted him to be there.

'Elaq!' he bellowed, scaring the children playing in the garden so they squealed.

His estate manager and oldest friend came at a run, alarm creasing his features and a knife clutched in his fist. 'Spear?' Pilos handed him the message and Elaq read it. He blew out his cheeks and shook his head. 'No way. Not a fucking chance. She'll kill you and say these peace-weavers did it. If there even are such people here. What sort of title is peace-weaver, anyway?' He waved away his own question as irrelevant. 'It's a bad idea, Spear.'

'I know,' Pilos agreed and relief flickered over Elaq's rugged, scarred features. 'But what does Enet know of negotiation?

What does she know of the types of concessions warriors make or the sorts of agreements they reach to end further bloodshed? Of course I'm going.'

'Then I'm coming with you and we'll both be armed. And more than that, you'll be carrying three antidotes with you. Don't eat anything Enet doesn't eat from first.'

Pilos held up his palms, laughing. 'We've got until dusk, my friend. Plenty of time to lecture me on the finer points of not being killed by our resident viper.'

'I'm not sure that's long enough,' Elaq complained, but there was a glint of amusement in his deep-set eyes.

'Peace-weavers,' Pilos mused. Whatever his reputation might be among the council and the city, Pilos would happily take a peace agreed over duskmeal than one won on the battlefield. Though, he admitted ruefully, sharing a meal with the Great Octave was surprisingly similar to fighting for his life. 'Their information could be of use in council tomorrow.'

'If you live long enough to get there,' Elaq muttered darkly, but Pilos chopped his hand through the air – the song-laden, magic-rich air, through which the Great Octave herself could be listening. The old eagle nodded and held his tongue, but his words had planted the seed and Pilos let it sprout. In truth, he would need to be very, very careful this night.

As the Singer's chief courtesan, Enet's estate had always been a lavish affair, but there were two new wings to her palace, and the gardens were deeper, lusher than before, the trees filled with tame birds. She'd even had a private offering pool dug and a small streamlet diverted from a larger tributary to feed it, as if she were a member of the Singer's own family. Pilos caught the flash of a fish as he paced towards the house.

She might not be the Singer's blood kin, but she's Great Octave, her power second only to his, he reminded himself.

He still couldn't quite believe the old title had been brought back – and then given to her. Of all people, to her.

There's no telling what she must be able to talk the Singer into these days. My position as Spear – even as High Feather – could be in jeopardy. Maybe I'll wake up tomorrow and find myself destitute and living on the streets with the other beggars, prey to every Chooser who comes looking for offerings.

'Your slave is to wait here,' Enet's door slave said when they reached the building.

'My *eagle warrior* will wait outside the dining chamber,' Pilos corrected him as Elaq bristled. 'If your mistress tries to punish you for letting him through, send word to me and I will purchase you from this house – and not for offering,' he added when the slave's breathing roughened. 'Elaq comes with me.'

'As the Spear wills,' the slave said and Pilos noted how his fingers tightened in the folds of his kilt. Even if the man took him up on his offer, it was unlikely he'd get word to Pilos's estate in time to be saved. Pilos decided to put in a good word for him over food. Mostly, he acknowledged, to annoy Enet.

The Great Octave herself was lounging on thickly padded mats before a long, low table. She had removed the ridiculous headdress of her station and wore instead a single turkey feather over her right ear, as if she were a warrior. Pilos's jaw tightened at the insult, but his hand went reflexively to his right ear to check his own was still there, and then back to the fan of eagle feathers plaited into his hair. High Feather of the Melody. Proven warrior. Aristocrat. More than a match for the python coiled before him.

He touched belly and throat before turning his gaze on the peace-weavers. They sat opposite Enet – a slender young man and an older woman with heavy muscle in her shoulders and forearms. She sat on one heel, the other foot planted before her, ready to launch to her feet. Pilos inclined his head in her direction, one killer to another.

Each wore a full crown of turkey feathers, adding height and dignity, though the man had neither the bulk of a warrior nor the heft of a farmer. A born talker, and the blue on his forehead and lip marked him as a northern shaman. Unlikely to be a threat, unless he was also a poison-caster with the sleight of hand such people cultivated. Pilos made a conscious effort not to touch the pouch of antidotes swinging from the ornate belt around his hips.

He sat cross-legged on the same side of the table as Enet and favoured them all with a polite smile. 'Great Octave, I thank you for your hospitality. Peace-weavers, I am High Feather Pilos, commander of the Melody and Spear of the Singer, his military adviser. It is a pleasure to meet you here, under the song.'

The woman twitched. 'I am Betsu, warrior of the Yaloh,' she said shortly. 'This is a Tokob shaman, Tayan.'

The man pursed his lips; Pilos had the feeling they were about to cover old ground. 'It is true, High Feather, that I am no warrior as Betsu is. I hope my presence does not offend you. My people thought it would be better to send a different representative to offer a balanced view. I wish you the blessings of my ancestors.'

Pilos waved away the comment as Enet chewed slowly on a slice of mango. 'There is no offence, peace-weaver. The Great Octave is no warrior, after all. Wisdom can be found in many places, not just at the end of a war club,' he added before she could respond.

'Do you all have two roles within your society?' Betsu asked. 'Do you not find that hoarding all the power among a small number of people makes you vulnerable? To attack, or disease. Or corruption.'

'Our elections run on eight-yearly cycles in accordance with the movements of the Great Star who appears at morning and evening. Enet and I are the only ones who hold more than one role. For me, promotion to High Feather came in the last days of our efforts to bring the Quitob under the song fourteen sun-years ago, after our previous High Feather's death. The Singer saw fit to ratify that promotion when I returned home. I was awarded the position of Spear only three years ago.' He stole a look at Enet. 'And you, Spear. What did you do this last sun-year to achieve the status of Great Octave?'

Enet was calm. 'Served our holy lord to the best of my ability and in his interests,' she said without pause. Pilos could have applauded. 'But you hold two roles each as well, of course,' she added with sweet malice, gesturing at Betsu. 'Warrior and peace-weaver; shaman and peace-weaver. That must be a difficult compromise for someone used to getting her own way through violence. Perhaps it explains . . .' She trailed off, but the muscle flickering in Betsu's cheek told Pilos she had struck a nerve.

'Yes, the Great Star,' the shaman said eagerly in a clumsy attempt to change the subject. 'To Tokob and Yaloh he is the Watcher. When he disappears below the horizon during the grand and little absences, he carries our prayers to the spirits awaiting rebirth and those trapped in the Underworld. Is it so with you?' He looked at them expectantly.

'It is not,' Pilos said. 'As five rotations of the Great Star equal eight sun-years, new appointments to the council and other important positions are made at the beginning of each cycle, but our gods are the holy Setatmeh and the Singer. It is they who deserve our worship, they who mediate with the ancestors and adore and protect the world spirit, not a light in the sky.' He reached for a slice of monkey sprinkled with chillies. 'There is an old story that tells of the Great Star becoming Sky Jaguar, a mythological hero who fights the lords of the Underworld. It is a good excuse for a festival to mark the beginning of the grand absence.'

'And do you have many shamans? I would be pleased to meet some, to exchange knowledge of plants and medicine,' Tayan said after a pause to put away any disappointment that the Pechaqueh did not share their primitive beliefs. 'I am a healing shaman, though I have some skill in journeying and ritual. As well as medicine, my interest lies mostly in poisons and their antidotes.'

Pilos paused with the meat at his lips and Tayan grinned at him, popped a slice into his own mouth and chewed with relish. The High Feather acknowledged the jest – if jest it was – with a brief nod and ate the meat, imagining Elaq's squawk of outrage as he did.

'And how go the negotiations?' Pilos asked when they'd finished eating, making barely a dent in the feast laid before them. Enet had sent for honeypot rather than beer and Pilos cradled the tiny cup between his fingers, but didn't drink. He wanted to keep a clear head.

'They do not,' Betsu said shortly. 'Today we were taken to a fighting pit to watch slaves hack at each other with weapons, with little skill and less enthusiasm. A pitiful, barbaric spectacle of unnecessary death. We were subjected to much the same five days ago. Every day is filled so, with anything and everything but meaningful discussion.'

'Which—' Pilos began and then stopped. He looked to Enet, who was wearing an expression of almost constipated innocence. *My fighting pit, of course, when all that were scheduled were death-fights. That is why I was invited here*

173

tonight rather than earlier, and she will not have told them who owns the pit in hopes of making us all angry and embarrassed.

'Peace, Betsu,' Tayan said, and though the words were gentle, there was tension in the shaman's hands and jaw.

'I will not peace,' the woman snapped. 'We came to negotiate, with a very limited timescale imposed by the Great Octave; instead we are insulted and subjected to barbarism and make no progress.'

'Barbarism?' Enet said quietly. 'And here was me thinking you looked quite lovely in that shawl.' She gestured gracefully to the garment draped over the Yaloh shoulders and the woman flushed a dark red. Pilos wasn't sure what was going on, but the peace-weaver's fury was clear to them all.

Betsu tossed back the honeypot and slammed down the cup. 'Now you are here, *High Feather*, we can finally make progress, warrior to warrior, as it should be. What will it take?'

Pilos sipped his drink, just enough for its warmth to spread though his chest and throat. The others might not understand why someone so short-tempered had been sent to make peace, but Pilos appreciated the warrior's directness. It was refreshing to speak with someone who wanted progress. Who understood the passage of time was not a slow-moving river but a storm, moving in stutters and leaps across a landscape, hurrying and then dawdling and impossible to predict, with the will of the gods and the might of the Singer the lightning and thunder and lashing rain.

'What will what take?' he asked.

'For the last fifty years, you have expanded in every direction, with our lands in the north the last to remain free. You and your song spread like maize-blight. In three generations, you have taken nearly all of Ixachipan. And as soon as you have dominion over a land, you steal its people and give it to strangers to farm. You upset the balance, not only with your expansion but with your very methods. The earth will not stand your depredations forever – the theft of tree-cover that protects the soil when the rains come, that gives homes to animals and medicine to people. When the land fails, what will you do then? When your numbers are so great that even the richness of the soil cannot sustain them, how will you proceed?'

Pilos cocked his head. 'You wish to discuss our farming methods?' he asked and sipped again. 'My concern is defence of the Empire and its expansion in accordance with our Singer's will, not crops and fallow fields and' – he waved his free hand – 'the spreading of shit.'

'That is not what my colleague means,' Tayan said, swallowing hard when Enet caressed the bare arm of the slave kneeling by her side. Pilos ignored her: he knew from experience that there was no one with as much talent at getting under the skin of others as the Great Octave.

'We are here to discuss how to end the war,' Tayan finished.

Pilos shrugged. 'Agree to join us in the Empire. Allow us to bring you under the song, for your own benefit and to learn of the Singer's great love for all people. If you spurn this gift we offer you, then what choice do we have but war? It is the will of the Singer and therefore to your own glorification.' He spread scarred hands. 'Though I am a warrior and some would say my trade is death, it would please my heart to welcome you as friends with no more blood between us.'

'There will always be blood between us,' Betsu grunted, 'because every pyramid you build is mortared with it. Your entire society is built on death and the cold-hearted murder of innocents to feed your fucking Drowned. I said *I don't want any!*' she snapped to the slave offering her a platter

175

of fruit, shoving him away so hard she tipped it out of his hands. He stilled in horror and then spun to Enet and prostrated himself. Pilos could smell the fear on him even from here.

'The fault was mine,' Betsu said quickly, realising her error. 'Your . . . This man did nothing wrong. Forgive me.' She reached for the fruit and Enet raised her forefinger, stilling her.

The women watched each other for so long Pilos thought the air – and the slave between them – would catch fire. He knew Betsu would go to the slave's defence if Enet passed judgement she didn't like, regardless of how it affected this peace-weaving. He wondered if that was the Great Octave's plan.

'As you say,' Enet said, cutting into Pilos's thoughts as Tayan began to squirm in the smothering tension. 'Clear up the mess.' Betsu reached out again and Enet clapped once. 'Not you, honoured guest,' she said gently. 'The slave must do it.' Just the slightest emphasis on the word, enough to tighten lips and raise hackles and Pilos knew Enet had no interest in negotiating a peace. Had never had any intention of allowing this meeting or these people to be anything other than tools in her own ongoing scramble for ever-greater power.

And there is only one status higher than Great Octave.

'Now then, where were we?' Enet continued as another slave, a girl this time, knelt next to her. Enet's caresses of this one were more overt, challenge heating her gaze more than desire. 'The Singer has decreed that Yalotlan and Tokoban will become part of the Empire, and so they shall. You would both do well to agree now to lay down your weapons and be brought under the song.'

'You speak as if your Singer already rules us,' Betsu said hotly. 'He doesn't.'

'We all do the Singer's will, you included, though you know it not,' Enet snapped, her temper shortening as fast as Betsu's.

'We go around in circles,' Tayan said, clearly trying for diplomacy, though his tone was defeated. He looked at Betsu with sudden wariness. 'What proposal would you make to see the war ended?' His hand shot out impressively fast for a non-warrior and clamped down on Betsu's arm, his fingers digging into the corded muscle. 'Peace, Betsu. I am just asking.'

Enet raised her eyebrows but she answered readily enough. Pilos affected nonchalance, but he was curious what concessions she would make – without first consulting the Singer or council or, indeed, the High Feather whose warriors would oversee the transition of power and people.

'The song will be heard in every part of your lands. Our pyramids will ascend the Tokob sacred hill and nestle deep in Yaloh jungle. You could potentially remain in your lands, though Pechaqueh overseers would be in charge.' Tayan and Betsu exchanged an excited glance even as Pilos felt a slow heat of anger begin to kindle in his belly. What was this? Remain in their lands?

'You will tithe half your crops each year; this is standard. Your children will be fostered in Pechaqueh cities for two Star cycles. The most apt will join the Melody as dog warriors.'

Pilos shifted as the anger burst into flame.

'You will give us full access to your songstone mines. And, of course, you will cease killing the holy Setatmeh.'

Pilos's anger settled. The terms were impossible and Enet knew it. That was why she'd offered them. She watched the peace-weavers with the calm, unblinking serenity of a snake.

'We cannot give you an immediate answer,' the shaman said, his voice strangled. Hollow. 'We need time to discuss it.

The issue of the Drown— of the holy Setatmeh in particular. You would have us worship these creatures who kill us? You would ask us to change our religion to suit you?'

Enet opened her hands. 'Of course not. Your religion is your religion, though I had not realised god-murder was part of your worship.' She put her head on one side, quizzical.

'It is not,' Tayan said heavily. 'It is a means of surviv—'

'Then we are not asking you to change your religion, are we? In time, I hope, you will come to understand the joy of gods living among you and will see our beliefs for what they are – the truth. But either way, the killing of the holy Setatmeh would be met with the direst of consequences.' The Great Octave picked a piece of honeycomb from a bowl, popped it in her mouth and chewed; then she leant back on one elbow, licking the stickiness from her fingers. Her smile was warm and promising.

'My answer is no. The answer of every Yalotl is no,' Betsu said. 'I will not have this fucking song defile the forests and homes of Yalotlan. I will not give you my children for one sun-year, let alone sixteen. It is an impossibility, and, worse, you know it is. Don't you, you fucking snake? *Don't you?*'

Pilos tensed, ready to fling himself on Enet and pull her away from the warrior who would gut her like a rabbit. His mouth opened to yell for Elaq, and it stayed open when Enet did . . . nothing.

'If the Tokob hill, which I understand is also your goddess, is the birthplace of all creation,' Enet said calmly, 'then it must also be where the song came from. As such, it is no defilement to welcome it back to its place of origin, is it?'

There was a long silence in which Tayan begged Betsu with his eyes not to provoke their host further and Pilos was sorely tempted to join him in that plea. The Yalotl drained her honeypot and slammed the cup down again, barely avoiding striking the slave who leant forward to refill it.

'I have spoken with the other shamans who keep our histories,' Tayan said eventually, an edge of desperation clear in his tone. 'The song was not birthed by Malel for the song is – forgive me for speaking so bluntly – unnatural. Beautiful, yes, and clearly powerful, but it is bad magic. It is a manifestation from one of the nine levels of the Underworld. The lords of death have deceived you.'

'Please, honoured guests,' Pilos said, his own calm beginning to fray, 'do not insult the song. We have done you the courtesy of listening to your beliefs without demur. You shame yourselves by not doing the same.'

'Forgive us,' the shaman said, blushing, and he seemed to mean it. 'You are quite correct. To us, it is beautiful the way the blinding tree is beautiful. The song signals the end of our way of life.'

'But the start of a new, greater one,' Pilos insisted. There was something, some connection. He could feel it. Perhaps they truly could weave a peace, he and this strange, intense shaman from Tokoban.

'I will cross no more words with you,' Betsu interrupted and the moment fled like a darting hummingbird. Pilos exhaled, the heat of the moment tempered by the cold in her voice. 'I will speak with the Singer himself and none other. I will ask him to explain why he thinks he already rules us when he does not and never will. I will discover whether he is right to be as arrogant as the great black cat or is instead merely as stupid as the sloth.'

'*Betsu, peace!*' the shaman gasped. 'Spear Pilos, Great Octave, forgive—'

'You dare speak so, you who wear the peace feathers?' Enet demanded before he could finish, rising from her place

179

on the mats without grace, so the girl slave had to scramble from her path. Betsu barked a laugh and ripped the turkey feather crown from her head as she leapt up. She threw her arms wide in challenge.

Enet was shaking and they were all standing now, Tayan babbling something, though none of them bothered to listen. 'When we come to your land, when we rip you from your pathetic, petty delusions of gods and monsters, when we enslave your entire populations, when we sell your children to the brothels, I will make sure to buy you first, *Peace-weaver Betsu*. And you will serve me in ways you cannot begin to imagine—'

'Enet, that is enough,' Pilos barked, reaching for her. She wrenched away, nearly overbalancing as Betsu's hand spasmed at her belt for knife or hatchet. 'You goad your guests; you seek to disrupt these proceedings for your own pleasure. The peace-weavers have visited us with honest intentions and you deliberately antagonise them.'

'How dare you speak to me so in my own house,' Enet hissed, and now she was even more snake-like than before, her eyes glittering in the glow of torches. The hairs stood up on Pilos's neck and he had to bite back the urge to call for Elaq. 'And how dare they? I am Great Octave. I outrank all of you. I act on the Singer's orders and his alone. You would be wise to step aside, *Spear*.'

Pilos adjusted his kilt to hide the instinctive grab he'd made for a weapon that wasn't there. 'Then it is the Singer's direct order that you delay the peace-weavers here on your estate? Singer Xac wishes you to treat them with contempt, does he, to threaten and provoke them in order to justify a vicious campaign instead of a peaceful one? He told you he craves their blood, did he? Those were his orders?'

It was a gamble, because from what he'd seen in the

council over the last days, Pilos wouldn't put it past the Singer to order just that if one of his favourites proposed it – and Enet was the favourite of favourites. And yet her face betrayed her. She snapped her fingers and house guards stepped from the along the walls, clubs in hand. Betsu raised her fists and Tayan patted frantically at the air, trying to calm them all, his words lost in the rumbles of threat and the clanging tones of the song singing in the blood, the ears, the balls. Elaq shoved through the door, club in hand. He palmed a knife to Pilos and took his place at his shoulder.

'We are done here,' Enet snarled. 'See they are returned to their room – and put a guard on their door. I trust them less than a snake curled around a child.'

'Child? If you had children, your sour milk would send them to the Underworld before they knew so much as your voice,' Betsu growled and Enet's face suffused with blood.

'*Betsu, fucking peace!*' Tayan shouted, his voice so unexpectedly loud that everyone stilled. 'We beg your forgiveness, Great Octave, and yours, Spear Pilos; our world stands on a cliff edge and the balance teeters with us. Malel and the ancestors have not prepared us for such, such reckless indifference to harmony. Perhaps in the morning, when we are all calm, we could try again.' Tayan didn't wait for their reactions, just dragged Betsu towards a doorway in the far wall, armed slaves striding after them.

'Tomorrow is new moon,' Enet called after them, her voice thick with spite. 'You'll be begging to surrender then.'

Pilos didn't relax until the door shut behind them. 'Well,' he began, 'that was—'

'And you,' Enet said, her voice the dry rustle of scale on scale, portending death. 'Get out.'

Pilos hid his smile, touching belly and throat in mockery

181

of obedience. 'Under the song,' he said and turned away before she could reply. He and Elaq slid through the door just before a platter of fruit smashed against it.

TAYAN

Great Octave's estate, Singing City,
Pechacan, Empire of Songs
159th day of the Great Star at morning

The guard had remained outside their door all night, while a second stood watch by their window. The same young girl slave brought them fruit and steamed buns at dawn, and then they were left alone as the morning brightened and the rains came and then the afternoon began to fade.

It was new moon, the day of offerings, and Tayan thought – *hoped, prayed* – that Enet might have forgotten them. The estate had been busy all day, slaves rushing through the gardens with their heads down even further than usual, moving with a speed born of terror. Would Enet choose one of them as her so-called offering to the Drowned?

The song was exultant, seeming to build in a crescendo to a climax that never arrived – or perhaps was constant. Tayan found himself tapping his fingers or feet to it as the day wore on. The garden visible through the window was an immaculate profusion of flowers and plants that attracted

183

butterflies, tiny frogs, and many-hued hummingbirds. Not a petal, not a leaf was out of place. So perfect it was a parody of nature, as their tiny, strangled strips of jungle between expanses of farmland were a parody. The balance demanded each creature lived in harmony, not taking more than it needed, not exhausting the soil or the game. The Pechaqueh either didn't understand that most basic of necessities, or they thought themselves immune to its consequences. Slaves and cleared jungle, monkeys in cages and sacrifices to the Drowned – the Pechaqueh were so far out of balance that only catastrophe could set them right.

When Enet finally came to fetch them, Tayan wondered for one arse-clenching second whether catastrophe had found him. It wasn't just her own slaves the Great Octave could choose from, after all. 'Honoured guests,' she said, smooth as honey as if the previous night's confrontation had never happened, 'it is time. Please come with me.'

A child, a boy of perhaps nine, scampered ahead of her. He had the monkey from the cage in the gardens on a thin, supple leash and was pulling it along. It opened its mouth to screech and Tayan saw its canines had been pulled out. He shuddered.

Betsu was silent and obedient, again draping the gifted shawl around her, and Tayan was immediately suspicious, though of course he wore his own as well. They followed Enet and the boy and his monkey out of the house towards the litter. 'Can I walk, Mother?' the child asked and Enet smiled.

'Of course, Pikte. But keep the monkey under control, will you? I won't have you running off after it again. If it gets free this time, that will be the last you see of it, understand?'

The boy pursed his lips in consideration. 'That's all right. I saw the other one you got. I'm going to teach them both to dance!'

'The other monkey is for your father, that's why I haven't put it in your pet's cage,' Enet said as she climbed into the litter. The peace-weavers followed her in, ducking so their new crowns of turkey feathers, more lavish than the previous ones, didn't scuff the roof. Tayan was mortified; of course Enet would show off her son after what Betsu had claimed the previous night. Shame twisted in him and he wished, for what felt like the hundredth time, that the Yaloh had sent anyone else but her.

'Is the Singer allowed a monkey?' Pikte asked and Tayan's neck cracked, he twisted so fast to look at Enet. Pikte was the Singer's son?

'I am Great Octave now, Pikte. And I would never do anything against the will of the holy lord or to hurt him. You know that. Now keep hold of that monkey, remember.'

The gates swung open and slave warriors hurried out first, clearing a path through the crowd. The litter followed, Pikte and what had to be the boy's personal bodyguard to its left, and then more guards around and behind them. Last came a tight knot of slaves with their eyes down and their shoulders hunched. They stank of fear.

The limestone road was heavy with traffic, all heading in the same direction. Dozens and then scores and then hundreds of people, and several litters with groups of slaves behind them. The rain had stopped and the sun was slanting through breaks in the cloud, great bands of light that lay across fields and city like veins of gold in rock.

The rain had washed away the smell of so much humanity and there was a hint of night-blooming flowers from some of the gardens. Egrets flew above them, seeming to follow the slow-moving procession – towards what Enet had called the Blessed Water. If not for their destination, Tayan would have delighted in the festival atmosphere.

They reached that wide expanse of dirt, now churning to mud, and the river at its end. More people now, and on the other side too, pressing close to the water. Pechaqueh and free were relaxed, happy, even excited. Anyone wearing undyed maguey, though, stood in mute and cowering dread.

And we are here to bear witness. The shaman gave Betsu a warning look; the Yalotl licked her lips and fidgeted. The brightness of her skin had dulled, flesh pulled taut over the bones of her face. She was afraid.

Pikte ran ahead to a small group of Pechaqueh children, squealing happily, the monkey clinging to his shoulder. Enet smiled. 'Youngsters,' she said with affection. 'Every new moon the same, treating this sacred event as a game.'

'Yes, I like to play with my friends when we've sacrificed innocents to monsters,' Betsu said, but the words were toothless. Enet didn't even acknowledge her.

'Come, friends. As we are blessed with wealth and status, we repay the holy Setatmeh who have so granted us this rich life. We have an offering to make, and so we will take our places at the water's edge.'

She exited the litter and beckoned; six slave guards surrounded the three of them, and four more herded along Enet's own slaves. Tayan recognised some of their faces and wondered whether any of them would be the offering.

'Will the Singer be here?' he asked, trotting to catch up with Enet.

'No. The song-magic is tied to place; the Singer must remain within the source. He has a private offering pool, of course, and will honour the gods if any visit him.' The Great Octave glanced at Tayan almost fondly. 'Have you decided what you will do, then?'

He and Betsu had done little other than talk about Enet's ultimatum and the potential ways they might combat it, or at least soften it into a form their people could live with. He tried to focus on that now, as the scent of the river grew in his nostrils and the ground, already soft from the Wet, grew muddier. 'We . . . have not. Perhaps we might talk after this, this *ritual*' – Tayan almost choked on the word – 'is completed?'

But Enet was no longer listening. They had reached the front of the crowd and the river was only a dozen strides away. The shaman stopped abruptly when he saw it, and had to fight down a scream and the urge to run when he saw the Drowned. Five, eight, nine, eleven and then more, Lesser and Greater, their heads breaking the river's skin one after the other. The crowd fell into rapturous silence.

Tayan, peace-weaver and shaman, called the stargazer, felt his spine turn to liquid and he realised with a bitter incredulity that he'd never believed it. Somehow, despite everything, every indication to the contrary, he hadn't actually thought they would do it. That they *could* do it. He hadn't thought them capable. Cruel and indifferent, yes. Manipulative, definitely. But not actually, really capable of it.

And then Enet stepped forward in all her glory as Great Octave, enormous headdress of feather and jade and precious stones perched atop her head, so large that she had not been able to wear it in the litter. There were blue stripes on her kilt, as if she were a shaman who could commune with the gods. But then, perhaps she could. She believed the monsters in the water were gods, after all. She raised her arms and faced the river and the Drowned glided closer.

One's head broke the water completely and Tayan saw the bulge of its throat sac inflating. He tensed to run, knowing he wouldn't make it out of earshot in time but unable to do anything else, but instead of a song, it uttered a trill, almost birdlike, almost inquisitive. Tayan's breath stopped in his chest. The sound had no power over him; it commanded nothing. Instead, it . . . asked. It was an enquiry. And he could almost understand it. Fascination warred with revulsion, curiosity confined to this one thing to the exclusion of all else.

The Pechaqueh can talk to them? Is this a skill to be learnt? Is this . . . Enet's ultimatum included the prohibition on killing Drowned. That was the condition that no Toko would agree to. *But what if I could speak to them? If I could learn their language . . .*

The Drowned trilled again and beckoned, blinking heavy, clear lids over liquid-black eyes. It cocked its head.

Tayan had never seen such behaviour. No eja had ever reported such things. In Tokoban they were monsters who killed without thought or mercy. Predators, pure and simple. *But so are dogs if left to roam wild.*

His breath stuttered.

They can be tamed.

'Holy Setatmeh, you wise gods of rivers and lakes, you who command the rain to fall and the crops to grow, we honour you.' Enet's voice was loud and carrying and all around her Pechaqueh were advancing, their arms raised in supplication. It dragged Tayan's mind back to the ritual, breaking his feverish, fascinated reverie. All along the banks of the river, elite members of the city repeated her words.

'Sacred spirits who guard the world spirit, who have been blessed with the long life of your kind, who have known this world and now the world of song, who hold the world spirit in your hearts and who trace back in unbroken lineage to the first Singer, Tenaca herself, we worship you. We honour you. If you call, we will come. If you yearn, we will respond. If you ask, we will answer.'

Enet paused and a thrum of ecstatic fear lanced through the crowd and drove the air from Tayan's lungs. She was asking them to sing! She *wanted* them to. Curiosity was replaced by primal fear once again, the switch in emotions so rapid Tayan nearly staggered. Betsu appeared at his side and gripped his hand in hers, her warrior's calluses so like Lilla's that it stole him from the horror of the moment and into a memory – the first time Lilla had taken his hand, gentle and nervous, and the kiss he'd pressed to Tayan's knuckles. The shaman drew in a shuddering breath, so deep his lungs ached. In, out. Just his breath and the picture of Lilla in his mind. Carved upon his heart.

Get a fucking grip, Tayan. Watch and learn. Think.

Three slaves brushed past him, dragging a fourth who walked with vacant eyes and mind, stumbling as if drunk.

'You gods of waters and of fields, you children of the world spirit and ancestors of our great Singer, our holy lord, we do you honour and reverence. Accept this offering, and go in peace.' Enet took the slave by the arm – the clean, unblemished, exquisitely dressed slave who cried silently but made no move to free herself – and walked forward into the river.

'Fuck,' Betsu breathed and Tayan's hand spasmed on hers, clenching hard. What was this? Was the Great Octave sacrificing herself as well? The song seemed to swell in his veins, to caress his heart, whispering its greatness and its glory to his body, not his mind.

The Drowned who had . . . spoken, glided closer to the pair and made another noise, almost a chirp this time. But Tayan felt this one, in balls and bones. An imperative. *Give.* It was then and only then that the slave began to struggle. She let out a single high-pitched scream and turned for the shore.

It was too late. The Drowned rose up, as tall as Enet, who flinched despite herself. It wrapped a long-taloned hand around the slave's screaming face and pulled her against its chest. It did this without looking; it was looking at Enet. It chirped again, the same imperative, and Tayan could have sworn it was amused.

The Great Octave's chest heaved and she stumbled in the water, half a step towards it, and then stopped. Cords stood out in her neck. 'Holy god,' she croaked. 'Ask and we shall answer.'

The Drowned paused, considering her as the slave continued to struggle, pushing against its slick grey-green skin. Blood was sheeting down her face from the claws in her cheek. Considering whether to take Enet instead. Then it wrenched the slave's head back and tore out her throat with its teeth, blood spraying high into the evening and splattering into the Great Octave's face. It arced backwards into the water, taking the dying woman with it, throwing up a great splash of blood and river-water that drenched Enet.

The Great Octave put her hands on her knees, her belly undulating as she sucked in air. Three great breaths, and she straightened again. 'Holy Setatmeh, gods of rivers and of rain, of crops and of life, we honour you. Go in peace under the song. Until we meet again.' Her voice was high and girlish, thick with the aftermath of terror.

'Go in peace under the song. Until we meet again.' The people surrounding the peace-weavers chanted the words, and Enet walked out of the river slowly. Her face was speckled with blood, her tunic and kilt plastered to her skin with water. Up and down the Blessed Water, Drowned took slaves, one after the other, their screams ringing thin and piteous with distance, with hopelessness. With the betrayal of those who had been promised peace and wealth and stability within the Empire of Songs.

The same peace and wealth and stability Enet had offered Tokob and Yaloh.

Betsu's grip on Tayan's hand tightened and he jerked convulsively and faced her, almost dizzy with adrenaline and conflicting emotions. 'We run,' she breathed. 'There is no reasoning with such madness. Tonight, Tayan, when they sleep. We fucking run.'

It was dark and it was still. After the ritual there had been a celebration. As the Drowned feasted, so did their worshippers, though the meat in this case had been turkey, dog, and lizard. Baskets of food, firewood, mats had been brought to the bank of the river, and there, in sight and sound and song of the Drowned, the people of the Singing City had celebrated.

Now, hours later, the house was quiet with the aftermath of death and feast and Tayan and Betsu crouched in each other's shadow and whispered.

'What do you mean you're not coming? Are you moon-mad? Didn't you see what they did?'

Tayan allowed that it was quite possible he was moon-mad. But as the feast had progressed and they had been completely ignored by their host and everyone else – as they had, in fact, been left more in the company of slaves than free – he hadn't been able to tear his mind away from what he'd seen.

Tayan had only seen a Drowned up close once before, one of the lesser, smaller variety. Child-sized. As a walker upon the spiral path, he had thought the journey-magic might give him the same immunity as the spirit-magic and that, with its power wrapped around him and a spirit guide at his side, he could observe the Drowned up close. Try and find a weakness. He had drummed for his guide, Old Woman Frog, and then he had walked towards the Swift Water, Eja Billa reluctant at his side. She had been there to protect him, and she had. With her life.

Tayan's fingers trailed along the claw scars that ran from thigh almost to ankle. The Drowned – the child-sized, less dangerous Drowned – had given him these in the second before they realised the journey-magic did nothing to stop his ears. He'd fallen and lain there, blood pumping from his leg and venom coursing through his body, as Billa was eviscerated in front of him. Her dog had done its duty and dragged Tayan, not her, to safety. And she was dead. Because of him.

So yes, moon-mad was probably an accurate description. And yet . . .

'I will stand no more of this. We are leaving. Now. We were weeks on the road here and will be weeks back again, trekking through the Wet. It's time to leave.'

'And do what? Tell our councils we've failed?'

Betsu blinked, astonished. 'Yes. That's exactly what we do. And why? So we can form a fucking defence! So we can plan! We do nothing here but aid our enemies by delaying our return to the people who need to know that we'll be fighting.' She jerked her thumb at her own chest. 'I'll not die a slave in this place. I'll not serve these people knowing I didn't do everything I possibly could to save us all. This was a fool's errand and so it has proved. Who are we to negotiate with an Empire that has stolen the land, livelihoods, and identities of so many? They may sweep over us eventually, but I'll not stand by without a weapon in my hand and watch them do it.'

She grabbed a blanket from the bed pillows and fastened it around her throat as a cloak against the weather. She ignored the shawl Enet had gifted her. 'We can win, Tayan. I truly believe that. So I'm going to make sure we do. Are you coming?'

Tayan pressed his lips together and then shook his head. Betsu didn't even blink. 'I can't,' he whispered. 'I'm no warrior and I don't have your stamina. I can't keep up, and I can't see well enough – you know how I was on the way here, and that was moving at an easy pace.' He held up his hands. 'But you should go. I'm going to agree to their terms. I'm going to say that if they return *after* the Wet, we'll accept the song. No, listen – it's just about delaying them now. I'm going to give you as much time as I can. If Malel is watching me, I pray she'll make me convincing. If I am, they're going to come to Yalotlan as builders and administrators, not warriors. Kill them all, because it'll be bloody after that and it's the best I'll be able to give you.'

She did react at that, gave him a slow, approving nod. 'You're a good shaman and a good peace-weaver, Tayan,' she said, surprising him, 'but you're no fighter; if they put the brand on you, there'll be nothing you can do to stop them.'

'Then make sure you come back here and rescue me,' he said, only half joking. Acid swirled in his stomach and the urge to go with her was growing every second.

'Arm the farmers and shamans and artisans; train everyone,' he emphasised in a low voice. 'But don't move into the stolen land – not yet. No actions that can get back here to put the lie to what I'm going to tell Enet.'

Betsu sucked her teeth and then growled in frustration. 'I agree. But make it convincing, or you'll be the next one thrown to those fucking Drowned.'

Tayan felt sick, but he pushed it down. 'Don't worry, I'll think of something to get away. In a, a month or so.' She nodded and tears pricked suddenly at his eyes. 'And tell Lilla . . . tell my husband I'm sorry and I love him and I'll see him soon.'

'Well,' Betsu murmured. 'Turns out you're braver than you look after all. Ancestors guide you.'

'And you. Under the—' he paused, both of them aware

of what he'd been about to say. 'It really does get into your head, doesn't it?' he finished weakly.

Betsu gave him another of her inscrutable stares and then left. Just went, no more words, no supplies or weapons, just a blanket around her shoulders and through the window into the night.

Tayan knew the guards wouldn't see her if she didn't want to be seen. He sat on the bed, lower lip caught between his teeth. Around him, the song pulsed and arced. More and more, he'd found himself caught up in it, drifting away on its liquid seduction. It lived inside him, a watchful, ever-present thing coiled in his guts that never got any quieter or more distant, or louder or closer. It didn't react to worries or fears or joys but instead inhabited them, so everything was experienced alongside and *through* the song. It was just there, heard not with the ears but the whole body, a musical resonance stringing through his soul and connecting it to something bigger, wider.

He wondered for a second if it was anything like how Xessa experienced the world, how she could turn suddenly and know he was there, even though she couldn't hear him, as if the wind or the earth had told her of his secret approach. As if her skin tasted him.

It's as if there's a message in the song that I can't quite understand. The same as with the Drowned. If I can learn their language, I can understand them. I could weave a peace with the Drowned.

The audacity of the idea, the scale of it, took his breath away. But if he could do it, if he could take this knowledge back home, then once the war was over, everything, *everything* could change.

If he could get Enet to tell him the origins of the song and the link between it and the Drowned . . . *She said they were the Singer's ancestors,* he remembered as the memory slid from behind the horror of the slave's death. *She said all the way back to the first Singer in unbroken line . . .*

Understanding the song was the key to it all. The song and the Drowned, the songstone, the magic. Understand the song; learn the language of the Drowned. This was his purpose. Deceive the Great Octave about the war and then get her to open up about their magic. Easy. Tayan snorted and lay back, listening to the rain drumming on the roof. Scents drifted in from the garden and reminded him of home.

Grief welled in him, homesick and heartsick and missing Lilla and Xessa. He wondered even now if he could catch up with Betsu and knew he could not. But he would be lying if he pretended there wasn't a seed of excitement in his belly, too.

For good or ill, now, he was walking this trail to its end.

'Good morning, Great Octave. I trust you slept well?'

Enet managed a reasonably sincere smile when he entered, but it faltered when Betsu didn't follow him in for dawnmeal. 'The Yalotl is unwell?'

Tayan knelt at the table and helped himself to fruit, noting with distant indifference that his hand was shaking. 'We accept your offer. After the Wet, when you return to Yalotlan and then Tokoban, we will lay down our weapons. We will embrace the song.'

Perhaps she had not expected it. Perhaps she had taken them to see a woman eaten by monsters in the hope of provoking a war that would benefit her in some mysterious way, Tayan didn't know. What he did know was that the Great Octave, Spear of the City, was speechless.

Tayan ate the fruit while she studied him, the initial shock quickly hidden behind a neutral, calculating mask. 'I see.

Then allow me to welcome you under the song, Peace-weaver Tayan. And yet you have not answered my question. Where is the Yalotl?'

'Of course. Betsu is returning home. When we agreed that this was the best – the only – way forward to preserve some tiny remnant of our culture and heritage, we agreed that one of us should take the news back as soon as possible. Of the two of us, the warrior is the natural choice.'

A tiny crease appeared between her eyebrows. 'And that necessitated leaving in the night, in the rain?'

Tayan helped himself to cornbread, though it was too thick and chewy and bile rose in his throat. He made himself swallow. 'Betsu was distressed by the events at the river, Great Octave. She was angry – you have seen how her temper ignites. Though the agreement sits ill with her, once it was made, she refused to remain here any longer. I am sorry that she did not bid you farewell. I hope you can forgive her haste.'

Tayan's skin crawled at the length of the silence that unfurled, at Enet's serpent-stillness. 'My slaves did not inform me she had asked to leave.' She still hadn't blinked.

Tayan's shrug was elaborate as he chewed more tasteless cornbread. 'Betsu is a skilled warrior; I doubt they were even aware she had left the estate. But again, I apologise on her behalf.'

Fury flashed across Enet's face and just as swiftly vanished. And then she ran her finger down her jaw, her throat, and into the open neck of her tunic. 'And yet you have stayed with me,' she purred and Tayan nearly choked on the bread. Enet was undoubtedly the most beautiful woman he'd ever met, and if she lived in the Sky City he'd have thrown himself at her feet long before and begged for her favour. But as displays of power went, it was crude and ineffective – mostly.

'I have. We thought that the more I could learn about your society, and particularly the song and the Drown— the holy Setatmeh, the better. As I know you can appreciate, there will be much resistance to the outcome of this peace-weaving. The more I know, the better equipped I will be to answer any questions.'

They watched each other, like snake and rat. There was no mistaking which one was Tayan. 'You wish to know even more of our society?' she asked eventually.

'I wish to know of the song and the holy Setatmeh, Great Octave.' Tayan spread his hands and looked at her with complete honesty. 'I want to know all about them.'

'Interesting,' Enet murmured. She gestured at the table. 'Eat. I have business in the great pyramid today, but perhaps we shall speak more on my return.'

'Under the song,' Tayan said, but she had already left.

PILOS

Pilos's eyes opened and he stared into the blackness above his bed. It was hours before dawn, but the guard hadn't passed his door. At home, at the fortress, on campaign, or while travelling, every six hundred heartbeats a guard would patrol past him, as regular as sunrise. The lack of footsteps woke him as surely as if someone had screeched an alarm.

Pilos slid out of bed and reached for his salt-cotton, slung it over his head, and then took his club from its place between the bed and the door. He slipped a knife into the waistband of his loincloth and pressed himself to the cool plaster wall. Silence. A long silence. And then the very softest scuff of sandal on stone. Pilos flexed his fingers on the handle of his club and waited.

The door opened with a slight creak and Pilos let them come in. *Three? They should have brought more.*

He was standing behind the door and, when the three

198

figures had entered, he barged it with his shoulder and slammed it in the faces of any others who might still be outside. The assassins jumped and spun to face him, but Pilos's club had already crushed the skull of the man closest. He pushed the falling corpse into the arms of the second.

The third leapt sideways, avoiding the scuffle, and then lunged with a short spear. Pilos parried it diagonally downwards with the club and let out a bellowing war cry that would alert any of his household still alive. She pulled the spear back and jabbed again; again Pilos batted it away, but he was a step further from the wall now and the second man scrambled free of the corpse and advanced on his other side. If one of them could get at his back, out of his eyeline, it was over.

Pilos drew the knife with his free hand; the man hesitated, but then came on. He, too, carried a short spear. Good for them, bad for Pilos.

The woman thrust high and the man low. Pilos blocked the stab to his head with the club and tried to bat the second away with his knife; not fast enough. The spear tip sank in just above his right knee and then tore out through the side of his leg. Hot blood pumped and the limb trembled. He roared as pulsing, searing pain shuddered in sick waves up into his groin.

Pilos threw the knife. The blade lodged high in the man's chest and he let go of his spear to clutch at it. Pilos caught the falling weapon in his free hand and smacked it into the woman's arm, battered her spear down with the club and then smashed it into her sternum. It was an awkward move, a jab more than anything, but the club's head was a smooth polished ball of granite and it had all of Pilos's bodyweight behind it.

The woman stumbled backwards, fighting for air, giving

Pilos the space he needed. He reversed the spear in his off hand and sliced it through the man's groin and belly.

The door slammed open and Elaq staggered in, bleeding heavily, three house guards behind him. Pilos fell back against the wall. 'Take them alive,' he gasped, the pain beginning to work its way past his barriers. 'I want to know who ordered this before I peel their skin from their bones.'

'High Feather, are you sure?' Elaq fretted as dawn bathed their faces with pink and gold. A glare was enough to prevent further protest.

Pilos rubbed grit from his eyes and hissed between his teeth as the stitches above his knee tugged against the raw flesh. The man had died early from his wounds, but birds had begun to sing the sun's arrival before the woman finally broke. Pilos had been deeply unsurprised by her revelation.

'It is vital that I attend the council this morning, and not only to say farewell to the Singer. I have finally gathered enough support in the council to be given leave to raise my proposal – which is likely why the attack came last night.'

'But why would she think it a bad idea?'

Pilos shrugged and then yawned. 'Who knows what goes on in her head? This way, she'll be off balance at my appearance – at my survival – and might make her opinion known when the proposal itself is put to council. Now, are you well enough to act as escort?'

Elaq sucked in an outraged breath and Pilos winked before he could expel it along with a protest. The retired eagle had taken a javelin in the shoulder and a cut across his forearm in the fighting, he and the other guards dispatching half a dozen more assassins who'd fought a holding action to give the trio time to reach Pilos. He made no complaint about either wound.

'And during the council meeting?' Elaq continued, noting Pilos's hiss of pain as he flexed his leg again. 'With everything we now know . . .'

'If I am not safe in the very presence of the Singer himself, I'm not safe anywhere.' He ignored the supreme irony of that statement: the Singer could order him killed and the words wouldn't have time to stop echoing before the deed was carried out. Still, not even the councillors or Xac's favourites were stupid enough to attempt an assassination in the source itself.

'Then you'll have a guard of three plus myself on the way to the pyramid.'

Pilos nodded, knowing that Elaq wouldn't be swayed from this and secretly glad for it. The eagle closed the curtains to his litter in sombre rebuttal of the morning.

The doors to the compound creaked open and the sounds of early morning rushed in; turkeys and dogs and children all chasing each other through the streets, the first vendors hawking their wares even though dawn had barely kissed the sky. The stands of palm and bamboo growing on every corner rustled as they passed.

Pilos set his eye to a gap in the curtains, watching for further attacks, his club in his lap and knives in his belt.

'Spear of the Singer Pilos, High Feather of the Melody, requests entrance to this council.'

As expected, half a dozen heads whipped around to look, and Pilos took careful note of which ones they were. Not only that, but the translucent hanging hiding the Singer's cronies visibly rippled and an urgent whispered conversation began behind its screen. The Singer wasn't here yet, and Pilos could guess who sat in splendour back there and suddenly had so much to say.

He didn't so much as blink as he lowered himself to his knees on the cushion at the back of the council, though the fierce pull of his wound brought a surge of nausea to his throat. He pressed his forehead to the ground and then sat back on his heels, breathing slowly.

'Our great Singer will not be in attendance today,' came a low, melodious voice from behind the hanging. Enet's head, complete with the Great Octave's enormous and elaborate headdress perched precariously atop it, appeared around its edge and deliberately she drew the curtain back, then settled onto her heels again. Her snakelike eyes bored into Pilos's and he stared back without emotion.

'The holy lord leaves the day's matters to his council and his . . . closest advisers.' There was little doubt she meant herself and the others of the Singer's favourites clustered behind her. They all wore identical, sanctimonious smiles. Pilos breathed.

'Are you quite well, Spear?' Enet said suddenly with such fake solicitude that his mouth crimped as though he'd eaten something bitter. Again, all eyes turned to him.

'Quite well, Great Octave,' Pilos said casually. 'I had a matter to place before the Singer. I will petition to see him later, in private, if it is his will.' Enet's eyes narrowed in calculation and Pilos allowed a small smile to touch his face. 'I have had . . . interesting discussions recently. There is something on which I would like the Singer's wisdom.'

'If the holy lord has left today's business to his council, then there is no reason why you cannot share this information with us,' Councillor Yana said, and Pilos inclined his head at the old warrior. Yana could smell danger from a stick away and again he was allying himself with the High Feather, this time openly against Enet. Pilos's respect for him grew.

The pain yammered for him to denounce her, to reveal to the entire council what she'd done, the words that had spilt from her assassin's own mouth to condemn her. Pilos breathed and was silent, and Yana's face showed his understanding.

'Later perhaps, then. To the first scheduled matter: there has been an outbreak of disease in Quitoban,' the old warrior said, changing the subject smoothly. 'Reports of at least two hundred farming Quitob dead, with double that number in the towns struck down so far. Some Pechaqueh have been caught up in it, Setatmeh protect them, and are secluding themselves on their estates. The shamans are working hard but it is spreading.'

'There will be food shortages in the Singing City without their harvest,' a councillor piped up, sounding panicked. 'Prices will increase, looting and banditry—'

'Indeed, but the sick Quitob?' Yana asked. 'How can we help them?'

Pilos admired the old man's tenacity, but he was speaking to the wrong people if he wanted to help the sick. Enet and the Singer's familiars had no interest in spending jade to save the lives of slaves, even when those slaves provided the food and goods that would see them through the year.

'Quarantine the district and let the illness burn itself out,' Enet said, waving a hand and almost dislodging her headdress. 'When the sickness has passed, send some of the new Yaloh slaves there to bring in the crops. I want a list of names of Pechaqueh in Quitoban. Spear, we will require dog warriors to escort them out of danger. Next.' And as easily as that, who knew how many slaves, who had come under the song only because of the promises of safety, security, and glory, were condemned to death.

She hadn't even asked his permission. Pilos breathed.

'The holy lord, great Singer Xac, 174th Singer since the founding of Pechacan, graces this council with his presence.'

Chorus Leader Nara's voice boomed through the source and stilled the muttering of the councillors. A choir of honey-voiced children entered, singing the song of Xac's accomplishments in the eleven years he had ruled so far. Six Chorus followed, their spears held horizontally across their bodies. Then Nara. Pilos saw the Singer's shadow on the wall before pressing his forehead to the mat.

'Draw the curtain,' Nara said, his voice imperious, a tone he would never take with any of the councillors, let alone the Great Octave, under any other circumstances. But this was the Singer, and to look upon him was forbidden. Pilos knew when the Singer entered: the walls of the source almost seemed to bulge and flex to accommodate him. The song's intensity strengthened within the blood, like taking a draught of honeypot on an empty stomach.

Pilos's leg throbbed its complaint; he ignored it, though a glance told him the bandage was staining red. But the Singer was here. *Thank you, holy Setatmeh, for speeding Elaq's words to the Singer's ears.*

'Speak, High Feather,' the Singer said without preamble and his voice was musical, throbbing with power and magic. The council sat up, nervous, uncomfortable. Several exchanged anxious looks and Pilos wasted a second savouring the furious worry that must be eating at Enet's perfect features and blackened heart. She'd come to sit on their side of the hanging now, while the Singer's favourites retreated to the far wall.

'Thank you, holy lord, for the honour,' Pilos said and bowed his head briefly. 'The Melody is in need of new warriors. While we have many new slaves, it will take time for them to be trusted to fight in lands they once counted theirs. Not even the Xentib, four sun-years under the song, are reliable enough to send to Yalotlan once the rains stop. To be so close to their tribal lands could prove too much. In addition, since returning to the Singing City I have seen the aftermath of the most recent purge. I have seen hundreds more people begging. As the wisdom of our forebears forbids slavery of full-blood Pechaqueh, these unfortunates clutter our plazas and bring disease and ugliness to our streets. They breed faster than the Choosers can offer them to the holy Setatmeh. And so my proposal, great Singer, which I submit to your wisdom, is that the disinherited are drafted into the Melody as indentured warriors and engineers, pyramid-builders, weapons-makers, cooks. They have had everything taken from them and now they turn our beautiful city into an eyesore. I propose that they redeem themselves and earn their freedom and their wealth back through war and expansion of the Empire in your name.'

'You would name them eagles?' Yana asked with a tinge of distaste.

'Absolutely not. They have lost their honour; I will not see them tarnish the honour of eagles. I propose a new caste of hawks. With a similar system to that which we operate for the slave and dog warriors, we could ensure a steady flow of new blood into the Melody, a reduction in the number of beggars and instances of disease in the Singing City and our other cities – the Great Octave has told us of the outbreak in Quitoban, for instance – and a way for the disgraced to continue to serve the Empire and glory. When each had paid off their debt and shame in years of service, they could farm the new stretches of Empire they themselves helped to conquer, with half of their crops tithed to Pechacan, as is usual. Their honour will be won by their own hands, some wealth and status within society regained. All at no cost to the Empire other than that expended in housing, feeding, and training them. Still a small sum for guaranteed flesh to hurl at our enemies.'

There were murmurs from the council now, a few scoffing but many, those he had spoken with over the previous weeks, hushed and approving. Yana dipped his head in a tiny nod, satisfied. Enet remained motionless, offering no opinion either way. She would do as the Singer wished – and right now she had no idea what the Singer's thoughts were. She couldn't afford to jump the wrong way and incur his ire.

Jump, you bitch, Pilos willed her. *Jump and condemn yourself.*

He pressed a finger to the bandaging hidden by his kilt and let the flare of pain clear his thoughts. 'As they are, the disgraced do nothing but stink up our cities and die in its corners. They have no purpose and they have no honour.' He took a deep breath. 'They shame us.'

Enet's face hardened. 'You speak of shaming Pechaqueh?' she screeched, one painted fingernail aiming between his eyes. She gripped the hanging as she rose. 'You who cannot even subdue—'

But the rest of the council had fallen on their faces as the material tore and exposed the Singer to public view. Pilos, too, dropped forward in obeisance as Enet flushed, realising the enormity of her error. He glanced up for a brief instant – like a lightning strike in the dark. Her headdress had slid over one eye and she shoved at it, mouth open. She was standing while the Singer sat, she had exposed him to the council, she had raised her voice in his presence, threatening the very song. Any one meant death, should he wish it.

The Chorus rushed from their stations about the walls, casting aside their spears and fumbling with the cotton, tying it ragged and crooked to the hooks above and once more screening the holy lord from unworthy eyes.

'Leave,' the Singer rumbled and the council began to rise in shocked silence. 'Enet. Leave.'

Pilos felt an uncharacteristic surge of triumph and pushed it away, concentrated on keeping his face averted until the hanging was secure and the council had settled once more. He'd seen enough, anyway. Enet stood in sodden silence, the jade and onyx and feathers of her headdress – feathers like Pilos's own and denoting high military position – *a deliberate fucking insult* – nodding and bobbing as she resettled it on her head with awkward, wooden fingers before stumbling out into the gardens, her back rigid with fury and shame.

'Your proposal is accepted.' The Singer's voice sparked with magic and the song flowed into something dark and majestic that reminded Pilos – reminded the whole Empire of Songs – just who and what their holy lord was. He swallowed and concentrated on the Singer's words.

'Victory is all and glory is our purpose. Round up the destitute and make of them what you can. Those who cannot fight can carry supplies and make weapons, cook meals and be offered to the holy Setatmeh to ensure success. Find a use for as many as possible, but the rest take their chances with the cats and snakes and Choosers – they are the visible face of betrayal and it does not do for people to forget what happens if they break our laws. My laws.' The council bowed again.

'With grace and humble thanks, great Singer,' Pilos said. 'I will leave the Singing City for the Melody's fortress tomorrow. With your permission, I will order a hundred warriors to begin the process of selection in my absence. They will be sent to the fortress in batches, where their training will be fierce and fast through the Wet.'

'Do it. This council is over.'

'Under the song, holy lord,' they chanted, prostrating until he had left. Whispers surged up in a storm as soon as he had disappeared deeper into the source, his favourites following and several turning to stare over their shoulders with cold eyes. Those ones were Enet's, he guessed, even as they pretended to be Xac's.

Pilos waited until most of the council had exited before forcing himself to his feet with a muttered oath. The muscle was throbbing, the leg shaking as the blood flowed back into his feet and bloomed through the bandage. Yana was waiting for him and pointed – there was a fresh red stain on Pilos's kilt. 'Cut yourself shaving?' he asked with a grin.

Pilos clapped him on the back. 'Little girls playing with knives,' he said.

'Ah. I suspected as much. You have my support, High Feather, both against the Yaloh and here in the Singing City.'

'Still taking risks, eagle?'

Yana's hand went to the feather plaited into his greying hair. 'Some habits are hard to break. You be careful. There're more things with claws in this city than cats.'

'I know it, councillor, and, truth be told, I am keen to be away,' Pilos said. 'But your support means much. Under the song.'

LILLA

It was time. The peace-weaving would not yet have concluded – would barely be halfway through its course – but the councils had argued, bitterly and at length, and the members of the shamanic conclave, advisers to the council, had journeyed to the ancestors and to Malel herself for guidance. In the end, agreement was reached.

It wasn't unanimous, but as the Wet strengthened, even Lilla couldn't help but see that they needed to do something. The enemy were building another line of pyramids, this time in Yalotlan hill country far too close to Tokoban's border to go unanswered, and there had been another desperate influx of Yaloh refugees to strain Tokob villages and cities. Yet they were not going to war, despite some of the more strident voices on the councils and among the Paws.

Instead, they would destroy the stockpiles of wood and stone and paint that would become pyramids. They would not take life unless they had no choice; they would not hunt down the builders and kill them, for they were likely to be slaves. They would simply . . . halt construction. Resistance without violence, as far as possible, to prevent the magic within the pyramids being brought to life and thus all the land through which it rang belonging to the Empire.

But before Malel would grant her blessing, she had a demand. And her first children had listened.

Tokob wore their finest tunics and salt-cotton, their best jewellery and paint. There were so many drums that the plaza shook with sound and Lilla could feel it through his chest. The ejab had space at the front of the crowd so that those whose hearing was stopped by the spirit-magic could still take part.

Two thousand warriors of the Yaloh and Tokob were grouped behind the ejab, and as many others as could fit into the biggest festival plaza crowded its edges, its streets, the roofs of the buildings lining it.

The bone flutes joined in, a jarring, skirling, skating sound as though the spirits themselves were flooding into the flesh world with bloody intent. And then the rattles, a low sliding counterpoint slithering between the drumbeats like the Snake-goddess who helped bring the world into being. Malel's second creation, the wise and patient predator who gave strength and kinship to the ejab.

The heartbeat of Malel. The wails of the spirits. The hiss of the Snake. Lilla's heart waited, sweat beginning to break out on his skin. And then it came, rushing out of the dawn from a hundred shamanic throats. The coughing roar of the Jaguar, brother to the Snake. The warriors' god.

Lilla's heart gave a great liquid thud and began pounding faster than the drums. Malel was listening and so were her daughter and son. Listening to the first children and their allies. They crouched close, their presence felt in wind and cool and pressure. The Jaguar called again; the Snake hissed; Malel's heart beat. The people crammed into the plaza moved in time, swaying and stamping their feet as the music and the gods swept them up into one creature, a single form with thousands of eyes and mouths and hearts and hands.

At the top of the plaza, above the steps where the musicians knelt, on a platform open to sky and wind and rain and sun, the shamans roared and whirled in a complex dance around the prisoner. Lilla's heart ached; Tayan should have been up there. The dance grew faster, the leaps of the shamans more exuberant, their roars now interspersed with wails and whoops and Lilla felt it, felt the gathering magic, felt the closeness and tension, a blanket of power sitting heavy across the Sky City.

And then, at some unseen, unknown signal, the shamans fell still and the music halted. Between one beat and the next, one breath and the next, silence.

'Malel, mother, goddess of all the world, hear our prayer.' Vaqix's voice, normally so reedy, throbbed with power and control. He had stood immobile next to the kneeling prisoner throughout the commencement of the ritual, but now all of its magic was gathered in him.

'Snake-sister, Jaguar-brother, hear us. Spirits of before, spirits of now, spirits yet to walk the world, hear us. Ancestors, hear us. We do not call to you all through some petty need; we call to you from danger and dire terror. We call to you, O Malel, O Snake and Jaguar, O spirits, O ancestors! We call to you for our very lives and our very way of life.

'And so that you might hear, and so that you might listen, and so that you might intervene, we offer you a life. One life for thousands, O Malel, that you extend your protection over Tokob and Yaloh. That you purge the threat from our borders. That you grant us life in which to honour you, O Malel.'

Aez, the Axib Coyote of the Empire's Melody, had been washed and dressed in a long, belted tunic, blackened with charcoal. His fine hair had been shaved at both sides and the remainder braided. Vaqix and the Yaloh high elder, Zasso, pulled him to his feet. He didn't resist: to fight a sacred, ritual death would be to condemn his spirit to the Underworld.

The two shamans cut the seams beneath Aez's arms and lifted the tunic from him. His face and body were covered with thick, alternating stripes of chalk and charcoal. Even from this distance, Lilla could see his chest heaving, though he worked hard to keep his expression neutral.

'Thank you,' Lilla whispered, as did thousands of others, a susurration of noise lifting from the plaza. 'Thank you for the honour of your life.'

'O Malel, O Snake, O Jaguar! O spirits and ancestors, hear our prayer! O world that was, and world that is, and world that will be, do not see your children cut from your skin. Do not see your children in bonds and degradation. Do not see your tribes broken and scattered to the winds. Accept this life and this blood; accept this courage and this strong-beating heart. Accept this man, as he accepts his time for rebirth is at hand. We call to you from despair, O Malel. Answer us!'

Vaqix turned to face Aez, who took one single step backwards and then halted. In the silence, Lilla heard a sound, small with distance, a cut-off plea. And then Aez flung his arms wide, baring his chest. To preserve the spirit, his body would die. The high shaman smiled behind the blue of his paint. 'Fair and noble warrior, your death will carry our prayers to Malel. We honour you. We thank you. Go now in honour and in thanks. Go without pain. Go with peace.'

Vaqix struck, a single hard blow that entered just beneath

the ribs and angled upwards, cleaving stomach and lung and then heart. The Axi shuddered once and opened his mouth, but the knife had stolen his breath and whatever sound he made this time didn't carry to Lilla's ears. His knees buckled and Zasso and Vaqix caught him. They lowered him gently, reverently, to the platform and he disappeared behind the ring of kneeling shamans.

Lilla's breath whistled through a tight throat. 'Thank you,' he whispered again. Malel was close, her god-born were close, and spirits and ancestors gathered around them. Magic overlaid them. And then a single drum, a single beating heart, that stuttered and skipped, and finally stopped.

Lilla thought his own heart might do the same as the goddess filled him and filled them all. A flute screamed, so unexpected that he jumped, and then the drum started up again, a wild celebration, a rattle bursting through. Next, a cacophony of instruments. On the platform the shamans spun out of their positions and began again to dance, screeching and roaring, flinging themselves into the sky in twisting leaps, clawing fingers reaching for the magic, the spirits, Malel herself.

In glimpses between their whirling bodies, Lilla saw Vaqix and Zasso making the final prayers over Aez's body, cradling his head and his hands. There were tears on Lilla's face, tears of joy and thanks. Aez had begun as an enemy; he had died carrying all their hopes and dreams. Had died an ally; a friend. His name would be remembered among Tokob and Yaloh alike.

The shamans split and leapt down the steps over the heads of the kneeling musicians and whirled into the ejab and then the warriors grouped ready to march. They carried bowls of animal blood and whisks of feathers, and as they spun they flicked it high into the air to rain down in blessing.

Lilla turned to Lutek and Tiamoko and swept them up in his arms in turn, planting kisses on their cheeks and smearing the fine sprinkles of blood that peppered their skin. 'Malel will listen,' he said. And it wasn't just as Fang reassuring the warriors of his Paw that he spoke. He *knew* it. 'Malel will send us her aid. The Pechaqueh will be stopped. But more than that, the magic will reach Tayan and Betsu, too, even so far from our soil as they are. It will lend its strength to their weaving and they will return home with word of peace. And we will escort the Melody from Yalotlan and then lay down our weapons. Malel will listen,' he repeated, but softer now as they hugged again and he was jostled by spinning shamans and dancing warriors.

The gods had listened. And they would act.

The shamans had taken Aez's body up to the womb to hasten his spirit's passage to Malel, and to honour the life he had given in service of theirs. The long snaking procession was gone, the musicians were gone, much of the crowd was gone.

The plaza was quieter now, subdued, and the goddess's presence had faded from Lilla's body, replaced with a cold rain that washed the blood and paint from his skin in long smears that stained his armour and kilt. It seemed fitting, somehow. The magic would linger in them, waiting until it was needed.

His Paw would be one of the first to leave, marching with five others to meet up with those already in Yaloh territory.

They would creep like the snake and the jaguar through the hills and jungle of Yalotlan and destroy every pyramid that reared above the green and living canopy. They would smash the supplies and free the slaves and only kill where there was no other choice. Those were the tasks for which Aez had died and for which they had begged Malel's aid.

Ossa pranced towards him, his tail wagging furiously, and Lilla bent to scratch his ears, a smile curving his lips as the dog whined and wriggled with pleasure, collapsing onto his side to have his belly rubbed. 'Wanton,' Lilla murmured, but he obliged nonetheless.

Xessa hugged Lutek and Tiamoko for long seconds, kissing them both, before she clicked her fingers and Ossa sat up, alert. She pulled Lilla to his feet and then wrapped her arms around him too, standing on tiptoe to reach around his neck. He hugged her hard, a flower of anxiety blooming in his chest. *If they go after the Drowned with both Tayan and me gone . . .*

He pushed it away. Tika was leading the planning and practice; she would ensure they were ready before any attempt was made. He lifted Xessa off her feet and squeezed, then put her down and planted a kiss on her head. She was smiling when she looked up at him, but her eyes were shadowed with worry.

'Be safe,' she signed simply. Lilla nodded. She hesitated, then she licked her thumb and pressed it to his temple and he stilled, shocked, before a rush of affection and gratitude surged through him. She had gifted him a piece of her courage, her spirit, to aid him in the war. She had named him family.

He pulled her into another embrace, almost overwhelmed. Over her shoulder, he saw Toxte, Ilandeh, and Dakto approaching. Lilla let her go. 'Look after this one for me when I've gone,' he signed to Toxte.

Xessa's eyes narrowed and her hands began to move, but Toxte interrupted, cocking an incredulous eyebrow. 'She's the one who looks after me and you know it,' he replied. Xessa's irritation turned to a blush of delight and Lilla hoped they would hurry up and become lovers before he got back.

So much blood in their faces when it should be much further below. He grinned, but didn't say it.

'What's wrong with those two?' he signed instead, pointing at the Xentib who were arguing in low, intense voices.

Toxte shrugged. 'They've been like it all morning, far as I can tell.'

'Dakto,' Lilla called, suddenly wanting to part with everyone on good terms and make sure Ilandeh did nothing to antagonise Xessa again while he was gone. 'Everything all right?'

Dakto hurried over, Ilandeh trailing behind looking furious and bewildered and a little bit scared. His stomach turned over.

'Fang Lilla,' the Xenti said, 'do you have room for one more in your Paw?'

Something that sounded suspiciously like a sob broke from Ilandeh's mouth and she half turned away. Xessa, unsure what was happening, nevertheless went to her and put an arm around her shoulders.

'You have been ordered to fight?' Lilla asked, surprised.

Dakto shook his head. 'No, but I want to. I've been out with you before. I'd like to fight at your side. With what's coming – what you're trying to achieve – I thought, well, I want to help.'

Lilla looked from Dakto to Ilandeh, staring at them from the protective circle of Xessa's arms. Her expression was mingled betrayal and fury. He could see Ilandeh's thoughts as clearly as if she signed them: *Don't say yes. Please don't say yes.* He stared around the plaza at the warriors scattered across its immensity with their families. The rain was steady and cold and they were all soaked, but few made their way to shelter. Time was slipping on, and at highsun they would form into their Paws and filter down through the city and out, down into the treeline, the jungle, gone.

Lilla still had to say goodbye to his mother and sisters, and yet here he was, dealing with the Xentib again. He swallowed his sigh. A flight of green and red parrots caught his eye, heading from someone's allotment in the city down to the orchard. He watched them go, breathing in rain and stone and home. Ilandeh's eyes were like coals on his skin.

'It is dangerous, Dakto,' he said eventually. 'We risk much. We risk everything. Especially with the prohibition against fighting unless there's no other choice.'

Toxte signed his response for Xessa and she tightened her arms on Ilandeh as the woman sagged. She was too shocked to cry.

'I understand, Fang. This is . . . this has begun to feel like home, and we haven't had that in a very long time.' Dakto's voice was low, but Ilandeh heard him anyway.

'Then stay,' she begged, on her knees in the rain now. Ossa licked her neck; she shoved him away. 'Stay, Dakto. Please. I have no one else.'

'You have Xessa and me,' Toxte said immediately, signing the words. Xessa nodded.

Dakto crossed back to her and pulled her to her feet. 'This is home,' he repeated. 'And I have the skills to defend it. I have to do that. Let me do that. Let me fight in Yalotlan, for our gods. Our future.'

'We need all the help we can get, Ilandeh,' Lilla said softly.

Ilandeh's face crumpled. Dakto wouldn't stay for her; he'd made that clear. Maybe if a Toko made the decision for them, it would be easier to live with.

'Take him and go, and Malel watch over you both,' Xessa signed, maybe coming to the same conclusion. 'I love you.'

'I love you too, crazy eja,' Lilla signed. He wanted to tell her that Tayan would be back soon with news of the peace-weaving, but he feared the words might conjure his husband's ghost. That perhaps a ghost was all that was left to them. 'Come on then, Dakto,' he said and Ilandeh finally began to cry.

Lilla looked to Toxte. 'Look after her,' he signed again and this time Xessa had to press her lips hard together against the storm of emotion.

'I will,' Toxte said aloud. 'I swear. You just come back, Fang Lilla. We need you. Xessa needs you and him both.'

Lilla flinched that Toxte had conjured Tayan after all. *Please, Malel, watch over my husband. Send him back to me alive. That's all I ask.*

Dakto extricated himself from Ilandeh's grip and returned to Lilla's side. 'She may never forgive me for this, but I feel it, in here.' He rubbed his chest. 'This is the trail I'm supposed to walk. This is right.'

'I make no promises to you, nor have I made any to the rest of my Paw – I cannot promise you will come back alive. I can promise I won't risk you unnecessarily.'

Dakto looked at him; they were of a height, and the Xentib face was calm and clear. 'That's enough.'

The city was behind them. The best part of the day was behind them and they were deep in cultivated jungle, the trail just wide enough to walk two abreast as the cloud and the trees combined to steal the light. They'd have to rest soon.

'Do you know any of our touch-sign?' Lilla asked quietly, breaking the comfortable silence between him and Dakto.

The Xentib warrior skipped over a tangle of vine that crept across the trail, brow furrowed. 'Touch-sign? What's that?'

'We've taught most of the Yaloh warriors; you should know too. It's sign language for the dark.'

Dakto scowled, slowing. 'But if it's dark . . .' he began. 'Do you take me for a fool?'

'Well, you did volunteer to destroy pyramids when you could have stayed at home.' Lilla laughed as the man's scowl deepened. 'No, look, let me show you.' He squinted down the trail. 'Looks like we're making camp anyway – there's a clearing up ahead that should squeeze us all in. Come on.'

They pressed forward until the trail lightened and they could see the sky again, filtering out into a clearing and finding a rotting tree to use as a lumpy seat. 'Give me your arm. All right, touch-sign can never be as eloquent as full sign, but it's still really useful. Here.' He held Dakto's forearm in his left hand and with his right drew a long straight line and then a triangle at the end – a basic arrow – with his fingernail. 'Direction.' Next, he drew a big cross. 'Negative. So the arrow and the cross mean don't go that way.'

Lilla drew a large loop from inner wrist, up the forearm and down to outer wrist. 'What do you think that one is?'

Dakto looked up, biting his lip. 'Apart from ticklish?'

'Apart from ticklish,' Lilla confirmed with a grin.

'Well, supposing we are at the start point, it might be . . . go in a circle? Circle around?'

'Retreat. See? You've gone back to the start. Circle is just that, a circle,' and he drew on Dakto's inner arm. He showed him a few more, making the Xenti close his eyes to really understand the feel of the instructions.

'Good,' he said a few minutes later. 'Of course, we'll have to practise, but—'

'Let me try,' Dakto interrupted and Lilla obediently extended his arm and closed his eyes. Dakto's fingers were gentle on his arm and then his fingernail scratched a crossed arrow.

'Don't go that way,' Lilla said, pointing and grinning.

Dakto let out an annoyed huff and drew another sign. Lilla frowned. 'Again.' The sign again, lighter this time, even harder to read. He started to open his eyes when Dakto's lips touched his, soft and hot and faintly salty. He sucked in a surprised breath and jerked away, his eyes flying open. 'Dakto,' he breathed.

Confusion flitted across his features. 'But I thought . . .'

Lilla pulled his arm out of the man's grip, embarrassment flaring hot. Had he missed the signs? Had there even *been* any signs? He didn't think so. 'No. I'm sorry if I led you to believe . . . but no. You know I'm married.' He stood up, wiping flakes of bark from the seat of his kilt, flustered.

Dakto scrambled to his feet, too. 'We're going to war,' he said in a low voice, his hand on Lilla's arm to stay him. 'We could die. Tayan might never come back from the Singing City.'

Lilla managed a small, pained smile. 'I know.' Dakto leant forward again, but Lilla put his hand on his chest, firm. 'I know all that. And yet I am married. I'm sorry, my friend, but that's all we can be. There are enough warriors around you who are free, though. Both Lutek and Tiamoko, for two. I could—'

'I don't want Lutek or Tiamoko,' Dakto said and there was such despondency in his tone that Lilla almost felt guilty. 'Forgive me, Fang, I have misread . . . everything. It won't happen again.' He moved to the other side of the clearing and stood there with his head bowed, ignoring the quiet industry as the camp was prepared.

For an instant, Lilla was tempted to call Dakto back and apologise again, but didn't. Doing so would only give the man fresh hope and there was none to be had.

Tayan's quick mouth and lively eyes flashed across Lilla's mind, and his absence was suddenly sharper than obsidian.

The words Lilla had spoken at their parting came back to him: 'You're taking my heart with you. Make sure you bring it back.' And Tayan's reply, whispered against his mouth as he stretched up for a final kiss: 'I leave mine here, my love. Look after it.'

'I will,' he promised quietly. 'Always.'

XESSA

Sky City, Malel, Tokoban
168th day of the Great Star at morning

Otek's house smelt of chillies and honey: the scent of her childhood.

Xessa sat with Otek, Kime, and Toxte around her, her first father draped in the heat of three big dogs, each trying to cram into his lap or under his arms or against his neck. They were as gentle as ever, but Xessa watched closely to make sure Otek didn't just give every morsel of food to the drooling animals. He was too thin these days, barely eating unless someone was with him, and the Wet had increased Xessa and Kime's duties so that he was alone for long periods.

But as always, Otek's face relaxed when he was around the dogs, and the animals all understood; they were never exuberant around the old man, instead sitting close, in Otek's lap if they could manage it, heads pressed against the thin chest or under his chin. And Otek's old hands would stroke them and fondle their big ears and a little of his spirit would return to his flesh.

It was a special duskmeal, and she was warm in the love

of her family and quietly delighted that Toxte had agreed to come along. Tika had stopped by earlier as well, to check Xessa and Kime were ready for tomorrow. When they'd attempt to capture a Drowned.

Will. When we will *capture a Drowned.*

She pushed the thought away and clicked her tongue when Ossa tried to steal food from Otek's hand. The dog's ears went low and he gazed at her as if he'd never been fed in his entire life, but he didn't try again. Xessa made sure her father ate it instead and was rewarded with Ossa's wounded betrayal. The corner of her mouth twitched up despite herself.

'Do you understand?' Kime was signing, and Xessa focused back on the conversation. There was a good chance, after all, that neither of them would come back from the Swift Water tomorrow; she hated the thought of Otek not understanding where they'd gone.

Xessa, Tika, and Kime had spent a lot of time with him, explaining what they were going to attempt, and a few times the conversation had sparked something in him. He'd told tales then of his days as eja and the battles he'd fought, the nets and spears and dogs he'd lost. The friends. Xessa had listened, joyous despite the subject, despite knowing all of these stories better than he did now, just glad to have him back for a while. Her father.

When he finished signing, she'd leant against his side, tucked into his armpit as she'd done as a child, even though now she had to scrunch down to fit, and she'd pretended she was that girl again, and her father still existed in the flesh world, and nothing could hurt either of them, despite the duty he performed and the risks he took.

Though now the duty and the risks are mine.

'It is a very good plan,' Toxte signed and said at the same time, the movement bringing her back to her surroundings, small and cosy and filling with the particular, heady scent of the man who every day burrowed his way a little deeper into her heart.

She put her hand gently on Otek's knee, nudging Ekka's haunch out of the way as she did. The dog shifted in his lap and her rump slid onto the mat. They were all far too big for laps anyway, not that it stopped them trying.

'We have built a cage, a strong but light cage,' Kime was signing as Xessa's eyes flicked from his hands to Otek's face. '. . . a Drowned, and take it to the—'

Otek's hand grabbed Xessa's; she started and met his gaze – his present, entirely-in-the-flesh-world gaze. Her heart flooded with love and relief and she smiled, raised his hand and pressed her lips against it; then she held it to her cheek. It shook. 'Capture?' he said and she nodded. She suddenly didn't want to think about it, talk about it, not while Otek was here with her.

Kime had taken his other hand and Otek looked between them, his wrinkled brow creased further by a deep scowl. And then he took his hands away from them both and pointed at Toxte. 'Who is this?' he signed.

'Toxte is my duty partner,' Xessa signed and caught a glimpse of his mouth drop open. Confusion flittered over his features. 'And my friend,' she added hurriedly. That didn't seem to work either. 'My . . .'

'We are becoming intimate,' Toxte signed and Xessa felt a blush creep up her neck. 'I care for your daughter very much, honoured ejab,' he said, looking at Kime as well.

She waited for more, but Otek was wandering again, the brightness of his eyes beginning to fade. 'Good,' he said. 'None of you die.' He was gone before they could even raise their hands to assure him they wouldn't – whether or not that might be a lie.

Still, he'd seen Toxte. Known him and what they meant to each other, even if she had fumbled the admission so badly. That was something, a small precious pearl more valuable than any traded by the coastal villages.

Kime tapped her knee. '"Becoming" intimate?' he asked with a grin that made her blush come back. 'Then why are you here with two old men? Go on, off with you.' He shooed them away with a smile and Xessa thought she might burst into flame from the heat of her embarrassment, but Toxte seemed more than willing to do as they were told.

He rose to his feet with a fluid grace that nearly stole her breath, and then held his hand out to help her up. He grinned and signed something to Kime and Otek she didn't see, then whistled for the dogs and dragged her through the curtain and out into the evening. He turned abruptly so that she collided with him and wrapped both arms around her and kissed her thoroughly until she was breathless for real.

Toxte let her go long enough to sign. 'What does my duty partner and my friend want to do now?' he teased and Xessa bit her lip. The thought of taking Kime's advice was both embarrassing and deeply appealing. Maybe he realised that, because he signed 'Drink?' and she accepted gratefully. Hand in hand, their dogs ranging ahead and behind, they wandered down through the city to the entertainment district.

Despite wanting it to chase away the anxiety, the beer was too sweet and Xessa didn't dare risk the hangover that came with honeypot. Instead, they strolled again as night fell and the late markets lit up with braziers and candles. There were more people than usual on the streets; the whole city knew what the ejab were going to attempt the following morning and more and more people came to offer blessings and prayers for her when they saw her pass. Eventually, Toxte read the growing panic in her eyes and led her firmly and quickly back to her home.

It was one of four houses in a square around a communal garden and firepit, and though the pit was red with embers, no one sat in its meagre light. Xessa breathed a soft sigh of relief and ducked under the curtain and in. She lit a couple of candles and then Toxte's arms wrapped around her waist from behind and he kissed her neck. She leant into it and then he was turning her to face him.

'Are you scared?' he signed and it was like dousing the heat in her blood with water.

Xessa hitched in a breath, not wanting to think about this now, of all times, but the words smashed the wall she'd built to hold back her emotions. Her vision narrowed with a suddenness that frightened her and her breathing was rough as bright, jagged panic carved through her without reason or warning. She thrashed against it, but still its waters closed over her head.

She barely registered sinking to her knees, Toxte following her down with his big, warm hands stroking her shoulders and back. Xessa's body was slick with cold sweat, her head too light and her limbs too heavy, and the walls were pressing in and out as if they were breathing, as if she'd taken some magic.

Dimly, she knew Toxte was helping her purge some of the fear so she'd be calmer tomorrow, but the knowledge was distant and drowning under the ocean of her terror.

And then Ossa's face was in her face, his tongue in her ear as he wriggled between them. She didn't have the strength to push him away, knowing that if she let go of the double handful she had of Toxte's shirt that she'd collapse. Toxte's hands slid beneath her arms and tugged her forwards; he shifted to wrap his legs around her hips until she was cocooned in his limbs and Ossa was in there too, somehow, sprawled across their legs. Toxte pulled her head to his chest and the dog stilled, his breath fugging the tiny space between them.

The aftertaste of beer roiled in Xessa's stomach again but then it settled, the only part of her that didn't seem to be screaming. Her muscles and bones and heart and spirit all clamoured that she should run, run high and far and fast and never come back.

Toxte rocked her and let her cry, and she was embarrassed for him to see her like this. But the panic was still a roaring beast with claws hooked deep into her spirit and she could do nothing other than fight it, pulling on his strength, focusing on his body and his scent and the heat of his skin beneath her cheek. On the real.

She supposed that answered Toxte's question about whether she was scared. Between them, dog and man brought her through it and back into the world, the panic receding like storm clouds, hovering on the horizon, threatening but no longer immediate. Her fingers were clenched in Toxte's tunic and she uncurled them with difficulty. He leant back to look down at her and she managed a half-smile, half-grimace of apology. His brows were drawn together, worry etched across the fine bones of his face, and his full lips were thin with pressure. Xessa ducked her head as embarrassment began to seep in again, but he put his finger under her chin and lifted her face up; then he kissed her softly.

'You should sleep,' he said and she shook her head. 'Tomorrow is—'

Xessa sat up enough to sign. 'There is no tomorrow, there is only now. Make me forget tomorrow, Toxte. Please.' She hesitated. 'I mean, that is if you want,' she began but he caught her hands in his and kissed them until they stilled, before placing one against his heart; its beat was strong and slowly accelerating and she wrapped her free hand in the thickness of his hair, stretching up to him and pouring everything she had – and everything she wanted – into another kiss until her heart was full to bursting.

She inhaled, sharp, and her hand on his chest tightened and then found the neckline of his tunic. Her fingers slipped inside, onto warm, smooth, soft skin. He broke the kiss long enough to shove the dog away and slide it over his head, pulling free the long hair, plaited and beaded, that tangled in the material. The meagre candlelight outlined him in gold and pooled him in shadow, a hero from the old tales. First of the first children. She blushed at the absurdity, but then he was kissing her again, all the warm, hard expanse of his chest and belly and shoulders hers to roam.

The kiss didn't end, not for a long time, not until there was fire flashing across Xessa's nerve endings and she could barely breathe, barely see. She was still in the circle of his legs and shifted now, up onto her knees to tug off her own tunic and then the cotton band that held her breasts tight against her chest. She swung her leg over his, her kilt riding high, the thick sweep of her unbound hair framing his face as she grabbed it and kissed it again, feverish now. Wanting. Needing.

Toxte's hands were on her hips, pulling the kilt higher and then tugging at his own, and Xessa pulled back from his face long enough to watch his expression as she shifted and sank onto him. His heat filled her, his arms tightened convulsively around her waist and back and his mouth sagged open. More than need in his face, more than desire. Love.

Xessa drank in the sight of him as they moved, her left hand pressed to his throat to feel the noises he made.

She sucked in air and let her head hang back far enough her hair brushed his thighs, let mouth and hands and body work their very own, very special, and ancient brand of magic. Slow but insistent, unstoppable, a rhythm that lit fire inside them both, a shared and sacred burning until fingers became claws and pleasure battered at them and swept them up and consumed them and the world cracked and broke open, drenching them in light.

ILANDEH

The womb, above Sky City, Malel, Tokoban
168th day of the Great Star at morning

High Elder Vaqix knelt on a woven mat before a beaten copper bowl from which incense rose and curled and twisted and was pulled away through fissures in the ceiling. He prayed in an ancient language that Ilandeh understood only imperfectly – a word here or there that was almost known to her, a phrase that hinted at meaning but then concealed it, taunting her with almost-understanding where she stood in the mouth to the cave the Tokob called the womb.

The rhythms and cadences of his prayer were familiar, tantalising, tickling at her memory. But most importantly, the chant echoed and built and reverberated, introducing harmonics that hadn't been in his voice, as if the cave itself sang the other half of the prayer back at him.

The womb, sacred to the Tokob, was alive with magic. The torchlight glittered from a multitude of tiny crystals embedded in the rock walls, and from the hundreds of jade and obsidian and wood and bone ornaments placed on shelves carved into the rock. Lumps of gold, polished stones, and gleaming wood decorated every surface, reflecting the light even further. Bunches of feathers hung twisting on thin cords from the roof, stirred by tiny zephyrs too faint for Ilandeh to feel. Malel's breath. Beyond the kneeling high elder, at the opposite end of the small cave, the floor dropped away, and there glittered the still surface of the pool the ejab had made. This was where they'd bring it, if they caught it.

'High Elder?'

Vaqix's chant ended in a yelp of surprise and the old man spun on his knees to the entrance where Ilandeh stood. He gaped. 'What are you doing here?' he demanded after an incredulous pause. 'The womb is not for foreigners, unbelievers. This place is forbidden to you! None but Tokob may set foot in here.' His outrage made the words and his thin cheeks alike quiver, though his eyes were black as jet above the wicked hook of his nose. 'Get. Out. Now.'

'It is made of songstone, isn't it?' Ilandeh asked, stepping up into the cave and staring around. Small deposits of it were everywhere, but she pointed to a particularly thick seam in the far wall, as wide as the span of both her arms outstretched. 'There. Songstone. Do you know how valuable it is?'

'Songstone?' he repeated dumbly, scrambling to his feet so quickly the incense plume sputtered and billowed with his movement. 'This is our holiest place. It is Malel who gives strength to our prayers, the ancestors who—'

Ilandeh bit her lip. 'Oh, High Elder, you are so wrong. Songstone is holy, yes, but it does not speak in the tongue of your goddess or ancestors. It is its own thing, carrying its own sanctity and that of the world spirit. I fear you have been misled. I fear your whole society is built on a lie.'

Vaqix drew himself up even taller, his shadow long and

twisted by the candles that made the cave overly warm. 'Get. Out.'

Ilandeh cocked her head to listen to the echoes of his voice, smiling. Raw songstone, unrefined and yet as full of hidden, coiled power as a constrictor lazing on a branch.

'I can't do that, High Elder,' she said with genuine regret. She'd come to like the old man, in her way. He looked past her to the entrance. 'Your guard won't be joining us, I'm afraid.'

'What have you done?' Vaqix demanded, his voice a whisper now, cracked and beginning to fear. 'Who are you?'

Ilandeh took another step into the cave, confident now that she understood where the sense of sanctity came from. *I'd actually begun to think a god lived here.* She snorted at her own foolishness; she'd spent far too long among these people. 'I want you to know I'm sorry.'

Vaqix's fists clenched. 'I said, *who are you?*' he shouted and the songstone took the violence of his words and amplified it, not just the echoes or the volume but the emotion, casting the Tokob anger and violence back at himself, rebounding against him.

Ilandeh didn't flinch – the songstone's emotions weren't hers, weren't meant for her. 'I am Ilandeh, High Elder. Who else would I be?' She pulled the knife out of her belt. 'I'm afraid this heretical plan to capture a holy Setat and your childish idea to sabotage our pyramid-building in Yalotlan has forced my hand earlier than I would have liked. I still had so much to accomplish here, but . . .' She trailed off and spread the fingers of her free hand. 'Even the most meticulous plans can go awry. So, you are going to cancel the ejab attempt to capture a holy Setat tomorrow, and then you're going to recall the warriors you have sent to commit sacrilege in Yalotlan. Yes?'

'How did you get out of the city? There are guards at the walls,' the old man tried, clutching at anything that might make sense. He kept glancing behind her, as if hoping someone would come and explain to him what was happening.

'High Elder, please focus. You cannot allow the attempt tomorrow to take place. You must not allow any more slaughter of the holy Setatmeh.'

'Holy Setatmeh? You're a *Pecha*?' Vaqix demanded, using the question to try and distract her so she didn't notice the dart he pulled from its wooden holder on his belt.

He was a shaman as well as high elder and Ilandeh treated that knowledge with the respect it deserved. That dart could be smeared with anything: sedative for treating those in pain, even a poison. Despite a year spent observing the city and council, she didn't know Vaqix as well as she'd like.

'I am Ilandeh,' Ilandeh said again and saw how it angered him, 'and that is all you need to know. For the last time: your answer, High Elder. Cease the slaughter of the gods and recall the warriors from Yalotlan. Your choice will impact all your people. Your children. Think carefully.'

His answer was violence. He took her by surprise, throwing the dart underarm so Ilandeh almost missed the cast. She spun away and heard the faint clatter as it hit the wall behind her and then leapt forward, stabbing the old man up under the ribs, pivoting past him – a flailing arm catching her across the cheek and making her eyes water – and a second strike, down behind his collarbone into his chest.

He was dead on his feet, the songstone reverberating with the spilling of blood in wild echoes unformed and uncontrolled by the will of a Singer, when Ilandeh stepped up close behind him. 'You disappoint me, High Elder, but know this: for every holy Setat your fucking ejab have murdered, I will take vengeance in blood from your people. Under the song.'

She wiped the knife on his tunic and sheathed it, touched her belly and throat and inclined her head towards the song-stone, then walked back out of the womb and along the low passage leading out onto the hillside. She didn't look back at the sound of Vaqix collapsing. The night's storm had broken by the time she exited the womb and the darkness was heavy with rain, slicking back her hair and washing away the sweat of confrontation. She stepped over the corpse of Vaqix's guard – *shouldn't have left him to stand outside alone in the dark, blinded by torchlight* – and hurried downhill.

She still had much to do.

'May I ask how the day went?'

Eja Elder Tika blinked as Ilandeh sat next to her on the waist-high wall marking safe distance from the Swift Water. 'We are ready for the attempt,' she said, her voice loud – the spirit-magic was within her, muffling her ears.

'And was it wise for you to take the spirit-magic today if you must take it again tomorrow?' Ilandeh asked, watching Tika's dog sniff around among the shrubs and rows of medicinal plants below.

Tika ran her fingers down the four pale lines of scar on her throat. Ilandeh knew they'd been dealt by a holy Setat – one that Tika had gone on to slaughter, even injured as she was. She kept her shoulders relaxed and breathed through the horror and the rage and visceral, aching need to spit this woman on her own fucking spear.

'Why are you so interested?'

'What do you think they are?'

'Animals,' Tika said, shrugging. 'Vicious beasts.'

'The Pechaqueh say they are gods,' Ilandeh said softly.

'The Pechaqueh are children who break things they cannot have – including tribes. They understand nothing of the balance and the world or the poison of their song and that these monsters are bound up in it. Break the song, kill the Drowned, I say.'

Ilandeh's face was neutral. 'They call them holy Setatmeh. Do you know why?'

Tika squinted at her. 'I've just said—'

'It's because they are, both holy and gods. Back when the world was new, it sang to itself and each note created life – trees, plants, fish, birds, animals. That song remains, for those who know how to listen. It's trapped in the stone, the very bones of the world. The Singer knows how to free it, and the holy Setatmeh sing with the world spirit's own voice to claim their offerings and show us a hint of glory. The Singers birth the song of the world, bringing plenty and wealth, bringing the rains that swell the crops. The holy Setatmeh take away, maintaining the balance you say you are so fond of and that we do not understand. And yet you kill them and call them Drowned. I think it is you who doesn't understand.'

Tika was silent, assessing, and Ilandeh smiled. 'Now do you see the Singer's purpose? When he restores the song to all Ixachipan, he will wake the world spirit and it will sing with him. And all will be bountiful. No more hunger or disease. The lords of the Underworld will hold no fears for us and all will be music. And the longer you resist, the longer you prevent that glorious world from coming into being. How selfish you are, to deny us all such eternal beauty.'

'Who are you?' Tika asked, and now her voice was soft and her dog, Yalla, was standing looking up at them, alert, tail unmoving.

Ilandeh chuckled. 'You people, you're all so obsessed with identity. Why does it mean so much to you?'

Tika licked her teeth and eyed the distance between them.

She seemed unreasonably relaxed, and Ilandeh matched it – the calm looseness, the even breathing, the utter focus of the warrior. She hadn't killed an eja before – not in combat, anyway, though she had employed many of her quieter skills in the last year in this city that stank of heresy.

'We've learnt that in the Empire, identity means little, and status means everything,' Tika said eventually. 'If you're a Pecha, you're at the top, whether you gather shit or sell the finest obsidian. And if you're anything else, you're below, whether you gather shit or sell the finest obsidian. Any rational person can see how ridiculous that is, but another thing we've learnt is that the Pechaqueh aren't rational. No matter how skilled or dedicated, it seems that a person's blood places them in a hierarchy that ensures the Pechaqueh are on top. Which seems very convenient, doesn't it?

'You, though' – Tika jabbed a finger in Ilandeh's direction – 'you've pretended to be a Xenti this whole time. Lived in Xentibec, undertaken the rituals of the Xentib at festival time. I can't imagine a real Pecha doing that. But I also know – all Ixachipan knows – that Xentiban was only conquered four sun-years ago. So my question for you, *Merchant Ilandeh*, is this: did it only take you four sun-years to betray your people and your beliefs and all you hold dear; or did you actually *lower yourself* to pretend to be Xentib? Have you sullied your blood in order to spy on us? And will it ever be clean again?'

The ejab words were like rotten fruit in Ilandeh's mouth, bitter and vile and rank with poison, and she spat a low snarl against their invasion.

Who she was, what she was, had nothing to do with this woman or this place or these uncivilised, god-killing, frog-licking heathens. She was moving, but so was Tika, and Ilandeh had a bare instant to regret not just stabbing the woman in the back of the neck when she had had the chance. But no, this would be better. Staring into the eyes of a god-killer as she killed her, as she made amends for all the deaths she'd been unable to prevent.

'You have no idea who I am or what I'm capable of,' Ilandeh growled as she bounced to her feet on the wall.

'Then show me,' Tika snarled in response, her short stabbing spear in her hands as she jumped off the wall and landed on the side closest to the city. 'Fucking come on and show me.'

A knife against a spear was only ever going to go one way, so Ilandeh used the height of the wall to her advantage, drawing a viper-quick strike from Tika, even though the spirit-magic must have almost left her, making her tired and shaky.

Ilandeh leapt high over the sweeping horizontal blow intended to cut her legs from beneath her, throwing herself at the eja even before the swing was finished, her knife reversed in her grip. One knee caught Tika in the chest and her hands came down on the backs of her shoulders. But Tika stumbled under the impact, somehow twisting as she went down, and the knife only ripped off a few bamboo scales sewn into the salt-cotton before they were both on the ground.

Ilandeh rammed her left elbow into Tika's throat as the spear cracked across her shoulder blades and then the dog was there, coming in low and fast and silent, only the thud of its big paws alerting her. Ilandeh grabbed the back of Tika's armour and jerked her into the dog's path as it pounced, spoiling its leap so it twisted in mid-air, and her knife ripped open its flank as it landed. The dog screamed and so did Tika and the woman punched her in the eye and crushed her onto her back, wrestling for the knife.

Setatmeh, she was strong. Ilandeh thrashed and managed to slide half from under her, though the moment of inattention nearly cost her her life as Tika prised at her fingers wrapped around the knife hilt and tried to twist it so the blade pointed down at her own chest. Roaring, the bones of her wrist grinding, she fought Tika's strength, fury, and body weight until she managed to plant her foot and drive up, twisting her hips and throwing the older woman back towards her dog again – not to fend it off, this time, just to roll her, keeping hold of Tika's wrist as she did.

Ilandeh knew the ejab trained in some ground-defence techniques, but not as many as the Melody, and once she'd got one leg free she kicked it up. The eja reared up just slightly to avoid her flailing sandal, but it was enough. Ilandeh's calf caught her across her throat and chest and she bent her knee to lock it around her neck and slammed her down with all the strength of her thigh and arse and back, twisting up as she did. Tika hit the ground back first, hard enough that her hands jolted on Ilandeh's knife hand. Ilandeh wrenched free and pushed the blade into the woman's side, ripped it out and drove it in again.

The urge to stab her for every heresy and every insult and every disparaging comment burnt at the back of her throat like bile, so strongly that her muscles trembled with it, but Ilandeh kicked free of the woman and rolled to her feet, putting space between them. The eja wasn't dead yet, and that was important. Sucking in air, Ilandeh put the dog out of its misery and then clubbed Tika in the temple with the butt of her knife, before eyeing the dark expanse of hill between them and the city. The terraced fields and orchards and water temples appeared deserted, and no voices were raised in alarm despite the noise of their fight.

'Thank you, Setatmeh,' Ilandeh whispered fervently.

Swearing at the weight, she dragged Tika up and pushed her over the wall onto the other side – the river side, and then followed. Panting, she hoisted Tika onto her shoulders. The woman's blood began seeping down her back, but it was the least of her worries. Staggering but moving as fast as she could, Ilandeh made for the Swift Water, beginning to pray as soon as she could hear the rushing of water.

'Holy Setatmeh, gods of the rivers and the streams, you who bring the rain that makes the crops grow, you who speak with voice of song and world, accept this your offering. Accept this eja, this enemy of your blood and mine, as your just reward.' She could barely see where she was going, let alone if her prayer would be answered, but the thin rind of the moon brightened just a little behind its veil of cloud. Just enough to see three Setatmeh rise from the shallows. Ilandeh waded in to her knees, fear fluttering through her – *I stood by and let them be killed; though I did everything I could, it still feels as if I did nothing* – and lowered Tika with a grunt.

The eja roused at the chill of the water. She sucked in a breath and then her eyes widened so much the whites were visible all the way around. She flailed out with one hand, begging perhaps, before the gods dragged her below.

Ilandeh waded back to shore. 'Accept your offering, sacred spirits,' she said again. 'Forgive me for what I have allowed to be done to your kin while I have been here. But soon the song will echo from these hills. Soon you will be free – and all the world will be music.'

ENET

Enet rattled the carved jade and bone dice in the cup. She knelt opposite the Singer, carefully adorned for maximum effect – meaning, on this occasion, without the Great Octave's headdress. Better not to remind him of her status lest it be taken from her.

Eleven days since she had suffered the disgrace of being cast out of the council meeting. It was the longest they'd been separated since she'd become his courtesan, let alone Spear or Great Octave. Two missteps in the last few months. Enet rattled the dice again. She could not afford a third. She would not survive a third. And so she would act.

She had been pleased to see the monkey in its cage when she entered, that despite her disgrace he had kept it, a reminder of her and their son both.

Enet's mouth softened at the thought of him, her beautiful, dutiful, quick-witted Pikte. The best parts of both his parents, and song-born, too. He was special to the Singer, and Enet

240

used that to remind the holy lord that she, too, was important to him. Vital. He needed her if he was to complete the conquest of Ixachipan and wake the world spirit. He just needed reminding of that. Of what she could offer; what only Enet could bring him. And one sure way to do that was with the dice.

Xac's own divinations were by the stars and the histories and through the holy Setatmeh themselves, and were usually focused on the fate of the Empire of Songs and the path to the waking of the world spirit. Enet's divinations were smaller but no less crucial to the holy lord's great destiny, and of all the councillors and shamans who served him, hers were the tellings he trusted the most.

Enet breathed on the dice and cast them and together they watched them bounce and stutter across the mat and then stop. The mat was an exquisite work of art, painted with the four cardinal directions and the centre of the world, the centre of magic and power and life-giving water. The fountain and the firmament laid out in vibrant inks between them.

Across the face of the mat the jade and bone dice skipped and rolled, their images and their positions telling the present and the future. Xac's future. The Empire's future. Enet's future. The black cat, a Setat, a shard of obsidian, a jade amulet, a liana-wrapped tree. And, rolling to a stop off the edge of the mat, the storm.

Enet let the images and their positions float across her consciousness, breathing deep, palms on her thighs. The Singer was silent opposite her. 'Black cat, water god, obsidian, jade, wrapped tree. Storms from afar.' She met his eyes. 'There is untruth in your council.' She pointed to the die nearest the world centre. 'You, of course, are the holy Setat, and the black cat crouches behind you, waiting to pounce.

You cannot see it, facing forward towards your Empire, but it is there. Biding its time. Patient.'

The Singer's gaze was fixed on the dice, his fists tightly clenched. She had no idea whether this prophecy would match his own; all she could do was tell him what she saw. 'The Empire is the wrapped tree.' He looked up sharply at that. 'While you have cut many of the vines strangling it, others still remain. Perhaps they are external – the Yaloh and Tokob that Pilos has not yet dealt with – or even internal. A stifling of your glory, and by extension, of the Empire's glory. A . . . smothering of your divinity.'

The Singer grunted and leant a little closer, his eyes tracking from the black cat to the holy Setat to the tree. 'And these others?' He stabbed out a blunt finger, nearly but not quite touching the dice.

'The shard of obsidian may be a weapon, holy lord.'

'Lying between me and my Empire? Assassination?'

'Not necessarily. Perhaps a weapon that you can reach out and take for yourself. Perhaps something of value, but see how its colour matches that of the cat that threatens you? A weapon against those who would do you harm. Or a prize won from those who would seek to hurt you.'

'What else?'

'The jade amulet. See its shape, pointed at the top? Like a hill. Perhaps the Tokob lands. It may be that they hold greater significance than we had thought.'

Xac sat back with a growl. 'Than we had thought? *We?*'

Enet swallowed and concentrated on maintaining a neutral expression. 'You, holy lord.' The monkey began screeching and throwing itself around its cage, perhaps in response to the sudden weight in the room, like a storm's approach. Enet didn't miss the flinch and sudden anger that crossed the Singer's face.

'Are you Spear or are you Singer?' he growled.

The hairs stood up on Enet's arms. 'Merely your humble Spear, holy lord.'

Xac leant forward and cupped a hand around his ear. 'What? Speak up when you address me.'

'I am merely your Spear,' she repeated a little louder. *Adoration. Awe. Love.*

'And how many more years do you have to serve?'

She started – he wouldn't dare. The election of a Spear was endorsed by the holy Setatmeh themselves, was pronounced at the first sighting of the Great Star at morning after its grand absence. Spears served for a Star cycle, no less. To cut short such an appointment was a disgrace that could not be borne.

'I have five sun-years left as Spear, holy lord.'

He stared at her until she looked down again, and then carried on staring; she could feel it. Almost a physical weight. The monkey screeched again. When the Singer spoke, his voice had harmonics that made her stomach flutter. 'What else?'

'The storm sits far from the universe,' she said after a while, pointing. 'Some upset in the world of the gods or among the lords of the Underworld. Perhaps something invades the world spirit's dreams. The Tokob god-killers, perhaps. I have been asking the shaman at my estate about it and—'

The song, low and soothing before, clanged out of harmony, reminiscent more of the grunts and screams of battle than the sure and smooth praising of power. Enet felt it spike her blood and set her heart racing. Sweat popped out on her brow. Here, in the source itself, the song's power was undeniable, its emotion a storm inside her skin. Everyone in the pyramid would feel the same storm and know the

Singer was displeased with the prophecy – and with her. *The third misstep?*

Enet shuffled backwards on her knees and pressed her forehead to the ground, careful not to touch the painted world.

Outside the pyramid, the song's changes and effects would be less noticeable, but they would be there. Enet's chest heaved. The monkey flung itself at the bars of its cage again and the Singer suddenly swept up the dice cup and hurled it across the source. It bounced off the bamboo bars and the little animal went berserk, racing around the cage and screaming. Enet didn't move, filling her mind and spirit with devotion and reverence.

Singer Xac was reaching the fullness of his power and she could feel it swelling the source and the song alike. If Enet didn't consolidate her own power before he began to wane, all her plans would come to naught. And they were such plans. Such plans.

He may not wane. It may be that he is still strong when the time comes to wake the world spirit. It may be he who walks Ixachipan at its side for eternity.

And so it should be. Enet filled her mind with love for her lord.

He snapped his fingers and she sat back up, ready to continue with the reading, but the Singer's eyes roamed the sanctuary, the suite of twenty-seven rooms within the great pyramid that collectively made up his home and the source. His skin was flushed red with blood and tinted gold with magic; Enet caught her breath when she looked at him, a small, involuntary murmur of appreciation slipping from her. He flexed the muscles in his arms, head cocked to listen to the corresponding flex of the song, and grinned, but the triumph lasted only a heartbeat, before being replaced with weary bitterness, almost resignation.

'I never realised the thrill of opulence would fade,' he said, as if to himself. 'I never realised how the power and the divinity are so inextricably bound up with the responsibility and the sacrifice.' He swept an arm out to encompass the room. 'Sculpted gardens, a tamed stream and offering pool, wide verandas with views over the city, and the platform at the summit beneath the songstone: the heart of my power. All colourful and pristine, populated with only the most beautiful slaves, courtesans and sculpture. The finest musicians and actors, jewellers and dressers. The most talented potters and artists to paint their wares. Everything so . . . Fucking. Perfect. It makes me sick.'

Enet flinched. The song tore at her with teeth and claws, made nausea surge at the base of her throat and heat build between her legs. Beneath the anger sat Xac's lust – for life and death and cock and cunt and everything in between – desires impossible for any in his presence to ignore.

It was the official reason, the most obvious reason, why Singer Het had failed so soon – she'd been a child at the mercy of feelings she had neither name for nor familiarity with. They'd frightened her and then they'd consumed her. Children should not be Singers; they had not the experience to control the changes. Even Xac had struggled to contain his impulses in the first years of his divinity.

The Singer rubbed a hand across his face, weariness souring his lovely, song-brightened features. His lips peeled back from his teeth and Enet squirmed where she sat, wanting him and him knowing it. His denial of her desire bringing him more pleasure than acceptance would. A dark pleasure, a spiteful pleasure, and that too entered the song. All through the source, harsh words would be spoken, parents might pinch their children just to make them cry, secrets would be spilt and arguments started. Chorus warriors practising their weapons might spill blood in earnest.

'These rooms and gardens, maybe the slave quarters if I wander down there: they're all I will ever know,' Xac continued, surprising her again. She'd expected angry sex or dismissal, not confession. 'All the years I had before my selection and what did I do with them? Nothing. Barely travelled, never visited the untamed jungle or saw the dead plains. Never fought a battle. Never took a life except when making an offering. And *I* don't take them even then.

'This is it. This is the rest of my life within these walls and gardens. This sacred prison. The Tokob murder my divine kin and I sit here unable to help them.'

Enet swept up the dice and moved them and the world mat to the side, then shuffled forward on her knees until they touched Xac's. She put her hands on his face, unable to be away from him any longer. 'But you are the Singer,' she said with ragged passion. 'You are glory incarnate.'

'I am a prisoner in a luxurious cage. And I am sick of fucking luxury.' He slapped her hands down. 'I am sick of beauty and hymns of praise. I am sick of pretty slaves and pretty courtesans and pretty food. You, Enet – I am thoroughly fucking sick of you.'

But despite his words she could feel his desire pressing against her like a hurricane. She flipped up his kilt and hers, swung a leg across his hips and lowered herself down, driving a long groan from both their throats. His fingers would leave bruises in her flanks.

'You know when I feel most alive? When I watch the holy Setatmeh accept their offerings,' he gasped. 'Not even *this* compares.'

Enet grabbed fistfuls of his hair and pulled hard; she darted her head forward and bit his shoulder. It wasn't enough; she could tell by his face that all these sensations were no longer enough. Still, he didn't stop her as she rose and fell in his lap, squeezing and rocking, long, painted fingernails scoring his flesh. He shuddered once, twice, and then stiffened with a roar part release, part frustration. She wasn't there yet, though she was so close it was enough to make her want to scream her own frustration, but she didn't protest when he shoved her off. The sex, the divination, the discussions of the war – none of it had soothed him. She knew what might, if she dared. If Enet had the courage to take the next step on the path of destiny.

She could still taste the residue of the tonic she'd drunk before coming here, the tonic that had set her on a trail she couldn't now turn back from. She was already on that path. Committed. She ran her tongue over her gums and let that taste strengthen her, the flicker of magic in her mouth and belly.

'I want to experience something . . . anything,' he panted, reaching for honeypot and throwing it back in one gulp. 'I want more. I *need more.*'

And I live to serve you, great Singer. 'Then, holy lord, I have a gift for you,' she said, fighting against the throbbing, sullen ache of unfulfilled desire at her core. She bowed shallowly and then stood and crossed to the bamboo cage. She opened the lid and gently picked up the little creature. It struggled and bit the meat of her thumb, but she took it back and placed it in his lap. Reflexively, the Singer grabbed it before it could run off.

'Something else I'm sick of,' he roared. 'It does nothing but screech and throw its shit at me.'

Enet nodded. 'Then kill it,' she said over its noise. Xac paused and looked at her, and the Chorus warrior at the far wall stiffened, his gaze snapping to them. He made no move to interfere, as she had known he would not. His loyalty belonged to her. Still, her words were more than dangerous – they were sacrilege.

'It's just an animal. Kill it and we can eat it later. You said you'd never killed anything. You haven't experienced the taking of life and perhaps you should. Perhaps when the Melody returns to Yalotlan after the Wet, that newfound experience will weave through the song and strengthen our warriors. Your experiences are what shape the song, after all. Your knowledge; your magic.'

She leant closer and sucked at the bleeding bite on her hand. A little obvious, perhaps, but, judging by the way Xac's throat moved convulsively as he watched her, effective. She swallowed blood. 'Feel,' she whispered. 'Feel something new, my love, and weave it into a song that will last forever.'

The Singer lifted the squirming monkey in one hand and squeezed, tentative at first until it squeaked, and then his face turned ugly and the song *jumped* and he squeezed again, hard and furious and delighted, until its frightened squealing was lost beneath the cracking of its bones. Enet watched, dizzy and wondering at her own audacity as the tiny death rumbled through the song, swelling it with sudden power, and Xac's skin flushed golden-red again. It was proof. It was what she needed and now that she had seen it, taking the next step was easier.

'That was not the gift, holy lord,' she said in a smoky voice as the Singer examined the little corpse. He glanced up, his brow furrowing as the body flopped in his grip. 'The true gift is not another monkey. It is not pretty or musical. It is dangerous, Singer.'

The song will change if he accepts this, change maybe forever, and my future will be secured. Or my death.

No. It is worth the risk. We are too close to the wakening. It has to be now.

'May I send for it?' Enet asked. When he didn't answer, she rose from the mats and straightened her kilt as she strode to the courtesans' entrance, then signalled for her guards to bring it in. She took the cloth-wrapped package one proffered her, hummingbirds taking flight in her belly.

Enet hurried back to Xac's side, noting the wary confusion in his face as they brought in the hooded, bound figure and kicked it to its knees. She flicked fingers in dismissal of her guards and let the Chorus warrior take over, standing above the prisoner with his club ready.

'Great Singer,' Enet said and pulled off the kneeling figure's hood. 'This is Betsu, a Yaloh spy and a warrior who insulted your name and our Empire. She came here under guise of being a peace-weaver, and then she fled my house in the night and was spotted trying to rouse slaves in the flesh markets to rebellion. I have kept her secure – and she has been brought here in secret.'

Enet watched for the Singer's reaction as she unwrapped the cloth from the bundle. 'Great Singer, divine god, I offer you the stone knife.'

The Singer stared at the weapon lying between them, the ritual blade of rare pale quartz knapped to a wicked sharpness, the handle carved from the leg bone of a jaguar. Unique and beautiful and full of magic. Forbidden, ancient magic not used in centuries. The gold in his skin pulsed and flowed as if reaching towards it, urging him to take it up, to wield it on flesh and bone.

Enet's mouth was dry as the Singer didn't move. 'Prisoner, lower your eyes. You have no permission to look upon the holy lord, our living god, our great Singer,' she snapped. Her voice bounced from the plastered walls to mingle with the choir of children singing somewhere out of sight, the trickle of water, and the chirr of cicadas from the gardens. Beneath them all clanged the song and Betsu's ragged breathing. The

Singer's own breathing wasn't much better; his nostrils flared like an exhausted deer's as he dragged in air, not quite believing what was happening.

'You shouldn't have fucking brought me here then, should you, if you didn't want me to look? Get your stinking hands off me!' the Yalotl shouted as the Chorus shoved her head down onto the mat and held it there. 'Not that he's anything to look at. Hands are soft – has he ever tilled a field or held a weapon?' The words were muffled but loud enough to reach Enet's ears. And the Singer's.

'What is this?' Xac whispered, his eyes as round as those of a holy Setat. 'Is this a joke – or am I the joke here?' The danger in his voice made Enet's bladder tighten.

She ran her palm up his arm, across the thick shoulder and down his back. 'No, holy lord. You want sensation. You want experience. You want to kill, and more than just monkeys.' He twitched at that and Betsu began to struggle.

'It is forbidden,' the Singer said, his words slow and unsure.

They all knew why it was forbidden. The Singer must be surrounded with beauty and strength at all times. The Singer must not be upset or experience strong emotion of a negative nature. The Singer must not be exposed to horrors or criticised or angered. And the Singer must never, ever revel in death, lest it seep into the song and corrupt the millions of spirits bound up in its glory. A strong song meant strong people. A bloody song, though . . . or at least, that was what the legends said. Enet's research indicated otherwise and here, now, with her influence and status hanging by the thread of the Singer's changeable whims, she had no choice but to accelerate her plans.

She lowered her voice to a purr. 'This woman is no one. She is . . . invisible. Expendable. Sensation, great Singer: that is my gift to you.'

'Return to your place.' The Singer's voice was a throaty growl.

The Chorus warrior hesitated. 'It is my duty to protect you.'

'Do not disobey the Singer,' Enet snapped, trembling with adrenaline and triumph and not a little terror. *There's no going back. Am I really doing this? Are* we *doing this?*

The warrior hesitated again, testing the very bounds of duty and obedience despite his loyalty to Enet, and then he let go of Betsu's neck and took a single pace backwards. The Yalotl came up faster than a striking snake, got her feet under her and was halfway to standing when his club smashed into her shoulder and drove her back onto her knees. Enet squeaked at the sudden movement, but the sound was lost under the Yaloh bellow of hurt.

A moment later the Singer's fist buried itself in Betsu's gut. She folded over and Xac hit her again, hammering into her cheekbone, snapping her head to one side.

'*Who is your god?*' Enet shouted when the warrior instinctively stepped back in, panic flushing his features at the breach not just of tradition and protocol but of ritual. *The Singer must never be exposed to violence. The song must not be blooded.* The single most inviolable rule – and the one that Enet was deliberately breaking.

Because it is wrong.

Her question brought the Chorus stumbling to a halt, obedience warring with duty, and in that moment, it happened.

The song *brayed*. Raw power crackled from Xac, lifting the hairs on Enet's arms and neck, a frisson of energy and need and dominance tingling from scalp to soles. She shuddered and rocked under its intensity, and then Xac was on Betsu, straddling her waist, fists driving into her head and neck and chest, bellowing with joy, swelling with the thrill

251

of the song, his body expanding, muscles engorged and golden beneath glistening skin until he *glowed*.

The knife was next to them, within reach of the peace-weaver – if she could free her hands. Another thrill shivered through Enet and she shifted on her knees, facing the Singer, avid, living his joy through the song, buffeted by the storm of his emotions.

The Yalotl was on her back, helpless to avoid the beating, her head snapping one way and then the other. Whatever she was shouting was garbled, lost amid the punches raining on her jaw and mouth until they faded into grunts. Blood and a tooth splattered from her mouth and across Enet's tunic, up in a line of dots across her throat. Xac paused, staring intently at the blood on her skin, and then he leant forward and licked it from her neck.

The source was swimming with power, so thick Enet couldn't help but breathe it in like pollen, like sunlight, until it filled her with radiance and need and she found the abandoned knife and shoved it into the Singer's hand. The Chorus dropped his club and fell to his knees at her side, his hands clenching and unclenching with brimming, uncontrolled need as they watched Xac work, song-driven lust and bloodlust filling them both.

Enet watched her holy lord, her great Singer, her lover, as he peeled the Yaloh face off with the knife and wove her screams into the song until it roared and beat at them, beat inside them until they were all three growling like animals and everything was edged in golden radiance, in *power*.

Xac pulled Betsu's face, still blood-warm, over his own and showed it to her. She screamed louder, somehow still fighting, but the Singer was invincible in his magic now and he lifted her in one hand and dragged her, clawing at his arm, to the offering pool.

A Setat rose with a need greater even than the Singer's. Its song filled the source, filled them with such yearning, such inescapable delight amid the carnage and the power that Enet orgasmed as Betsu, faceless and yet somehow, she knew, smiling, freed herself from the Singer's grip and walked into the water, arms out to receive the Setatmeh claw-tipped embrace.

They watched the waters turn pink and the Singer threw the woman's face into the pool and then he returned at a run and fell on Enet like an eagle, his lust swallowing her whole.

And the song roared on.

THE SINGER

The source, Singing City, Pechacan, Empire of Songs

The song is mine, my will and creation, my duty and my glory. I craft my greatness into music. My flesh and mind, my soul and intentions. My divinity.

I know the song's needs; I know the Empire's needs. None may gainsay me or stand against my will.

My magic drives all hearts and stirs all souls, music that resonates through every mind and from every pyramid in this great Empire. Which I have made. Empire and music both.

I am the Singer, glory incarnate. Song incarnate. Magic made flesh. My strength cannot be measured for I have come into my power like the Singers of old and I will raise the Empire to heights none have ever achieved.

I will wake the world spirit. I will do whatever is necessary for glory. The song is mine and it can never be undone, unsung, unheard.

The song is mine . . .

I am the song.

I am the song that beats in the blood of millions. I am

the song that lulls them to sleep and rouses them to war, that succours the fearful and strengthens the weak.

I am the song and the song is me. I know what it needs; I give it what it craves. I strengthen myself to strengthen the Empire.

To be without me is to be without hope, without faith, without will or might or cunning. To be without me is to betray, to lie and wail and know defeat. To be without me is to die.

I am the song and the song is me. I am unlike all others and my song shall be the lasting melody of the world. I am the sum and pinnacle of all life.

It is my song that raises us up. It is me. My will. My divinity.

My blade.

For I am the song. And the song is me.

TAYAN

Death stalked him.

He'd promised Betsu he would wait a month before leaving, but he was half convinced he wouldn't live until duskmeal, let alone another two weeks. Something had happened, something momentous that had changed the song, driving it out of its usual beautiful strength into something . . . lustful.

It had taken hours to settle, imperious as ever, but there was a wildness to it even now, two days later, an edge of danger, as if it danced on the very cusp of madness and the Singer was unable to tame it. Or perhaps he did not want to.

Tayan hadn't seen Enet since it had happened and none of the slaves would answer his questions or allow him anywhere but the few rooms he'd been granted access to and a small part of the gardens. He ate and sat and walked in silence, in

256

isolation. He didn't know what had happened, and without the usual excursions the Great Octave had taken him on, he had nothing to distract himself from wild speculation.

Since Betsu's departure, Enet had taken him into the city most days in a blatant attempt to overwhelm him with Pechaqueh society. They'd visited gardens and fighting pits, markets including flesh markets, where she pointed out how they selected the appropriate profession for the new slaves, and they'd visited temples to admire the murals of holy Setatmeh and Singers past. He had seen much and learnt very little. It was all empty, a formal nonsense intended to cow him into submission, to reinforce the belief that they could never defeat the Empire of Songs and that the proposed surrender was the only rational choice. Even worse, a small, traitorous part of him was beginning to believe it.

Tayan barely slept, and not just because of the nightmares he'd suffered ever since the ritual at the river. The slave's face, barred with the Drowned's fingers and claws, bleeding. Each night, the face changed – sometimes it was Xessa's, other times it was Lilla's. Once it had been his own. And through it all the song, worming through his skull and bones like a million ants.

But now, finally, she had summoned him to the so-called small room with its views of the garden. Tayan hadn't seen most of the other rooms, so its size meant nothing other than that it was almost as big as his and Lilla's entire home.

They sat, a pitcher of honeyed water and fine pottery cups on the low table between them. 'Is the holy lord quite well, Great Octave?'

Enet jerked and looked at him. Her eyes were bright – too bright – as if she'd swallowed journey-magic, and although she sat apparently composed opposite him, her hands were rarely still. Her fingers twined and curled about each other like a nest of mating snakes and flickers of emotion raced across her face that she seemed unable to control. She kept running her tongue around her gums, as if she had seeds stuck in her teeth. He hadn't thought she could be so preoccupied, so vulnerable.

'What? Of course. The great Singer is in perfect health,' she said, waving a hand in poor imitation of airy dismissal, and that's when he identified it. Deep inside, behind the walls and masks of power, privilege, and arrogance, Enet was frightened. Terrified down to her bones.

And that frightens the shit out of me.

Something had happened. When the song had veered so wildly out of control, when it had reverberated with fury and lust and a dark, red-edged cruelty that had made his pulse thunder in his ears, something had changed for Enet, too. While she had remained frustratingly vague on the magic that powered the song, he knew enough to recognise that something momentous had occurred. He'd witnessed the hunched shoulders and lowered voices of the slaves, the hurried, anxious whispers as they went about their tasks. He'd seen the ones in the gardens staring at the estate wall as if they could see through it all the way to the pyramid and within, to learn the cause of this change. And what it meant for them.

Perhaps it was the sound of the Singer's decision to go to war. Perhaps Tayan's ruse had failed. Enet had assured him that she would tell the Singer and the council that the Tokob and Yaloh had agreed to surrender to preserve their lives, but maybe she hadn't, or he hadn't believed her. Maybe what Tayan was hearing now was the call to war, summoning the Melody from their massive fortress somewhere to the south.

Betsu will warn them. They'll be ready.

But the song didn't just sound different. It *felt* different.

It was similar to those times he used old journey-magic ingredients whose potency was diminished – he still journeyed, though with difficulty, but when he came back he felt . . . grubby. On the inside. As if he needed to shuck his skin, turn it inside out, and scrub it clean.

And none of that explained the fear the Great Octave was struggling to hide.

The shaman had become so used to the song in the last weeks that he didn't think of it any more. The change had reminded him and now it was as it had been those first days inside the Empire: he couldn't ignore it. It was in everything, flavouring his food and colouring the things he looked at. Affecting his mood. Because this song was victorious; it was triumphant; and it was vicious. It made Tayan want to be vicious. Earlier, he'd even insulted a slave who hadn't made his cornbread with enough chillies.

As if I'm a fucking Pecha. The shame of it – and the insidious, creeping fear of it – filled him. *This is what the song does. I feel what it feels, what it tells me to feel. And it is telling me that I am better than these slaves.*

And I am not. But he didn't like how long it had taken him to remember to add that qualification. He clutched at the yellow marriage cord around his neck, running his fingers over the familiar knots and tiny charms to ground himself. It didn't help; was he becoming like them?

'What happened to the song?' he asked abruptly. His voice came out too loud, too demanding, and he flushed, but again Enet barely seemed to notice.

'What?'

'Why is it different? What has happened? Is it some sort of Empire-wide message?' He tapped his fingers against his knee in indecision. 'Is it broken?' he added and Enet flinched.

Her hand jerked up in a short, abortive gesture that nonetheless took in the room and beyond. 'You live within the song now. It has taken you and woven you into its whole. You are a note within it. Tell me, does it feel broken to you?'

Tayan considered her, fidgeting and afraid and trying hard to hide it. 'Not broken,' he said slowly, 'but not . . . controlled, either. It no longer whispers; it shouts. Why has it changed?'

The Great Octave forced a derisive laugh. 'Why would I discuss such things with you?' she asked.

He took a soft, slow breath in. 'Because you can't discuss them with anyone else,' he suggested and she started, eyes widening and then, an instant later, narrowing with suspicion and contempt.

'Are we friends now, peace-weaver of the Tokob? Should I confide in you?' She sniffed and looked away, shaking her head as if at a foolish child.

'Do you want to?' he asked and she forced another laugh.

'I think not,' Enet said softly, and then straightened, as if reaching some sudden decision. 'We are done here.'

Tayan's smile congealed and then slid into polite puzzlement. 'I'm sorry?'

'You yourself have said you will surrender, and so the peace-weaving is concluded. I am too busy to waste any more time on you, and have done you courtesy far above your status. You will return home today.'

The change in the song had unsettled him, planting a seed of anxiety in his belly that was swiftly growing. He'd wanted to leave, had spent much of the last two days trying to work out how to escape unscathed, half convinced that he was going to be killed in some ritual to calm the song. Now here she was, pushing him out, eager to see him gone, something like relief breaking like sunlight across her face as she spoke and yet he was . . . reluctant.

When he crossed eventually back into Yalotlan, he would

no longer hear the song. Which was a good thing. Soon after, he'd be back in his land, surrounded by the spirits and his ancestors and his family. His husband. And yet. Tayan felt a part of something greater now, the way he did when he journeyed but *all the time*. It was powerful and it was seductive and he could no longer imagine what it would be like to not hear the song.

No. No, Tayan. Get a fucking grip.

Deliberately, he thought of Lilla, the tilt of his head when Tayan said something stupid, the curve of his mouth in the dark, the heat of his flesh and the strength of his body. He thought of his laugh, low and infectious and more beautiful by far than this fucking monkey-chatter. That was the real music of his life. The only song he needed was Lilla's voice.

'You will be escorted to Yalotlan; I trust you can make your way home from there, carrying your message of surrender as you go and warning the Yaloh who remain in their land to be ready to give it up.'

She leant over the table, so close Tayan could taste her breath. 'Make sure you stay alive, little Tayan. You're pretty enough to have tempted me, despite those ugly scars on your leg, and clever enough that I would relish having you in my house again.'

Tayan jerked back as if she'd spat in his face. 'And what would be my status in this house?' he asked, folding his arms across his chest to prevent his hand dropping to his scarred left leg.

The Great Octave's laughter pealed, bouncing from the walls and the elaborately painted stucco, but again it was a little too false to be convincing. 'Let's not get ahead of ourselves, pretty Toko, eh? Everyone starts somewhere, for their own good and the stability of the Empire,' and she made a collar of her fingers and thumbs and slotted it around her own throat. She laughed again at whatever expression was on his face. 'But you are a special case, Tayan, because I can see that the song already breathes inside you. You would not be a long time branded, I think.'

She stood and crossed to a second low table, this one scattered with bark paper, ink, and brushes, her energy matching the urgency and brutality of the song. As did Tayan's, for he had a sudden image of her face purpling as he put his hands around her neck and squeezed.

'Under the song,' she added without turning her head and snapped her fingers at her kneeling estate slave.

The man rose from the mats and handed her a report as if Tayan wasn't still sitting there, numb. 'The latest numbers from the songstone mines, high one.'

Enet grunted, and two of her slave guards approached Tayan and gestured him out of the room. He looked back as he went, but the Great Octave of the Empire of Songs was deep in discussion with her slave. The man was pointing to a column of figures and speaking with the confidence of a free.

And then he was in the garden, waiting in the early morning rain until four slave warriors hurried out carrying weapons and packs of supplies, including his own. The quartet surrounded him and marched down the path.

The estate's tall gates creaked open and they swept out into the flow of traffic. It was over. Tayan was alive – and he was going home.

XESSA

High Elder Vaqix was dead. High Elder Zasso of the Yaloh was also dead. Both had been murdered.

Tika was missing. Her dog had been stabbed.

The Sky City was in uproar.

They had sacrificed a life to Malel for strength in the coming war and she had answered by striking at the heart of their society. And they didn't know why. What had they done wrong? Why was the goddess angry with them?

The training of the new Yaloh ejab stuttered to a halt and many seized the opportunity to rescind their promise to walk the snake path completely. The Tokob ejab continued to rotate the spirit-magic and the duty between them, all the while trying to suppress hurt and dread and the sharp teeth of grief at the losses. And the Wet continued, and the Drowned became bolder, and people died.

Toxte and Kime both lived. For that, for them, Xessa was deeply grateful – and guilty for it. But Ilandeh was missing,

263

fled or dead as far as they could tell, and as the days passed and no sign of her was found in the streets or the fields or the jungle closest to the Sky City, worry became suspicion, not just of her but of all those living in the Xentib quarter. Their people had been conquered and stolen by the Empire of Songs; perhaps Ilandeh had been offered a way out, or safety for her family, in return for killing the elders.

Xessa remembered Ilandeh arriving at the Swift Water, remembered assuming that it had been fear that had caused the woman to prevent her from killing the Drowned that attacked them. But it hadn't been, she was convinced of that now.

She saved its life by risking mine and her own. She arrived at the river when it was not singing. Nothing drew her there; she came to stop me and try and get me killed. She wouldn't have done that to save the lives of family held hostage to her co-operation. She did that for love.

Love of the Drowned.

The deaths had also destroyed their plan to capture one of the monsters. Tika had been the heart of the scheme; without her there was no way to proceed. In the initial aftermath, when dawn had broken and Tika hadn't arrived, and then Zasso had been found with her throat slit and Vaqix wasn't found at all – not for hours until warriors made the climb to the womb and found the corpses – the plan and its importance had meant nothing to Xessa. Now, as the days passed and the grief settled on them all, humid and stifling, the need to learn what these things were, to have one at her mercy the way people were at theirs, grew again in her stomach.

If she couldn't take her vengeance on Ilandeh – *her friend Ilandeh* – then she would slaughter the monsters the woman likely believed were gods.

And not just Ilandeh. That fucking Dakto had gone with Lilla and his Paw, right into enemy-held territory. Who knew what he'd get up to. She'd gone to the council in a frenzy, barely able to sign she was so anxious, but they'd already thought of it. Dakto wasn't the only Xentib refugee who'd gone, and Elder Apok sent twenty warriors off in pursuit to try and find them and warn the Paws they were with. Another dozen were combing the jungle below the city, looking for the killer.

The killer. Xessa snorted. It was Ilandeh and they all knew it. It had to be. That *bitch*.

Some of the residents of Xentibec argued that Ilandeh was another victim, not the killer, but that just caused relations between the tribes to sour further as the Wet strengthened and stores began to run low. There had been one mass brawl and two stabbings since the murders, and now armed warriors were guarding the district, as much to keep the Yaloh out as the Xentib in.

Malel, however we have angered you, know that we are sorry. If the Axib life was not enough, I pray those newly dead redress the balance. Watch over us, Malel, and you, our ancestors. Guide our hands and steps. Snake-sister, grant us your cunning.

Xessa sat in the doorway of her house and stared at a sky the grey of a dead fire, brooding. It seemed fitting, somehow, but nothing easy ever came on a day when the sun hid its face. Fitting, too, was the sudden cramp in her stomach, deep in the bowl of her pelvis, radiating out to sit in her hip bones, sick and hot.

She heaved herself to her feet and went inside, crossed to her clothes chest and pulled out the loincloth she used during this phase of her moon. She folded a thick pad of cotton into it, cursing her body when her nights with Toxte were still so new and intense, despite everything that had happened. Perhaps because of it.

Another cramp seized her as she tied the loincloth, squeezing her insides, wringing the blood free and spiking nausea up through her chest to sit at the base of her throat. She coughed and straightened against the pain, pulled on a pair of doeskin leggings and returned to the doorway, unsure whether she was watching the dawn or watching for assassins.

Toxte had left when it was still dark to take the spirit-magic without interruption. Already the house felt empty without him and Ekka, but she wouldn't distract him from his preparations. Xessa's head jerked up at movement between two houses and her hand reached for a knife. Ossa reacted to her sudden tension, leaping down the step, but then he relaxed and she saw it was her fathers.

Kime had a basket and she registered the smells of bread, meat, and avocado. Of cacao. Her eyebrows rose at the luxury and she wasted no time in shifting off the step to allow them to sit and taking the pot of cacao and setting it in the firepit to reheat. Knowing Kime, there would be a hint of chilli in the drink as well, just enough to warm the throat and mouth.

She kissed them both and held Kime's hands tightly – Tika had been his duty partner for two decades and her death was a gaping wound in his spirit. His smile was wan but he flicked his head in dismissal; he wasn't ready to talk about it yet, though he already had a new duty partner. The ejab were stretched so thin he wasn't even allowed time to mourn.

Xessa fetched Otek a blanket, which he ignored, and tended the pot in the coals until the drink was bubbling. She poured them each a cup.

She sat at their feet and breathed in the chocolatey steam in heady inhalations. The first hot mouthful caressed her tongue and she closed her eyes and became the taste, a small world of heat and flavour and pain in her cheeks as her mouth watered. She sipped again and let the scent mingle with that of Toxte's sweat still clinging to her skin.

Kime passed Xessa a plate of hot strips of turkey wrapped in cornbread and half an avocado cut into thick, creamy slices. Her gut rebelled, but she made herself eat. The pain in her stomach spread from her navel to the small of her back, washing down into her hips and groin and up as far as her bottom ribs. A low throbbing, as if a weight swung inside her or a deep bell had been struck at her core.

She sat with the discomfort, with her thoughts, with the tastes and scents of turkey and cacao tickling her senses. She waited for the sun to come up and the world outside to wake and shiver the air with life and movement.

Toxte came back soon after they'd finished eating. He squeezed each man's hand and kissed Xessa's mouth with soft hunger. She painted the glyphs for speed and skill onto the backs of his hands, and then his forehead and cheeks. Grief and pain combined in her stomach – Tika had done this for her after she'd been injured. Then she painted Kime and he her, while Toxte shivered at the spirit-magic moving in him, making his fingers and eyelids flicker.

Eventually, he nodded his readiness and they gathered their weapons and made their way downhill through the city. Otek wandered along behind them. It was Xessa's turn at the river, and she left him and Toxte behind in the water temple, Kime angling away to the west and his own part of the river.

The cage. The cage was still there, between the temple and the Swift Water, mocking her with Tika's absence, Tika's death. Xessa's heart was cut free of its place in her chest and beating its way up out of her throat. She swallowed, pushing it down, and walked past it towards the river, Ossa prowling at her side.

Bulbous skulls, hair drifting like weed, and dark, dead eyes rose above the lip of the water. Faces emerged, mouths open to reveal needle teeth, and no doubt the song rang across the slope and the fields from four speckled throats. Four. She'd never dealt with so many at once – wasn't sure she could.

Tika could. Xessa took a steadying breath and even smiled a little. *All right, Tika, you're an ancestor now, and I know that probably makes you really fucking angry, but there it is. So if you could lend me a little of your aid, some of your strength and cunning, I'd appreciate it. I don't want to die on this riverbank.*

She cast Ossa left and three Drowned followed his movement, drifting with the current. Xessa used the distraction to check the pipe; it seemed intact. The fourth Drowned rose into the shallows, squatting on long, webbed hands and feet like a frog. The ejab lip curled as she took a step forward. There was a flicker in its eyes and it beckoned, the gesture so human it sent a shiver down Xessa's spine. She took another step, her peripheral vision marking the three to her left, almost out of sight now.

Thump-*thump*. Faint but there: the heartbeat of the world. Ossa, signalling her. Xessa ran back half a dozen paces, spear up and ready by her jaw, and then looked left. Ossa jumped, back feet, front feet, and then pointed right, beyond her.

Kime in the shallows. Xessa's heart stopped and then she began to run and Ossa outstripped her in moments. She had a confused glimpse of Eja Nallet, her father's new duty partner, sprinting downhill from her water temple, but they were both too far away. Kime was waist-deep now and it was swirling red and green about him, his blood and

Drowned blood mingling. Xessa was screaming as she ran, faster than she'd ever moved in her life. He had one Drowned by the throat and another tangled in his net, but a third and a fourth rose behind him. Xessa hurled her spear. The weapon flew true and hit a Drowned in the back, knocking it over but barely penetrating the thick plates of its hide.

Ossa was black lightning as he streaked towards Kime, his own dog, Pit, a mess of bloody fur being dragged from the bank into the shallows. There were still three Drowned, the fourth injured or dead, but the water was more red than green. Kime's left arm came up and most of his hand was gone. He saw Xessa coming and pointed his only remaining finger at her, and then uphill to safety.

They dragged him under.

Xessa splashed into the shallows, her hands flailing below the surface in the hopes of finding him and pulling him to safety. She was in up to her knees when Ossa and then Nallet's dog grabbed her padded sleeves and began to pull her backwards. She thrashed, but they were implacable and she had to step back or fall.

When she was on the bank they stalked her, teeth bared, herding her away from the water and towards Nallet and the distant, running Toxte. He was gone. Kime was gone.

Xessa dropped to her knees and dragged up handfuls of mud and flung them at the water, screaming.

Nallet arrived, and then Toxte, and eventually Otek, and Xessa's heart broke anew at the sight of him as he stood there, looking between her and the river with such confusion on his lined face. Such loss. Toxte held her, both of them on their knees in the mud, and then Otek too. He pulled Xessa out of Toxte's arms and into his own and she clung to him, sobbing. The symbols of strength and courage that Kime had painted on the backs of her hands were smudged and smeared, their magic broken. Useless.

They held each other and Ossa shoved his head in between them, his hot breath adding to the fug of bitter sweat and bitter tears. Eventually the first storm of grief passed and Xessa's sobs subsided. Otek patted her back and kissed her brow and by the time he pulled away, her father was gone and the spirits crowded his eyes once more. She wasn't sure if he even knew Kime was dead.

He let her go and stood. He walked away with a wandering gait, and didn't look back. Hatred flashed into Xessa's throat, hatred for the Drowned and spirit-magic, for the spirits themselves. Hatred for Otek, that he had left her and Kime both, not just now but years ago when the magic broke him. Shame followed it, cold and vicious, but it couldn't quite smother the burning hate. Toxte was kneeling at her side; the other two water temples had both been successful and the Sky City would live another day.

Kime won't. And I'll have to break the news to Otek every time he asks. I'll have to tell him, over and over, that his love won't be coming home, and watch it shatter him.

Toxte touched her arm but she shook her head and stood and walked past him. He let her go. Xessa got halfway home and then changed her mind; she didn't want anyone to be able to find her. She turned away and lost herself in the streets.

It was the end of the afternoon and the ejab had finished in the water temples hours before when Xessa and Ossa returned to the Swift Water. Her spare spear was smooth in her hand and her net swayed from the back of her belt with each step. She also carried a club, borrowed from Tayan and Lilla's house.

She didn't pray; she didn't wear her paint. She did wear her armour, but a second layer of protection, formed entirely of cold, calm rage, encased her heart. The dirt and mud and shrubs were wet and cool from the rain, and rain ran from her hair down her face and back. Her salt-cotton was saturated and losing its tension, but the bamboo scales above and padding beneath would do enough. Or not.

Xessa stopped a hundred paces from the Swift Water. The bamboo cage lay where it had been left, big but light, the cords wrapped in hardened rubber to defend against the Drowned's claws. She pushed the handle of the club into her waistband and then dragged the cage through the shrubs, its corner leaving a furrow in the earth behind her. Ossa shied away from it and his tail wagged uncertainly once or twice, but he was at the water and that meant he was working.

Xessa took a deep breath and wiped sweat and rainwater from her palms and face. She put the club down on the dirt a few paces behind her. Then she cast the dog along the bank to wake the Drowned.

Come on then, fuckers. Come and get me.

Spear in her left hand, net in her right. Waiting. It didn't take long.

It was a Greater Drowned that responded, bigger than Xessa, with the characteristic dark vertical band down both sides of its throat. They were much rarer than the lesser variety, which they appeared to dominate. Xessa merely adjusted her strategy, her mind very cold, very sharp. She had wanted one of the smaller ones; she'd got this. So be it.

It drifted towards the steep bank and beckoned to her. The corners of Xessa's mouth turned up in a snarl. She raised the hand holding the net and beckoned back. The Drowned stilled in the water, its head on one side in much the same way Ossa looked at her when he was confused or playful. Or unsure. Xessa beckoned again.

The Drowned leapt out of the river, its powerful legs

springing off the riverbed and propelling it onto the bank, where it paused, considering. Its throat sac bulged and then deflated, as if it knew its song held no power over her.

Ossa was stalking it from the other side, his hackles raised and one ear turned towards the river in case there were more.

Xessa let her spear hang point-down, unthreatening, in clear violation of every lesson she'd ever been taught. The Drowned skittered towards her on hands and feet, sideways like a crab, its head swaying on its long neck. Curious. Almost birdlike. She'd never seen behaviour like it, but the knowledge slid off her and left no impression. Smoke in the wind, there and gone.

A little closer and Xessa clicked her tongue three times. The dog stopped moving; the Drowned rose a little higher on its back legs. Its throat sac bulged and then deflated; had it imitated her? She didn't care.

Come on. Come on.

Xessa rested the spear against her chest and extended her empty hand. The Drowned copied her, its own hand turning palm up as hers did. She stopped breathing. She blinked the sweat from her eyes. She watched death watching her. And she snapped her fingers.

Ossa erupted into motion, streaking towards the Drowned, and it reacted, spinning on those long, muscular legs to face the dog. Her dog. Her Ossa, who obeyed his training even though she was sending him to die. But she needed to draw its attention away.

Xessa flung the net underhand, the cord wrapped around her wrist. It unfurled in the air, the tiny pebbles tied to its edges spinning it wide and bringing it down over the Drowned's head and shoulders. The eja raced after it, spear reversed in her left hand. She whistle-clicked to put Ossa into stalk, not attack, but it mustn't have come out right because he kept running for the thrashing Drowned.

She clicked once, hard and desperate, to make him stay, and then sprinted towards the monster herself, screeching to hold its attention. The spear was reversed in her hand and she smacked it around the Drowned's head, splitting skin and releasing green, stinking blood. It was tearing at the net, already ripping holes in the tough fibres, but the blow staggered it and it went to one knee, claws of one hand tangled. Xessa let go of the long cord and brought the spear down again with all the strength of her shoulders, back and thighs. Like splitting wood.

The haft snapped in half, the splintered, obsidian-tipped end spinning away into the water. The Drowned hit the mud, its tangled hand unable to break its fall and she hit it again, across the back of its neck this time, while Ossa danced in and out of reach. It lay still except for the fluttering of its gills and then the lift and fall of its ribs. The dog, stiff-legged and hackles up, stalked in front of it, throat rippling as he barked his challenge.

She picked up the club and circled around to come at it from behind – closer to the water, Ossa on guard. Gaze flickering between river, dog, and Drowned, Xessa crept in, stepping carefully over its splayed legs. Then, before she could change her mind, she smashed the club into its knee.

The Drowned spasmed, rolling over and over towards her, pushing her back to the edge of the bank. Ossa leapt in, burying his teeth in its shoulder and Xessa used the opening to leap over the monster's struggling, netted body, away from the water just before it boiled apart and another Drowned swiped for her.

The eja scooped up the trailing cord attached to the net and jerked, arresting the creature's desperate wriggling towards safety, but the other one hopped over it and came for her and she only had a club.

A low, dark shape passed between her and the advancing Drowned and an instant later there was green blood and white teeth before it darted back out again. The Drowned – this one a lesser – chased it, but someone leapt in after their dog and raked it across the face with a spear. Toxte, of course, with Ekka. The Drowned fell into the river and didn't come back up.

But the day was getting late and the spirit-magic would be leaving him and this was exactly why Xessa hadn't wanted him here. If he died because of her, if one more eja or Toko or anyone – even a fucking Xenti – died because of a Drowned, then Xessa knew she would die too.

I won't fail this time. I will not.

Toxte's net settled over her Drowned, wrapping it more securely, and he began to haul it away from the riverbank. She stepped closer to it, and when he paused between pulls, she crushed its other knee with the club. It curled in on itself like a spider, mouth wide. Hurt. *Trapped.*

A weary, bone-deep satisfaction began to spread through her, a righteous, hard-edged, foul sort of vengeance, which lasted right up until the magic failed and Toxte tried to give himself to the Drowned.

It was only a few seconds before the dogs were driving him backwards and Xessa clubbed it in the head to silence it, but those seconds were an eternity that scrubbed her raw and salted her with fear. Because she hadn't thought this far ahead, had she? So consumed with grief, and the coward part of her hoping she'd die too, just to stop it hurting, she hadn't thought of the ejab who'd need to help her with this next part.

Xessa made the dogs guard Toxte, because now he'd found her – now he'd been so *stupid* as to approach the river at the end of the magic's effectiveness – he wouldn't leave her alone. When he was a hundred strides away, she grabbed the two nets and rolled the Drowned more securely in them, then hauled it into the cage. The rope to tie the lid shut fed through a clever combination of hollow sections of bamboo so the Drowned couldn't reach it with its fingers or claws and unpick it.

And then it was done. Captured. And they had until the sun had moved a finger's width closer to the horizon to get it somewhere with a water source, or it would die and everything – all of it – would be for naught.

LILLA

He'd worried that things would be awkward with Dakto after the kiss, but the Xenti had accepted his rejection with only minimal hurt. If he volunteered for most of the advance scouting missions, or made himself scarce when Lilla stripped off to scrub sweat and dirt from his skin in the evening, then the Fang didn't stop him. If anything, his absences were a relief and in the last days, as they moved deeper into Yalotlan, things were easy between them again.

Their three hundred warriors in ten Paws had so far evaded two patrols, been forced to annihilate a third, and destroyed one partially built pyramid. The force of slave and dog warriors they'd encountered had been almost fanatical in their commitment to the Empire of Songs, and Kux and Lilla had had to give the kill order, leaving none alive.

It had been different at the pyramid. They'd faced a hundred warriors – what he'd learnt over the past year was called a pod – and three times as many slaves who slept tied

276

in lines of twenty and staked to the ground. They at least hadn't been a problem. Still, it hadn't been a sudden skirmish they'd found themselves in this time; in order to destroy the pyramid, they'd had to kill the warriors guarding the slaves and the stone. They'd had to creep in and slaughter as many as they could before the alarm was raised, and then fight the rest. Stabbing people while they slept didn't sit well with Lilla. Nor with most of them. But as Kux said, it was better than waking them up and asking for a fair fight.

The slaves were a mix of Quitob and Xentib, and the difference between the two was more extensive than their hair and tattoos. The Quitob had been under the song for nearly two Star cycles; the Xentib for half of one. When offered freedom, the latter had leapt for it and Lilla had given them directions to the Sky City, elated and yet concerned. They could be trained in defence, yes, but they were more mouths to feed and water. But what else could they do?

Dakto's reaction had worried him, though. Seeing his kin enslaved was more traumatising than any of them had expected and he'd taken himself away from the pyramid clearing, unable to bear the brands in their flesh and the thinness of their cheeks. Even the renewed vigour in their eyes as the thick leather collars were sawn from their necks hadn't soothed him and it had been some hours before he'd returned, quiet but composed.

But the Quitob, oh, the Quitob were different. Slaves, yes, none could doubt that, and out from under the song for the first time in sun-years, but its absence had done little to break their fervour. To Lilla, they'd seemed almost as zealous as the warriors who guarded them and at least forty had died when they'd thrown themselves between his war party and the enemy, even tied to ropes as they were.

The debate had raged for most of the day as they'd escorted the Quitob away from the pyramid clearing and left a Paw behind armed with chisels and hammers to smash the stone blocks. Escorted? Guarded, more like, and just the memory turned Lilla's stomach.

'We can't send them to the Sky City alone, and we can't be sure what they'll do when they reach it. We can't take them with us and I won't have us roping them and staking them out at night to sleep like animals,' Lilla had said. 'We're not Pechaqueh. We have to let them go.'

'You let them go and they'll bring the enemy down on us,' Dakto had said flatly, arms crossed over his chest. 'Keep them captive or kill them: those are the only choices we have. We're in a war, Lilla, and sentiment has no place in war.'

Kux opened her mouth and Lilla knew instinctively she would make a scathing remark about Dakto's own response when confronted with his enslaved tribe: he glared her into silence.

'It's not sentiment; it's who I am. Who we all are. I won't become a slave-owner and I won't kill innocents. We let them go,' Lilla insisted. They all agreed, all but Dakto.

'I've seen what happens next,' was all he would say, but Tokob were not Pechaqueh, and neither were Yaloh. The Quitob were people, and if all the tribes had stood together back when Chitenec was first invaded in their grandparents' time, none of this would have happened. If freeing them now was all they could do to even begin to redress that balance, then they would.

But not blindly. Kux had sent a Paw to follow the retreating slaves and nominated a meeting point, where they'd rested until the trackers got back. They'd been disappointed but not surprised to learn that the slaves had indeed fled to another pod that was standing guard over construction of another pyramid. And from what they could tell in the dark, this one seemed almost finished, looming taller than the tree canopy – a brooding, malevolent presence that promised violence and poison and the end of all things.

They stared at it now. Lilla told himself it was just wood and stone, but although he could barely make out the painted carvings that had been fixed to the outside, the shiver up his neck half convinced him they were watching him. Monsters. Conjurations of the Underworld. Drowned.

Dakto's lips were a thin line of tension, as if he was chewing over words best left unsaid as they crouched a dozen strides into the treeline. It was the still, cool hour before dawn. Birds were not quite stirring and fruit bats were still leaving scratches of black against the surface of the night. Insects droned and night flowers bloomed, sickly and cloying. There was a sudden rustle and a thump above them and Lilla held his breath, staring up into the blackness, but whatever was in the tree was staying clear of the multitude of humans below and he could see nothing.

Lutek was on Lilla's left, Tiamoko to his right, and the rest of the Paw stretched out to either side. Kux's Paw was to their left, and the others had stealthily, slowly fanned out on three sides of the clearing. The fire and the torches around the pyramid had burnt low, barely casting enough light to show the long lines of sleeping slaves, huddled on beds of palm leaves, and the warriors in hammocks strung in the edges of the treeline.

Lutek shifted, just a fraction, and her fingers tightened on Lilla's arm. She tapped it, a slow countdown from ten, and fear surged in his gut. He swallowed three times, his mouth dry, and when they reached zero the two of them rose a heartbeat ahead of the rest. They crept through the jungle, slow and sure.

Kill the warriors. Free the slaves. Smash the stone.

And the slaves who don't want freedom? The slaves who now outnumber us two to one? Who will have told the story of our destruction of their pyramid and that the Xentib have run for the Sky City with our blessing? What of them?

The enemy camp was quiet but for a dozen warriors on guard, making slow rounds of the clearing, stepping between the rows of sleeping slaves with as little care as if they walked past rolls of woven cloth. They had no fear the slaves might rise up and attack them; Lilla marvelled at their arrogance.

Kux's Paw shot first, arrows and poisoned darts thumping into the figures in the hammocks and then the moving guards. The other Paws shot and alarm calls went up through the jungle as screams tore the last of the night into rags. One volley from three sides of the clearing and the war party charged into the burgeoning chaos, their cries ringing from beneath the trees like vengeful spirits.

A man reared up out of the gloom, a wicked hatchet in his hand and already swinging for Lilla's chest. Lilla pivoted away from the weapon, smashing his spear down onto his attacker's wrist, and then stabbed him in the gut, out and into the thigh. The hatchet came in again, a strike that would open him up, armour or not, but Lilla spun the spear and cracked the butt into the side of the man's jaw. He fell, limp, and Lilla stabbed him in the throat and leapt past him.

He'd been close, right there as soon as Lilla entered the clearing. Where had he come from? He hadn't been one of the patrolling guards. Tokob and Yaloh were screaming and slaughtering people in or near the hammocks and the perimeter, people who put up little resistance, while flights of arrows and darts rained down from the pyramid itself and the shadowy figures perched there. Not carvings after all.

And they had been watching him. They'd watched them all and allowed themselves to be surrounded.

Fuck.

'Trap!' he bellowed. 'Look to the pyramid!' As he spoke the enemy warriors, concealed on and around the structure – *Shit, so those in the hammocks are slaves, we're killing slaves* – began shooting darts and arrows and throwing javelins of their own. The slick, co-ordinated attack by the Paws faltered and then a woman slammed into Lilla and they went down in a tangle of limbs and weapons, Lilla's spear trapped between them and her knife arcing for his face. He seized her wrist in his left hand, but she had weight and momentum and the blade edged closer to his eye.

Lilla snarled, thrashing his legs and trying to throw her off, straining to get his other hand onto her wrist. She smacked it away and landed a clumsy punch into his throat that stole a little of his breath. He grabbed the back of her neck in his right hand to pull her sideways, but his grip slipped and the knife lurched closer. Lilla bellowed and slammed his hand into her face, pushing her head sideways and up until she couldn't see him and her balance shifted. He bucked his hips and threw her off, rolled with her and tried to prise the knife from her grip, but she lunged up off the dirt and her teeth closed on his ear.

Lilla screamed and punched her, trying to keep the knife out of his ribs and her teeth out of his flesh. He worked his hand around her face, nearly losing his thumb to her teeth this time and then jamming it into her eye. She shrieked, twisting her head away as his thumbnail popped through the yolk of her eyeball, and he pulled the knife from her hand and stabbed it into the side of her neck two, three, four times until her hands fell and she shuddered beneath him.

Lilla spat out her blood and slid off her, then retrieved

his spear and used it to regain his feet. He kept the knife and spun in a circle, looking for the next attack, the next enemy, the next kill. In the confusion and beneath the constant rain of arrows and darts, the fight had become a slaughter on both sides, slaves falling alongside warriors in an orgy of bloodletting.

'Stop!' Lilla shouted. 'Stop. Spare the slaves!'

The warriors closest heard him, but many were too heavily engaged and fought on, heedless, and it wasn't easy to identify slaves from warriors in the flickering torchlight anyway. Lilla saw an Empire warrior stab three slaves rather than allowing them to be freed; he was cut down from behind by Lutek, but by then it was too late. Lilla ducked as an arrow whickered overhead and another clattered through the leaves behind him, but those on the pyramid had little protection and the war party, too, had bows and blowpipes. And ample cover.

There was just enough daylight for Lilla to pass the orders in sign to the Tokob nearest, and the Yaloh saw his plan soon enough. Those who could disengage concentrated their arrows and darts on the pyramid, and when the enemy couldn't stand the withering rain any more, they leapt to the ground and charged those shooting from cover.

Lilla deflected a spear with his own, slapping it out of the air, but then a dart took him in the thigh. He ripped out the palm-long missile with a roar and held onto it, as weapon and to identify the poison if there was any, and if he lived long enough to take any of the antidotes in the pack he'd left back in the trees.

Someone screamed his name and his skin flushed with cold when he saw Tiamoko surrounded by three enemies. Lilla snatched up a fallen blowpipe, slapped in the dart, and shot. It lost much of its power on the too-long flight between them but grazed one warrior's arm, just enough to distract her so she didn't block Tiamoko's punch to her jaw. She went down hard and the young warrior stamped on her throat and left her to suffocate, ducking the axe of the second and spinning him into the path of the third to spoil his blow.

Lilla threw his spear, catching one in the back of the thigh, and chased after it, but Kux and a handful of Yaloh got there first, hacking into the enemy while Tiamoko backed away, his eyes wide and wild. Lilla kept going anyway, more slowly. He knew the look of panic on Tiamoko's face and how quickly it could become unmanageable fear.

The shouts, grunts, and screams, the thuds of falling bodies and the meaty smacks of flint and obsidian cleaving flesh, of clubs smashing bone, began to fade, though the sun had risen by the time it was done. The clearing fell still and silent but for the groans of the wounded and the sobbing of some of the slaves. Of some of the warriors. The enemy fighters, dog warriors and Coyote commanders only – not a Pecha among them – were herded to the pyramid and executed. Swift deaths. Clean if they could manage it.

Too many of the slaves had died this time, killed by Empire weapons, killed by the Paws, but still most of the Quitob survivors refused the offer of freedom.

Lilla wanted to shake sense into them; his fists itched to hurt them, but he didn't. They were still bound in their hearts, holding firm to the habits of invisibility and obedience that had seen them survive this long. He had no idea whether their stated love for Empire, Singer, and song was a survival mechanism or the truth; all he did know was that he was faced with the same dilemma as before, only with almost double the number of slaves. *People, not slaves,* he reminded himself. *It's not their fault.*

Yet when Lilla tried to put himself in their position, he

couldn't. He'd fight until he died. He wouldn't surrender and end up like this – broken and meek, stinking of fear-sweat, expression glazed with hopelessness. The slaves made him profoundly uncomfortable and he began to understand a little better why Dakto wouldn't go near the Xentib. What would he do if he saw a Toko wearing a collar and a brand, after all? He shivered, head to toe, at the idea.

This is why we fight, so that this doesn't happen to any more people – of any tribe. It's not just survival now, it's to free slaves and help them find themselves again, help them return to the world and reconnect with their ancestors. Help them to be themselves again.

'If we let them go, the same thing happens,' he said to Kux as they rested, several sticks from the pyramid clearing.

Dakto was sitting halfway up a tree above them, keeping watch and idly carving patterns in the branch. 'You know my thoughts,' he muttered, as if to himself. 'Sooner or later they'll lead us to a force that outnumbers us and that'll be it. Lead us to our deaths.'

'We're not killing them,' Lilla said, sharp with irritation.

'Then let's send them to the Sky City under the . . . protection of one of the Paws,' Kux said. 'We can keep pressing forward with only nine. They can escort the Quitob to your city and, I don't know, keep them well fed and secure and healthy. Not prisoners, but definitely not slaves. The longer they're out from under the song and among free people, the faster they will . . . recover.' She didn't sound sure, though.

'People like that will never recover,' Dakto said. 'They don't know how.'

The decision among the Fangs was unanimous. The Quitob would be escorted to the Sky City by a Tokob Paw. The slaves – *the Quitob* – and those thirty lucky Tokob would be home and be safe, if only for a while. Lilla stared south into the dappled greens of the jungle. Where he was going, nothing was safe.

Dakto dropped out of the tree and clapped him on the back. 'Let's find some Pechaqueh, have ourselves a little chat,' he said and winked. Lilla grinned, sharp as a cat, and followed his friend deeper into Yalotlan.

XESSA

The womb, above Sky City, Malel, Tokoban
183rd day of the Great Star at morning

There must have been a hundred torches and candles burning to chase away every last shadow and leave the Drowned nowhere to hide. It lay on its side at the far end of the cave, both gills and lungs having to work to keep it alive in the shallow pool. Its twisted legs were stretched out in front of it, the remains of the net still tangled around its upper body, and they'd managed to get a thick, rubber-coated collar and rope around its neck while it was still in the cage. The rope was secured around an outcrop high in the vault of the roof. It couldn't stand, let alone climb the wall, in order to pull the tether free. It was as restrained as they could make it.

Xessa crouched at safe distance, her spear in her hands, and watched it. It didn't move, didn't even seem to register she was there, but she could feel it watching her. Thinking. She had no doubt it recognised her as the author of its agony.

Ossa stood at her side, hackles raised. The dog refused to remain outside whenever Xessa visited – the Drowned's cold, alien smell invoked all of his protective instincts. Even after a week of its captivity, he had yet to relax, and Xessa was glad of it. On the other hand, it meant she couldn't spend as long here as she wanted to. She couldn't allow Ossa's training to be confused by prolonged exposure to the Drowned's presence and scent, and besides, the constant threat fatigued him. It wasn't fair. But the dog wouldn't leave her side. He knew she was angry and grieving and he did all he could to raise her mood.

As did Toxte. Xessa bared her teeth, but still the Drowned made no move. Her lover had nearly died at the Swift Water with his stupid heroism, his insistence on interfering. She knew her anger had nothing to do with him – and, thank the ancestors, so did he – because he bore it stoically and silently. And then, when she inevitably broke down, he held her and let her cry. Never any reprimand, never any recrimination.

Nor did he complain when she woke him screaming. Kime's wild, agonised face, one eye obscured by his hair, fingers missing, and the Drowned rising up behind him, cursed her dreams. It recurred multiple times each night until the thought of sleep terrified her and she was hollow-cheeked with fatigue and Toxte wasn't much better.

But they did their duty at the Swift Water, because they were needed, and then Xessa visited Otek and told him Kime was dead – again and again – and waited until his friends arrived to sit with him – and tell him, again and again, that Kime was dead. And then, when rage and grief climbed her throat until she choked on them, she came here. Came to watch her captive struggle to live, throwing chunks of meat at it, refilling the pool as water seeped slowly through the stone, keeping it alive. Mustn't die. Not yet. Couldn't die yet. Xessa hadn't learnt enough from it yet. Xessa hadn't *hurt it* enough yet.

Of course she hadn't learnt from it. How could she, with Tika and Kime and Tayan and Vaqix all gone? They were the clever ones, the ones who would have known what to look for, what to think or do. Xessa wasn't clever; she was a killer. She hadn't been fast enough to save Kime. She hadn't thought he might need her and so he'd died. She hadn't been clever enough to see through Ilandeh's ruse, fuck what the other Xentib were still saying about her innocence. Hadn't suspected Dakto, and by now he'd probably killed Lilla.

Xessa jabbed the Drowned's foot with her spear, her movement so sudden and unexpected that Ossa leapt and barked, and she could feel the vibrations of his challenge swirling around her. She hesitated, concentrating. She *could* feel vibrations. And so could the Drowned. It moved. Finally. It had done little more than twitch when she poked it, but now its head rose and it blinked those round, black eyes and it cocked its head as if listening.

Xessa snapped her fingers and the dog quietened. She studied the Drowned. It reached out a long-taloned hand and caressed the wall of the womb and the eja was suddenly sickened. Their most holy place, befouled by this creature. The Drowned opened its mouth and began to sing, its throat sac bulging and emptying. The vibrations returned, stronger than before, fluttering in Xessa's bones, but this time they seemed to grow in intensity, as if the womb itself was reacting to the song of the Drowned.

Ossa began to bark again and then stopped. His ears pricked and his head cocked to one side just as the Drowned's had done. And then, tentatively, his tail wagged.

A fresh, poisonous rush of fury swept through Xessa and she jabbed its foot again, this time hard enough to pierce. Its body jerked and perhaps it made some squeal or sound of pain, and the womb echoed that back too, and suddenly Ossa threw back his head, his legs straight and stiff as he howled.

Xessa leapt to her feet and backed away, her fingers tight in Ossa's scruff until he came with her. She paused one last time at the corner and the Drowned was watching her. Watching, and tapping a long talon against the wall. Amused.

'We should kill it. I don't trust it. It's doing something.'

Xessa's hands were shaking so badly she could barely sign, and she was breathing hard after running from the womb. She'd told the ejab on guard up there to be extra vigilant and then come straight to the new elder's house. Elder Rix had been elected by the surviving ejab to take over from Tika, but he was cautious. No doubt he'd relish killing their captive.

Toxte had spotted Xessa as she ran through the city and followed her, not wasting time asking questions. He knew where she'd been, of course, and therefore that the news couldn't be good, but he looked rattled when she explained what had happened.

'Of course the womb has magic,' Elder Rix signed now, with more calm than seemed appropriate. 'We have known this forever. It was likely the goddess attacking it.' He paused, thinking, and then nodded, as if that explained everything.

Xessa gaped. 'It didn't look attacked. It sang and Ossa *wagged his tail*. He responded positively to it. He's knows a Drowned's song is a warning – all his training reinforces that. And then it did something else and he howled. It, it *knows something*.'

Rix laughed. 'The Drowned know nothing other than the hunt and the kill and the imperative to breed. Just because they have hands and can stand on two legs does not make them like us.'

'I never said they were like us,' Xessa signed, fuming. 'I said it was clever. You wouldn't say a jaguar or a snake is stupid; they are perfectly adapted to their environment and—'

'And a Drowned's environment is not a cave two hours' walk from a water source,' Rix signed, his face darkening. 'It is captive and it is hurt. It was probably just . . . whimpering.'

Xessa knew she'd get nothing else from him. The elder still hadn't forgiven her – or Toxte – for their reckless behaviour in capturing it in the first place, without telling anyone, without preparing the city or readying the stops along the way where they could put it in water to keep it alive. All those things had been done in a hurry, in the frenzied moments after Xessa had had to set Ossa and Ekka both on Toxte to keep him back from the Drowned and then club it in the head to stop its song.

The city was on edge enough; the fact they had captured one of their greatest predators hadn't been greeted with any great enthusiasm by anyone. And the fact that it was in the womb now, of all times, when they needed that sacred place's solace, just made things worse.

Xessa had been at the ceremony in the Snake-sister's temple when Kime and Tika's names had been painted onto the wall, below all the others. Two walls filled now. Two whole walls of ejab dead. The air had been tight with pain and thick with rage and the need to hurt. Even the retired ejab had come, the spirit-haunted who had their own wall and their own list, for theirs was a living sacrifice and was honoured just as profoundly.

Yes, Xessa understood that need; even now the sensation of the club bucking, of the creature's knees coming apart under impact, echoed in her hands and sent a ripple of righteous joy through her. But for Rix to dismiss what she said . . .

'Thank you for your time, elder,' she signed formally. 'If

the shamans have any other experiments they would like me to conduct on the Drowned, please tell them I will be at home this evening and tomorrow morning.' She rose and left before she could sign anything she might regret.

Xessa and Toxte walked home hand in hand. He let her brood, and if he had any thoughts on the matter himself, he didn't sign them. The dogs raced ahead, playing and twisting among the stalls and shoppers. Their joy was lost on her. She was sour and frustrated and exhausted, but dreading the night to come and the nightmares she knew waited for her.

Xessa was secretly relieved when Toxte elected to stay at his own house that night. He needed uninterrupted sleep and she was poor company anyway. She sat in her doorway and watched his tall, muscular frame disappear into the distance. The whole city was sour, not just her. Xentibec was still under armed guard and the Xentib within were increasingly angry. Tokob were being forced to fetch water for them and Xessa had seen one woman spit into a jar before she'd left it for the Xentib to collect. And liquids worse than a mouthful of saliva were being added. Xessa had heard of three Yaloh hauled before their elders for conspiring to scrape frog-venom into pitchers before they delivered them. It could have killed people – children or the elderly. This was what Ilandeh and Dakto had done to them. The other three houses around the central firepit were all empty and the evening was still but for the swaying of palms and water vines, of ripening beans and corn in the allotment, and of the dozen gourds hanging from the eaves above her head. Ossa snuffled around their allotment and then flopped down by the wood-pile. She longed to ask him what the Drowned had done.

Tika had written out a list of things, experiments, that she'd planned on carrying out on the Drowned when they caught it. During the aftermath of her death, when they'd gathered to dance her to rebirth, Xessa had asked after those notes. No one had been able to find them. They'd vanished along with her body and now that they had a Drowned, they were fumbling around doing little more than poking it with sticks and making sure it didn't escape.

She didn't know what to *do*.

Tayan would know.

The thought hit her like a club to the chest. Xessa missed Tayan with sudden, biting intensity and that yearning drove her onto her feet. Taking a candle from inside, she crossed to Tayan and Lilla's house, suppressing a twinge of guilt at intruding into their home without permission. Again.

The house's interior was so familiar that it brought a lump to Xessa's throat. Bunches of herbs and medicine hung from the roof beams, as well as charms and feathers and items of clothing. Lilla's spare spear stood inside the entrance, and their spare sandals were lined up neatly as if they'd just stepped out for the evening. But it smelt empty, the herb-smell long since faded. Shelves of pots and jars and sealed gourds containing mysterious substances lined a wall. She ignored them and ran her gaze along the shelf below instead. Bark-paper books, eight of them. No. Xessa tapped her fingers against her lips, looking around the room, thinking. The storage chamber? She dragged the mats free and then lifted the wooden lid: empty but for a few beetles that shrank out of sight behind a dusty pitcher.

Come on, Tayan. You didn't take it all the way to the Empire of Songs, did you?

She replaced the lid and the mats and stood again. The last shelf contained bedding, bandages and a few more folded items of clothing. She rummaged beneath the blankets and lifted the basket of rocks and pieces of wood and trinkets and . . . things. Tayan insisted they were all for some lofty shamanic purpose, but she and Lilla knew he just liked interesting shapes and shiny stones, and collected them for the simple reason they brought him pleasure.

And there it was. Another bark-paper book, but much thinner and written in Tayan's own hand. Xessa hesitated, not quite touching it. It was an invasion of his privacy, a terrible violation of his trust, but if her friend had written down his ideas for capturing a Drowned anywhere, it would be here. And not just capturing it, but what he'd do afterwards. He was the most curious person she'd ever met and they'd spent enough lazy evenings discussing what they thought Drowned were that surely he'd have made notes somewhere.

Sorry, Tay, but you're not here and I need you. I need to know what to do. And what it is I might have done by hurting it and putting it in the womb. What I've shown it.

She didn't go back home: to take the book out of Tayan's house felt even more like stealing. Instead, she sat leaning close to the candle and opened the book, trying her best just to skim the words until she found mention of the Drowned.

Xessa saw her own name more than once, and Lilla's, too, and the urge to read about herself was almost overwhelming, but when she glanced up Ossa was watching her and his faith – his loyalty – reminded her of her own. Even so, it took an immense amount of will not to read what her friend thought of her deep in his heart.

Drowned. There. Peering closer, Xessa began to read.

The darkness was complete and the winds were strong, roaring up the streets and the hill, lashing the gardens and door curtains and stands of bamboo and vines. Fires were torn to rags, their light dancing and mocking the eye, hiding and revealing and making the roads treacherous. Xessa's foot slipped into a carved drainage channel more than once, and her ankle was sending a spike of pain up to her knee with every step by the time she reached Toxte's house.

Xessa clapped twice and then knocked on the wall. No response. She stamped on the wooden rocker that would wake him, even though he hadn't taken the spirit-magic today so should have heard her knock. Still nothing – and no Ekka, either.

Xessa lifted the door curtain; the house was empty. She turned in a circle, grinding her teeth in frustration. Where would he have gone? Her emotions had been wild since Kime's death and the murders before it, and the constant simmering anger she felt now threatened to spill over into rage. He'd said he was coming home. Where the fuck was he? She needed him.

Xessa began moving back uphill, but not home this time. She headed for the upper exit and the path to the womb. She headed for the Drowned. Ossa padded at her side, enjoying the novelty of walking the city late at night. His head was high as the gusting wind brought him all the scents and probably many of the sounds of the jungle far below.

She hadn't come out with a spear or a net, but she had her knife and the ejab on duty at the womb would have weapons. Not ideal, but now that the idea was alive in her, she had to act on it. Tonight. Now.

They passed through the northern gate and onto the trail to the womb. 'You too?' the warrior on duty signed in the flickering light from a fire-pit. 'Everyone wants a look, don't they?'

'Eja Toxte?' she guessed and he nodded. Xessa's stomach churned and her temples pounded with sudden tension. She thanked the warrior and left the city, breaking into a run as soon as she was out of sight. *What are you doing, Toxte?*

And why pretend you were going home? What don't you want me knowing?

She fell twice in the dark, the wind so strong at her back that it seemed to want to blow her into the rock, and even the toughened skin on her feet struggled as she scrambled and scuffed unseen stones. Her knees were bleeding and the palms of her hands were bruised by the time the trail began to descend into the womb.

The dogs belonging to the ejab on duty spun at her approach, alerting their owners, and Eja Nallet brandished her spear before Xessa came into the flickering torchlight. 'What's going on?' she signed, sucking in cold air that chilled the sweat on the back of her neck.

'Toxte. He's—'

But Xessa had seen the rope in Eja Quin's hands and understood what her lover was doing. Toxte hadn't taken the spirit-magic today. He could hear. 'How long has he been in there?'

'He said pull him out after a two hundred count. He insisted. Said it wasn't right to risk anyone who wasn't an eja, and that you thought it was up to something. That it was clever.' Nallet shuddered.

'Pull him out now. Now,' she emphasised, and then snatched up Nallet's spear from where she'd rested it to sign. She ducked past the pair and followed the rope into the gloom, towards the distant glow of the womb. Her heart was in her throat and sweat prickled her palms and her back, cold and sour.

Not Toxte too. Please, Malel, please, ancestors, not Toxte too. If a life is owed in here, you can have mine.

Xessa worked to steady her breath and her hands, so that she would not be surprised by what she saw. It didn't work. Toxte was on his knees in the water, at the limit of the tether that was knotted across his chest and beneath his arms, tied securely in the middle of his back in such a way he couldn't reach it and free himself. The rope was taut but he was fighting its pull, one hand hooked around a little bump of rock to hold him steady.

The Drowned was opposite him, propped upright against the wall, singing. Toxte's other hand was on its leg, fingers feeling around the bones of the knee. His chest was heaving, but Xessa couldn't see his face. Ekka was at the edge of the water, barking, her tail curled under her. She wasn't obeying her training; she wasn't dragging him clear. It made no sense.

Toxte's hand stilled on the Drowned's leg and then he gave a sudden sharp wrench. The Drowned threw back its head and whatever sound it made wasn't song; Ekka and Ossa both cringed and Toxte's hands flew to his ears, pressing against the sides of his skull as the Drowned thrashed – but the leg moved and bent again, the bones set back in place.

Xessa stepped past Toxte and prepared to strike even as he was jerked backwards by the rope harness, but his hands closed on the spear she held, jerking it from her hands. She spun to face him and could see his expression now, twisted with yearning and a terrible, blank need, a desperate urge to give himself into the arms of death. Xessa slapped him as hard as she could, the sting vicious in her palm, and shoved him hard in the chest to get him moving towards the exit. She ripped the spear back out of his hands as Toxte slid backwards in the water, on his knees, clinging on to the walls to slow himself. As she had at the river, Xessa gave both dogs the guard order and now Ekka responded; they sprang at him, barking and snapping until he flailed onto his feet out of their reach and was immediately pulled over onto his arse by the rope.

Pain creased his face as his tailbone struck stone and then

he was gone, hauled out of the source. Xessa turned back to the Drowned and it was just climbing to its feet – or foot, anyway. The other leg was still twisted. It must have been in agony. Xessa didn't give it time to stand; she brought the spear around and swept its foot from under it. The Drowned crashed into the pool, the impact shivering through Xessa's feet and a great splash hitting her and the wall. Its throat sac deflated and its song ended, and the weird, oily vibrations that had been echoing through the womb and her bones began to fade.

Meaning Toxte would be free of its song and able to reach his feet and run.

Xessa watched it lying in the water. *Tayan has such ideas and, Malel bless him, he wrote them all down for me. But I think I've already learnt enough for one night.*

She didn't have a club and doubted she'd able to re-break its knee with her spear. Maybe she could hack its foot off, but it was more likely she'd take a faceful of clawed toes and the venom would send her blind. But if it could stand, it might be able to reach high enough to untie the rope from the stalactite. And then it could get out, and then it might get into the city and even if it died there, there'd be more than the sixty-three dead this time. It could just sit in the plaza and sing. And those deaths, too, would be on her.

Xessa stepped within range and dropped the spear. The Drowned kicked out, its mouth a rictus of needle-sharp teeth, muscles standing out in neck and chest at the pain of movement. Xessa caught its ankle and its claws scraped the underside of her arm. Before it could pull back, she ripped her knife free and jammed it into the Drowned's calf, sawing at the thick muscles.

Throat sac bulging, it wrenched back and its leg slipped from Xessa's grasp, the skin smooth and cold and wet. The limb splashed down and then the Drowned slid through the shallow water on its back towards her to snatch at her ankles. If she went down it was over, she was dead. She leapt back, praying that her knife had done enough damage.

The Drowned lay on its back, gills flapping rapidly, water greening with blood, and Xessa stared at the length of it, at the thick, toughened plates like an armadillo's that covered its stomach and chest and lower back. How many times had she seen arrows and darts bounce off those plates? How many times had her own spear clattered free or drawn only a shallow wound in the shoulders, where no real damage could be done?

You could break their limbs. She'd proven that, though she hadn't known for sure when she'd tried it. But it took strength and leverage to pierce that armour and that meant being right there with it, not shooting arrows from a distance. Xessa's gaze returned to its face and she jumped; it was watching her, and she could recognise both pain and intelligence in its regard. Though she knew it was clever, it was still unnerving to find it studying her even as she studied it. Slowly, it dragged itself away from her and brought its bleeding leg up to its belly and lay there, one gill in the water. Still.

Wary, her knife up to ward off any sudden attack, Xessa bent and fished around until her fingers bumped Nallet's spear, and with a shudder of relief, she dragged it out of the water. The eja backed out of the womb and then turned and ran, up into the night and the darkness, towards Ossa and Toxte. Fucking Toxte. Oh, she had some questions for Toxte. The torchlight grew as she fled back to the ejab and then Ossa was there, and then Toxte, and all Xessa's constant, bubbling anger cooled and settled, because he was sitting on the floor with his arms and legs wrapped around Ekka, and the torchlight molten in the tears on his face.

Nallet and Quin reacted violently to her appearance, Quin even lunging with his spear before recognising her, and then there was a babbling flurry of hands as they demanded answers. Xessa slashed hers through the air to still them. 'It's contained. It's still tied – and it's still injured.'

Toxte was watching her. A shudder went through him at her words and he clutched Ekka tighter. The dog was sitting still in his embrace, giving comfort, her tongue working patiently at his neck. Xessa stood over them and shame filled her. She wasn't the only person who grieved for Kime and Tika, even if she had been kin with the former. Yet she'd done nothing since the deaths but batter away at Toxte, wallowing in her own mourning and ignoring his. She'd provided him with no comfort, yet she'd demanded it in turn. And he'd gifted it to her, selflessly, day after day.

'Can you check on it?' she signed to Quin. 'Both of you together. I stabbed its right leg, near the calf. Check it's still down but other than that don't touch it.'

Nallet and Quin were reluctant, but they went.

When she was alone with Toxte, Xessa knelt down next to him and took his face in her hands. 'I'm sorry,' she mouthed and he frowned, confused. She didn't explain, just kissed him, with tenderness and the first new growth of love, until he transferred the tightness of his grip from Ekka to her and shared the bottomless depth of his fear with her. He stank of it, his skin wet with it, and she held him all the tighter, his trembling becoming hers until she took it all from him and he was still.

Xessa helped Toxte to stand and untied the rope still crossed over his chest and back. There were ugly burns on his collarbones from where he'd struggled against it, but he submitted now without protest, and they waited for the ejab to come out of the womb and nod it was still contained, and then he let her lead him slowly back down the path in the blackness, and into the city, and home.

Xessa lit every candle she had and then made him strip and washed the sweat from him and lent him a shirt and kilt, though he couldn't get his shoulders into the former and sat with a blanket around him instead. She pegged the door curtain shut against the wind, fussed with food he didn't want and beer he did, and then finally sat opposite him. Ossa put his head on her thigh; Ekka was squeezed onto Toxte's lap, head and legs spilling across his knees.

She snapped her fingers and Toxte looked up, eyes dark with a haunting that had nothing to do with the spirits. She had so many questions, but she asked the most unexpected one she could think of to take his mind off what he'd seen – and done. She tapped her ear. 'What did it sound like? The song. Show it to me.'

Toxte paused, swirling beer in his cup, and reluctant wonder slid across his features. He put down the cup and rubbed both hands over his face. 'It was . . . You know how sometimes you can sit on the steps to the council house and watch the sun set, unobscured by the city? Just you and the sky and how any clouds there are turn gold and the rest of the sky is pink and red and orange? You know how sometimes it's so, it's just all so big and you're so small and yet it feels as if it's there just for you? And it's all you can see, it sweeps you up in it until you *become* the sunset? Until *you're* gold and pink and orange and as vast as the sky herself?'

He put a gentle hand on her chest, between her breasts. 'You know how it makes your heart hurt that it's so beautiful?'

Xessa nodded convulsively, bitter, wondering tears stinging her eyes.

'That's what it sounded like. It sounded like the sunset looks. It sounded like all the world is there just to make you gasp with wonder, to open your heart so wide that it can absorb all that beauty and hold it and be it and never lose it, no matter what. That's what the songs of the Drowned sound like.'

He had tears in his eyes too, but then the wonder in him vanished and the moisture was burnt away in dark fire. 'And that's why they need to die. Every last one of them. Forget studying them; just kill them.' He seized her hands. 'We just have to kill them, Xessa. All of them.'

ILANDEH

The Neck, Xentiban, Empire of Songs
184th day of the Great Star at morning

Ilandeh was exhausted, but everything lifted – her mood, her fatigue, the constant anxiety of discovery and failure – when she crossed the border into Xentiban and heard the song once more.

She was back in the Empire. She was home. The commander of the Melody's Whispers stood still, her arms out from her sides and fingers splayed, drinking in the song through her skin and ears and heart, breathing it deep into her lungs like the finest incense, like sunlight. The gaping wound inside began to close, the song's every note a stitch that pulled her edges together until she was whole again. Scarred, but alive.

A whole year, give or take, she had been without this majesty, without this constant reminder of her orders. Of the trust that the High Feather had placed in her and in Dakto so very long before. Ilandeh sank onto her knees, the rich earth warm and wet and heavy, teeming with life. Tears splashed onto the ground, adding their load of moisture and

302

precious salt. She stared at a busy, organised line of leaf-cutter ants marching back and forth before her and grinned. The song filled them and enhanced their purpose. They, too, worked for an empire and a high ruler, for glory and for peace.

Ilandeh stretched out her hand and let an ant climb over it and carry on its business. 'Overcoming all obstacles,' she whispered approvingly. 'Go with the gods, little warrior.' She sat back on her heels and a laugh of pure joy burst from her.

She was filthy and exhausted, hungry and desperately thirsty, but she could just see the trees thinning ahead, more sun filtering down through the canopy. A clearing. A pyramid. A Listener and eagles and warriors and home.

Grunting, Ilandeh climbed back to her feet and pushed on, weaving among untamed jungle until she reached a well-worn trail. She turned onto it with relief and checked the scarlet feather in her hair, restored after so very long to its proper place. It was ragged and dirty and bent, because it had been sewn into the seam of her tunic beneath her arm for a year and had been much abused, but it was there and it was hers. She was Flight Ilandeh, commander of the Whispers and the macaws of the Fourth Talon, and she said as much when two eagles emerged from the forest to confront her.

And then she was in the clearing and fresh tears pricked at her eyes as she looked upon the magnificence of the pyramid, gleaming red as fresh blood, carvings of holy Setatmeh and Singers and of the world spirit itself parading around its sides. 'Praise the Singer,' she breathed and the eagles escorting her were respectfully silent.

'How long have you been out,' one asked eventually.

'A year.' There were low murmurs of surprise and appreciation, and their regard filled her, mingling with the song until she was full. 'Is the Listener available?'

One of the eagles chuckled. 'I think for an assassin and spy of the High Feather himself, and one who's been in the heart of the enemy for a year, he'll make himself available.'

They left her at the base of the pyramid and she climbed the sacred steps and passed into the cool and the shade. The Whisper left sandals and weapons at the entrance, conscious of the grime, of her smell, in this holy place. The doorway was so low she was forced to kneel, to enter with her head bowed in humility and her neck exposed in supplication, as was right. She crawled down a short, black-painted passageway, the light from the chamber ahead growing and blinding her, and then slithered down onto the sunken floor, graceless and defenceless.

As was right.

The chamber was airy and wide, and if the outside had been majestic, the inside was the song made manifest. Each wall was a story painted by a master artist, a lesson, a revelation. The Listener who occupied the centre of the room, by contrast, was unreadable and barely there, so deeply connected with the song that Ilandeh didn't know if he'd noticed her come in.

Light from four high apertures spilt down onto the elaborately dyed mats where he sat, and Ilandeh remained on her hands and knees to cross over to the appointed place opposite him. The song was stronger here, pure and clear and vibrating in her bones. She looked up and saw the base of the songstone cap itself above her head. If she stood and reached, she could touch it. The thought sent a shiver of awe down her back, and although her fingers twitched, she didn't dare act on her desire.

'Where do you wish to go?' The Listener's voice was melodious and contained the same rhythms as the song. Ilandeh jumped and looked closer; his eyes were open to slits, glittering with intelligence and magic. She cleared her throat; her own voice was scratchy with thirst and from disuse. She had made the journey from the Sky City in sixteen days, longer than she would have liked, but she'd been forced to creep past war parties and avoid unfinished pyramids in case slaves captured by the Tokob told of her passing. Now, she wanted nothing more than to drink a dozen gourds of water and then sleep for a week. She could not.

'If it is possible, Listener, direct to High Feather Pilos. If not, then to his Listener, Citla, with my thanks.'

The light gleamed from the Listener's shaved head. 'It may be done,' he said and held out his hands. Ilandeh placed hers in them and let herself be swept into the current of the song, the Listener's skill and the burning of the incense and those black, black eyes taking her, swift and sure.

The Whisper's spirit tugged from her flesh, a whipping flag trailing behind her, touching the raw magic of the song itself and she heard a whimper that she knew to be her own, but didn't – couldn't – look away. The Listener's mind had claws in hers and led her forward, both with and against the current at once, across the sticks, across the jungle, into Pechacan and the Singing City and far beyond, to Pilos. To the fortress. To home.

Ilandeh felt the shock of connection, the confusion as the Listener contacted Pilos and he responded, and then he drew her into her High Feather's mind, into a small, shuttered place of darkness and water, cut off from the rest of his thoughts and feelings. Protected. Private.

'Flight Ilandeh?'

Ilandeh tumbled in the song and in their shared consciousness, striving to control her emotions – relief, delight, something akin to love – as his voice echoed all around her. 'High Feather!' Her inner voice was golden with relief, sparking within the liminal darkness.

'You are early.' His words entered blue with caution, tinging to red alarm. 'What has happened?'

'Three thousand Tokob and Yaloh have marched to southern Yalotlan to free slaves and destroy the pyramids before the peace-weaving is made official, in case part of the agreement is that the Empire keeps all land newly beneath the song.'

The space they were in blazed purple, iridescent as a hummingbird's wing: rage. Ilandeh quailed before it. 'Forgive me, High Feather,' she began.

'Could you have prevented it?' he demanded, the purple fading, though not by much.

'No, High Feather.' She wanted to apologise again, but the truth was there was nothing she could have done to stop them. 'Dakto has gone with one of the Paws. He will endeavour to contact a pod and spread word as well as he may without alerting the Tokob to his intentions. I had hoped you might have heard from or of him by now?'

'We have not. I thank you for the advance warning. I will have to let the Singer know they are using the cover of the Wet.' There was a pause. 'It's going to be Quitoban all over again,' he said, almost to himself.

Ilandeh knew she flashed yellow with anxiety at his prediction, could do nothing about it. She wasn't as skilled at concealing her emotions when communicating through the song. At least Yalotlan didn't have sticks and sticks of swamp and tidal marshes to navigate, the way Quitoban had.

'What else?'

The Whisper collected her thoughts. She'd been tired before the Listener had swept her out of her body; now she was nearing exhaustion and her emotions painted the darkness of the space they were in, the rich, living black of fear and the grey of grief streaking from her. 'I . . . Their high elders

are both dead, as is the elder of the Tokob ejab. I stayed as
long as I could, but, High Feather, they were going to attempt
to capture and torture a holy Setat. I could not let that
happen, not when I have been witness to so much. I had to
act, I could not . . .' She trailed off at the remembered horror.
Pilos had wanted her in the city for the duration, even up
to their attack so that she might disrupt the defence if she
could, but the sheer spirit-horror of listening to ejab
discussing slaughtering her gods, over and over across a year,
had shattered her.

'I killed the leader of the frog-lickers and stole the list of
. . . of *things* they were going to do to the god if they
captured it. It will delay the attempt but no more, I fear.'

Pilos was silent, but the space around them pulsed a
deep, angry purple again. Just once as he fought to control
his emotions.

Ilandeh didn't know if it was directed at her. 'Forgive me,'
she whispered again.

'You have done well,' the High Feather said eventually.
'Give the Listener a full and detailed report and have them
transmit it to Citla. But first, your observations.'

Ilandeh pulsed gold with relief. 'The city can be defended,
but the walls are more to prevent line of sight for cats
than any real barrier. We can be over them easily. Arrows
and darts from above will be a danger. There is a rope
bridge over the river below the city, but there are longer,
slower routes past it that bypass the water. Those will be
heavily guarded.'

She paused again; still no response. Pilos's control now
was total. 'The Swift Water – the river – is populated with
holy Setatmeh but the Tokob have a way to transport water
through pipes uphill to the city. I have learnt the method,
and I know too the ingredients and proportions of what

they call the spirit-magic, which allows their god-killers to be deaf to the call of the holy Setatmeh. Also journey-magic, which is something their shamans use to commune with their ancestors or their goddess. They'll be in my written report.'

Still Pilos was silent, but Ilandeh was used to that – had remembered that about him, now. Pilos sat and absorbed the information, and the quieter he was, the more people spoke, drawing out things they might have forgotten and that they now fumbled for to fill the silence.

'I left them in as much chaos as I could. There are a few hundred Xentib living in the city who fled from us four sun-years ago. I spent time fostering discord with Yaloh refugees, so with luck that will have broken into outright hostility if they connect the deaths with my absence. Which shouldn't be too difficult. And there is a cave, High Feather, high above the city. Tokob believe it is the womb of their goddess. It is not. It is songstone; the whole thing is veined with songstone. More than I've ever seen.'

The space flashed with intense colour then, green interest as bright as new leaves, before Pilos re-established his control. 'Your work is exemplary, Flight,' he told her and she knew she flushed pink with pleasure; couldn't prevent it. 'Your efforts, and Dakto's, will be remembered and rewarded. For now, bask in the song so that it might cleanse you and finish your report as I instructed.'

'As the High Feather commands.'

'I will inform the Singer of your revelations. I expect we will be ordered to Yalotlan immediately. Wait at the Neck for me and rest. Acting Flight Sarn and some of your Whispers are in Xentiban; the eagles will know exactly where. Take back your command and make sure your authority is unquestioned by the time I arrive. Stay out of any fighting until I've spoken to you face to face.'

'Of course, High Feather.' Ilandeh hesitated, unsure, and he read it.

'Speak. Quickly,' he added, and she became aware of the strain in the Listener. Connecting the two of them through himself and through the song was draining.

'My face is known among the Tokob, High Feather; when the fighting starts up again, I'll be a target. We can . . . use that, probably. Their anger will draw them to me and we can set ambushes. But . . . as far as Dakto's concerned, I'm still back in the Sky City. News is going to reach the war party he's with eventually about what I did. He's learning all he can of their plans and he intends to slip away with it, but if they find out before he can . . .'

'I know, Flight,' Pilos said, and he was now – deliberately – warmly soft brown with gentleness. 'And yet you both accepted the risks. You've made it out, and you've brought far more knowledge than I ever expected, and I know it's been just the two of you against them all for so long, but if Dakto is taken . . . well, his sacrifice will be remembered and his glory will be great.'

'Yes, High Feather,' Ilandeh said and did her best to keep her tone transparent, though that in itself would tell him much.

'Rest now,' he repeated.

'Under the song,' she said, but the Listener was already retreating and taking her with him. Ilandeh tried to cling to Pilos's mind just a little longer, for the comfort, but he was gone and they were swirling back through the song, across the landscape so fast it made her dizzy, until they slipped back into their bodies. The Whisper's spirit was still billowing in the song even as her consciousness returned to her flesh and she let out a frightened little squeak, but the Listener enveloped her once more and showed her the way.

She was slumped, heavy and full, as if her mind were a big meal weighing her down. The Listener was trying gently to extricate his hands from hers, but it took her several breaths before she could remember how to work her fingers. He was patient, though sweat ran through the lines of exhaustion carved upon his face. 'Thank you,' she gasped. 'Thank you.'

The Listener drank deeply from the pitcher of water at his side and she watched his throat move, reminded of her own thirst, but he needed it far more than she. And then panic filled her; she did not have an offering for him. She had not brought anything – had been so desperate to impart her news that she had forgotten entirely. Except . . .

'It is not much,' she croaked, 'but it is . . . I have had it a long time.' A string of four jade beads, two either side of a small jet pendant fashioned like a tiny jaguar's head. She pulled it over her head and placed it on the mats between them. It looked shabby there, travel-worn and old. 'It was my mother's,' she added and distaste flickered across the Listener's face, but he scooped it up and nodded at her. Her Xenti mother.

'I will write the report for you to transmit to Listener Citla,' she said, but already he was sinking back into the currents of the song. Ilandeh bowed again and crawled back out of the chamber and stood. Her neck felt bare and empty, but she relished it with a sudden, fierce intensity. She was only a half-blood, but she was loyal. The song was everything to her: it was music and fate and freedom; it was status and honour and respect. She could do nothing about her blood, other than be fiercely proud of her Pechaqueh ancestry and leave the rest behind. The necklace had been the last possession she had owned that was her mother's and here, back beneath the song after so long, it was right that she gave it up.

310

I am Pecha in my heart and my spirit and my flesh. I am Pecha in every way that matters.

Not every way, and not in everyone's eyes, but enough. It was enough. She was enough, and she refused to believe different. A little unsteady, Ilandeh made her way out of the pyramid and into the infrequent sun. The song cradled her, and in the distance she saw some of the Whispers who had been under her command before, coming to meet her.

PILOS

*Melody fortress, the dead plains, Tlalotlan, Empire of
Songs
184th day of the Great Star at morning*

Pilos, High Feather of the Melody and Spear of the Singer, came out of the song and slumped, breathing harshly. The Melody's Listener, Citla, was kneeling opposite, holding Pilos's hands in her own, tight and comforting. She hadn't been in there with him, but someone had noticed him being pulled under and sent for her. Once he was settled back in his body, he let go and gratitude flickered through him. Citla smiled and waited, patient. There would be messages to send in reply, she knew.

Pilos had come out of the song alone many times, but it was harder and far more dangerous. Even those experienced in such communication could be lost, their minds unable to find their bodies and their spirits stretching ever longer between the two until they snapped. Madness and death always followed. Always.

Feather Ekon was kneeling behind the Listener and he

312

bowed as soon as Pilos straightened his spine and nodded. 'Feather Atu has been sent for,' he said. 'Is there anything you need until then?'

There was a cup of water next to Pilos and he gulped it down. 'There will be a full report coming from Whisper Ilandeh via a Listener in the Neck,' he rasped. Citla nodded. 'The enemy are destroying pyramids, freeing slaves, and killing warriors in Yalotlan. I must inform the Singer.' Citla nodded again and Ekon swore, very quietly. 'When Atu arrives, let him know and then get me every Feather in the fortress. And the administrators. We can't count on either the new slaves or the hawks or the Xentib slave warriors, so I need to know who we *can* count on.'

Pilos's mind spun with logistics, racing across the various Talons and where they were based, who he could pull back and replace with Xentib, which parts of the Empire were currently peaceful.

It was too much, coming so soon after that awful moment when the song had jarred out of its natural rhythm so wildly and then taken almost three days to return to normal. Something momentous had happened that had changed the Singer or his grip on his magic. And now Pilos knew instinctively that they would be marching to war – in the Wet – because Ilandeh's information made that inevitable. At the very time they should be strengthened by the song and the Singer's magic, the fortress was alive with rumour and whisper and concern.

Pilos's mouth turned down as he remembered how helpless he'd felt, here in the Melody's own fortress in Tlalotlan, far from the Singer's side and unable to aid him. He had tried to contact Enet through the song in the immediate aftermath, but her Listener had simply said there was no danger and that he was not to return to the Singing City. He had sent her frantic letters, asking what had happened, but she hadn't bothered to reply.

Not for the first time, he wished for a Whisper in the great pyramid, one of his finest assassin-spies secluded among the administrators, Chorus and councillors, but only full-blood Pechaqueh could hold such positions, with a written lineage to prove their right to serve the Singer. Whispers were half-bloods, for no Pecha would risk their honour by undertaking the quiet, bloody work the Whispers were made for. In this, though their loyalty was without question, their credentials were lacking.

'I'll have Feather Atu draw up some recommendations for when you have finished with the Singer, High Feather,' Ekon said, pulling Pilos back to the current crisis.

Yes. Concentrate on the Singer first. He didn't have all the information, but he couldn't wait for Ilandeh's full report; the holy lord needed to know now, and perhaps Pilos might be able to ascertain the holy lord's health for himself during their communion. Citla looked at him, magic in her eyes and veins and sweat already gathering on her shaven scalp. Pilos took a deep breath, took her hands, and allowed himself to be swept away.

At his request, Citla had bypassed the source's Listener and attempted to contact the Singer himself. They did not slide into his mind as Ilandeh had into his; instead Citla held open a space in herself and let Pilos and the Singer fill it. The High Feather was dimly conscious of the Listener's hands closing on his with bruising force when the holy lord entered her mind, his might and power overwhelming. He didn't understand how Citla could bear it, how she could contain so much without losing herself entirely.

Pilos bobbed helplessly, feeling himself unravel into the Singer until somehow his Listener stopped it, containing him

314

and keeping him separate. The Singer's unspoken question – *Why?* – flooded through him and the High Feather poured out the sea of images and information received from Ilandeh. Words were almost impossible to form in the raw, unconfined presence of the Singer and the crackle of his magic, but Citla formed them for him, shaping his impressions and gifting them to Xac one at a time. A lifetime of training had prepared her for this, and Pilos could do nothing but trust her.

There was . . . a pause? An absence? Something, during which Pilos tried not to lose parts of himself, and then the Singer was gone and Citla was guiding him back into his body and there was new knowledge in his head and no memory of it being put there.

When he opened his eyes this time, the Listener was still kneeling but she was slumped against his chest, their hands still gripping tight. Her breath was a high, thin wheeze and Pilos looked up – Feathers Atu, Detta and Ekon were all with him. He nodded very carefully so that he didn't fall out of his body again, and Atu moved behind Citla, ready to catch her if Pilos faltered. The High Feather was shaking as he supported her weight and laid her gently on the mats. There was a wet stain on his tunic – drool or tears or sweat – from where her face had pressed.

As soon as she was prone, Atu helped Pilos to stand and they left her alone. Touch and voices could do her more damage in the aftermath of communion with the Singer than solitude. The High Feather's knees wobbled as he staggered out of his office and into another room, bigger, more comfortable. The Feathers followed and they all waited until he was sitting cross-legged with a stool under one elbow as support.

'The Singer will consult the stars and the prophecies and inform us when we need to move,' he croaked. His head was pounding with tiredness and strain and his lower lip was swollen from where he'd bitten it. Strange tingles and twitches plagued the muscles in his forearms and lower legs, but he ignored them. His state was far better than Citla's. 'It will be soon. We're going to throw every experienced Talon at them until they break, so I want options for the security of the Empire with our best in the north. I want to know who we can call back and how long it will take to march them direct to Xentiban.'

His Feathers looked at him, intent and focused.

'Get to it.'

They'd planned and argued and counter-planned until Pilos couldn't see straight and he'd dismissed them – or rather dismissed himself to bed, where he'd slept three hours past dawn and woken feeling vaguely alive again.

And despite the frantic hurry – or because of it and what it meant – he'd ordered the Feathers and the Third Talon to assemble and he'd finally elevated eagle Calan to Feather, a leader in her own right with three hundred eagles under her command, all full-blood Pechaqueh of course, all warriors of exquisite skill and renown. They cheered as Atu and Detta braided the war feathers into the command fan at the back of her head. When it was done, the trio faced Pilos.

He pressed his hand to his belly and his throat. 'Feather Calan, welcome. For the glory of the Empire and the holy Setatmeh, you have been gifted the feathers of command. Use them wisely, learn from your elders and betters, and fill me with pride when next we go to war.'

'For the Singer!' Calan shouted, returning the salute and then bowing her head at Pilos, unable to disguise the width of her grin. 'For the holy Setatmeh, for the Empire, and for High Feather Pilos.'

Pilos permitted himself another small smile; he should

probably put a stop to it, but the war in Yalotlan had been bloody, and the Melody had taken to chanting his name when they achieved victory.

As long as mine comes after that of Singer, Empire and Setatmeh, I suppose there's no real harm.

'Back about your work, eagles, there's a lot to be done. Atu, I want the first of the new slaves brought up; they've been stewing in their own filth long enough. Let's see how many are willing to fight and die for their Empire. We may as well make a start on them while we're still here.'

'Yes, High Feather,' Atu said, and dismissed the eagles to their barracks and training. On one side of the huge drill yard, dog warriors trained under the watchful eyes and eager whips of their Coyote commanders, the rain washing the sweat from their bodies.

On the other, the new hawk caste worked their way through basic spear forms. They were slow and awkward, but they were eager, knowing it was their only chance to put their shame behind them and regain honour and status again.

Pilos's view of the hawks was cut off by the appearance of hundreds of stumbling, squinting, filthy, chained men and women: the Yaloh warriors who had survived the first battles and been captured. Pilos had left them baking in the underground cells for the last five moons, coated in their own filth and scrambling for the rations dropped through the slats from above.

Only the strongest would have survived that, and the sound of more Yaloh being forced into the neighbouring pits month after month as the war progressed would have hardened them and given them an edge like the finest obsidian. Only those who were proven or suspected warriors were at the fortress. The rest – the old, the children, and the obvious non-combatants – had already been sold. For moons, this

317

batch of slaves had listened to the pitiful cries and brava-do-filled curses of their way of life ending, filtered, always, through the glory of the song that showed them what they could be, how great they could be. Now Pilos needed to turn the remains of their hate and rage against a target other than the Pechaqueh who'd defeated them and the Empire that would, given time and good service, raise them up to heights they couldn't imagine.

Pilos picked up his heavy war club. Swinging the weapon idly in his hand, he wandered up and down the ragged lines.

'Warriors,' he said in a loud voice. 'Fighters. Killers. Proud and upright and strong and fierce. No fear and no regret.' Some Yaloh watched the club as he passed, a few watched his eyes, most watched his feet, and some watched his chest. Each meant something different – those watching the club thought it the biggest threat, those watching his eyes would likely not bend, those watching his feet were broken. Those watching his chest, though, oh, those were the ones he wanted. They were waiting for him to strike, club or foot or hand, ignoring the lies he'd tell with his face and eyes and focusing on his body to give him away. Those ones recognised that more than just the club was dangerous. Those were the warriors who would win the world for the Melody and the song.

'You fought gloriously for your people and your way of life, and I honour each and every one of you in my heart, those who stand before me and those who fell. You fought gloriously – and for the wrong reasons.'

A few more eyes snapped up to his face then, a few fists clenched, a few shoulders tightened. Pilos wandered on, undaunted. Feathers and eagles bracketed the lines and a few stood behind him, all relaxed. Strength and confidence would win them to the cause, not brutality. At least, not unless he had no other choice.

'For moons now you have been under the song. You have heard its ever-changing beauty, its power, its glory. It has slithered into your hearts and spirits and now will never truly let you go. But it does not need to, for the best among you will be inducted into the Melody, to fight for the song and its Empire, for glory, for the Singer and the holy Setatmeh.'

A woman, taller than Pilos and almost as broad in the shoulder, sprinted from the front line behind him. The shift in the prisoners alerted him, that and the prickle along his spine. She didn't come screaming her war cry; she didn't come cursing.

She was three strides from him when he spun, club swinging up on the diagonal. At her peak, before her moons of incarceration, she would have been terrifying. Even now Pilos gave her the respect she deserved. She dodged the club, slamming into his chest, the edge of her left hand chopping into his right wrist and numbing his fingers, loosening his grip on the weapon. But it didn't matter, because the knife in his other hand had opened her from womb to liver. Blood sprayed between them, a puff of crimson almost lost in the sticky grey of the afternoon.

Her left fist was moving before she knew she was dead and Pilos jerked his head to one side so her knuckles just caught his cheek instead of breaking his nose. The hand with the club came around her back and supported her as she realised what had happened. Her eyes swivelled downwards and then back up to his.

'Under the song,' he said and lowered her to the limestone blocks of the drill yard. Blood coated his shirt, his belt and kilt and left hand to the elbow. Blood pooled beneath her, bright against the pale stone, the greying of her skin. 'Your ancestors will be proud.'

Pilos stepped back, sheathed the knife and took a

two-handed grip on the club. 'Mercy,' he said loud enough for the front rows to hear, and swung, crushing her skull. He pointed the bloody end at them. 'Each and every one of you will have the chance to prove yourself in battle. Those who prove outstanding, and who commit to serve as a slave warrior for five years, will be able to provide the names and descriptions of their families.' More eyes looking up, dragged away from the leaking corpse on the stone or their own broken sandals or bare feet. Looking at him but not in defiance now, not in hate. Desperate, ugly hope blazed in every face.

'Five years as slave warriors during which your families will be kept safe and together, parents with youngsters, old folk with your siblings, if you so wish. They will serve together in one house, somewhere in the Empire. Well treated, not abused, fed and clothed and healed when sick. Your children educated.'

There were murmurs among the ranks now and Feathers cracked whips and called for silence.

'After five years of successful service, your deeds and accomplishments will be tallied up. Those of you who have captured slaves for the Empire, who have committed acts of outstanding bravery, who have saved the lives of your fellow warriors . . . those who have tallies enough will be promoted into the dog warriors.'

Pilos gestured behind him with the club. A few drops of blood pattered to the stone. The dog warriors there were training hard, their unarmed combat fluid and fast and lethal.

'Dog warriors are not slaves. Dog warriors are paid good jade for good service!' Pilos shouted, drawing all eyes back to him. 'When word is sent to your families of your promotion, they too will be elevated, from slave to servant. Servants are paid good jade for good service!'

He paused and grinned at them. 'When between you and your families you have earned enough to buy your freedom, you may do so. A few years only, in most cases, sometimes less, and you can all be reunited. If you wish to earn that freedom faster, you can. How?'

The Feathers chanted the answer. 'By capturing slaves, by acts of bravery, by saving lives.'

'I know you are more than just warriors. You are farmers, artists, weavers, hunters, shamans. We are all, at the end of the day, hunters, gatherers, and farmers first. Warriors last. We pick up weapons only out of necessity. Once you and your family have bought your freedom, you will be given a plot of land within the Empire to farm. Half of your crop will be sent as tithe to the local governor of your district; the rest is yours to do with as you wish. Mostly, I recommend you eat it and grow fat and fuck your partners and have more children. But I leave that choice up to you.'

There were a few half-smiles in the throng and Pilos's grin outmatched them. 'This is how you earn your freedom. This is how you earn the freedom of your families. This is how you return to the lives you led before, but this time under the song, in its power and glory. Seven years, maybe eight, and freedom and land and family are all yours. Eight years – one Star cycle, no more. Just a Star cycle.'

He paused to let that sink in and then the timbre of his voice dropped, roughened. 'Refuse this gift, and your families will be slaves until the day they die. Your children will never be permitted to take a partner and any children they do have will belong to the people in whose homes they work. If they disobey or rebel, they will be offered to the holy Setatmeh in ritual. Neither education nor medicine will be theirs, for you show us by your refusal that their lives have no value. Your line will die. They will die.'

The choice that was no choice at all.

'Attend!' Feather Atu bellowed. 'Dog warriors, fall in.' The four hundred dogs drilling across the yard sprinted into position. 'When I give the order, ten slaves and ten dogs will fight. We want to see your skill, your aggression, and your footwork. We do not want to see death or crippling. We are here to assess you, not execute you.'

They'd lose a score of dogs, probably, and a quarter or more of the slaves, regardless of the order against killing. But those who were left would swear oaths to the Singer and replenish his numbers. When they could be trusted, they'd be sent into peaceful, happy Chitenec to enforce the Singer's laws. In the meantime, the Melody would march to Yalotlan and bring it beneath the song. And the cycle would begin again.

It was the end of a very long day, filled with far too many demands on his time, and Pilos would have already been snoring if not for being wound so tight about . . . everything.

'High Feather? Anything you need?' Atu was a shadow against the night as he paused in the doorway. Pilos shook his head and beckoned him in and onto a stool, sloshed beer into a second cup and handed it over. Atu knocked it back and then groaned. 'Thank you, Setatmeh,' he breathed and Pilos snorted, sipped at his own cup and gestured for his subordinate to top up his own.

'How long do you think we'll have?' he asked.

Pilos rubbed the back of his neck. 'It's seven weeks, maybe eight, until the Wet begins to taper. Under normal circumstances, we'd set out for Xentiban a week or so after that. But these aren't normal circumstances, so I think we'll be moving in four weeks and fighting up Yalotlan's hills and dying in mudslides a few weeks after that.'

Only because it was Atu, and only because it was late and he was a little drunk, did he allow those words to pass his lips, tight and bitter.

'The Singer's will,' Atu said quietly, and although there was no reprimand in his voice, Pilos sat up straighter.

'Look at Quitoban,' he said. 'A flooded delta in the east, tidal marshes in the south, and the worst Wet in living memory. We won there; we'll win in Yalotlan.'

'And the Quitob make up the bulk of our dogs now,' Atu added. 'The older ones will be useful in assessing the ground for danger. And of course, we'll be able to access Yaloh populations that have to stay for the harvests. That will make things easier.'

Pilos nodded; it had been the biggest difficulty they'd faced before the Wet, making significant progress in a society mostly comprising small villages. Even Xentiban had a few decent-sized cities that, once taken, had crippled any cohesive counter-attack. In contrast, the Yaloh had fled his advancing Melody and then returned to their villages and fields once they'd passed by. But harvest time would be different.

'We can supplement our own travel rations,' he confirmed as Atu suppressed a yawn. 'Point taken, Feather. Get some rest. I want twenty good eagles overseeing the new slaves at dawn. We're in for a tough war season and I want to know we've got replacements ready to go if we lose Feathers. Rotate any with promise into training and leadership roles with the hawks in the time we have left and get me a short-list for review.'

'As the High Feather commands,' Atu said and then hesitated. 'This is my favourite time, you know,' he added and then blushed. 'Forgive me.'

Pilos raised his hand to still him. 'No. Tell me,' he said, intrigued.

The Feather shifted, uncomfortable, and then said in a rush, 'When they first swear, High Feather, whether reluctant or not. When the slaves first swear and we have this chance to show them . . .'

'To show them how honour and discipline can bring peace to the spirit and joy to the heart,' Pilos said softly. 'How the loyalty of the pod, the Talon, the Melody becomes the new tribe, the new identity.' Atu nodded, bright with the warmth of it. 'Me too.'

They stared at one another for a long second and then Pilos cleared his throat and tapped his fingers on his cup. 'Get some rest,' he said again.

Atu touched belly and throat and inclined his head. 'Under the song, High Feather,' he said softly, and left. Pilos watched the door and then gusted a sigh. *A good man, that Atu,* he thought wistfully. *A good, married man.*

The slaves had done well, with fewer than fifty refusing to fight. Those ones had been marked as failed and put back in a pit, to be offered to the holy Setatmeh in the river outside the fortress. They'd be given one by one in return for the gods' blessing. Their fate would terrify them, the agony of waiting, and so the warriors incarcerated around them would be more likely to swear when their turn came. It was crude, but it was proven to be effective, too.

The rest had fought, and some had died or been damaged beyond repair. The latter would be used in the kitchens or fields, or sent as scribes if they could no longer walk. A few had chosen it as a way to kill themselves, and Pilos admired their resolve even as he was disgusted they would abandon their families in such a way. The survivors were all his, blooded and sworn into the ranks of the Melody's slave warriors and moved to the barracks of the Seventh Talon, where there was soap and water for washing, fresh clothes, fresh food, and clean sleeping mats. Small luxuries that would mean everything after so long beneath the ground, bathed in the sweat and shit and blood of others.

A second army of flesh-merchants had emerged to take the names and descriptions of their families, the locations where they'd been taken captive and when, or their descriptions if they so far remained free. They'd be identified and their details entered next to the slave warriors' in the central records. Wherever they ended up serving, their fates were tied together.

Though some had probably not expected it to be true, Pilos hadn't lied: their families would be kept safe where possible and, as long as they didn't break any rules or attempt to flee or kill their owners, they'd be looked after. If they did rebel, they would of course be offered to the holy Setatmeh for their crimes. If their slave-warrior relative survived to become a dog, they would be told then of their family's disloyalty and a year would be added to their service. By that time, most were more loyal to the Melody than to their kin anyway.

Pilos drained half his cup of beer as another form appeared at his door. Citla. He beckoned her in, noting her pallor and the tremble in her hands. 'From Councillor Yana,' she said as she held out the bark-paper. 'Confidential.'

He eyed her and then took it. 'Are you all right?' She nodded, swaying a little, and then padded away. Confidential information could be sent through the song, but it was difficult, involving the Listener receiving the communication while chanting a particular melody as the information was dictated to them. It ensured that once the message was written and handed over, they remembered nothing of what they had heard.

Pilos untied the message hurriedly.

*Honoured High Feather, Spear of the Singer and servant
of our holy lord, greetings.*

*In light of the information provided by your spies,
the Singer has viewed the skies and read the histories
and the prophecies. He has communed with the holy
Setatmeh here in the heart of Empire and cast the bones
and dice. He orders that the Yaloh are to be brought
under the song immediately, as are the Tokob, whose
deicide can no longer be ignored. He charged me with
the honour of informing you, for which I am obliged.*

*Upon conquest of the Tokob Sky City, he commands
you to bring him examples of these so-called ejab, as
many as you can find. If you must kill every Toko and
Yalotl to get to them, then that is your order. The
god-killers must be stopped.*

*You are to march on the 210th day of the Great
Star's appearance at dawn.*

Pilos stared at the letter and the deadline for moving an
entire army – through the Wet – to the border and war. It
was even shorter than he'd expected. Twenty-five days. A
laugh bubbled up in his chest and overspilt in a very undig-
nified, slightly hysterical snort. He slapped his hand over his
mouth and took a deep breath.

*Calm, Pilos. We knew this was coming and we've already
begun preparing. All will be as the holy Setatmeh decree.
There's a war to win. Against two tribes. In the Wet.*

Another laugh threatened and he suppressed it; then he
checked the timeline again. The two hundred and tenth
day. Right.

'Atu!' he bellowed, and then scanned the rest of the letter.

You will know better than I that the fever in Quitoban remains out of control. Despite my repeated requests, the order remains for quarantine and to let the illness burn itself out. Those Pechaqueh who have been able to flee to estates outside the major cities and towns have done so, and trade between Quitoban and Pechacan has ceased for now. Whichever Talon you have there will not be permitted to withdraw to aid you in the war.

Pilos dropped the letter again. 'Shit.' The Fifth were in Quitoban, and the Fifth were good. Experienced and steady – the very reason they'd been sent to calm a panicking populace.

'Where is— *Atu!*' he bellowed again.

I pray they remain safe from contagion, though if matters there get much worse, they are likely to be ordered to massacre anyone showing so much as a sweaty brow, and for what? Our shamans may have found a medicine, but they are not allowed to test their theories. No, the consensus is to lock them up and let them die. A pity and a waste.

The Singer is much distracted these days, High Feather. I'm sure you understand. Disappointing him would not be good for your health.

Under the song.

Your friend, councillor and retired Feather, Yana

Pilos puffed out his cheeks. That would explain the confidential nature of the letter then. Those were dangerous words no matter to who they were spoken. Yana was dancing with fire by even hinting that the approach in Quitoban was wrong. Again the old Feather was throwing his support behind Pilos instead of Enet. Were divisions in the council so great Yana was anticipating a coup, even all-out war? If it came to it, he'd take Yana's support with gratitude, though he had no desire to squabble over a position at the Singer's side. The holy lord would judge his service as he would – if Pilos was chosen to ascend with him, it would be because of his honour, not his political manoeuvring.

He snorted, knowing it was a naive and dangerous stance, but one he found it hard to change. As a warrior and then High Feather, politics had never been something he'd had to concern himself with: he was more used to being courted than courting others. It was different when he became Spear, with a voice that had real weight in council, but he'd always trusted his blunt honesty was enough to win him allies and reverse the way that Enet would poison the Singer's heart against him every time he was away from the Singing City.

I should have done more when I was there.

Pilos blinked away the worry. It meant nothing when he had only twenty-five days to organise the Melody and get them ready to march.

Not enough time. And yet the Singer's command.

'*Atu!*'

TAYAN

Fifteen days they'd travelled north, through farmland into forest, and only in the last few had the slave guards begun to answer his endless questions, more out of frustration than anything else, it seemed. As a peace-weaver, Tayan could be charmingly persuasive; as a shaman he was relentless. He'd known they'd give in sooner or later.

They were Chitenecah, supposedly the most loyal of the Pechaqueh subjects because they had been part of the Empire the longest. They had been born slaves, which didn't sit quite right with everything Enet had told him, but Tayan had expected no less. Secrets and lies and half-truths were her armour, and she wore them well.

Like the male estate slave in Enet's house, these men had more freedom to act and speak than Tayan would have expected. Though still property, they were fiercely loyal to Enet, and within that framework of obedience and at the mercy of her whims and tempers, they had carved for themselves a life that was bearable. They bore weapons and wore finely woven, though undyed, maguey, as well as jewellery, to reflect Enet's wealth and status rather than their own. Two were married, a third had children, and all were vehement in their love of the Empire. Enet trusted them, and their pride in that fact was conspicuous.

She had told Tayan that when he returned he, too, would be enslaved, and he remembered the estate slave with his quiet competence and respectful familiarity, how the Great Octave trusted him and had even listened to his opinions on occasion. Tayan could picture himself alongside him, advising, scribing and researching. A far better fate than to become another of the empty-eyed, exhausted creatures toiling in the fields. He knew it was the song inviting him to choose the manner of his servitude, but once the seed was planted, it grew sturdy and fast.

All those thoughts came to a crashing halt when they crossed into Yalotlan and, a day's march later, the song ended. It was as if a threatening lightning storm suddenly retreated, lifting pressure from Tayan's skin and skull. His head filled with a high, protracted whine that was almost painful, and then his ears popped one after the other. He winced and shook his head as the hairs stood up on his arms and the back of his neck.

'We'll go no further. We have done as the high one commanded, but we'll set no foot into this cursed place,' one of the guards said. They were huddled together, fearful, back within the invisible border of the song's magic. 'It is death.'

'Wait, please. At least leave me a weapon and a gourd for water. I'll die out here,' Tayan begged. His pack was empty of all but his paint and journey-magic and the shawl Enet had given him; the guards kept all food and water to themselves to make it less likely he'd attempt to escape.

They were already backing away as they conferred, but when they were only a blur in his vision, one bent to the ground and perhaps placed something there. And, as easily as that, they were gone.

Tayan squinted. He'd have to cross back into the song to collect whatever they'd left him. He didn't know if he could. 'Well, it's that or die,' he said aloud, to combat the awful loneliness inside his skin. The silence frightened him; his yearning frightened him far more.

He wiped his hands on his tunic and took a deep breath, then began to sing one of Lilla's favourite songs. He crossed back into the magic and within three steps his voice faltered, and then his feet, and he stopped and let it fill him again. Sunlight on his skin. Lilla's mouth on his throat. The warmth of honeypot in his belly. *Song.*

No. *No.*

He focused on the items the Chitenecah had dropped and broke into a run, counting his footsteps aloud, shouting them until he got there. A gourd, a sling, and a short blowpipe. Far more than he had expected. Tayan scooped them up, dragging up a handful of leaves and dirt in his haste, and ran back, still shouting numbers, until he passed into the silence of Yalotlan. He kept going, kept running through the maddening absence, faster and faster, the trail jerking and wobbling in his vision, until he couldn't run any further and had no idea where he was anyway. He knew southern Yalotlan was rife with pyramid-builders, slaves, and the warriors guarding them. It wouldn't be long before someone found him.

And then they can send me back.

No! I'm going home to Lilla. To quiet and peace and love.

Tayan walked on through the afternoon, forcing himself north when his feet and belly and spirit yearned to head south, into the song. The jungle was loud with birds, insects, and monkeys and yet somehow silent. The music of the balance between life and death wasn't the music his spirit craved. It didn't live within him as the song had, ushering him towards the glory to be found in surrender.

Stop it.

He found a clump of water vine and broke one open with a stone, filling the gourd and drinking what was left, tepid and faintly sweet. He kept going, following the winding of game trails and singing prayers and chants to combat the absence of the true song. The only song.

Stop it!

Tayan decided to spirit-journey as soon as he was in Tokoban. If he could reunite with his spirit guides and his ancestors, then the loss of the song would mean nothing to him. Nothing. He could tell them everything that had happened and beg their wisdom. And in the Sky City, he would find Lilla and Xessa and all the rest. He'd tell the councils everything he'd learnt, about Pechaqueh society and culture, their class system, the little he knew of the song and the Singer and the holy Setatmeh. The ruse of their surrender.

Swift-growing saplings competed for height and light in a clearing where a huge pom had fallen, and the shaman paused there in the open, turning his face up to the breeze. Clouds of finches and flycatchers flittered between the trees and darted across the open space almost too fast to see. Just flashes of bright colour against the flint of the clouds, there and gone among the trees and the shadows.

'Tayan?'

The voice was so unexpected that he screamed and fumbled for the sling and a stone, jerking around in a circle. There.

'It's me. It's Dakto of the Xentib, from home. From the Sky City. It's Dakto.'

And it was. Tayan squinted desperately to confirm it. The Xenti stood on the far side of the clearing, almost invisible. He was very still, examining Tayan and the trail he'd come along. His hatchet was in his hand and then he glanced casually back behind himself, just for a second.

'What are you doing here? You're . . . earlier than we expected.'

The stone fell out of the sling as Tayan clutched at his heart, trying to will it to slow, but it insisted on beating danger at him and he couldn't gather his thoughts to answer. Half a day out from under the song and he was a mess. *It'll get better. I just need to adjust.*

Dakto approached, softer than a shadow. He paused for a heartbeat of time, and then slipped his hatchet back through his belt. 'No, wait, it doesn't matter, you can tell me later.' He pointed behind him. 'About a stick, maybe two. There's someone who's going to want to see you.' His smile faded at that and his lips thinned, but Tayan barely registered it. His heart was thudding again, just as hard, but for a different reason.

'Lilla?' he whispered, all other thoughts swept out of his head at the whisper of that promise. Here, now, not in another two weeks when he finally made it home. Here. Lilla was here.

'Go on,' Dakto said. 'I'm going to check your backtrail. How long have you been out here alone?' he added as Tayan began to step past him, a manic smile pulling at his mouth.

He paused and managed a wheezing laugh. 'Half a day, so clearly Malel is smiling on me that I come across a friend so soon. My Chitenecah slave guards – I was seen by Enet, the Great Octave, herself, and the guards were hers – left me at the border of the song. But why are you all the way out here?'

'Enet sent you?' Dakto asked, his tone sharp. Tayan blinked, but then the Xenti was waving him away. 'Never mind, go and find Lilla. Go on, go. He'll kill me if he finds out I kept you here talking.'

Tayan squeezed Dakto in a brief, affectionate hug. 'It's so good to see you again,' he whispered, but then he let go and his dignity broke and he began to run, stumbling over roots and vines, his sandals skidding on rocks.

The gourd's string handle fell from his shoulder to tangle his hand and he cast it away, perhaps foolishly, but then how else would Lilla know it was him? He always teased Tayan that foolishness was his defining trait, and he couldn't let his husband down now. A laugh bubbled up and he let it out and ran faster, pounding along the trail. There were flickers of movement to either side and someone called out for him to stop, and he didn't want to, but he didn't want to get shot either, so he slowed and turned in a circle so they could identify him.

Someone stepped onto the path ahead and Tayan squinted hard. 'Lilla?' The figure moved, began to walk and then to run and he grew clearer and Tayan ran too and they collided so hard he almost bounced off his husband's chest – would have if Lilla's arms hadn't closed around him and crushed him tight.

'Malel, thank you, Malel,' Lilla was saying and Tayan wrenched his head down and stopped the words with a kiss that was hurricane and soft mornings and bodies moving in the dark and he was crying and it didn't matter. Lilla was *here*.

Voices from the trees, curious and then fading to give them privacy and Tayan never wanted the kiss to end, but his lungs were screaming for air and Lilla was still holding him too tight. He broke the kiss and pressed their foreheads together instead, breathing, fists in his husband's hair and chest to chest and belly to belly. And safe.

'You're back,' Lilla whispered, and Tayan slid an arm around his waist to press even closer. His chest hitched on a little sob. 'You came back to me.'

'I brought you your heart, as I promised,' he said, his voice rough. 'I will always come back, I swear by the ancestors.'

'And I to you. But you're early. The peace-weaving . . .'

'I bought us time. I bought us the rest of the Wet.' Disquiet twisted in him. Hadn't Betsu told them this already? Or was it simply that they'd left the Sky City before her return? That reminded him that Dakto had dodged the question of their presence so far south; Tayan wouldn't let his husband do the same. 'Why—' he began but then Lilla kissed him again, harder this time, and despite himself he let it soothe the worry that crept beneath his skin. The world went away again for a while as he concentrated on chasing Lilla's love with lips and tongue.

Lilla finally pulled away enough that Tayan could look at him properly. He was thinner, a little, and there were fine lines around his eyes and lips, where they'd been too tight for too long. But the same smoky intensity burnt in him, the same deep love of land and gods and home. No new scars that he could see . . . No, that wasn't right. A long, ugly slash in his forearm that Tayan spotted as Lilla gently brushed his hair behind his ear. He seized the hand and examined the wound. It was fresh but clean. Tayan met his gaze. 'What are you doing so far south?' he asked, reluctant to lose the moment but determined to understand.

Lilla sensed the shift and lost a little of the light in him. Immediately, Tayan wanted it back and cursed himself for speaking.

'Our war party's destroyed three pyramids so far and

freed, sort of, five hundred slaves. That's a bit complicated, though. We're—'

'War party?' Tayan shrugged out of Lilla's grip, his skin prickling warning and their reunion firmly behind them. 'We're at war now? In the Wet? *What were you thinking?*' He grabbed his husband's hand and dragged him towards the cluster of gathering warriors further down the trail. 'Tell me.'

'We offered Malel a sacrifice,' Lilla said. Tayan blinked. Of all the reasons, he hadn't expected that one. 'We offered and Malel accepted and told us to push forward, to reclaim Yalotlan and free the slaves and smash the pyramids. I wanted to wait until we thought the peace-weaving would have concluded, to keep you safe, but . . .' Lilla spread his hands helplessly. 'The goddess spoke. And it's not open war; we're not engaging with the Melody. We're *freeing slaves*. Breaking the pyramids means the land can't be claimed by song. We needed to retake as much as possible in case the peace-weaving stipulated the Empire could keep what it had captured. The Yaloh would accept nothing less.'

Lilla's tone was flat with the last words, but Tayan saw the way Kux glared.

They were all staring at him expectantly. 'The peace-weaving?' the Yalotl demanded, her fingers tight around her spear.

It was like trying to swallow past a stone in his throat. 'Betsu isn't back, is she?' he asked quietly.

Kux frowned. 'No. Why, did you get split up?'

'Then you don't know.' Tayan took a deep breath. 'There is no negotiating with the Empire of Songs. They were immovable. In the end, with Betsu's agreement, I told the Great Octave that the Yaloh and Tokob would surrender after the Wet.'

He was cut off as everyone within earshot began to protest, their voices shrill with fear and fury.

'Enough!' Lilla bellowed, though disbelief had twisted his voice high and young.

'It was a ruse, nothing more, intended to give us the rest of the Wet to train the non-fighters. Betsu escaped two weeks before I was sent back. She was coming here to tell you to appear defeated to buy time to teach everyone to fight, whether they walk the jaguar path or not. Time to build defences. But now, with this . . . they'll know. They'll know the peace-weaving meant nothing and they'll be coming. Maybe even during the Wet.'

Tayan closed his eyes. He'd accomplished absolutely nothing. 'The plan was that if they were expecting a surrender, they'd send pyramid-builders, overseers, and officials, and only a Talon or two at most to protect them. We'd wipe them out and gain the advantage, then retake Yalotlan while they sent for reinforcements. But that's obviously not going to work now. They can communicate through the song itself. Any warrior who escaped your ambushes could have crossed into the song and used the magic to tell the Singing City what is happening. They'll be coming. Maybe only days behind me, depending on when you started killing them and how quickly they passed word.'

Tayan looked from Lilla to Lutek and Kux and Tiamoko and all the others. Took in their shocked, disbelieving, deter-mined faces. He had to make them understand that everything they'd learnt through a season of war was just the beginning. That they *had to win*. 'I saw an offering made to the holy Setatmeh and I heard the prayers they spoke to it. I saw the . . . utter belief in the Pechaqueh at what they are doing. They call us frog-lickers and god-killers and if we don't win then we'll all be offered to the holy Setatmeh when they finally bring us into the glory of the song.'

337

'Glory of the song?' Kux demanded, her voice a bark of outrage.

'Holy Setatmeh? Surely you mean Drowned,' Lutek said at the same time and Tayan felt heat crawl up his throat to stain his cheeks. 'Be careful, shaman: you of all people know the magic in words. And as for us,' she added, folding her arms across her chest, 'we asked Malel herself for guidance and she answered. Is she less powerful than this song you're suddenly so fond of?'

Tayan didn't – couldn't – answer her. He turned away and walked into the trees. He needed time to think, but it was so hard, in the silence. Without the song.

'Tayan? Tay?'

Lilla's voice was low, almost as if he didn't want his husband to hear him, and for one bitter instant Tayan was tempted to pretend he hadn't. The words he'd said – the turns of phrase he'd used – echoed in his head and spirit and filled him with fear. He held out his hand behind him without looking and Lilla took it, and he let the taller man draw him gently around and into his arms again. Into that warmth that smelt of home and hope.

'You really sacrificed to Malel?' he whispered.

'We did. She told us to stop the song. I . . . don't know what's going to happen now, or why she would make us do something that deliberately draws the enemy to us early, but I trust her. It's done – or at least it's begun – and now we know they're coming. Thanks to you.'

Tayan sighed and nestled closer, rubbing his cheek against Lilla's salt-cotton. 'But no extra warriors, no element of surprise. And a two-week journey on to the Sky City to tell them. By the time I get there, the Melody will be here and you'll be outnumbered.'

Lilla's breath caught and Tayan slid his hand beneath the salt-cotton and the shirt to the hot, soft skin of his husband's back. He wanted to ask him to come home with him, to leave this patch of jungle where he would fight and bleed and kill and maybe die. He didn't. Tayan's job was to bolster Lilla's courage, to be his spine when his own lacked, his conviction in the night when Lilla's faltered. His home and hope in reply. He would never put down that burden. Lilla would never find him wanting.

'But then, if you hadn't decided to press forward, we wouldn't have met here and now,' he added and the edge of his mouth turned up as his husband pulled him even tighter. 'I'd spend the next week stumbling through the jungle falling into ditches and getting bitten by snakes and still believing I was so very clever that I'd fooled an entire empire.'

Lilla kissed his hair, his temple, his cheekbone. 'You are very clever,' he whispered fiercely. 'And you are a fool.'

Tayan pinched him. 'Rude,' he whispered. 'I've come all this way only to be insulted. Ancestors preserve me, but sometimes I do not know why I love you.'

Lilla smiled and pressed his lips to the corner of Tayan's mouth. 'Yes, you do,' he whispered.

'Yeah. I do.'

They stood quietly, wrapped in each other, remembering the feel and shape and smell of how they were together, but then Lilla suddenly stepped back. 'How did you know where to find me?' he asked. 'You were running, as if you knew I was here.'

Tayan shrugged. 'Dakto told me. He asked which direction I'd come from and said he'd check my backtrail.' He stared around. 'Isn't he back yet?'

Lilla swore. 'How many times do I have to tell him not

to wander off on his own this close to the border? Come on, we better find him.'

The war party was scattered into its Paws over half a stick to cover more ground and to better filter through the thick tangle of jungle. By the time they'd all confirmed Dakto wasn't with them, the Xenti had been missing for two hours and the light was failing.

'We're supposed to head east tomorrow, Fang, to link up with the next war party,' Lutek said into the worried quiet. 'Dakto knows that; if he can, he'll catch us up, but we can't miss that meeting for the sake of a single warrior.'

Tayan shivered, but no one contradicted her.

Lilla grunted and then nodded. 'Pass the word. We go now and we don't stop until midnight.'

They didn't make it to midnight.

In the dark, fewer than five sticks further on, arrows and darts cut into them from both sides, from below and above and seemingly everywhere. Out of the trees; out of the ground. Out of the black.

There were screams and over them the unmistakable lilt of a Pechaqueh war cry and Lilla threw Tayan into the mud and crouched over him, shouting orders to fan out, press on at the front, fall back at the rear. Split up, get out of the ambush site, then take them from two sides. He jerked and grunted, swore viciously, and cold flooded Tayan. He scrambled up and peered around, squinting, but it was impossible to see anything in the dark. Impossible for him, anyway.

Lilla pushed him into the mud again and an arrow whickered by overhead. 'Stay,' he growled and was gone, lunging into the blackness. Tayan lay on the trail for a frenzied eternity as screams and curses and thumps shattered around him, and then he rolled onto his hands and knees. He couldn't just stay here. He'd find Lilla.

Someone grabbed him around the neck before he'd moved far and he swung blindly at them. 'It's me. Lutek. Follow me and stay low.'

A body dropped next to him, coughing and clawing at the dart sticking out of their throat. An awful bubbling scream shuddered out of them and Tayan jerked forwards on instinct. He was a shaman; he could help.

Lutek grabbed a fistful of his grubby tunic and dragged him backwards. 'Now,' she growled in his ear. 'Fang's orders.'

'What?'

'Lilla says to get you out. So move.'

'Where is he? Is he all right?' Tayan babbled, struggling. Lutek transferred her grip to around his chest and wrestled him away. Into the night. Into the black.

Away from Lilla.

ENET

Everything she'd read indicated the song would only need blooding very infrequently, anywhere from once a year to every few months, only collapsing into discordance when another offering was needed to strengthen it.

Between offerings, the song would roar triumphant, filling its people with might and determination. It would strengthen the Melody marching to war; it would increase the loyalty of the slaves and the reverence they held for every Pecha. The song would increase crop yields and prevent blight and disease. The blooded song would make the Empire invincible and with that might Enet could hasten the waking of the world spirit. All the books said it.

The books were full of shit.

A mere three weeks since the Singer had blooded the song and already it was growing dissonant. Hungry.

Perhaps it was only the Singer's anger. The news from the north was uncomfortable – despite the reinforcements Pilos

342

had authorised from Xentiban, the Empire continued to lose territory and building materials and slaves in Yalotlan. The Singer was keeping as close an eye on the calendar as she was, keen to see whether the Tokob peace-weaver's guarantee of surrender would prove true. Enet knew it would not.

She hadn't let Tayan leave because she'd believed his little story. She'd sent him away because he'd asked her to confide in him – and the temptation had nearly overwhelmed her. To confess everything she'd done, everything she was working towards, to this pretty enemy shaman. An unburdening she could not possibly afford, but that she craved nonetheless.

The High Feather promised the Melody would be ready to set out by the date the Singer had divined as auspicious, but until then, they were being beaten, and the holy lord was ill pleased. He twitched and half turned towards her as they walked in the gardens on the pyramid, and Enet projected thoughts of humility and love, clearing her mind of all else.

It wasn't enough. Xac roared at the choir standing in the opening to the source. They stuttered into shocked silence, and then fled. Enet knelt among the flowers and put her forehead in the dirt. Singer Xac did not want beauty; he did not want charm or clever excuses. He wanted blood and death and retribution. He wanted to take up club and spear and go to war himself, spilling his own divine blood. Dying to save the holy Setatmeh, the living past, was a price he would pay without thought and his intentions rose like steam from his skin.

But he couldn't. All he had was his song – and it was not enough. Unless it was blooded again.

The song deepened into a mourning dirge, a weight in the hearts and spirits of all who heard it. It spoke of formless, nameless catastrophe and the dread it instilled might feed rebellion among the slaves, spark unrest among the rival families vying to be the next to put forward a candidate for Singer, take the spines from the warriors marching to Yalotlan. The strength she had given it – had given the Singer – was already fading.

It should not be like this. Not this soon.

'Holy lord, the song . . .' Enet began, speaking to the flowers beneath her face. 'It will worry your people.'

Xac stamped through the garden until he loomed over her like a storm front. 'Let it. Let them know my fury. I am their Singer and they will rage when I tell them to fucking rage. Mourn when I tell them to mourn.' He bent and latched a big hand around Enet's slender throat, dragging her up onto her toes.

'You wove your stories about enemies in the council, about how Pilos could not be trusted. You warned me to beware Yana.' He shook her so hard she had to cling to his arm to stay upright, her teeth clicking together. 'Yet you did not see how the peace-weavers distracted you while they planned to capture one of my kin for torture! Blinded by your own ambition.'

'Holy lord,' she tried.

'What have you done for me that was not also for yourself?' he mused. 'You tell me to beware Pilos when he is the only one of my Spears to do my bidding for *my* glory, not his own.'

He hurled Enet through the colonnade into the source. The air in the room flexed, the walls seeming to contract in and then bow back out, struggling to contain his power. The song's tone changed again, a warning and a promise, and both were full of blood.

He wanted. The *songstone* wanted.

The pale, crystal-flecked stone was the truth and foundation of all life, the very stuff of creation put in the earth by the world spirit. And the Singers were its children, its protectors and the living manifestation of divinity to which all aspired. To sing with the voice of songstone was to sing with the voices of the gods. To *be* gods.

And yet our gods can die. Plans can be laid to capture and torture them. Tokob can march down to their fucking river and kill them. Their magic is powerful. Perhaps even enough to rival the Singer's.

Enet lay in a tangle of limbs, gasping, but over her own voice she heard a thin keening wail. Panic flooded her and she lunged upwards. Pikte was cowering near the entrance to the source, fists up to his cheeks at the sight of Enet sprawled and – she realised belatedly – bleeding. The boy's pet monkey screeched on the end of its tether. Enet shooed Pikte out, but the Singer crossed the space between them in a few long strides and snatched him by the arm.

'What are you doing in here?' he yelled. Pikte only cried harder; life for children of the Singer was pleasant, luxurious. It did not include screams or violence or their mothers being thrown across rooms.

'I'll take him away, holy lord,' Enet said as the panic tightened her throat. The Singer grabbed the monkey and snapped its neck, and the boy screamed as if his own body had been broken. Xac raised his hand to him and Enet leapt up, dragging at his arm. The blow that had been meant for her son was loosed on her. She hit the rugs again, her head ringing and her cheek a hot, swollen agony.

Hauling Pikte by one arm, the Singer crossed to where she lay and squatted, examining her features. She shrank away from him and he flushed in pleasure at her fright, and so she forced herself upright and reached for Pikte's other arm. 'Hush, boy. Hush now.' She licked blood from her teeth, tasting the last of the grit from her tonic – her own magic – against her tongue. It was powerless against the holy lord's might.

For now.

'You think me a fucking fool, blinded by the delights between your legs?' the Singer shouted, wrenching the boy out of her grip. Xac spat in her face and she snarled, fury of her own rising to match his. She was his chief courtesan and mother of his eldest song-born. She was Spear and Great Octave. He had no right to treat her so.

This is what scheming brings you to, whispered a voice in her head. She quelled it savagely. She could still save this; save everything. Save the Empire of Songs, which was her true and only desire—

'You have steered me false ever since I took the song inside me,' the Singer said abruptly, tiny glimmers of gold sparking in his skin as the magic and the song swelled with his anger. 'I have no intention of naming you my heir, and as of now not even of naming you as one who will ascend with me. You are nothing but a body to enjoy and one that has produced only a single child.' He shook Pikte hard. 'A snivelling little shit that is as much use as a Tlaloxqueh vision-dancer. Your mind is weak and the boy you produced is worse.'

'I have not—' she began, disbelief coating her words. Where was this coming from? How could the firm ground of her status be so suddenly treacherous? Pikte was sobbing and she reached for him on instinct; Xac pulled him against his side, away from her. Taking him from her. 'I have given you something no one else would. No one else could,' she said, almost begging. 'I have done it for you, only you, so that your power knows no limits and your glory will span the world.'

Enet poured belief and sincerity into her words and into her mind. She believed this. She *believed* it and he would read nothing different in her.

Her words were smoke in the breeze, drifting past the Singer and making no impression. 'I rescind the status of Great Octave from you. There will be no limit put on my power, no leaching away of my authority into the hands of the incompetent and the greedy. No more lies whispered in my ears from your lovely mouth. I rescind the status of Spear of the City from you and name Yana in that place. At least he works for *me* and not himself.' Xac's great muscled chest ran with sweat. Pikte's sobs subsided to whimpers, his eyes squeezed shut and the flesh of his arm crushed and bruising under his father's grip.

'Holy lord,' Enet choked, collapsing to prostrate herself.

But the Singer wasn't finished. 'You are banished from my circle and from my sleeping mat. The boy is cast out. He is no longer song-born. No longer my son. And if you breathe one more word in defence of yourself or of him I will send you to join him. I will seize all your property and cast you onto the street for the Choosers and the beggars to fight over. But not before I ensure you're not pretty enough to tempt anyone into taking you into their home.'

Three Chorus warriors stood guard around the source, their usual impassivity vanished as they stared at the scene with shared expressions of horror: Enet was their patron; her fall from grace would be theirs if she so chose.

Enet could barely breathe, crushed beneath the weight of his pronouncement. With his words she had lost everything, and the work of twenty sun-years, work that had begun long before Xac was made Singer, was undone. She looked at Pikte, at his wide eyes glazed with incomprehension and his smooth, soft skin.

He would not survive on the streets for more than a day, and although it was a crime to sell Pechaqueh into slavery, there were those who would risk the city's wrath to have and to break a boy so tender. She swallowed her tears, for they would frighten him, and she made her heart into stone.

Everything I do, everything I am, is for the Empire of Songs. I am a tool of the holy Setatmeh, honed and working to awaken the world spirit. It is my sole purpose.

A sob broke from her throat as Enet rose onto her knees, reached behind her back and withdrew a sheathed knife from the waistband of her kilt. A blade of pale quartz; a hilt carved from the leg bone of a jaguar. Sacred and magical and obscene.

As the song had begun to grow in hunger and the Singer in aggression, she'd taken to bringing it with her, praying it would never be needed but unwilling to risk his wrath if it was. And here, now, in the darkest and cruellest of circumstances, when the very Empire hung by the thread of Enet's fraying power, it was needed.

Xac stiffened.

'Upon your word, I have no status among your council or within the source. I do not raise my voice in protest but offer you the stone knife for your glory. Do not take Pikte from me.' Enet splayed her left hand on the mat and drove the blade down before she could change her mind. The quartz edge bit into her little finger and she let out a hoarse scream, working it back and forth in the joint, severing muscle and tendon, popping apart the bones with a wet crack, pain like lightning arcing all the way up her arm to her shoulder, into her neck. Sweat ran down her cheek and she screamed again as she focused on the hand – *not my hand, not mine* – and kept cutting until her finger was severed at the middle knuckle.

She blinked against sweat and tears, snorting through her

nose and packing the screams back inside with the pain, and then met Xac's dumbfounded gaze. Pikte was shrieking and writhing in the Singer's grip. Would it be enough? The song thrummed with darkness, a bloody need unsated by her pain. Enet looked at her hand and wondered if she had the strength to take another finger. *The Singer has that strength and he can have them all if I can have my boy.*

Shuddering, Enet stared at her blood so bright against the pale stone blade. Then she held it out to the holy lord. 'Spare my son and I gift you my—'

'Not one word or you join him,' the Singer repeated, excited now. Calculating. His strange amber eyes, product of the magic, glowed almost like a jaguar's in the dark.

And yet there was nothing but emptiness in his expression. Emptiness and a terrible hunger that Enet knew, like a twist of a knife in her heart, that she had put there. And it was her fault, just not in the way he thought. She had blooded the song. Now she could do nothing but drink deep of its crimson depths and pray not to drown.

Enet looked at Pikte and another scream threatened, one that had nothing to do with the bleeding stump of her finger. 'Please,' she breathed, too low for him to hear. '*Don't.*'

'Choose, senior Chooser of the Singing City,' Xac mocked her. 'Choose what happens next.'

Don't.

'Choose,' he hissed suddenly and she jumped. Jumped – and chose.

Enet shuddered, dizzy with pain and cowering at the promise of more to come, pain such as she'd never known and that would never leave her.

For the Empire.

'You have cast out our son. He will live and die unknown and unmourned.' She sobbed out breath, sobbed out her heart and her spirit and cast them to the Underworld. 'I do not raise my voice in protest but offer you the stone knife.' The ritual words were obscene upon her tongue as she made a tiny, innocent-seeming gesture with the tip of the blade.

She could not save Pikte. Whether on the streets or here in the source, he was already dead. But she had this chance to save herself and so elevate the Empire into glory brighter than it had ever known. To do the unthinkable in order to reap the unimaginable.

If she would offer the Singer even this, how could he cast her aside? No other would feed his spirit this way. Only Enet. Only his beloved Enet.

'Nothing you do is wrong, holy lord,' she whispered as the song began to swell and in her cowardice she did not look at Pikte's tear-stained face. 'You are the Singer. You are divine. And I offer you the stone knife.'

He's dead anyway. Dead anyway dead anyway dead anyway.

There had never been anything Enet would not do for the Empire, for the glory of them all and not just herself. For the world spirit. But never had she been pushed so far; never had her choice been so difficult, or felt so wrong despite being right.

Setatmeh, please. Setatmeh, tell me this is right.

The Singer snatched the knife from her and she flinched. His power made her dizzy, squashed her to the size of an ant beneath his gaze. 'Nothing you do or desire is wrong, holy lord.' The words were foul on her tongue.

'And if I ram this into your eye?' he breathed. The song rumbled in the background, the lust inside it building.

Enet swallowed. *Do it. Do it and leave my boy alone. Do it.* 'Then I will watch your greatness through the other.'

The Singer hefted the knife and Enet tensed against the

promise of pain. Power surged through the source until the air crackled as if with pent lightning and Xac's skin flushed golden-red with magic and he tightened his grip on the boy's arm until Pikte howled, a howl abruptly cut off by the blade crunching through his bird-delicate ribcage and into a lung.

Enet screamed as her son's blood splashed her kilt, as agony sank its fangs deep into her heart.

Her breath shuddered out as rage, lust, hate, and sheer fucking joy boiled along her nerve endings, as the song flexed and her son's father plunged the knife back into the little body she'd strained to birth, into the soft undulating belly this time. She screamed again, but still it grew, the power, the need, and the release, towering above them all like a mountain and crushing Enet's grief into nothing, compacting it down small and hard until it was diamond.

The song roared upwards as it had done with Betsu, and the Singer stabbed again and again, grunts of ecstasy throbbing from his mouth as red, red, *red* blood poured over his hands, hot and sticky. So much blood in such a small body and every drop of it was wrung from Enet's own heart; every drop was a knife that flayed her until she was raw.

Coward that she was, she let go of the diamond of her grief and threw herself headlong into the song until it engulfed her, swallowing any emotion other than those the Singer projected, hiding from the pain behind his lust. She reached out and dipped her palm into the crimson, this last vital remnant of her child. She smeared it across her face and then across the Singer's, marking them both in their son's death and life. Hoarse wails tore from her throat.

Xac reared back in surprise, blinking at the stickiness on his eyelashes, and then he roared his satisfaction and stabbed the stone knife in again and again until the boy was meat and the song careened out of control all across the Empire.

351

The Singer lusted, the song lusted, and Enet could do nothing more than exist within that lust. Inside her, the diamond burnt – as it would forever. Her diamond child.

'The song needs this,' the Singer said when he finally cast the knife to one side and reached bloody hands for her, pulling her onto him. Sickened at his need and her own, Enet took him into her with a sodden, hateful cry of black satisfaction.

'The song needs blood and war. I know this; I know the song. I know what it needs: I and no other. And if the council and the Chorus don't fucking like it, they can join the boy in death, to *my* glory.' He squeezed the stump of Enet's missing finger, making her scream until fresh tears streaked the gory mask of her face.

'*I. Am. The. Song.*'

THE SINGER

The source, Singing City, Pechacan, Empire of Songs

I am the song and the song is me. The song is bloody and needful and will be fed.

This is my will, and cannot be opposed.

This Empire that I have created resounds to my song, my name. The people are mine to use as I need. It is my will that drives them, my rule that cows them, my desires that shape them. I exist in the blood of them and they will give me blood in return. It is I who allows them to sleep and I who rouses them to war. I who strengthen the weak and discard the useless.

I will feed from them and my song will grow.

I am their strength and will, and they are the knife and club of my retribution and we will sweep through the Yaloh and Tokob and batter them into the ground. Their fields are mine, their homes are mine, their lives are mine.

Their blood is mine.

The Melody will bring these ejab to me and I will peel their flesh for the Setatmeh to feast on. I will cut their spines from their bodies. I will roast them over coals from the feet up and feed their meat to my council.

My song will drive them to ruin. Those who live will do so in the agony of their wrongdoing.

I am the song and it is bloody.

I am the song and it is war.

LILLA

So thirsty, and throbbing pain in his head and jaw exacerbated by dehydration. All around him the groans and mutters and low, hopeless laments of Tokob and Yaloh.

As he had for the last however many days, Lilla woke and tried to remember what had happened. Just fragments, scattered, parts of it coming to him at odd moments or out of sequence, other parts of it lost, maybe forever.

There'd been darkness and then arrows, he knew that. Shouting orders, one of them for someone to stay low and hidden, but he didn't know who. Couldn't remember their face or name. Warriors in the dark, and a dart that went into his elbow, sharp and hot like fire, and then he was running and fighting, but his arm was going numb and his tongue was getting thick in his mouth. Warriors, more fighting, and he couldn't find a clear space to stop and identify the poison or the medicine to counter it. His throat was a thin hollow reed that whistled and his tongue flopped over it, blocking it, and he couldn't breathe and he was on his knees and there was a club, arcing into the sky above him and then falling, falling, falling.

And then nothing.

And then pain in a band around the back of his head, in his ears, and his jaw that clicked whenever he worked his mouth. Pain that made it hard to think, that made him slow to hear and to respond and to move, his limbs not under his control.

Lilla lay in the leaf-litter with the others, some huddled together against the chill, the rest separate, as far as the ropes would allow them to get. Together or apart, each was alone, locked in a private misery of hurts and fears.

Footsteps passed his head and Lilla tucked his chin to his chest and tensed his sore muscles. Nobody hit him this time and slowly he uncurled and blinked at the greying dawn and the small fire where the dog warriors of the Empire of Songs were clustered.

'. . . awake? Lilla, you awake?'

He knew that voice. Maybe. Blearily, and wincing at the clicking in his neck, he turned his head. A woman. A warrior. Scar on her chin. Couldn't remember her name.

'Are you with us? We're going to do it today. In an hour, just before we start to march. All right? You're with us, Fang, yes?'

Lilla put his head down in the leaf-litter and closed his eyes. Fang? The constant whine in his head was a little quieter today; perhaps whatever had broken inside him was healing. Would heal faster if he had some water. So thirsty.

Daylight bright behind his eyelids and sudden chaos. Lunging and shadows flickering. A wrench on the rope around his neck, the one that tied him to the others, and Lilla's eyes opened and he squinted. Eight lines of twenty. Eight long ropes with twenty warriors on them. He knew that; he'd counted that. Yesterday?

The warriors on Lilla's rope were on their feet, kicking and lunging, trying to scramble away or grab weapons from the dog warriors, but it was hard; everyone had a second rope around their waists, and their hands were tied to it. They had some movement, but not enough to wield a knife at anything other than the closest of quarters. The dogs guarding them, of course, didn't need to get close. They had spears.

He rolled onto his knees, pain lancing through his head so he made a noise low in the back of his throat. He stayed there a few seconds, fighting down nausea, and then planted his right foot and pushed, stood wobbling.

'Fight,' screamed the woman with the scarred chin. 'Lilla, fight.' But then she couldn't say any more because there was a spear in her chest and it had stolen her words and her breath. Her heart. Her life. They ripped the obsidian out of her body – a pretty green glass, unusual and winking in the sun where it wasn't stained red – and she fell, and all over the clearing other people were falling, strings of them, one after another or in clumps. Some were screaming or praying and a few simply cowered, and everyone on their feet was cut down.

The man next to him pulled back onto his knees. 'Stay down. It's over. Fucking over,' he said. Young, he was, and big. Lilla didn't know his name.

He tried to make sense of it all, to understand the faces that leered at him and screamed up close, jeering and prodding him with the butts of spears. Were they spirits? His ancestors? Something hit him in the back, pushing him off balance. He tried to put his hands out but they wouldn't

357

leave his sides – oh, the rope – and his cheek slapped the dirt and the pain exploded in his head again and it went dark. Not the world, just his eyes. Black.

Water. Blood-warm and sweet, in his mouth. Nectar. Lilla swallowed and there was more, the pressure of a vessel against his lower lip, and the sensation of someone lifting his head, their fingers digging into the monstrous hurt that was the base of his skull, but the water . . . oh, the water was good.

He drank again, and again, and they let him have as much as he wanted in small, patient sips and the more he swallowed the clearer his vision seemed to get until eventually he looked up and saw a face he knew. Male, a string of red beads in a braid hanging by one ear. A small wooden stud in his lower lip.

'Hello, Lilla.'

'Hello,' Lilla whispered, but then the name floated away again.

'Time to walk. Up you get.' The man helped him to stand, carefully. 'You've got some stitches in the back of your head and the shaman thinks your skull might have cracked. You should be feeling better by the time we reach the Singing City and they'll assess whether you can join the Melody.'

Lilla nodded, not understanding most of it, just happy to see a friendly face. The line of people in front of him began to move and there was a tug on his neck as the rope tightened. Lilla followed.

The movement and the water focused his mind as it had focused his eyes and he looked around. They were moving east and south, as far as he could tell. And now that he concentrated, he recognised most of the faces around him, sullen and bloody and filthy though they were. The warriors – the survivors – of his war party.

Stay.

The word echoed in his head and Lilla remembered it. Remembered saying it as the ambush was sprung and his people began to die around him. *Stay.*

Tayan.

Stumbling, Lilla scanned the lines for his husband's familiar slender form, the blue of his kilt or the particular set of his head when he was being stubborn. Couldn't see it. Couldn't see him.

The survivors of Lilla's war party gathered together, tied like sheaves of palm, and Tayan wasn't with them. Tayan, called the stargazer. Shaman. Peace-weaver. The keeper of Lilla's heart. Gone.

Lilla put his head on one side and let a thick cable of wet hair fall across his mouth; he sucked the rain out of it, licked the moisture from his own shoulders, his upper lip. It wasn't enough.

As if he'd been waiting for this, the familiar man, the face he knew, appeared at his side. He matched his pace to Lilla's and held a gourd to his lips – the warrior managed a few awkward gulps that were gone too soon, barely wetting his throat. But then, there in his mind, as if washed clean by the water, was the name.

'Dakto,' he breathed.

The Xenti smiled. 'Ah, you're back with us. You've been unconscious or just gone for days now – we were starting to think you were permanently damaged. I suppose you still might be. We'll know in time.'

'What are . . . Why . . .' Lilla looked at his own bonds and then glanced back at the warrior behind him; she was staring at Dakto with fixed, unrelenting hatred. 'Why aren't you roped?'

'Because I am loyal.'

'I don't . . . I don't understand.'

Dakto snorted and gave him a little more water, brushing the hair back out of Lilla's eyes for him. 'Of course you don't,' he said. 'You've got a broken head. The others all figured it out days ago. I am a Whisper, a macaw of the Fourth Talon of the Melody. Ilandeh and I were sent to Tokoban to learn about you so that we could bring you under the song with the fewest possible lives lost. To save you.' His smile seemed genuine and Lilla smiled back. It was only polite.

'I don't understand,' he said again, apologetic.

Dakto squeezed the back of his neck. 'Don't worry: everything will make sense when you're under the song – we're only a few sticks away now. Everything will change then, Lilla.'

They walked for a while in silence. None of it made the least bit of sense. 'Where's Tayan?' Lilla asked suddenly, remembering.

Dakto's mouth went thin. 'Dead, most likely,' he said. 'I'm sorry, but it's best just to forget him now. Concentrate on carving a new life for yourself. One dedicated to peace and discipline and prosperity for all. You'll love it, Lilla,' he added, light in his face. 'Oh, how you'll love the Empire of Songs and the knowledge you're part of something truly great, truly unique. A warrior with a purpose.'

'Malel. The ancestors,' he managed, but his mind was clouding over again as if Dakto had stuffed it with too many pictures and ideas. He could only cling to one. Tayan was dead. *Tayan was dead.*

'Lilla?'

Knees striking dirt.

'Lilla? Wait, stop! One of the injured is down again.'

Black.

* * *

'So you're a Pecha?'

Dakto grinned at the belligerence in his tone. 'Someone's feeling better. You look it, too. Don't have that moon-mad, blank-eyed gaze your frog-lickers walk around with any more.'

Despite the insults, he was quick to hold a gourd of water to Lilla's lips. It was warm and bitter with herbs. Lilla balked at the first mouthful, but then identified the familiar taste of healing medicine. He drank it gratefully and his head, which hurt just as much today but seemed to work better, cleared some more.

'But to answer your question, I'm half-Pecha. My mother was a shaman of the Xentib. Her ancestors told her that Xentiban would be brought under the song. When she tried to tell her village elders, they refused to heed her word. Blind and stupid, like your people, like the Yaloh. She lived near the border with Pechacan, so she crossed over and she listened to the song and she learnt its truth. Its greatness. She tried again to tell the village the best thing they could do when my people – my father's people – came was to embrace the song. Again they would not listen, but this time in their ignorance the elders banished her. She returned to Pechacan and offered her services as a shaman to my father, as a paid servant. He agreed, intrigued by her cleverness. A few years later, I was born.'

'She sold herself into slavery?'

Dakto's punch doubled Lilla over, and the warriors he was tied between stumbled as he dragged, wheezing, at the rope around their necks.

'My mother was never a slave. And neither am I.'

Dakto hauled Lilla upright. 'I am half-Pecha and a Whisper. I am elite among the macaws. You are nothing, lower than the mould beneath my sandal, and you will die as nothing unless you take the song within you and become a Pecha in your heart as you never can be in blood.'

361

Lilla breathed around the fire in his ribs. Dakto had held nothing back in that punch and it had woken the agony in his skull. He pushed, regardless. 'Nothing, am I? That's not what you thought when you wanted to fuck me,' he said and blew a kiss at Dakto. The warriors tied before and behind him jeered and whistled. 'Do you have to practise being Pechaqueh in your heart, too? Seeing as you're only a half-blood.'

'Nothing you say will affect my loyalty,' Dakto said, but without heat.

'You knew freedom in the Sky City for a year,' Lilla croaked after a long pause to collect his scattered thoughts. A half-blood would never be as respected as a full Pecha. Perhaps that gave them some common ground. 'You had friends among the Tokob, a home, and food. You hunted with us; you fought with us. You had a life with us, Dakto. You could have that again. A partner, children. Freedom.'

'I am already free. And I am loyal to the Empire.'

'You may be loyal, but are you really free?' Lilla asked. 'Your mother may never have worn the slave brand, but it sounds like she sold herself to your father nonetheless. How much did she get to choose what happened to her after that – and how much do you?'

The medicine had dried his mouth and added an almost manic edge to his thoughts. He had no idea whether his words were making sense, or what Dakto's reaction to them might be. He did his best to brace himself for another punch.

The Whisper was silent for twenty steps. 'Fuck you, Toko,' he snarled eventually, and stamped off towards the head of the column.

'Nicely done,' the woman behind him said. 'That piece of shit.'

There were still many things Lilla couldn't remember, but

the pain and rage he felt confirmed one definite truth: Dakto had been a friend, part of Lilla's Paw, and a trusted warrior. And it had all been a lie.

In return for his betrayal, Lilla would find his weakness and he'd slip a chisel into that crack and split him open for the vultures to feed upon. He clung to the notion, gripping it tight so that he didn't have to acknowledge the agony in his head or the persistent scream in his ears. Or Tayan being dead.

They walked for a few more hours and then the song was there, without warning, impossible and overwhelming and there, outside him and inside and everywhere in between. Music in his blood and muscles, in his bones and organs, heart and balls. Entrancing, beautiful, possessing. As if he belonged to it. The string of captives came to a ragged halt, those on the other side of the invisible line of magic asking what was wrong, those within the song stumbling, shaking their heads like dogs dislodging flies.

The dog warriors were laughing, though surely it had been the same when they were first captured.

'Here.' Dakto had appeared by his side again, a lightness in his step and smile. He reached out and put both his hands over Lilla's ears; the song continued unabated and unmuffled. He wasn't hearing it normally, the way he heard everything else. It was *inside him*. Lilla's mouth dropped open.

Dakto was watching him intently, that lopsided smile still there. He removed his hands and took a deep, satisfied breath. 'Now do you see who we are, the blessing and power of our magic? Now you know the merest sliver of our glory.'

'Glory?' Lilla asked, raising his voice over the song and provoking another burst of laughter from the warriors guarding them. 'How is being forced to listen to something glory? It's just another form of slavery – we have no choice but to listen, as your slaves have no choice but to obey.'

Dakto sighed, his disappointment clear. 'You'll learn,' he said. 'You'll come to understand it eventually. And I hope you do, Fang Lilla. You're a good man despite your pettiness earlier; I'd be pleased to fight alongside you for the glory of the Empire.'

Lilla bared his teeth. 'I will never fight for the song or the Empire. You don't have to fight for them either. If we're in the song, then we're in Xentiban. Your homeland. You could—'

Dakto laughed, cutting him off. 'I was born in Pechacan. The only time I've spent here has been while bringing these people under the song. I am a macaw of the Melody, a Whisper. I have Pechaqueh blood in my veins and the song in my heart.'

'You have Xentib blood in your veins too, the blood of free people enslaved. That blood gives you a choice.'

'No.' Dakto's voice was cold. 'Stop now, Lilla. Listen to the song; embrace it. You'll understand soon enough. And when you do, your life will truly begin.'

PILOS

Melody fortress, the dead plains,
Tlalotlan, Empire of Songs
204th day of the Great Star at morning

For the second time in a month, the song had swept out of control and cut through them all with clangouring hate and violence and need. And for the second time in a month, Pilos hadn't been there to help his Singer.

Again, Enet had refused to communicate with him, and all Citla could tell him was that the song contained a power she had never felt before. Enough to shake her spirit almost out of her flesh and send her into a faint from which she'd been slow to recover. The hairs stood up on Pilos's arms at the thought of what might have happened to him if he'd been communicating through the song at the time. He had none of Citla's strength or skill; surely he would have been lost.

It was because of the changes to the song, clear even now, ten days later, that they were ready to march early. Eagles, macaws, dogs, and even the more experienced slave warriors had tripled their efforts in response to the unknown threat to the Singer's safety.

The hawk Talon would accompany the Melody to the capital and take up residence in the large compound on the outskirts to continue their training there. If the war went badly – *praise Setatmeh it will not* – then they were already a week's march closer to Yalotlan.

Though if I do have to throw barely competent hawks at the enemy, we're truly fucked.

Feather Atu stood at Pilos's side. 'Feels strange to be heading out again so soon. In the Wet. Reminds me of Quitoban.'

Pilos snorted. 'You were still sucking your mother's tit when we brought the Quitob under the song,' he teased, for Atu had been one of the youngest Pechaqueh ever to become an eagle and his youth and wide-eyed innocence had been a constant source of amusement among the older warriors.

His second laughed. 'There was many a day I'd have gladly run back home for a cuddle during that campaign,' he admitted.

'Wouldn't we all,' Pilos muttered. The Quitob offensive had been bitter, drawn-out, and a fucking shambles, if he was honest, and though it was fifteen years in the past, the memory still bit at him. Forcing the final the battle in a flooded river delta, holy Setatmeh snatching the unwary on both sides, and warriors drowning in mud only strides from the fighting, sucked under before anyone could reach them. He'd lost an entire Talon of dogs and Coyotes and a full fifth of his eagles before the Quitob capitulated.

Now one in six of the dogs he was taking to war were Quitob, their tenacious, fierce determination put to work bringing peace to all Ixachipan. The glory of the song made manifest.

He didn't doubt the Yaloh and Tokob would fight like the

very lords of the Underworld in the moons to come, and he worried for the Melody as if each warrior, down to the lowliest slave, were his children. How many would they lose this time? How many offspring and partners would never see loved ones again? How many dog warriors, drunk on promises of freedom for themselves and their families – promises Pilos himself had made – would instead die screaming on Tokob and Yaloh spears?

Too many. The number, no matter how small, was always too many.

The eagles' feathered banner was hoisted into the grey sky and the march began, first to the Singing City where Pilos would seek an audience with the holy lord, and then on, through Pechacan and Xentiban, out from under the song once more, and, with the Singer's blessing, for the very last time.

Pilos's feathered cloak fluttered behind him as they marched down the limestone roads, eight abreast, weapons and shields bright, war paint fresh on faces and arms. There was a long way to go yet, but the paint focused his warriors' minds and reminded them that they didn't march to sport or their families. They marched to war.

They made the Singing City in a week, but there were no messengers from the source waiting under the ceremonial arch to tell Pilos that the council or the Singer wished to see him. Despite the second incident with the song. *Or because of it?*

Pilos gritted his teeth and marched in impenetrable silence and his Feathers faded back behind him to avoid being a target if his temper snapped. He didn't realise his mood had spread to the thousands of warriors marching behind him until Feather Atu coughed and then appeared at his shoulder.

'Perhaps a song to lift the heart, High Feather?'

Pilos grunted, eyes fixed ahead, but then Atu's words reached him and he consciously loosened his hands and shoulders. 'Yes, of course,' he said and then his gaze flicked sideways and he huffed a laugh. Elaq was marching off the edge of the road, unconsciously in step with the Melody and waiting for Pilos to glance over.

Atu touched belly and throat and vanished and, at a gesture, Elaq replaced him. Moments later the Feathers began the song of Chitenec, an old favourite. It rippled down the seemingly endless snake of warriors with its tail of cooks and builders and weapons-makers and offerings. Pilos and Elaq marched in silence for a while, listening to the voices settle into harmony. The song within the song.

'Atu's right; it does lift the heart,' Pilos said and clapped Elaq on the shoulder. 'Business or pleasure?'

'The former,' Elaq said, and Pilos sighed. Of course it was. 'About the Great Octave; about the song,' he added and Pilos was suddenly grateful for the singing of thousands of warriors behind him. He let it fill his consciousness, focusing on the rhythm and the story, so that as Elaq spoke, the words mingled in his mind and would be harder see. A poor imitation of the Listeners' method to transmit confidential information.

'Tell me about the song first,' he said. Whatever Enet was up to could wait; the changes to the song could not.

'Word from the source is that Pikte, son of the Great Octave and the Singer, is dead.'

'The song first,' Pilos repeated and Elaq held up a hand to still him. The eagle so rarely acted as Pilos's equal that when he did, it meant something, so Pilos bit his tongue and waited.

'Pikte was murdered. In the source, by Enet and the Singer. That's what caused the change in the song—'

'Stop,' Pilos interrupted, his stride faltering. 'This can't be right. Why are you saying this?'

Elaq marched in silence, sympathy mingled with grim reality twisting his hard face into something harder. Pilos felt sick and the warriors' singing suddenly seemed more like the wailing of spirits condemned to the Underworld. The afternoon was grey and windy – a typical end-of-Wet day – but it seemed more. Portents in everything.

'The Singer was casting Enet out, stripping her of title and status, and so she offered him Pikte and the old ritual stone knife from back before. He took it, Pilos. He blooded the song, against all tradition, against the law. He blooded the song with his own son.'

There was such bewilderment in Elaq's voice, usually so calm and capable, that it choked Pilos and he put his hand on the man's shoulder again, giving and taking wordless comfort even as his mind rebelled at what he was being told. It couldn't be true. *It couldn't.*

'Councillor Yana's nephew is one of the Singer's courtesans,' Elaq continued after a pause, as if hearing his thoughts. Behind them, the ballad was coming to an end; they didn't have much time. 'He heard it from another courtesan, who heard it from an administrator, who got it from the Chorus warrior *who was there when it happened.*'

'But—' Pilos began, but Elaq interrupted again, and he let him.

'The first time the song skewed, one of the peace-weavers, the woman Betsu, was brought into the source. The courtesan doesn't think she ever left. We think that was the first, because Enet let it be known that one of the peace-weavers had returned home. The other followed a couple of weeks later – and he really did go; I had people watching. But not the Yalotl, as far as we can tell. Yana thinks the Singer killed her, too.'

'Enet is blooding the song?' the High Feather whispered, dread dragging icy claws down his spine. 'Is she truly fucking insane? Does she know nothing of our history? She will destroy us all, destroy the Empire itself! *Why would she do this?*'

'Yana and I are making enquiries, High Feather, but at this stage we don't know whose idea it was. We don't know if the Singer decided to blood the song, or if she encouraged him and provided him with . . . the means to do so.'

'The Singer would not do that,' Pilos said immediately. But was it loyalty or truth?

'Her lust for power has no limits,' Elaq said quietly.

It was rare for Pilos to be lost for words, but he could do nothing other than stare around him in bewildered disgust. Despite its size and strength, despite its military prowess and wealth in food and jade and slaves, the Empire of Songs forever trod a knife's edge. The song lifted up the Pechaqueh and subdued and glorified the other tribes brought under its power, but if that song broke, if it became corrupted, even the most content slaves might become restless. The song was the resin that bound them together; Enet was wilfully, intentionally picking it apart. How would that bring them the stability needed to waken the world spirit?

'I'm almost afraid to ask, but is there anything else?' Pilos asked eventually, because Elaq had that shifty look he knew well.

'The other information I have for you is from Councillor Yana. He is almost certain Enet controls a songstone quarry, at least one, owned through a number of subsidiaries so that it cannot be traced back to her. For the last four sun-years she has controlled all the provision of songstone to the Empire. He says that through clever manipulation of the council she has been earning enormous sums selling it to the architects capping pyramids and expanding the reach of the song. When you forwarded on Whisper Ilandeh's report that Tokoban is rich in songstone and it was read out in council, Yana says Enet was furious. He thinks she fears the loss of her control over its supply.'

Pilos gaped again. The news, in its way, was just as shocking. 'Songstone is divine,' he spluttered. 'It is not to be, to be fucking *bartered* for like a slave or an ear of corn. How has the council allowed this to happen? She cannot just *sell it*. No one *sells* songstone.'

Elaq's mouth twisted with bitter humour. 'The costs have been cleverly disguised – the use of artisans to quarry and shape the stone before removal; the prohibitive costs of transport, both of materials to move the stone and in offerings to any holy Setatmeh encountered along the route; the alleged difficulty in accessing the stone itself and the increased labour required to chip it free. Not one of the costs has ever actually been attributed to the stone itself. That remains, for all intents and purposes, free and sacred as it always has been. The Great Octave has merely been requesting compensation for the labour.'

'That bitch-slut-snake,' Pilos growled. It made sense though. For years Pilos had tried to discover the source of Enet's influence and failed. The number of families who could afford the honour of commissioning a songstone cap for a pyramid – gifting the money directly to the source rather than to anyone who owned a songstone mine – was vanishingly small, and nearly all of them had a seat on the council. And . . . all of those councillors were loyal to Enet. 'So Enet can deny her rivals access to songstone if she chooses, or she can barter for information from them. Payment in knowledge if not in jade.'

Pilos turned to walk backwards and caught Atu's eye. He

circled his finger in the air and his second nodded, and as the last notes of the marching song faded away, he began another.

'That is the councillor's thought also,' Elaq said when their voices were covered by the Melody's. 'And the Great Octave sees you as her biggest rival. If she has as much power as Yana fears, it's likely why the Singer didn't meet you today. You need protecting, High Feather,' Elaq added. 'I'd like permission to come with you, to watch your back and front and every other fucking direction. I wouldn't put it past Enet to have assassins among your Melody – even your eagles.'

Pilos smiled despite himself. 'What an ignoble end for the mighty High Feather, to be gutted by one of his own, seduced from him by the snake in the council,' he said with mock solemnity. 'Peace, my friend. With fever in Quitoban, a conquest in the Wet, and the blooding of the song, my life means little in the grand scheme of things. Still, I promise to be careful,' he added, seeing Elaq's scowl. 'But you know I need you in the city. You and Yana are the only two people there I can trust. I need you working – discreetly – to discover anything else you can. Definitive proof of the blooding, for a start. And look at my wealth, too, will you? Start drawing up papers to have me buy any mining rights in Tokoban. I'll see it's worked and gifted as it should be. For free. For the song. The more we can do to loosen Enet's grasp, the better.'

'As the High Feather commands,' Elaq said with pointed courtesy.

Pilos gusted a sigh. 'Setatmeh preserve me from overprotective eagles and the manipulations of beautiful women. I'll be careful. And you be careful, too. You're living in the viper's den, remember. Under the song, my friend.'

TAYAN

Sky City, Malel, Tokoban
205th day of the Great Star at morning

They'd fled the fighting, deep into the darkness beneath the trees, moving fast and quiet until Tayan was thoroughly lost.

He'd sat in miserable, shivering silence through the rest of the night, and as dawn broke they'd returned to the ambush site. They'd found a few survivors and a lot of bodies. They didn't find Lilla.

Tayan stopped paying attention after that. His husband was gone. Not dead, not unless he'd crawled away and died in the undergrowth somewhere. Captured, then. A prisoner of the Empire of Songs. A slave. Lutek's mouth had moved and her arms flapped, but the shaman didn't care. He'd followed numbly when the survivors began to head north, taking the straightest route they could towards Tokoban and Malel. He was going home. He just didn't have anyone to go home to.

And now there it was, the Sky City a bright blur above them as Tayan climbed out of the jungle below the Swift

Water. After all this time, it was almost impossible for him to conceive it. It didn't take long for the relieved chatter among the surviving warriors to fade, though, as they made their way past the Swift Water's loop and towards the walls and no one challenged them.

Tayan managed to swallow his grief long enough to summon some worry. 'What's happening? What can you see?'

'It's what we can't see that's the problem,' Tiamoko said uneasily. They'd found him the morning after the ambush unconscious beneath two corpses, covered in their blood; the enemy must have assumed he was dead. 'No warriors watching the approaches and barely any farmers in the fields or the orchards. Only two pipes running from the water temples, not four. And . . . shit, is that smoke?'

Tayan squinted desperately to where the young warrior was pointing. 'Where?'

'Looks like Xentibec's burning,' he said, and at that, no matter their fatigue and their wounds, they began to run again.

The weeks of journeying had done more for Tayan's strength than he'd known until their flight from the ambush, and now he kept up with the warriors as they laboured up the hill and the images slowly resolved themselves in his poor vision. Smoke was billowing from at least four, no, five places in the Xentib quarter, and the gate leading out of it – the one closest to their route as they followed the boundary wall past the Swift Water – remained closed.

Tiamoko sprinted ahead, but he slowed before he got there and turned back. 'I can hear fighting!' he shouted and then hurled himself at the gate. It was locked from the inside and, even stranger, barricaded from without. They tore away the wooden props and the stones piled against the gate. 'Up and over,' he said when it was clear and Lutek ran at him, put her foot in the cradle of his hands and was thrown upwards.

She got her elbows over the top and stared down through the smoke, then scrambled up to straddle the gate.

The others were shouting questions, but she pointed downwards and vanished. The shouting and screams were clear now and dread was a punch to the gut. Was it the Empire? The gate creaked open and Lutek's face appeared. 'I don't know what the fuck is going on, but you need to get in here. There are Yaloh fighting Xentib.'

Everyone paused. 'What?' someone asked.

Lutek pulled the gate wider and they crowded through, into burning buildings and savage fighting. The Xentib were a mass of terrified citizens hiding behind their few score warriors, but the Yaloh were there in their hundreds, it seemed. Stones were being hurled from deep in the crowd. Blood spurted and a woman went down, screaming.

Tayan stepped forward. 'Xentib! Gate's open,' he roared as loud as he could. Those nearest looked back and then sprinted towards the gate without hesitation. Tayan and the rest flattened themselves against the buildings, urging them on. More and more left the protection of their warriors and began to flee, and the first were passing them when a flight of arrows arced against the morning.

'Stop shooting!' Tayan screamed, waving his arms. '*Stop shooting.*'

But the Xentib were moving as one now, all of them running, and more arrows were falling among them. One shattered on the stone in front of Tayan, the flint head ricocheting through the air to hit him below the eye. He rocked backwards at the impact and felt the immediate, hot rush of blood.

'Stop!' he yelled again as the Xentib raced past him and the Yaloh followed, faces contorted with mad and inexplicable rage and a terrible sort of justice.

Lutek and some of the warriors tried to get between Yaloh and Xentib, but they were too mixed in together now and the attackers were hacking spears and axes into the backs of the fleeing people. They were yelling too and being ignored, and the runners were slowing as they got trapped in the narrowness of the gate, fighting and snarling and screaming to get through.

More people racing into the street from the far end – Tokob, shoving people out of their way so they could get in. Tayan felt a moment of utter panic at their appearance, but then they too started dragging Yaloh out of the mass and forcing them back. Holding weapons to them until they backed away. The street echoed with conflicting voices and orders and screeching, and the shaman waded back in, hauling on the arm of a Yalotl with an axe raised. He fought for the weapon, shouting incoherently, clung on even when the man's other hand punched him in the face, right in his split cheek.

Tayan howled and headbutted him, pure instinct, and felt the man's nose crunch under the impact. He ripped the axe out of his hand and shoved him backwards. 'Fuck off,' he screamed right in his face, and stepped into the gap to stop the next, dropping the axe. He wasn't going to fight Yaloh, no matter what.

Too slowly, the Tokob overwhelmed the rioters and wriggled through their number to form a cordon between them and the Xentib, who continued to struggle out through the gate as the fires intensified, choking them all in black smoke. When the last Xenti had run through the city gate, Tayan went to look. None of them had stopped once they reached safety and the fastest were already disappearing into the jungle below.

He turned back into the city. 'What the fucking *fuck* was

that all about?' he shouted and a few sullen Yaloh turned to face him, hostile.

'You should know!' one of them shouted back, 'seeing as you were such good friends with her.' The noise began to build again and the anger was firmly directed at him now. The Tokob, a mix of warriors, ejab and others, tightened their lines and some began shouting back.

Tayan looked back to Lutek and Tiamoko, one hand pressed to the wound in his face that was beginning to take all his attention. 'What are they on about?' he demanded.

'There's been some trouble,' Tiamoko began, but then Elder Apok was pushing through the crowd with an armed escort.

'Peace-weaver Tayan? And . . . you're from Fang Lilla's Paw, aren't you? Come with me.'

'What's going on?' Lutek demanded. She grabbed Apok by the shoulder and spun him around. 'What's going on?' she repeated, louder now.

A warrior passed his spear between the pair of them. 'Please release the high elder,' he said respectfully. Lutek stepped back as if bitten and the shock of his words leapt from one to the other.

'High elder?' Tayan stuttered, the words tripping over each other. 'What has happened to Vaqix?'

'I am glad to see you returned, Peace-weaver, though in unfortunate circumstances,' Apok began when they were all seated in the council chamber. There were faces missing, not just Vaqix's.

'What are these circumstances?' Lutek grated. 'We're down there in Yalotlan freeing slaves and sending them here to regain their strength so they might fight with us and you're letting them be killed alongside Xentib who've lived here for years? What about the Quitob we sent? Where are they?'

'I'm sorry, but I must hear your news first. Peace-weaver?' The council chamber fell silent and Tayan filled it with the same story he'd given Lilla and the others in Yalotlan, Lutek and Tiamoko's presence adding to the horrible dreamlike sense that he was reliving those moments – but this time without his husband.

The councils of the two tribes descended into the same bickering that had swept the Paws, and Tayan sat in their midst, not listening. Exhausted. Heartsick. His face swollen and caked in dried blood.

Tiamoko stretched across Lutek and patted his knee awkwardly. 'Fang Lilla won't give in that easily,' he murmured. 'He'll stay alive, and when we defeat the Empire of Songs you can go and find him.'

The shaman managed to force one corner of his mouth up into some ghastly approximation of a smile he didn't feel.

'May we know why the city was on fire and Yaloh were slaughtering guests of the Tokob?' Lutek demanded when the councils had gone over Tayan's story for the third time without making any different decisions. Yaloh elders immediately began to protest.

'Are you saying we are not guests of your tribe?' one asked and Lutek tensed to stand. Tiamoko and Tayan both clamped a hand on her arms and stilled her.

'We seek to understand,' Tayan said quickly.

'There was an . . . incident,' Apok said diplomatically. 'High Elders Vaqix and Zasso, as well as Eja Elder Tika, were murdered, the day before Tika, Kime, and Xessa were to attempt to capture a Drowned. The Xenti woman Ilandeh vanished the same night and, over time, suspicion fell on her as the killer. Tensions between Yaloh and Xentib have been building ever since. What you saw was the latest in a series of riots that—'

'Vaqix is dead?' Lutek demanded.

'Riots? More like murder!' Tiamoko shouted.

'Ilandeh?' Tayan said, dumb. 'Impossible.' High Elder Apok spread his hands and the council began to argue yet again. From the look on his face, it was an increasingly common occurrence. 'She wouldn't,' Tayan said. 'She was a refugee; she was a merchant, not a killer.'

'Dakto,' Lutek said and Tayan frowned at her tone. 'Dakto found you and said he was going to check your backtrail. He sent you on ahead, knowing you'd distract Lilla and the rest of us with your news. Buying him time to find Empire warriors and set up the ambush. And he knows everything, all of our plans, where the other war parties are . . .'

Tiamoko was cursing, a long litany of expletives as his fingers tightened and loosened on his knees.

'That was our thinking, too,' Apok said over the babble. 'We'd sent people to warn you of our concerns, but clearly we were too late. I will need to know the details of your defeat,' he added and Lutek flushed, but he went on before she could retort. 'The biggest problem here, though, is convincing the Yaloh that the rest of the refugees are not similarly spies and assassins.'

'Prove it!' shouted the same elder as before. 'Prove they're not.'

Spies and assassins. Tayan would have laughed – *Ilandeh* would have laughed – if their faces weren't all so serious. Hysterical laughter, granted, but laughter nonetheless. The shaman was very, very tired. He stood.

'High Elder, if the council has no other questions, I would like to go home. I have been away for too long and my husband is dead or missing.'

Apok's face softened. 'Of course, Peace-weaver, of course.' He touched his belly and then his throat. 'Under—' he began, and then stopped. His smile was mirthless, but he ignored Lutek's questioning gaze and hurried out of the council house. He needed to get away.

Tayan stamped on the wooden rocker that would alert Xessa to his presence and waited for her clap. Inside it was the pretty much the same as it had always been, tidy floor space and messy shelves, only now there was an extra dog and an extra eja. Toxte. Tayan halted inside the doorway and drank in the sight of her. But then she was on her feet and in his arms, the familiar scent of her, the hard strength of her arms around his neck, her huffing laugh.

He hugged her back as hard as he could, a lump threatening to seal his throat and unstop his eyes, when she let go and leant back far enough to turn his head and examine the wound in his cheek. He batted her hand away and hugged her again. One part of his heart returned to him.

One part still missing.

He felt the hitch of her chest and knew she'd started crying and he squeezed and tried to lift her off her feet, ostensibly to make her laugh – she was far heavier than him – but in reality so he could shift to see Toxte's face and raise an eyebrow.

'Tika died,' the eja said. Tayan nodded. 'And Kime died, not long after. It . . . broke something in her. She went to the Swift Water on her own and caught a Greater Drowned.'

Tayan's arms locked even tighter around Xessa and his mind filled with a sharp buzzing. Kime. Oh, ancestors. She was sobbing on his shoulder now, full-body crying, and Ossa was whining and pawing at his legs and Toxte looked a bit teary himself. And so he put away his own fatigue and hurt, and he became the shaman they needed even as his mind reeled under the revelation that *Xessa caught a holy Setat.*

Gently, he pushed her away and wiped her tears with his thumbs before signing: 'I'm so sorry. Tomorrow, I'll journey you to the Realm of the Ancestors and you can say goodbye. And I'll make sure his spirit is on the spiral path to Malel, all right?'

She sobbed some more, but nodded, and Toxte was definitely crying now as well and Tayan had to carefully lock away his own grief. Kime. Father of the friend of his heart.

'Word is you've lost your mind while I've been gone. Going to tell me about it?' he asked as her tears slowed.

Xessa ducked her head and wiped her nose on the back of her hand, but he knew the set of her chin well. 'Tell me what happened to you,' she signed instead, and if she wasn't ready to talk about it all, he couldn't really blame her. Still . . . *she did it. We've got a Drowned. We've fucking caught one.*

He glanced at Toxte, who'd scooted forward and pressed his leg along Xessa's thigh as she sat within touching distance of Tayan. The eja nodded, and so Tayan summarised the previous three months and the ambush and the absence of Lilla, either as corpse or as living man.

'So. How do we get him back?' Xessa signed and the question was so her – and so him – that something in his chest cracked and he had to look away, fighting for control.

'Your news,' he signed when he could be sure he wouldn't cry. She protested, he insisted, and eventually she related everything that had happened since he'd been gone. It made as little sense this time around as when Apok had told him, but he could see the evidence stacking up against Ilandeh and Dakto both and in the end he had to concede that what everyone else thought was likely the truth. In light of everything that had happened, and even on top of the monstrous weight of fear and pain at Lilla having been ripped from him, he found their betrayal cut deep and wondered, for a single selfish, wallowing instant, whether he had the strength to carry this extra load.

And then he told himself to stop being a mewling little pup and help his friend.

'Haven't told me everything though,' he signed at the end and pointed to Toxte. 'What's the pretty little ornament doing here?'

The corner of Toxte's mouth turned up, and then again when Xessa blushed. 'Like you said, he's pretty. He amuses me,' she signed with studied nonchalance, but Tayan well knew the mischief dancing across her face and it lifted his heart to see.

'Amuse?' Toxte demanded in mock outrage. 'I'm the best thing that's ever happened to you and you know it. You save my life, I save yours, we have great sex. Regularly,' he added and waggled his eyebrows.

Xessa huffed a laugh but then she kissed him, a lingering kiss that had Tayan clearing his throat and fussing with the dogs until they were done. 'You are the best thing,' she signed simply and they smiled at each other until Tayan made dramatic vomiting motions and she threw a cushion at him.

The rest of the night passed with too much beer and too many tears until Tayan couldn't stay awake any longer. He desperately wanted to sleep on Xessa's floor, or even curled with her in bed as they'd done countless times before. The thought of returning to his and Lilla's empty house terrified him, but Xessa and Toxte were making eyes at each other and he couldn't intrude any longer. With luck, he'd have drunk enough to sleep.

Lilla had, of course, left their home clean and tidy, and Xessa had given him water and candles, though he didn't – couldn't – light them. Instead, Tayan kicked off his sandals before stepping onto the mats, and then stripped out of his travel-worn clothes, scrubbed his face and neck and armpits with water and fell into their bed. It smelt like Lilla, and Tayan cried.

'So, you want to see it?' Xessa asked casually as they sat around the firepit eating breakfast the next morning. There was still hurt in her – far too much hurt, and a deep-rooted guilt that he hoped the journeying would help rip out – but there was a hint of her usual mischief, too, and something else that seemed a result of her relationship with Toxte. Obviously, the eja could give her something he couldn't. *And frequently does, from the sounds last night.*

'I suppose,' he replied with equal indifference. 'If you think it's worth my time.'

Toxte raised his hands to the sky in supplication, before signing, 'I can see I've made a terrible mistake. Malel, save me from friends who think they're funny.'

Tayan pulled a slice of meat out of his dawnmeal and waited until he had both dogs' attention, then threw it at Toxte's chest and laughed as they flattened him, tongues and drool coating his face and neck.

Toxte fought himself free of the dogs and noticed Xessa and Tayan collapsed in each other's arms, laughing. 'Is this how it's going to be, really? This is my life now?' he demanded, and they looked at each other and dissolved into fresh giggles. Something loosened in Tayan's chest – not the weight of fear and hurt about Lilla's fate; nothing would get rid of that until his husband was back in his arms – but the need he'd had since he and Xessa were children to know that she was happy.

'Come on then, you monsters,' Toxte said as they finished eating. He glanced at Xessa. 'I'm going to tell him what happened, so he knows what to expect,' he signed. 'Get the weapons.' She waved him on and vanished into the house, and when she came back she was loaded down with nets, spears, clubs, and knives, so many that Tayan felt a lurch of unease. She handed one of each to Toxte and, as they made their way uphill through the early morning city towards the womb, the eja told him the story of what happened when he'd gone in on the end of a rope and listened to it sing.

'Ancestors,' Tayan breathed when he was done. 'I knew it. I knew I'd seen something significant in the Singing City. I knew they weren't just animals.' Xessa tapped his arm and he repeated himself in sign. 'I was . . . We had to observe an offering, the monthly ritual,' he continued. 'It was exactly as awful as you'd imagine, but before the actual . . . the death, one of them . . . spoke. Not in any language I could understand, though I did understand it – in here.' He tapped his chest. 'Enet – the woman we saw, a high official in their society – was in the water with the offering and the holy Setat beckoned and made a noise. A little, inquisitive sound. *Give*. It was telling her to give it the offering. I heard it. I knew it.'

'Holy Setat?' Toxte asked in a low voice and Tayan paused on the trail between Sky City and womb. Had he actually signed that?

'Too long under the song,' he signed briskly and then pushed on past, disquieted. Lutek had seen it, too, the unconscious use of an honorific for a ravening monster. And he'd almost used the song blessing when he left the council. *Shit*.

Toxte stopped well below the womb, out of earshot – he hadn't taken the spirit-magic and wouldn't risk getting too close. Tayan knew the ejab on duty by sight, but they weren't friends; he nodded politely. Now he was here, he was consumed with the need to see it. To hear it.

Since Toxte had told him what he'd seen and felt, he'd known the only way he could interact with it would be without a magical barrier between them. Still, he'd taken their warnings to heart and Xessa would go in with him. She knew him better than anyone save Lilla, and if he started acting strangely, she'd drag him out.

And how it reacts to her presence will be the first experiment: its ability to recognise threat. Can it differentiate between me and her?

'You've been here every day since you captured it, yes? Studying it?' he signed as an eja looped the rope around his chest and shoulders and pulled it tight, tying the knot between his shoulder blades where he couldn't reach it. He slid the knife out of the shaman's belt, too, and Tayan felt a little lurch of panic.

Xessa nodded.

'And how does it react to you? You captured it, you're keeping it here, you prevented Toxte from freeing it. What does it do when you go in?'

'Sings,' she signed. 'Always. It makes me feel . . . dirty. Vulnerable somehow. As if my body and my spirit know its singing, even if I don't. If that makes sense? But it never does anything else. Not even when I feed it. Just watches me and sings until I can't stand it any more. I can't learn anything from it,' she added with intense frustration.

'Maybe I can,' he signed. 'Have you got me?'

'Always.' She took a spear in one hand and a club in the other, and when he raised an eyebrow, she tapped her knee with it. Tayan winced at her casual brutality, but couldn't really blame her for it. Not after everything that had happened.

He wiped his hands on his kilt and then stepped down into the tunnel leading to the womb. He tugged at the rope around his chest fretfully, checking the knot, and when his feet slowed, Xessa gave him a gentle nudge. The torchlight grew and he could hear a splashing, abruptly stilled. It had heard him, too.

He paused before the turn into the womb. 'Wait here, out of sight,' he signed. 'I want to see what it does when I'm alone.' Xessa shook her head vehemently. 'Send Ossa in with me. He'll alert you if anything goes wrong.'

She licked her teeth and chewed at her lip, then gave him the club and waved him on. The dog, too. Tayan took a deep breath and turned the corner, pausing just inside the womb to blink in the light of the torches and candles. The cave was hot and smoky and the water at the far end was shallow and the Drowned . . . the Drowned was on its side in the water, gills flapping and lungs labouring. Suffering.

Ossa was growling, a constant low rumble of threat that didn't seem to stop even for breath. Tayan leant the club against the wall and checked the rope again, then scratched the dog's head to try and calm him. The rumble continued.

'Hello,' Tayan said, his voice cracking. He cleared his throat and tried again. 'I know you have language. I know you can speak, in a way. Do you understand me? I'm not going to hurt you.'

The Drowned watched him, and when he took a step forward it thrashed backwards, huddling up against the wall. The movement triggered a snarl from Ossa, but Tayan spread his hands. 'I'm not armed. I'm not going to hurt you. I just want to understand.' Gingerly, he squatted down to be less of a threat, ready to throw himself backwards at any second. The rope was almost taut behind him; he couldn't get much closer.

'Holy Setat,' he whispered and the Drowned's head came up. It stared at him with unblinking intensity. 'God of rivers and lakes, of rain and crops, you who give and take to maintain harmony.' Its throat sac bulged and he braced himself. It chirruped, tentative, as afraid as he was: he was sure of that now. 'Yes,' he said past the constriction in his throat, 'I'm a friend.'

Release me.

Tayan rocked under the command, issued in a low, bird-like warble. 'I can't do that,' he said. 'At least not yet. Soon perhaps. But we need to understand each other first. Do you understand? Understand my words?'

Release me. Hurt.

'I can't,' he repeated, filled with sorrow, and the holy Setat looked away from him and lowered its head back into the water. There was an ugly slash in one leg, and the other was dislocated or broken. 'Can I ease your hurt? Is there anything, any medicine you need?'

It looked up again and this time it sang. It was a song of yearning and loss and pain, a song of fear that broke Tayan's spine and heart and begged for aid, begged to be saved. And yet there was no imperative in it, no command to come to it that drew its victims and its offerings. It was alone and hurt and there was not enough water and so it must struggle, a constant pain throughout all its body as it slowly suffocated. Over hours. Over *days*.

And then Xessa was there, alerted by Ossa's response to the song, and she dragged Tayan backwards by his harness and stepped past him, spear up by her jaw. The shaman scrambled to his feet. 'No,' he said, 'no, you don't understand. It's not a threat.'

Xessa didn't look at his mouth or his hands and when he grabbed her arm she shook him off violently and pointed at the exit.

'No,' he tried again, desperate now, but she was implacable.

He backed to the cave mouth and looked at the holy Setat over her shoulder. 'I'll come back,' he promised it, 'and we will talk again.'

LILLA

*Outside Singing City, Pechacan, Empire of Songs
211th day of the Great Star at morning.*

He'd expected more than this. The way the dogs and Dakto spoke of Pechacan, calling it the heart of the Empire, he'd expected every home to be a stone palace or for the song to be stronger, purer, finer than before. But nothing was different. Nothing. It was just the same expanses of fields separated by tiny strips of jungle supporting nothing more than a few monkeys and birds.

The slaves were the same mix of empty-eyed and zealous converts. Their Pechaqueh owners were neither taller nor more impressive than the lowest of the dog warriors escorting them. Perhaps the hundreds of Star cycles they'd lived inside the song had changed them in some hidden, fundamental way, but Lilla thought not.

He was, being honest, disappointed. Where were the riches and the splendour? Where was the visible proof that this tribe was closer to the gods, or more powerful or beautiful, stronger or more intelligent? How could this be the people who had conquered nearly all Ixachipan?

But they did have one startling, incomprehensible difference, and the Singing City epitomized it. Pechaqueh built their towns and cities *next to* water, and in that water swam the Drowned – lots of Drowned, both Greater and Lesser. Captives and slaves alike shied away, but the dog warriors and Dakto made them stand close. Made them watch as one of their number was untied, marched down to the water's edge and shoved in. She screamed and thrashed and the Drowned tore her apart.

The sight had quelled the embers of rebellion more effectively than any beating could, and the days had passed in quiet, hopeless silence as they filed past towns and cities dotted among the farmland, ever farmland. As if there could be nothing else in the world but fields in various stages of green, abundant growth.

'I had expected beauty,' he said to Dakto when the macaw came to walk by his side for the final sticks to the Singing City. It grew on the horizon, sprawling and vast, and there were several other limestone roads winding towards it from all corners of the Empire.

'What you see is wealth.'

'No. Not wealth. Greed. Where is the balance in this, Dakto?' Lilla jerked his chin at their surroundings. 'We would never destroy the jungle or kill all the animals around our homes, tipping that balance from plenty into poverty. You have done all this and more, and all for greed. As children with honeycomb, you are likely to give yourselves a bellyache.'

He had been like this for days now, unable to stop himself poking, poking. Perhaps it was the continuing pain in his skull, the weakness it brought, or the endless high-pitched fucking whine in his head that not even the song could blot out.

The captured Paws had been absorbed into a much larger caravan made up of slaves from the Empire escorted by armed free. Dakto had remained with them when the dog warriors turned around to head back to the war.

Dakto, who still found time to talk to Lilla each day as the long lines of bound prisoners weaved through the naked, open farmland. The others must have been enslaved for years, because they weren't roped. Lilla watched them walk ahead on the road with a mix of horror and incomprehension, wondering why they didn't run from the tiny number of people leading them. But he knew why. He'd known why ever since he first heard the song.

The music was in his heart now, a worm twisting inside him, threaded through every limb and muscle and nerve. He knew the Pechaqueh were no better than him, but there was a small part that was grateful to them for bringing him under the song so that he might know its majesty. The song he'd sworn to die before hearing.

He worried that small part would grow like a cancer and eat away at who he was, so he sang songs under his breath as they walked, focusing on the old tales set to music he'd learnt as a boy. Yet always, within only a few lines of verse, he'd fall into the same rhythm as *the* song. It was as if it moulded his chants and hymns to itself so that even they became a part of it. So that his worship of Malel and the ancestors became worship of the song – and by extension, he realised with a sickening lurch, of the Singer, the Empire, and the so-called holy Setatmeh. He stopped singing after that.

'Those dog warriors feared you,' Lilla commented.

'As they should,' Dakto said, proud and haughty. 'I could kill any of them in combat without breaking a sweat.'

'What would happen if they disobeyed you?'

'They would die. Disobedience of superiors is not tolerated.'

'What if their disobedience saved your life? In battle, for instance? What if you told them to move away and then your life was in danger and someone came back and saved you? Would you still kill them?'

'Glory is won in the Melody in three ways: by capturing slaves, by acts of bravery, by saving lives. If a dog disobeyed me but saved my life, they would be rewarded. You will learn all this soon enough.'

'And if you were not saved?' Lilla pressed. Dakto wouldn't answer and the Toko forced a laugh. 'I see. So your slave and dog warriors only risk their lives for yours if they receive a direct order or there's a guarantee of success? Otherwise they watch you die and feel, well, not very much at all, I expect. Relief, perhaps. And yet you still believe they all fight for the same cause? You think they actually believe all this monkey shit about the song and Pechaqueh superiority? No, my friend. They've learnt the rules of the game and they're playing to win. Fight and stay alive until they're freed, then get away from Pechaqueh control as soon as they can. They may never get their land and traditions back, but they've got more freedom than you have.'

'Says the slave to the free man,' Dakto said, but his smile was tight.

Lilla shook his head, knowing he was provoking the macaw and yet caring nothing for the consequences. 'Says the free man to the slave,' he contradicted. 'Out of the two of us, I am the one with pure blood; it is yours that is mixed.'

Lilla didn't give a single shit about the purity or otherwise of his blood or anyone else's, and there had been enough inter-tribal marriages over the years for there to be no such thing as a full-blood anyway, probably, but he knew Dakto did care, and so he poked. And Dakto, for so long the garrulous warrior and friend, was tight-lipped. Lilla wondered whether anything the other man had said during the previous year had been true. Whether any of his traits or jokes or responses had been genuine. The cloak of his disguise had been perfect.

Dakto glared at him and Lilla made himself laugh again, though he could taste the sudden danger in the air. Sweat trickled down his back, itching.

'Once they're free, as long as they keep their heads down and pay lip service to your barbaric beliefs, they can do what they like. You, as a half-blood, will forever be at the mercy of their expectations. A free Axi fucks up? Well, they're savages, what do you expect? But if a half-blood fucks up . . . you betray every Pecha, don't you? You bring the blood into disrepute. Your shame is all Pechaqueh shame.' Lilla shook his head in mocking sympathy. 'Slave,' he whispered. 'Until the day you die.'

Dakto ripped his knife out of his belt and Lilla braced, breathing a swift prayer to Malel that she would find his spirit for rebirth. Instead of killing him, the macaw cut the rope at his neck free of the main line and dragged him away. He punched Lilla to his knees, kept on punching until Lilla was curled on the ground, teeth gritted, eyes squeezed shut and muscles tensed to try and absorb the impact. The pain in his head, which had finally begun to settle, roared back with a vengeance when Dakto punched him in the face.

Nobody came to his aid, not even when Dakto started in with his feet, not even when, heaving for air, he kicked Lilla onto his back and sat on him, ripped open his tunic and sliced into the skin of his chest with the knife.

Lilla screamed then, barely able to see Dakto through the swelling around his eyes and the pain that ripped through his head and chest. The cutting stopped and he lay there, gasping for breath, until he felt the man climb off him. He tried to roll onto his side but was kicked flat again, and moments later the macaw was back. He rubbed a handful of something into the cuts on Lilla's chest, making him screech again as it burned and grated in the wounds, as if he'd poured warrior wasps into his lung.

'Get up.' Dakto's voice was implacable. 'Get up and get in line or I'll cut your balls off.'

Lilla rolled onto his side and got to his knees, wobbling. He spat a mouthful of blood and half a tooth into the rich black earth at the edge of the limestone road. He held his breath and made himself stand, groaning. He staggered towards the line of prisoners, his balance gone and his hearing muffled in his right ear. The whine in his head was louder.

The cut ends of the cord were knotted back through the wide collar on Lilla's neck. He could feel Dakto's breath and body heat as the other man stood right next to him, far too close for comfort. 'Walk. If you slow us down I'll flog the skin from your back and make you eat it.'

Limping, gasping, and counting up his hurts one at a time so he'd know the exact number to repay, Lilla walked into the Singing City, through estates and gardens and craft quarters, over a flat bridge spanning a river that made his skin crawl with horror, and into a wide space of beaten earth filled with tall bamboo cages. The flesh markets of Pechacan.

Dakto sought him out one last time, and Lilla braced for another beating. The macaw stood close enough to kiss, so Lilla could see him through the swelling around his eyes. 'You told me once you would not have me because you were married.'

'I did and I am, even if Tayan is dead. Why? Are you going to buy me for yourself?' Lilla tried to sneer, but his stomach tightened. What if Dakto did exactly that?

'For what you did, how you made me welcome in your home, I give you this and only this.' Dakto lowered his voice and leant even closer, making a pretence of fiddling with Lilla's collar. The Toko fought not to shy away. 'I didn't find his body.'

Lilla rocked and the Whisper had to grab him by one arm to prevent him from collapsing. 'But even if he lives, you should not be married. It is how they control their slaves. If you defy them, they will kill your family one by one and send you their heads. If you want any sort of freedom despite your bonds, your brand, and the cage they'll keep you in – do not be married. Don't claim him. That way at least he lives, even if you do not.'

And with that he walked away.

ENET

Enet sat in the hidden room in her palace, the mute old body slave weaving in a corner, her estate slave waiting outside the door. The centre of the room was dominated by the large, roughly hewn block of songstone. Her hammers and chisels were stored on a shelf nearby, but she did not work the stone now.

Instead, she sat on a cushion at a low table, and all of the books of history and song-magic and legend and prophecy that she owned were scattered around her. She had the calendars in front of her, sun-year and Star cycle both. Twice now they had blooded the song, surely more than enough, and yet it was veering out of harmony *again*. Again it was hungry. She had read every book, cover to cover, seeking some tiny sliver of information that she might have missed before. All of the books gave slightly differing advice, but all agreed that the blooding should happen no more than four times a year at the very most.

396

Enet's heart spasmed with grief and she swallowed it down, refusing to let the edges of her mind touch that raw and gaping boy-shaped void. She could smell Pikte's hair. Savagely, Enet pressed the stump of her finger against the table and inhaled the pain, clearing her mind.

The blooding – *Pikte, my child, my heart* – had re-secured her position and her influence, as she had hoped. She had retained her titles and her position as chief courtesan. Pikte's absence from the source was noted and she had let the knowledge of his accidental death spread, along with confirmation the topic was never to be mentioned in her presence or the Singer's.

Taking a deep breath, she turned her mind back to the problem. Her books, so rare that she believed she had the only copies in existence, told a far different story to the accepted history of Pechacan. *The song must never be blooded. A peaceful song leads to peaceful citizens; a violent song to violent citizens.* Those imperatives had been repeated so often as she grew up that they beat in her blood much as the song did. And they were all lies.

But so are the books.

The Empire was only as strong as the song that united it, and Xac's song was powerful indeed. Powerful before the blooding, but even more so afterwards. If only they could find some equilibrium; if only the holy lord himself could exercise restraint and control the song, keep his demands for offerings to the accepted limit.

Once a month for the holy Setatmeh; once every three months for the holy lord. If he had already had two, then should the next offering be three months from the first one, or from the second? Or should it be six months? The books were worse than useless.

This morning, the Singer had summoned her and once

again told her to bring him something special. She had thus far managed to deflect him by bringing other treats – trinkets, food, jewellery. But he'd been asking for the last three days, and she wondered whether he might take matters into his own hands if she denied him much longer. There were more than enough warriors, courtesans, administrators, councillors, and slaves in the source for him to choose between, and none of them could even conceive of denying him – nor would they be able to withstand the song-magic when it roared and glowed within him. And if that happened, if he realised he no longer needed her to gift him this sensation and this strength, she would fail and all her plans would be dust.

Three months from the first, she decided, because she had to make a decision. She marked it on the calendar. She would have to ease him through the coming weeks, deflecting him with games and divinations and reports of the war. Pilos would be in Yalotlan within days and he'd station runners to return over the border to report through the song. Surely that would be enough stimulus for him?

Enet tipped the silver-white powder of her tonic into a cup and stirred it, ignoring the concern in her slave's eyes as the woman paused her weaving to watch. She drank, ignoring too the grainy texture and the dusty, somehow dry taste. She was used to them both by now. She ran her tongue around her gums, teasing out the fine grains that crackled and grated between her teeth. Her mouth dried and she drank some more, ignoring the faint hurt in her chest and stomach. It was worth it, and what did a little discomfort matter, anyway?

Pikte hadn't liked her to be uncomfortable, though. Enet's mouth pressed tight and she pinched the stump of her missing little finger. The house was quiet without him and her body slave had cried for a week in the aftermath, as if it had anything to do with her. The diamond of Enet's grief shifted in her chest, threatening to soften and so expand, to grow until it filled all Ixachipan and crushed her beneath its weight. She thrust it away again, back behind her heart, in the prison of her ribs.

The Great Octave ran her finger around the inside of the cup, drawing up the last of the powder and licking it clean. The tonic was a recipe from the very oldest and most precious of her books, something used by the very, very first shamans who shaped the songstone – and who went on to become Singers. The legend of it had been lost, and so when Enet discovered it in the book, which was otherwise useless, it had felt like more than coincidence. Along with the truth about blooding the song, she had finally begun to see a way forward. A path to greatness, not for her – for the Empire. Everything she did was for the Empire that she loved so much.

And yet the blooding is out of control. Who's to say the tonic won't likewise be a disaster? Who's to say it won't kill you?

Enet pushed away her concerns. When Yalotlan and Tokoban were safe under the song, the time would come to waken the world spirit. And when that happened, Enet needed to be in the strongest possible position, and the tonic would give her that. Strength of body and clarity of mind and a connection to the song deeper than any she'd known before. What did a bellyache matter in return for such gifts?

'High one? The latest report is in. I . . . think you should read it.' The estate slave's voice was neutral as he spoke through the door.

'Not now,' Enet snapped, staring at the books and the calendars in front of her and rubbing her stomach in soft, circular motions. It was here, the answer she needed to control the blooding. It had to be here somewhere. Why had none of the books discussed even the possibility that—

'It's from one of the eyes in the Melody, high one. Regarding intentions in Tokoban.'

Enet stared through the body slave, who had stopped weaving, awaiting orders. She swore and stood and the slave rose too, with a muffled grunt. She scurried ahead and opened the door for Enet, and the estate slave stepped back and bowed. He had the report in his hand, but she swept past him to the room facing her gardens and sat there instead. Her slaves brought water, honey, fruit, and incense, an extra cushion should she want it, and only then did the Great Octave hold out her hand for the report.

She read quickly, lips pursing as the implications became clear. Someone was watching her and they had gathered information that was not theirs to know. Potentially damaging information. Enet needed to consolidate her claim on the songstone in Tokoban, and she needed the Singer's approval to do it.

'Setatmeh be praised he didn't want to see Pilos when they passed the city,' she muttered, and then handed the report back to be filed with the others. 'Finest clothes and jewellery, and prepare those spiced monkey skewers the holy lord prefers. And a bath. And oils for my hair and skin. My formal headdress, and make sure the feathers aren't bent this time.'

The slaves bowed and scurried to do her bidding and Enet stood and began peeling off her clothes and jewellery.

Eyes watching eyes, she mused as she stretched and bent and reminded herself of the dances the Singer most enjoyed watching her perform. *I wonder which one of us will blink first.*

* * *

The song hungered. As Enet's litter moved through the streets towards the source, she saw the effect of that hunger. Her guards made the litter-bearers backtrack and take an alternative route when they came upon a mass brawl in one of the avenues. Choosers and city overseers were trying to break it up, but the level of violence they employed to do so only added to the chaos. Crowds were watching, jeering and placing bets on the outcome. The air smelt of blood.

Xac's song blared stronger than any Enet had heard in the forty sun-years of her life, louder and more imperious than his sister's or the two Singers before her that Enet remembered back to when she was a child.

'. . . ruined the entire meal. Of course, I had him killed,' a noblewoman in the cloth market said later as the litter floated past. 'The other kitchen slaves won't make his mistake.' Slaves killed for errors that would normally warrant only a whipping. And killed, not saved as offerings for the holy Setatmeh at the next new moon.

It was everywhere. The song's sharp edge cutting at the people within it, making them sharp in turn. Quick to anger; quick to hurt. And Enet needed to ease the Singer through almost two more months before he could be allowed to blood the song again. Her heart almost quailed at the thought, and so she unstoppered the gourd and drank more of her tonic, for luck. For courage. For magic.

They reached the great pyramid and Enet hurried up the long, steep stairs and swept in, removing her sandals and letting a slave wash her feet before continuing on into the source and the holy lord's presence.

The Singer lounged among the mats and pillows, appearing at ease, but she could see the glitter of his eyes, the eagerness. The hunger. And here in the source, the song was sharp enough to make her bleed.

'What have you brought me?' he demanded before she'd even made her prostration. 'Where is it? Tell me.'

Enet sat back. 'Spiced monkey, holy lord. Your favourite.' She gestured and her slave put the platter down next to her and then hurried to her usual place at the wall.

The Singer's face was blank. 'Spiced monkey?' he asked in dangerously soft tones.

'Yes, great Singer.' She picked up a piece in her fingers and shuffled across the mats towards him, lips parted as she offered it, everything about her appearance, attire, even her scent, calculated to arouse. Once she had taken the edge off, they could discuss the songstone in Tokoban. She proffered the meat and he knocked her hand away, not hard, but not casually either.

Enet's mouth was dry. 'No monkey?' she asked playfully. 'Very well, then how may I please the holy lord?' She knelt up so she was taller than him and began fiddling with the ties of her kilt, one eyebrow raised.

The Singer looked away from her. 'By bringing me another,' he growled. The song responded, too, not lustful at her antics but a rumbling threat. 'Now.'

'I . . . It is not the appointed time. It must be only on the third—'

'Get me something.'

Enet paused again, her kilt loose now. 'Let me please you, my love,' she whispered. 'I wish to feel your might inside me. We can talk afterwards.'

The Singer shoved her backwards into the pillows and she landed with a grunt. Finally. He straddled her and leant down into her face.

'Get me something or take its place,' he breathed and the smile died on her lips. 'Am I entirely understood?'

Enet reached up to hold his shoulders in clammy hands.

'Holy lord, your will is divine,' she managed. 'But it is too soon. It must be carefully managed, great Singer, so carefully, or there will be unintended consequences, for you and for the Empire.'

He reared back and pulled the stone knife from the waistband of his kilt.

'Wh-where did you get that?' she asked, shocked, for the ritual knife was stored in the source's treasure vault deep in the earth. Xac hadn't been down there in years.

'So be it,' the Singer said, ignoring her question, and there was no emotion in his voice or face, not even the bloodlust she expected. His skin began to glimmer gold and the song changed, darkening, demanding.

Enet put up both her hands. 'Wait, wait! As the Singer commands, holy lord. As the Singer commands. Give me one hour and I will bring you a prize.'

The knife was poised above her chest and Xac lowered it until the tip pressed between her breasts. Enet held her breath. He pressed, digging it in until it hurt, and then relented.

'Less than one hour,' he grunted and got off her. 'Run, little Enet,' he added and rubbed his hand hard over her cheeks and lips. 'Run. And fix your face before you come back.'

Enet scrambled to her feet and backed rapidly from the source, her slave hobbling after her. When she was around the corner she paused, leaning against the wall, dizzy. Councillor Yana watched her, Chorus Leader Nara by his side.

'Look what you've created,' Yana said, his voice low and throbbing with anger. 'You've broken the song and doomed us all, *Great Octave*. All that comes next, you have caused. All of it.'

Enet couldn't meet his eyes. She brushed past him and fled. An hour wasn't long enough to reach a decent flesh market. She hurried down the corridors towards the courtesans' rooms. One of them would lend her fresh cosmetics while she bathed.

A second would honour the Singer with their screams. Enet would work out how to explain their death later, but she knew, now, that Yana was right. She'd lost control. She wasn't even certain she'd ever had it. Those fucking books; all those fucking books had promised her an outcome she could manage.

And they had lied.

THE SINGER

I am the song and the song is war.

The song is death for glory and glory for the Empire and the Empire for death. The song is me, my will, my divinity that I choose to share with those mortals who crawl on their bellies and die and fuck and kill at my command.

I am the song and my will is inviolable. The song demands war. The song demands conquest and vengeance and the blood of my enemies to paint the walls of this sanctuary. The song demands war because I demand it. Because I am war.

There will be no rest, no surrender and no retreat. The Yaloh will fall under the song and embrace it. The Tokob will fall under the song and die for their atrocities, for ripping my divine kin from the world.

My warriors will bring me the god-killers and I will craft their screams into the song and they will echo for eternity through its power, dead and never dying. Their blood will make my song invincible. The world spirit will know my glory.

Anna Stephens

My song is war.
My song is blood.
And I am the song.

ILANDEH

The Neck, Xentiban, Empire of Songs
226th day of the Great Star at morning

The Melody was here. Pilos was here and Ilandeh's heart leapt.

The ten, hundred-strong local pods Pilos had sent in to Yalotlan in response to her communication through the song had already pushed forward, retaking land and destroying the war parties who had thought to take the Empire by surprise. They couldn't go too far in without reinforcements, but they'd managed to protect a string of pyramids from destruction.

Ilandeh stroked the single scarlet tail feather of a macaw that hung in her hair and then rubbed her thumb over the small tattoo of a chulul gracing the inside of her wrist. The symbol of a Whisper, elite among the macaws, and subtle enough not to be remarked upon. She'd missed the scarlet almost as much as the song. Neither could ease her nerves, however, as Pilos strode through the rain to the open-sided shelter she'd had built to receive him.

Ilandeh touched belly and throat and then knelt to bow.

'Under the song, High Feather. Praise the holy Setatmeh you are well.'

'Under the song, Flight, and you are welcome in it after such a long absence. Sit comfortably, please. We will rest here for two hours and then push on – the Singer is even keener than I to have this matter closed. The Third, Sixth and Seventh Talons will push into eastern Yalotlan under Atu's command. First, Second and Fourth are going straight through to Tokoban. If we can take their mountain, we cut off retreat for the Yaloh and close in from both sides.'

The Singer is even keener than I . . . He must mean the strange dissonances in the song she had heard, the ones that made the Listener in the nearby pyramid scream and weep. The ones that made every warrior there, whatever their rank or status, cringe. An anomaly. An abomination to the glory.

'We attack hard and without mercy,' Pilos continued and Ilandeh blinked and focused. 'The Singer wants ejab captives particularly and an inventory of the Tokob songstone – he cares little for the rest of them.' Pilos sat cross-legged on the mats. 'Your report on the city's defences can wait until the Feathers are gathered. For now, tell me of the ejab and their spirit-magic.'

'A concoction of fungus and herbs, plus a tiny amount of frog-venom. They eat it and then for that day they . . . the spirits either steal their hearing or plug their ears with spirit music. They hear nothing but that and it protects them, though the magic takes a terrible toll as the years pass. The oldest ejab are little more than shuffling madmen and -women, yet they are cared for, almost revered, for their sacrifice. The list of ingredients is here.' She handed him a report.

'And the songstone?'

'There is a cave high up on the hill above the city. It is their most sacred place – they call it the womb and believe all life issued from within it, all creation. There are rich lines of songstone in that cave. It's possible the entire hill may be veined with it. The echoes and hums and vibrations were consistent with those I have observed in other quarries.'

'And they don't use it?' Pilos asked, curiosity furrowing his brow.

Ilandeh spread her hands. 'The Tokob appear entirely ignorant of its true purpose and, indeed, ignorant of the world spirit itself. Unless this Malel is their understanding of it. Perhaps when we have shamans and historians as slaves . . .' She trailed off; she was babbling, more nervous than she liked to admit, and Pilos knew it.

Ilandeh took a deep breath and began again with her report. She talked and Pilos listened, to stories of ejab and civilians befriended and gently interrogated, of luring people to the river for the holy Setatmeh to take, of the killings of the high elders. Of how Dakto had ingratiated himself into a Paw and then, so she'd heard, arranged the ambush and destruction of a war party.

'And where is your Second Flight?' Pilos asked.

Ilandeh frowned. Where indeed? 'He chose to escort those captives to the flesh markets, High Feather,' she said evenly. 'I did not expect it, but in truth . . . it may be the thought of leaving the Empire again, of being outside of the song for more weeks and months, is affecting him. He will be disciplined on his return, of course.'

He watched her, silent.

'Forgive me, High Feather. I should have paid more attention to Dakto's words when we lived in the Sky City. I should have seen if there was restlessness growing in him. He was given much . . . responsibility by the Tokob. It may have planted unfortunate thoughts.'

The High Feather drummed his fingers on his knee as he

studied her. 'Then let us hope his time in the Singing City reminds him of his duty. Are there unfortunate thoughts growing in you, Whisper?' he added. 'Perhaps the Sky City's freedoms have turned your head, too.'

Ilandeh pressed her forehead to the mat as the breeze blew rain in at them in a fine mist and tugged at her scarlet feather. 'My loyalty is absolute, High Feather. Tell me how to prove it and I will do so.'

'If I told you to kill Dakto?'

She twitched, wanting to look up and scan Pilos's face for deception; didn't dare. 'Then I would kill Dakto. For the Singer, the holy Setatmeh, and the Empire. For you.'

Pilos was silent for so long that sweat broke out across her back. Then: 'Sit up. We will see what is to be done with him when he returns. In the meantime, Sarn is your new Second Flight. He commanded the Talon in your absence.'

'As the High Feather commands, though my previous Second Flight was Beyt. She did not have command in my absence?'

Pilos stood and stretched. 'Beyt was given other tasks. Come, there are many sticks to march before nightfall. Take a hundred out ahead and find us someone to fight.'

Sarn crouched behind her in the pre-dawn gloom beneath the trees. He'd made his displeasure at his reduction in status known, and had repeated some of the rumours she knew were flying through the Fourth Talon at Dakto's unauthor-ised absence. Had she been tainted too? Was her status as Flight in jeopardy? Her life?

Pathetic, she told herself. *They question their own devotion by questioning mine. If they doubt me, it is because their own faith is weak. My allegiance is total, my loyalty without reproach. I will prove it to Pilos. His belief is all that matters.*

It wasn't all that mattered, and everyone knew it. She dismissed the thought and slid on through the brush, concentrating on her task and ignoring the wet leaves rubbing against her face and hair and soaking her clothes. Her hands, knees, and feet were black with mud and clinging leaf mould. Bow and quiver were strapped to her back for ease of movement and her spear was in her right hand. The force they were tracking was both large and alert, and though most of it now lounged around a series of small, spitting fires scattered among the trees, others stood watch at regular intervals. Stood watch but did not see, for Ilandeh was a Whisper, and so were those who moved around her, quieter than snakes.

Ilandeh reached her left hand behind her back and gestured, fingers splayed open and then pointing left; she heard only the faintest scuff and knew Sarn and the others would be spreading out to encircle the camp, awaiting her signal to attack. But not just yet. They could get a little closer still.

A quick patter of raindrops from above told her Beyt was in position, hidden by the canopy. The woman could put six arrows in six targets in six heartbeats. She'd take out most of the guards before Ilandeh's team even reached the perimeter, clear their path to make a quick ending to the Tokob and Yaloh shits who thought to seize Empire land.

She scanned the camp again and the trees around her; the enemy she could see, but not her Whispers. Ilandeh wiped the mud off her hands and the spear shaft so it didn't slip in her grip. The obsidian tip gleamed green-black in the early light. She touched belly and throat and then gave a single long whistle. Beyt's arrows, and those of other Whispers in the canopy, flew before the note ended and Ilandeh followed them in as shouts and screams erupted in the camp, warriors leaping to their feet and snatching up weapons, staring blindly into the gloom and clearly outlined by their fires.

411

A dozen were down with arrows by the time she cleared the tree and lunged into the clearing to take a man in the belly just below his armour. The spear tip rammed in, scraping off his pelvic bone before sinking deep and he whooped in a breath, choked, his own weapons falling as he clutched, one hand on her spear, the other on her upper arm, as if unsure whether to pull it out or push himself further onto the blade. Ilandeh solved his dilemma, ripping the spear free and jabbing it in again, lower this time, down into the groin.

The Tokob legs gave out and the Whisper stepped back, spinning the spear and clubbing him in the head, sending him into the dirt. She skipped over his body to the next, a woman, blood already sheeting down her arm from an arrow wound and a shaft falling from her hand as she tore it out. Black paint from the bridge of her nose up to her hairline made her eyes disappear, only the gleam of firelight revealing where she was looking. Yaloh. Ilandeh saw the woman's feint too late; a club slammed into her sternum and sent her over backwards, lungs paralysed, mouth gasping, but no air left in the world for her to breathe.

Pain exploding through her chest, knives of agony shooting front to back and her spear lost by her side somewhere and the Yalotl approaching, mouth yelling something Ilandeh couldn't hear through the roaring hurt. The club went up, slivers of obsidian set into its length gleaming golden in the firelight – the last sight she would ever see.

Under the song. May Setatmeh and Singer bless me and keep me. May the ancestors . . .

Three arrows sprouted from the Yaloh chest and she faltered, the club wobbling as her arms lost their strength. She took another step, small, uncertain, and then one more before a final arrow took her through the throat and she toppled backwards like a felled tree.

'Flight? Flight, can you move?' Sarn asked, arrow clamped to the bow stock with his forefinger and his free hand dragging at her arm. 'Up you get, Xenti. More killing to do.'

Air rushed into Ilandeh's lungs and the pain roared its fury and then subsided, just a little, just a touch. A second, hotter fury at mention of her half-blood propelled her up to sitting – as though Sarn was any fucking better. Tlaloxqueh bastard. A pause to breathe again and she rolled to her knees and stood. Each movement of her chest caused a rippling coruscation of pain and the world lurched around her before her feet steadied.

Sarn handed her her spear. 'At least half of them fled; archers are mopping up the rest. Runners went this way.' He pointed and set off and Ilandeh had no choice but to follow. She was the Flight, but Sarn was leading them now, following protocol when she was disabled.

Only I'm not. I'm right here, three steps behind him.

If she wanted to retake command, she needed to shrug off the pain and start giving the bastard orders. Ilandeh pressed a hand to her ribs and sucked in a deep, deliberate breath, waiting for the scrape or creak that would tell her she'd broken ribs or cracked her sternum. Pain, a lot of pain, but she was intact as far as she could tell. No bubbling, no blood in her throat or mouth. Her armour had held then, just.

Ilandeh ran heavily after Sarn and the rest of her command, ignoring the urge to sit and rest, to hunch over. She was Flight, and she had a task. A duty to Empire, Singer, Setatmeh and High Feather all.

The Whispers were shadows in the gloom, flitting like moths across the face of a cloudy moon. Ilandeh moved among them, a little slower, a touch breathier, but with them. Sarn had the arrow's tip of their formation, while she laboured along out on one of the barbs. She told herself it didn't matter. She almost believed it.

And then screams and the faltering of the arrow, a structure that would've held strong if she'd been the tip.

'Line out,' she called ahead into the darkness, no need for stealth now. The Whispers re-formed and ran forward in a loose skirmish line, the better to encircle any enemy, dodging trees and tangles of shrub and vine. Ilandeh saw what Sarn had led them into, what his hubris had done to them in his desire to retake command.

The force they'd been tracking wasn't alone. The force they'd encountered had fled – back to its friends. Two, maybe three hundred Tokob and Yaloh warriors spread across a clearing – a full war party – and Sarn had led them straight into it. Fighting broke out immediately and Ilandeh threw herself into it, shouting orders to tighten up again. Where they could, her pod obeyed, falling into close formation to protect each other.

Ilandeh heard the distinctive sound of a blowpipe and leapt to one side – no idea if she was moving into or out of the dart's path. Nothing hit her so she kept moving, adrenaline speeding her limbs and smothering her hurts. She slipped beneath the flashing edge of a hatchet and ripped upwards into an armpit with her spear. Her attacker spun with the movement of his weapon and avoided the blow; she flowed into the next attack, letting the spear's momentum carry it and her forward, the butt rising to catch her opponent in the back as he turned and shoving him off balance. She brought the spear back down again in an overhand blow, the haft slamming into the top of his shoulder.

The hatchet was too short and he couldn't get close. She whirled around him and sank the spear tip into his arm, his arse, his thigh, none of them killing strikes as he managed to parry the full force of her blows, the hatchet's stone head chipping pieces out of her spear haft as they attacked and counter-attacked. An arrow hummed between them and both ducked on instinct, but no more followed it and Ilandeh thrust again. The Yalotl countered, but the crack of wood on wood was high and wrong, and the hatchet's head flew off the broken handle. He threw it at her and tried to grab for her spear; he got a hand on it, and pushed it wide and then jerked it back, free hand flailing for her. Ilandeh let go. The Yalotl stumbled back, unbalanced, and she kicked him in the thigh, where she'd grazed him with the obsidian.

He growled and began to swing the spear at her; Ilandeh spun in the same direction, just ahead of its arc, and punched him in the side of the neck; she kept going until she was at his back and snaked her right arm around his throat, grabbing the biceps of her left to complete the lock. She drove her right foot into the back of his knee, wrenching upwards at the same time. There was a grinding crunch and a pop, and his neck came apart in her arms.

Ilandeh held him up as a shield as she quartered the clearing. Most of her command was down: only fifty or so still fighting hard, and while their formations were holding, they were outnumbered two to one at least. She couldn't untangle the mess Sarn had dropped them in.

'Scatter,' Ilandeh screamed. 'Scatter!'

Those Whispers who could disengaged instantly, ducking, rolling, and sprinting out of reach of their opponents, weaving through the trees at the edge of the clearing and vanishing into the pre-dawn. Five were too heavily engaged to make it out and Ilandeh retrieved her spear and dashed for the closest, her ribs a forgotten hurt that would haunt her later, and scythed the legs from under the nearest enemy warrior. The Whisper didn't waste time thanking her –

together they helped a third and turned for the dark of the jungle, Sarn vanishing just ahead of them. The final two they left to their fate, and screams rose before they were ten strides into the treeline.

Fury boiled in Ilandeh's veins as she ran. The first engagement since Pilos had arrived – one intended to clear the route ahead of them – and fucking Sarn had got half her pod slaughtered. No, she reminded herself, *she'd* got half her pod slaughtered. She was Flight. The responsibility – and the blame – was hers, no matter what Sarn had done.

Ilandeh gritted her teeth. Knowing she'd disappointed Pilos hurt more than a club to the chest. She'd forgotten just how much the High Feather's good opinion of her mattered and how, despite the *utter purity* of his blood and lineage, his status and reputation, he never once looked at her with anything other than respect. Or he hadn't, before this.

They reached the camp. Ilandeh snagged Sarn's armour and pulled him close. 'With me, right now,' she growled, and strode towards the High Feather before she lost her nerve.

PILOS

Pilos walked through the latest ambush site to plague their advance as storm clouds bellied across the sun, their ragged edges turning pink and peach before fading back to grey. He picked his way among the corpses, analysing the arrows, the darts, the direction of flight of both warriors and weapons.

One man dangled by an ankle from a trip-snare, his head mashed to pulp, body twisting gently around and then back, around and then back, as the wind stirred the branch from which he hung. The clearing was silent but for the call of birds high above and the hum of insects enjoying a brief respite from the rain.

The High Feather dipped his fingers into the mess of crushed skull, then rubbed them together. The humidity had kept the blood fluid but it was thick, trying to clot. A couple of hours then.

Six days into Yalotlan, in the Wet, and the enemy was throwing everything at them. The Talons were ambushed

417

every day, sometimes more, from ahead and behind as small war parties crept past them in the thickness of the forest to pick off a dozen or score of their warriors before melting back into the undergrowth. It was a slow, patient attrition that had the Talons on edge, but Pilos wouldn't let them lose focus.

Here on this low hill, on the only trail wide enough for his Talons and so of course defended, sprawled forty-six dead warriors with not a Toko or Yalotl among them, from what he could tell. Feather Calan stepped in his footprints behind him, silent as a shadow. Second Flight Sarn came last; it'd been he who brought word. Ahead and behind, four eagles looked beyond the ambush site to the surrounding jungle.

However much Ilandeh knew about Tokoban, she could provide little intelligence on this land, with its sudden lines of hills that seemed intended to hinder their progress, its unexpected pools and hidden cenotes. He'd lost seven slave warriors the day before when a lip of rock hidden by a tangle of undergrowth had given way and taken them screaming down into a cave. Superstitious dog warriors had whispered of the lords of the Underworld aiding the Yaloh, and Pilos had been forced to punish them publicly for it. And now this.

Behind them, in the land they'd retaken, slaves and engineers were hurrying the completion of new pyramids with supplies dragged in from Xentiban. They were working through the night, building the pyramids small so they could be completed faster. The song would be weaker, but it would be there. Once Yalotlan was secure, grander structures would be built to properly honour the Singer and the song. Soon it would ring all through this land and all the way to to the edge of Ixachipan, stick after stick of majesty and hope. The peace of the Empire of Songs brought at last to these uncivilised peoples. Maybe then they'd stop setting fucking ambushes.

And when we are finally finished here, I will return to the Singing City for a conversation with Great Octave Enet, about so many things. And I will stand before the Singer and break her hold over him. And he will abandon the madness she has brought upon him. There will be peace across Ixachipan and a song of glory. And we will waken the world spirit and life will become music.

A dream for a different day.

Pilos pushed at the hanging man, setting his body to swinging again, the rope creaking like the slow laughter of one of the lords of the Underworld. He stared around the clearing some more, squinted up at the canopy. 'Sarn, you said the trail was clear. Now forty-six dogs and macaws are dead. My macaws. Your Flight's macaws.'

The Second Flight limped forward, a stretch of cotton bound around his torn calf. He wouldn't meet his High Feather's eyes and shame burnt in his face, hotter than the hidden sun.

'They had archers in the trees, softened us up before we knew they were there, High Feather. Must have taken out at least half of us with one flight of arrows. Then they swung down from the trees and came in to finish us with spears. I fought my way clear, injured two, but I could see they weren't taking prisoners, so I ran. No one else was getting out; they were mired in too deep. I would've given my life gladly if the cause wasn't already lost.'

'As Second Flight, you should've been at the front. You should've been the first to die,' Pilos snarled and spat into the dirt. 'And yet here you are, the only survivor.' He poked the man hard in the chest; Sarn flushed anew but didn't respond. 'I gave you this task to allow you to prove yourself after you led my scouts into an ambush. And here we are, and you . . . led my scouts into an ambush. Once can be forgiven, Sarn. But only once. I had thought you a Whisper; I had thought you a leader. Instead you are but a half-blood macaw, and you will march with the rest of your kind and fight with the rest of your kind. Give me your arm.'

'High Feather, please,' Sarn began.

'Feather Calan,' Pilos said softly and she caught Sarn in a chokehold and put a sharp sliver of obsidian beneath his eye. The Whisper stilled.

'Your arm,' he repeated and Sarn extended it. He was wheezing and his face was red, but his eyes pleaded. Pilos ignored them. The tattoo was just above the inside of his elbow – the little chulul. The mark of the Whisper.

'Please,' Sarn begged again, one last time. Pilos took the obsidian from Calan and slashed it through the tattoo, cutting the cat's head free, and then its tail. Sarn yelled and writhed, but Calan tightened her grip and choked off his protests. The blood was hot and fresh and pattered into the leaf-litter.

'Do you know where Flight Ilandeh's chulul is, Sarn?' Pilos demanded. The man was gasping at the pain, but he managed to shake his head in Calan's grip.

'The inside of her wrist. She told me when she made Flight the reason – so that if she ever dishonoured herself or displeased her High Feather, the destruction of the tattoo would kill her. That's how much it means. That's what a Flight is. Now get that seen to and make your way to the regular macaws. No stitches,' he warned, for he wouldn't be the first disgraced Whisper to try and save the tattoo. 'Cleaned and bound, no more.'

Calan let Sarn go and shoved him away, back down the

trail. She wiped her hands deliberately on her armour before accepting the sliver of glass back.

Pilos walked through the last of the ambush site, cleared of traps by those who'd died and those who'd secured the perimeter before the High Feather arrived.

'They know we're here, yet they're not pushing in. They ambushed us, now they're allowing us to regroup. Why?' he asked the trees.

And that, of course, was when the true attack came.

Pilos hadn't anticipated it, as such, but there was less surprise than admiration in him as arrows whined out of the trees to north and west and he threw himself into a stand of young chay, taller than he was and densely packed. A two-pronged attack on his position, and they'd held back long enough to ensure Pilos was barely guarded. They recognised him as High Feather and thought cutting the head from the snake would kill the body.

They were wrong, and not just because Atu was ripping them apart in the east of Yalotlan. Even if they killed every Feather in the Melody, he would still trust his eagles to bring them under the song.

Sarn sprinted down the track, calling for aid, his disgrace notwithstanding, while Calan came charging to her High Feather's defence. Sarn would bring everyone – eagles who wouldn't be held back from aiding their High Feather – and his elite would crush these bastards. They'd claim another stick of land, that little bit closer to Tokoban and peace.

Pilos just needed to hold out for a few hundred breaths and the fury of the Melody would fall on the enemy. He huddled in on himself as darts and arrows thudded into the soil and shredded the chay leaves, releasing their familiar scent and milky sap. Pilos wiped it carefully from his eyebrows and mouth. Such a small amount would do little harm unless it got in his eyes, but the situation was risky enough without adding in poison.

His armour, salt-cotton for the most part, like that of his warriors, was inlaid front and back with strips of painted mahogany in the same style and appearance as the toughened plates gracing the belly and back of the holy Setatmeh. It wouldn't stop a spear thrown from close range, but for now they weren't closing, so he had a chance.

And armour will do fuck all for me if I get a dart in the neck, he thought as one hit and bounced among the woody stems.

Calan was under a fig to his left, pressed against the trunk and watching him for orders. He could see her debating whether to sprint to his side and make herself into a shield, so he held up a flat palm, ordering her to stay still.

A scream from nearby, ragged and protracted – a bad wounding, maybe a poisoning. One of his warriors. The arrows and darts flittering across the clearing were coming from three sides now as the attackers kept them pinned down and worked their way around. They all knew it was a race to get to Pilos before reinforcements did. He wondered how many of the enemy had followed Sarn and whether his warning would reach the rest of the Melody at all.

Another scream as a second eagle found her cover insufficient against the new angle of attack. Pilos would be next, he knew. The chay was dense but the growing stems were slender and green, flexible, not enough to do more than disrupt line of sight and slow the arrows a little. He wormed further into their midst and then watched behind him. It was the only direction left open to them now and he knew all weapons would be trained on him the moment he broke cover.

A scattering of arrows and javelins whirred through the glade in the other direction. Not many, probably just those macaws stationed between here and the main camp below. The missiles pinning him down faltered, then grew even heavier as they tried to kill him before reinforcements got to him.

Pounding feet and the Pechaqueh war cry, and then the distinctive crack of wood on wood signalling hand-to-hand fighting. Pilos wiped his palm on his armour and gripped his club again; then he took his chance and joined the fray, leaping from cover and sprinting to the aid of a dog warrior. The head of his club crushed a Tokob warrior's shoulder and he fell at the feet of the dog; the man finished him, nodded shocked thanks to Pilos and then stepped between him and the flicker of a thrown spear. The weapon tore through the outer layers of his salt-cotton, its force stolen. It staggered him back two steps, into Pilos who caught him, grabbed the spear and wrenched it back out. A spray of blood followed.

The warrior grunted, then shook his head and pushed away from Pilos, hand pressed to his side. 'Go, High Feather. We'll cover you.'

Three Pechaqueh flowed around him, armed with small shields – eagles. 'No need, dog,' Pilos said and grinned as battle-joy surged within him. 'Kill them all,' he bellowed and the five of them charged the treeline, where the stutter and flow of movement gave shape to the enemy. To stay in the open was certain death; better to close with their attackers.

More eagles joined them, appearing from the trail or the surrounding jungle, and the dog warriors pulled back, let the eagles take their places around Pilos. Macaws ascended into the trees to support with darts and arrows of their own, shot from above.

Pilos aimed for the thickest knot of Yaloh and Tokob and

trusted to the holy Setatmeh and his armour. Screams and shouts erupted, leaves shivered down from the movement of Whispers in the trees, and the High Feather gave himself up to war.

In the end they'd held and then more than held, pushing their ambushers back through the hours and the rain and wind that whipped the treetops and fluttered the fan of wet feathers in Pilos's hair.

The macaws held the canopy and the eagles had the forest floor, dog warriors curving around on the flanks, and the Tokob and Yaloh were driven like deer ahead of a pack of grassland coyotes until they broke and scattered and not even the Whispers could track them through the gloom of storm and dusk. They lost nearly fifty dogs and half as many eagles before it was done, while the enemy dead numbered two-thirds that. They'd chosen the ambush site well, and they'd fallen back rather than fight to the death. It was no shame to admire a talented enemy, and Pilos did so even as he cursed their names and ancestors.

He walked among the wounded, shamans kneeling over them and bloody to the elbows, until he found the man. He squatted at his side. 'How do you feel? No, don't get up, that's an order.'

'Shaman says I'll live, High Feather. I'll be back in the line in a few days, less even,' the dog tried, panicking. Pilos squeezed his shoulder, hushing him. He looked for the nearest shaman for confirmation.

'A week, but yes, he'll live,' she said, wiping her hair out of her eyes and smearing blood across the blue paint zigzagged across her forehead.

'What's your name and how long have you fought?' Pilos asked, offering him a gourd of water.

The man looked terrified. 'Oteom of the Axib, High Feather. I have had the honour of fighting for four sun-years.'

'Four, eh? And before that?'

'My family are free weavers in Pechacan, High Feather,' Oteom said with deep pride and Pilos nodded his respect.

'You fought well. You fought bravely. And you saved my life. I'll see to it you're promoted to Coyote, Oteom, and your family and the Melody scribes informed of your change of status. Will you rejoin them when you have enough wealth?'

Oteom fought his way up to sitting, one hand clutched to the bandaging around his waist. His face was glowing. 'No, High Feather,' he said fervently. 'My place is here. My life is the Melody, for Singer and Setatmeh and Empire. For High Feather Pilos.'

Pilos grinned. 'Glad to hear it, Coyote Oteom of Axiban. Make sure you get your insignia from the scribes in the morning, yes?' The man nodded, overawed, and Pilos snorted at his expression and then left him with an instruction to rest.

They set a wide perimeter and the rest of the Melody moved up; no point returning to their established camp. 'Calan, pass word – we march at moonset. We've got ground to cover and I want to press our advantage – or at least make the enemy think we have an advantage and that that ambush didn't hurt us. Set dogs to string out in a wide skirmish line to either side of the main force so we don't get flanked. Whispers scouting a stick ahead and slave warriors behind them. If they trigger any more ambushes I don't want the eagles taking the brunt of it. We'll need them for the Sky City.'

'As the High Feather commands.'

'They're starting to piss me off now,' he added and Calan laughed.

'They won't live free to regret it,' she said with a grin

undimmed by the hours she'd fought. He smiled back and Calan touched belly and throat and vanished between the trees.

Pilos licked his teeth and then spat. 'Fucking Wet,' he muttered as the wind freed a cascade of droplets from the branches above. The advance was too slow, and every day they didn't reach Tokoban was a day more that those heathen bastards could be killing or torturing the gods. There were four days left until the Great Star began its grand absence, when it would vanish for ninety days and return in the evening, not the morning. Surely its absence would be long enough to conclude the war. They might even be home in time for its reappearance. That would be a good omen.

Patience, Pilos. The Wet will end, the ground will firm and the conquest will proceed as the holy Setatmeh decree.

And then peace. Finally. Once I've strangled Enet with her own entrails.

Pilos huffed a quiet laugh and made himself a nest in the roots of a strangler vine. Moonset was only a few hours away; best sleep while he could. It was going to get far worse before it got better, and not even the prospect of strangling the Great Octave was enough to distract him from the cold worry of what was to come.

XESSA

The Great Star had vanished.

All across Tokoban and Yalotlan, cities and towns should have been a riot of noise and colour as people celebrated the story of the Great Star's disappearance below the horizon as, in his guise as the Watcher, he took their prayers to the spirits awaiting rebirth and brought succour to those trapped in the Underworld.

During the ninety days of its absence, there should be rituals and prayers and festivals. There should be feasts and spirit-journeys and great day-long dances to lend the Watcher their strength. Instead, there would be blood. Oceans of it. The Great Star would return to the sky and the world beneath him would be soaked red. Choked with corpses and salted with tears.

The Sky City had begun the day with a muted celebration. Smiles were strained and prayers were whispered with a desperate, clench-faced fervour. At the very moment they

427

most needed the Great Star's guiding presence, he had left them to fight a battle of his own.

'He has not left us!' High Elder Apok had shouted out over the ceremonial plaza at dawn. 'He shows us the way. He shows us that strength and battle are our only hope now. He walks the trail that we too must walk, and where he battles the very lords of the Underworld to save those ancestors who are lost, we merely battle people. Let the Watcher's victories be ours, and ours his. We strengthen each other, for in this, too, there is balance. As he fights below, so we fight above.'

Now, Xessa sat on the steps of a small plaza in the circle of Toxte's arms, the weight of his chin on her shoulder, watching the shaman fight.

Xessa was surprised at how quickly Tayan had learnt, though she knew why, of course. Not even a captive Drowned could distract the friend of her heart from the loss of his husband, and he'd been more serious than she'd realised about learning to fight.

Lutek swung again, the head of her hatchet black against the grey sky, and Tayan leapt sideways and stumbled, his ankle rolling beneath him, but somehow he got his own axe between hers and his flesh and Xessa let out the breath she'd been holding. He was still wearing the paint from this morning's rituals and it was smeared into his hair with sweat. He looked wild.

Tayan's small wooden shield cracked under the next blow and Lutek punched him in the face when he hesitated to look at it. He sat down hard, blood already oozing from his nose, and she pressed her foot onto his wrist, pinning his axe, her own raised.

Better but not good. Not yet. Xessa wondered if he'd have long enough to become good, or whether the Empire would have killed them all by then. It soured the morning and she clutched Toxte's arms tighter around her waist and leant back into him, turning her head so they could kiss.

He shifted her sideways so he could sign, and alarm flashed through her at his seriousness. 'This isn't the best time to be talking about this,' he started and the wind was suddenly too cold and too harsh, stealing her breath, stealing inside her until she shivered. She wouldn't cry, not in front of him and Lutek. She promised herself she wouldn't cry.

'I understand,' she signed and shifted further away from him so she could stand. He grabbed her hand and pulled, making her look.

'I don't,' he signed. 'I don't know what you think's going on here, but that's not the answer I was hoping for.' Toxte hesitated and blew out his cheeks, then nodded once, sharp, to himself. 'I know it's early in our relationship, I know we haven't . . . Eja Xessa, will you marry me?'

The question was so unexpected that she just sat there, her mouth hanging open. *Marry?*

Anxiety was building in his eyes and his hands blurred with speed. 'I know we haven't been together for long, but the world is changing and there's war in the trees and we might all be dead in a month and I don't want to die without you knowing how I feel. I love you, Xessa, I've loved you for more than a year and I want to marry you. If you'll allow it . . . Will you allow it?'

Xessa's hands had started to shake. Her fingers were cold and clumsy. She couldn't even tell him how much she loved him, because her hands wouldn't work, so she pressed her face against his and then her mouth, and then her arms around him and her chest to his and he shifted and held her and scooped her into his lap and she closed her eyes against the promise of the day and gave herself to the promise of him. It was sweeter, and warmer, and more luminous than even the sun.

When she could finally lean back, he was a little astonished and a little confused. 'Yes?' he asked her and she laughed. She nodded. She kissed him again. Marriage during the Great Star's absence was considered unlucky, but he was right – they might be dead in a month. She wouldn't waste a single instant of their lives together worrying over that. Malel would understand. So would the Watcher.

'We should celebrate,' he signed, jubilant, but a shadow fell over them – Tayan.

'You're supposed to be watching my epic victory over the warrior,' he signed, but he knew. Knew and was trying to hide his grief for their joy.

Xessa unwound herself from Toxte and stood so she could wipe the drying blood from his chin. 'Go again,' she signed. 'Show me how you're going to save Lilla. And know that I'll be at your side to do it.'

Toxte stood. 'We both will,' he signed, and although Xessa hadn't thought it possible, she loved him even more for that.

Tayan slapped Toxte's shoulder. 'Welcome to the council of idiots,' he signed. 'And just know that if you ever hurt her, I'll hold her beer while she beats you to death with your own bollocks.'

'I'd expect nothing less,' Toxte signed solemnly. 'And, if you'd be the one to marry us, I would consider it a great honour.'

Xessa winced, because it would hurt him to do it, but Tayan forestalled her protest. 'If you had asked anyone else, I'd have held Lutek's beer while she beat you to death with your own bollocks. Now watch me fight!'

* * *

It had been a stolen moment. A lightning flash of joy in the darkness of the city's life as the war drew closer and gave good people the excuse to do bad things.

They'd come out of her house wrapped in secret smiles and stolen kisses, and they'd been on their way to Toxte's house to gather his belongings when they passed through the market and heard the news: the Quitob slaves rescued by Lilla and Kux's war party had been slaughtered. All of them: none left alive. They'd been housed in the Jaguar-god temple. Not guarded, but watched. Certainly not roped. Allowed out in the temple's gardens but just . . . encouraged not to leave. Shamans and elders had been visiting them each day to remind them what freedom looked like and how they might choose, for themselves, the shape of their lives to come. How if, after some time in the Sky City, they chose to return to their owners, then the Tokob would not stand in their way, though they hoped the Quitob would choose instead to stay with their new friends.

Only when they'd visited this time, to hold a smaller ceremony honouring the Watcher, the temple was awash with blood and the Quitob were dead, piled in heaps and droves, their blood staining walls and murals and idols. Death from spear and knife, arrow and dart, many of them poisoned. There had to have been screaming, but no one admitted to hearing anything. And so Tokob blamed Yaloh, Yaloh blamed Tokob, and the tension between the two tribes increased again.

The market was rife with gossip and speculation and Toxte pointed out how Tokob were trading only with Tokob, and Yaloh with Yaloh. 'Well, that can't last,' Xessa signed sourly. 'We're the ones providing food and water for them. When that runs out, they'll have to trade with us or starve.'

'They're just scared,' Toxte signed.

'They're not the only ones,' a passing merchant had

snapped. 'Not that we'll have time to starve if they keep on murdering everyone they decide they don't like. We should throw them out of the city.'

Xessa and Toxte hurried away. Xessa left her soon-to-be husband – *husband!* – arranging his belongings in her home – *our home* – and went to find Tayan in the womb. It was how he spent his days now – ritual in the morning, then training with the other non-fighters in the plazas, then the hours until duskmeal in the womb. He was getting thinner, but also stronger. But he was tired and she knew he was trying to fill his days so he didn't think of Lilla. As promised, he'd journeyed with her – in Otek's presence, though her father was too frail to journey with them – to the Realm of the Ancestors and Kime. Knowing he was safe and that his spirit was ascending to rebirth had leached some of the guilt from her, lancing the poison so that she could begin healing. She didn't know what she'd have done if Tayan hadn't come back when he had.

Ossa bounced at her side or raced ahead and then back, covering three times the distance as she jogged easily uphill, his tongue flapping and his tail high.

Xessa was breathing hard but relishing the burn in her legs and lungs and the freshness of the air by the time the trail began to dip into the earth to take her to the womb. The ejab on duty had the rope stretched. 'Tayan?' Xessa asked and they nodded. 'Who's in with him?'

'He said he'd do this one alone,' Esna said. 'The Drowned won't speak with an eja there.'

The Drowned won't speak?

Xessa shoved past them and lunged into the earth's embrace and pelted along the tunnel towards the glow of torchlight. She burst around the corner and skidded to a halt, squinting at the brightness. Ossa was at her side and she brandished her spear, blinking desperately. Tayan was already standing and facing her, his hands moving. 'It's all right. No danger. There's no danger. I'm perfectly safe.'

Ripples in the water told her the Drowned had shifted at her arrival, and now it was huddled against the rear wall again, one clawed hand clutching at the rock.

'You don't need to be scared,' Tayan signed to her. 'It won't hurt me.' The skin tightened on Xessa's face. *Won't hurt you?* She jerked her head at the exit. 'No, Xessa, not yet. Let me talk to it. Look at the book over there, look at everything I've learnt about it so far. The things I know, they're, they're incredible. And it's quite docile, I promise.'

Tayan was calm, but there was an intensity about him she didn't like, as if he'd taken the journey-magic. He gestured again but Xessa wouldn't look at the book. She frowned: there was something different about the Drowned. It was still curled against the back wall, huddled as far from her as it could get, but those eyes she'd once thought of as empty were anything but. They evaluated her, inspected her and her weapons, her dog. Her lack of armour. Its throat sac rippled and Tayan turned back to it. He was talking to it. As if it was human. As if it understood him.

And perhaps it did, because slowly the Drowned relaxed and sank back to put one gill beneath the water. Those big, black eyes flitted between eja and shaman and dog, back and forth, and its throat did that same ripple again. And again Tayan spoke to it. Answered it.

Xessa eased forward another step to try and read his lips, but again the Drowned thrashed away from her and Tayan whirled, his hands out. 'Please don't come any closer. Any time there's an eja down here, it's too afraid to communicate. Please, if you insist on being here, then wait over there.' He pointed to the cave mouth. 'Safer for everyone that way.'

433

Xessa licked her lips. This was wrong, but she knew the instant she put down her spear to sign, it would attack. If all she could do was stand and watch, then that's what she'd do. But not over at the fucking exit. The eja took five steps sideways, with her toes in the water and a clear line of sight between her and the Drowned. Unless Tayan did something spectacularly stupid, he couldn't get between her and it – and the rope harness shouldn't stretch too much closer to it anyway.

She caught a glimpse of Tayan's marriage cord hanging around his neck and suddenly wondered how it would feel to wear one herself. One given her by Toxte, knotted with the promises they'd make to each other. Tayan's was sweat-stained from his travels, but he wouldn't make a new one until he was back with Lilla. That was how it worked. That was what marriage was. Or one of the things.

Xessa blinked and gripped the spear hard, focusing. She could feel that weird vibration again, but when she looked the Drowned's throat sac wasn't bulging. She snapped her fingers and when Tayan looked over, she tapped her ear.

He shook his head. 'Well, not really. It's almost . . . humming. I think it's trying to comfort itself. It stopped communicating when you came in.' His disapproval was thick in the air and it cut at her, but she let it go. She wasn't the one in the wrong here. He got back to his observations, scribbling with charcoal in the book and seemingly asking it questions. Xessa had no idea whether it was answering – and how could it answer, anyway? It didn't have their language. Unless Tayan had somehow learnt its way of speaking. An eerie, unpleasant image of the shaman singing like a Drowned flickered before her eyes and she shivered and pushed it away.

Xessa's temples began to throb, thirst clawing at her. Ossa was sitting out of the water, his head drooping. Only

Tayan seemed energised. She thought of drinking the water, but the Drowned lived in it, ate in it, pissed and shitted in it too. No wonder it was stuffy and hot and smelly in here. Ancestors, but she was thirsty. She snapped her fingers again. 'Water?'

Tayan pointed vaguely and Xessa sidled in that direction, unwilling to turn her back, but there was no gourd of water in sight. She risked a glance, looked back: no change. Another glance, to her left this time, and back; the Drowned hadn't moved.

And then she saw it, sitting on a ledge just outside the cave mouth. She backed into the tunnel, fumbling for it. Her fingers bumped stone, and then bumped something else that wobbled, wobbled. Xessa made a grab for it on instinct and missed. The gourd fell, spilling its contents on the floor of the cave. Ossa slunk over and lapped it up and she groaned and rubbed her brow. Maybe she was getting ill. She pressed her face to the cool stone, feeling her heartbeat in her temples.

The eja took several deep breaths and then straightened up and looked back into the cave. Tayan was standing face to face with the Drowned, which stood perhaps half a head taller than he did. The shaman was reaching out to it, and the Drowned was reaching back as if they were lovers about to embrace and now she saw its throat sac fully extended and it was singing, singing.

Xessa gasped and scrabbled for the spear she'd leant against the wall and when she charged back in, almost tripping over Ossa in her haste, the Drowned was hunched against the rear wall and Tayan was standing with book and charcoal in hand. She blinked desperately, her heart thudding so hard her vision was pounding with it, but everything was normal. The Drowned was still roped and still huddled in the water. Tayan's harness was secure.

She'd imagined it. She *must have* imagined it.

She stayed close to the shaman after that, hurrying him along, and she insisted he leave the womb before her. Xessa paused before turning the corner and looked back one last time. The Drowned's fingers twitched in something that might have been a wave, and then it rolled over in the water and put its armoured back to her.

ENET

*Great Octave's estate, Singing City, Pechacan, Empire of
Songs
7th day of the grand absence of the Great Star*

Enet sat in the light from the window, enjoying a rare break
in the clouds, and mixed her tonic. She drank it down, barely
noticing the grit or the aftertaste any more.

Reports had come from both Pilos and Atu, confirming
progress was being made in Yalotlan. Once they had peace
throughout Ixachipan, it would be time to consider waking
the world spirit. And Xac with his red-stained song was
perhaps not . . . the correct holy lord for so delicate a task.

It was frightening but freeing to know she didn't need to
worry so much about the Singer reading her intentions
through the song any more. The holy lord was much preoccupied these days. Under her gentle, invisible guidance, she
had led him to concentrate his attention on demanding and
receiving updates on the war. The more stories of victory
and bloodshed filled his head, the more they might begin to
fill the gaping, black-toothed maw of hunger within him.

And of course, it kept Pilos accountable.

The song was a rumble of warning and impatience, summoning her as surely as any messenger or Listener. She would have to answer soon. She did what she could to keep his hungers in check, stretching out the days between offerings, but she also knew when Xac was reaching the point where he would take her if she didn't supply an alternative. These days there was always a pretty slave held ready in her quarters within the source.

The holy lord grew ever more voracious in his appetites, and she had let it be known he was coming into the fullness of his power as Singer. The gossip was the opposite: that the Singer was waning and beginning his ascension, and the resultant scrambling among his council was as predictable as it was pathetic.

By now, it seemed that the entire council and most of the nobles were aware of the blooding – or that the Singer's indulgences had gone wrong, at least. Some of his favourites had quietly disappeared from the source, likely fearing that they would be the next to leave a bloody stain on the mats. Those who remained redoubled their efforts to ingratiate themselves, hinting at the blooding and making approving noises. So far, none had attempted to procure an offering themselves, and Enet worked hard to ensure that one of the Chorus loyal to her was on duty whenever she couldn't be there. She couldn't afford for anyone else to start supplying the Singer with this particular experience.

Not that anyone would be able to harm Enet now, no matter their suspicions. Not Yana or the remaining favourites, not even Pilos when he slunk back from war like the blood-clotted dog he was. No one. Curving up the column of Enet's throat was a tattoo of a dark feather. The mark of a Chosen. Chosen of the Singer. Chosen to ascend with him – or even, perhaps, to succeed him. Singer Enet.

Xac had taken very little convincing in the end. He had seen the exquisite twin slaves she'd found for him and begged for them. Actually begged her, panting like a dog in heat and the song building in waves all around. Enet had cooed and flattered and placed the tattoo equipment into his hands. The Singer had complied without even a murmur. Quickly, while the slaves knelt at the edge of the mats with their eyes cast down in respect, he had dipped the thorn into the ink and given her the mark. And she had given him the twins.

Enet had inspected it in a piece of polished gold later that night when the Singer slept in his bloodstained glory – and then she'd summoned her own tattooist and had the design tidied up around the edges, so that none might mistake it.

Nothing could take this away from her now: Enet was Chosen, elite even among Pechaqueh nobility, as far above them as the sun was above the earth. The future was bright – incandescent – with possibility.

For now, though, Enet put such thoughts from her mind and slipped into a loose kilt and tunic, with a wide red sash bound from her hips up to her breasts. Another symbol of power. The body slave knelt near with the tray of cosmetics, but she could wait a little longer. The Great Octave reopened the letter and scanned its contents. Another potential source of songstone had been uncovered, in Chitenec of all places. She'd thought all those quarries had been worked out. She'd been told so. Now there was yet another challenge to her supply of the sacred stone and she still hadn't managed to successfully raise the subject of the Tokoban songstone with the Singer. Fixated as he was on war and blooding the song, he could fly into a spectacular rage when she mentioned anything that might increase her influence.

'You,' she said to her estate slave and the man bowed. 'I want an accurate report on the supply in Chitenec, and I don't want anyone to know it's me asking, so use at least four intermediaries to cover your trail. If it's rich enough, buy it but keep my name out of it. But if it's small, buy a stake in it – and do that publicly. We can afford to lose a little wealth for the status it will bring. But I want to know who buys the other stakes.'

'As the Great Octave commands,' the man said and bowed again. Frowning, Enet put the letter in a dish and touched a candle to it. She couldn't let just anyone begin supplying songstone, for new pyramids were always required, not just in the new parts of the Empire but to replace those that grew old or unstable, or where the songstone caps cracked and failed.

The construction of pyramids and supply of their crucial, magical capstone was an honour that could not be handed out thoughtlessly. While theoretically, anyone with the wealth to do so could contribute a songstone cap, the reality was that Enet had spent two Star cycles covertly gathering all the songstone supplies into her hands, and strictly monitored those whom she allowed to purchase from her. Not that anyone knew they were purchasing from her, of course. But controlling the pyramids controlled the flow of status, the height or depth within society of the family offering their wealth to their development. Let them scrabble for limestone and sandstone and timber; Enet didn't care for those. But for the songstone, for the source of the world spirit's own voice, its own dreams, perhaps? No. No, access to that must be strictly supervised, and who better to do so than the Great Octave herself?

'You. Do my face.' The slave scurried over and began to apply the cosmetics, the charcoal around her eyes and the staining for her lips. Another began fixing the feathered headdress to Enet's hair with pins.

'A guest, mistress,' her estate slave said moments later. 'Councillor Chel seeks entry.'

Enet grimaced. 'Show her into the garden room and provide refreshment. If she wants to see me, she'll wait.'

When the paint was correctly applied and the headdress secure, Enet padded sedately into the outer room and found Chel reclining on the mats and examining the new mural the Great Octave had had commissioned. Enet paused to admire it herself, to admire how well the artist had captured the tilt of her head, her demure obedience to the stylised symbol of the Singer before which she knelt.

Enet's gaze tracked from the image of herself to the curve of Chel's neck, left exposed by the hair piled atop her head and secured with jade and bone. An undoubtedly pretty woman. With the voice and manners of a starving rat. But few people in this world were perfect, and when the two of them were among the pillows it didn't matter, when Chel's abrasive tones gentled into urgent whispers, begging and commanding. It was only in the pillows that Enet allowed herself to be commanded by anyone other than the Singer.

She held her feathered fan before her. 'Councillor Chel.'

Chel twisted on the mat and craned her neck to look up. Her lips puckered in appreciation of what she saw. 'My, my, all for my benefit?' she teased. She waved away the need for Enet to reply. 'I have news, Great Octave.' Her use of the title didn't go unnoticed and Enet stopped preening and moved to the mat opposite, dropping down to sitting heedless of the fall of her kilt. Chel wasn't here for pleasure.

Enet gestured to the refreshments first, as propriety demanded, but the other woman shook her head. 'Speak then,' she said.

'There are concerns throughout the city, among the nobles

and some of the council. Concerns about the changes to the song.'

Oh, pretty little Chel. How bold of you. And unexpected. Do you come to me because I am Spear, and Great Octave, and principal courtesan? Or because you suspect my involvement? And how was it that you were the one chosen for this task, to be the sacrifice on the altar of my wrath? Pretty, yes, but not clever, I think.

They watched each other, cat studying rat, seeing who would blink first. 'Changes? You mean the swelling of power as the Singer exerts all his will to crushing the Yaloh and Tokob resistance? How he exhorts the pyramid-builders to work faster in Yalotlan to bring the succour of the song to those of the Melody stationed there? So that they may be as close to glory as possible? How his power waxes to its fullest might so that all Ixachipan might hear it?'

Chel twisted a strand of artfully dishevelled hair around one finger. 'Indeed. Perhaps the Singer might make a public announcement stating that is the cause, to reassure the . . . more superstitious among the population?'

The cat flexed its claws. 'What a good idea. Why don't I secure you an audience with the holy lord and you can suggest it to him yourself?'

The hair-twirling stopped. 'Thank you, Great Octave, but no, although the honour is great. For a start, my status is not sufficient for such a privilege. And also . . . well, it is rumoured that those who enter the Singer's presence at your side are never seen again.' Chel shrugged. 'My lovers would miss me if I were to, ah, vanish into his domain.'

Enet narrowed her eyes and let the fan fall. Chel's gasp as she saw the feather tattoo was gratifying. 'There are always rumours dripping from the tongues of the jealous and the stupid,' Enet said. 'Rarely do such rumours have any truth to them. But I will pass on your suggestion nonetheless. It is my life's greatest honour to advise the holy lord. If his people are restless, we shall do what is required to calm them.'

And she could say that now, 'we', because she was Chosen, and if Chel had thought to trade on their occasional intimacy she was very much mistaken. Enet enjoyed watching the other woman come to the same realisation.

Nothing could touch her now, not Chel's jealousy or Pilos's scheming or even Councillor Yana's quiet hostility. She and the Singer were almost one, their words and bodies joined, her divinity second only to his, her future secure and her past buried so deep none would ever unearth it.

And if they did, they would die before they could tell what they had learnt. They would not be the first.

'Anything else?' Enet asked.

'Well,' Chel murmured, sliding a finger into the neck of her own blouse and tugging gently downwards. 'Seeing as I'm here . . .'

Enet gave her the smile that made the sun seem dim in comparison. 'My love, I wish for nothing more, but I am the Singer's first and foremost and he has sent for me.'

Chel's hand fell back into her lap and her face smoothed. 'Of course, dear. The Singer's will is all. His appetites, though . . . well, they too are becoming the subject of speculation among the council and the wealthier nobles who hear of such things.'

'Yes, I am exhausted these days,' Enet replied, but said no more. And to that, Chel was unable to find a suitable response. They exited the house together and climbed into separate litters. Chel drew the curtains of hers; Enet did not. Let the Singing City see her, adorned in feathers and dripping with jade, that mark of the Chosen dark on her throat, as she travelled to the palace and into the Singer's presence.

Let them marvel at her. Let her glory steal their attention so that none would notice the two slaves walking behind the litter, the newest gifts for the Singer.

It had been ten days since the last. The holy lord needed to be fed.

THE SINGER

The source, Singing City, Pechacan, Empire of Songs

I am the Singer.

I am war and Empire and blood and fucking and death. I am screams. I am babes torn from parents.

I am the stars torn from the fucking sky if I choose. None can stop me. Here, now, in the darkness of my brother Sky Jaguar's absence, I am all there is to look upon and worship.

And I demand worship.

I am the Singer. Blood and Empire and glory are my legacy. I will be the one immortal at the world spirit's side. I will be its holy vessel. It is my strength that will awaken it; my strength that will nurture it. I will be loved as the world spirit is loved.

I am the Singer. I am the Empire. I am the divinity that restores the balance of this world: life and death; flesh and spirit; blood and magic.

I am the song. And my song is gore enough to drown the world.

445

PILOS

It had taken more days, more lives, and more fighting than he'd hoped, but less – just – than he'd feared.

Their advance had been torturously slow, though at least it meant they'd been able to dig in properly in Yalotlan, allowing the engineers and slaves to throw up small pyramids. The song now rang across almost all of western Yalotlan. Pilos prayed nightly to the holy Setatmeh that the same was true in the rest of that land, that Atu and the Talons under his command were making similar progress in their long, bloody drive to the coast. But now, finally, they were in Tokoban.

As he'd half feared and half expected – and so planned for – the war had degenerated into the same bitter, hard-fought mess that he'd faced in Quitoban so long before, but instead of river deltas and tidal marshes, they faced increasingly hilly territory, concealed ravines, and night attacks. Yaloh and Tokob fought not just for every stick, but for

446

every tree and vine and flower. They spilt blood as liberally as any holy Setat, their own and that of the Melody, and in the last two weeks they had made it clear that mercy was a concept unknown to them.

They set ambushes in areas prone to mudslides; they laid snares and pit-traps on the trails, they coated the leaves that hung across their path with blinding tree sap so that any who brushed against them were tormented by burning welts. Everything they did was designed to slow them. And slow them it did.

'How far to this hill of theirs, Flight?' Pilos asked as they stood in the shade of an immense fig, conscious of the fact this whole land was a series of hills of varying sizes. For all he knew, they might be halfway up this sacred mountain already.

Ilandeh clicked her tongue as she thought. 'On a clear run from here, seven days. Facing what we've been facing and with towns ahead of us? Two weeks. Could be more.'

'Well, it can't be more,' Pilos said. 'I'd prefer if it wasn't two weeks, either.' Every day he sent word back through the jungle to a pyramid where Citla, his Listener, waited to send updates to the Singer. The responses that came back were . . . confused. Many were clearly from the holy lord himself, demanding greater speed and reiterating, over and over, his desire that they send him the frog-lickers, but others required him to find shamans and keepers of lore and old tales, those who knew the history of their peoples and the creation myths.

Pilos had no idea whether these had come from the Singer or Enet. Neither filled him with much confidence as to the state of the Singing City and the wider Empire. His desire to return to his Singer's side and lance the infection rushing through the song increased with every passing day. His frustration – at the terrain, at the still-falling rain, at the Yaloh and Tokob shadows among the trees – grew with it.

'We need to conclude this campaign and get back to the Singing City,' Pilos said with quiet vehemence. 'Ten days. I need us at the Sky City within ten days. And I need a way in.' He pointed at Ilandeh. 'Flight, you're the only one here who knows the ground.'

He didn't add how much he could have done with Dakto's input as well as hers; Ilandeh knew it, and she blamed herself even though they'd been separated when the man had apparently made his own decision to wander all the way back to the Singing City to escort a few lines of slaves. Still, he could have been back by now, if he was coming. Pilos had sent a message to Elaq and Yana both to look out for the Whisper if he was still in the Singing City. He needed to know what he was up to.

The High Feather was glad Ilandeh blamed herself for his absence. It showed leadership, and out here, with time running out and Sarn disgraced, he needed warriors he could count on. Even half-blood macaws. 'How do we do this?' he asked.

'Pushing through Tokoban so far hasn't been easy, but I'm afraid it's going to get worse: the ground rises in hill ranges from here, plus their major settlements are all at the base of Malel, and of course the Sky City itself is high up on the mountain. We need to cross the ranges and then take these villages and towns at the base before we even start to climb.' Ilandeh pointed along the game trail they were using. 'The towns are spread around the base like a necklace. Five of them, plus the usual scattered settlements. It's five days to the towns and takes two to climb Malel to the Sky City. So with a ten-day deadline, that gives us three days to take the towns.'

She paused and puffed out her cheeks, then began to scrape a rough map in the mud with a stick. 'There are four game trails I know of that lead onto Malel and to the Sky City. Three are used heavily and lead past these three settlements. This trail heads straight uphill to the Sky City. But all four trails will be watched, and as soon as the first of these towns falls, word will reach the Sky City we're coming.'

'Clever bastards,' he muttered. 'And there's no way round?'

'No, and they'll be alert because of any forces we've driven ahead of us. I doubt even the Whispers could sneak past in any great number . . .' She trailed off and Feather Calan went to speak, but Pilos hushed her.

'But they don't need to be in great numbers, do they?' Ilandeh muttered and then coughed and winced, holding her chest. The blow she'd taken during the ambush had made her breathy, but she'd kept up with the march. Pilos knew it would take more than a club to the lungs to slow her down. It was one of the reasons he valued her so highly. That, and she was clever. 'May I?' she asked.

Pilos nodded. 'Please.'

Half a smile crooked the corner of her mouth and she shifted. 'Our noble adversaries like targeting work parties, killing overseers and warriors and freeing those slaves who would rather betray the song than die alongside their betters. Those freed slaves were being sent back towards Malel, but many of them will have stopped in these towns, especially if they're fatigued or wounded. It's likely that they all now have Axib, Quitob, even Tlaloxqueh refugees living with them. Many people. Many new, unfamiliar faces.'

Pilos grunted. 'I like where this is going. How many do you think would make a difference?'

'Ideally, a full half of the Whispers. I only visited one of these towns and I'd say it held a few thousand people. The rest, as far as I know, are of a like size. Fifty good Whispers in each to sabotage from the inside when you attack from without could be enough to tip the balance in our favour so they fall quickly. And we can cut off anyone trying to head uphill to warn the Sky City.'

'But how do we get you in there?' Calan asked.

'Seed them through the jungle in small groups and have them running scared for the war parties to find and take them home like the saviours they believe themselves to be,' Pilos said. 'They won't all make it, but enough will.'

'It's what we train for,' Ilandeh agreed with impressive equanimity. 'Blending in; avoiding suspicion. As you say, enough will get through to make a difference when the attack comes.'

Pilos knew she'd go if he asked it of her, despite being relatively well known in the Sky City and perhaps elsewhere.

'The Whispers' main priority will be to stop Tokob running uphill with word of our arrival. Second task will be opening gates and disrupting defence.' Pilos tapped his finger on the triangle of the Sky City. 'All right, I like it and I want the Whispers selected and sent off today. Once they've gone, they'll be on their own until we arrive at the Sky City. So how do we take the Sky City itself?'

Ilandeh began to sketch a second map. Pilos had already studied the one she had drawn while she waited for the Melody to arrive, but they could all do with a reminder now they were actually among the hills and jungle. Terrain always looked different when you were in it.

'Once we've taken the towns, we can split to use all four game trails for a swifter ascent. To the west, here, the land is bounded by the Great Roar; from what I learnt, no one lives there because the river is so wide and dangerous. There's a possibility they might flee that way to try and evade us, and I'd recommend sending a good number of pods there once we've taken the main territory just to clear it, but it's wild land, uncultivated, and they struck me as people who preferred the illusion of safety provided by stone walls.'

'Beyond Malel?' Pilos asked, gesturing at the crude map.

Ilandeh was shaking her head. 'Hardly anyone lives beyond the hill, or even on its northern slope. Their territory ends abruptly and the salt pans bordering it extend almost to its base and much of the lower land is poisoned from the salt blowing onto it.' She drew two lines, one heading up the triangle representing the hill, the other circling around to its rear before ascending. 'If we can co-ordinate it, I recommend a pincer, but the force skirting the hill to take its northern face should set out today – it gives them time to cover the additional distance while we take the necklace of towns.'

Feather Calan leant forward. 'Keep two Talons down here to fool them into thinking it's our full force while the third climbs its northern slope? Can we get up high without being seen?'

'They don't frequent the northern slope?' Pilos added, cautious excitement flaring in his chest.

Ilandeh grinned at them both. 'Yes, we can, and no, they don't. In all the moons Dakto and I were there, only shamans went onto the upper northern slope to collect medicine. They don't farm it; they haven't settled it. Plus, they say it's spirit-haunted by people who died trying to cross the salt pans. The most we should encounter are shamans and maybe a few scouts. Easily dealt with.'

Pilos glanced north, as if he could see the Tokob hill through the thick canopy. 'I like it,' he said.

It was audacious, and they stood to lose far too many spies and assassins if they were discovered, but the urgency in his blood, and the continued wrongness of the song, reported to him each day by Citla, drove him on. He didn't want to waste Whispers, but better them than his eagles.

'If I may, High Feather, what about what happened to Dakto? Is there a risk that the Whispers' loyalty might be tainted?' Calan asked. She blushed when Ilandeh narrowed her eyes at her, but it was a valid question. Pilos gestured for the Flight to answer.

Ilandeh grimaced and shifted. 'We don't know that anything's happened to my Second Flight,' she said, her tone neutral. 'Besides, we were in much deeper back then. We were among the Tokob for a year, tasked with making friends and earning trust by any means necessary. And during that time we were confronted with the slaughter of the holy Setatmeh and the abomination of the ejab. It would unsettle anyone. These Whispers will be in Tokob towns a matter of days, and those towns will be under assault. It's a completely different situation.'

He nodded. 'Do it. Flight, pick the smallest and lightest we've got, all genders. Get collars on them and get them out there – they're not to take food or water with them; I want them thirsty, filthy, and vulnerable. They're to stay a few days ahead of our front line – and any who get caught by our advance scouts get a beating. It needs to look real, and they need to be desperate to get out of harm's way.'

'As the High Feather commands.'

'And the slave brands?' Feather Calan asked. They stilled at that. Pilos watched Ilandeh; her nostrils flared but her face was smooth and blank.

'No. Put them in sleeves or bandages. They're to say, only if questioned, that they're hiding their brands the better to escape the Melody. But not to mention it at all unless they have no other choice.'

Ilandeh coughed again and then exhaled raggedly. She met Pilos's eyes. 'Thank you, High Feather.'

He looked at them both. 'It's going to be bloody and I want us ready to support our Whispers. I want us taking – and holding – territory, not just the towns; we want the people and we want the harvest. Easiest way to control a population?' he asked and looked to Calan.

The Feather grinned. It was one of the first lessons young eagles learnt when they joined the Melody. 'Control the children; control the council. No one fights when their offspring's at risk.'

Pilos smiled. 'All right, we have a plan and we have a set number of days to accomplish it. We move in an hour. Under the song.'

LILLA

*Melody fortress, the dead plains, Tlalotlan, Empire of
Songs
12th day of the grand absence of the Great Star*

The Melody fortress was immense, and it sat among huge
fields ripe with corn and peas. South, in the shadow of tall
hills that reminded Lilla of home, a salt pan stretched, white
and flat. The dead plains.

The fortress's walls were tall and patrolled by warriors
armed with bows. There was a wide training ground outside
where the eagles practised; the slave and dog warriors' own
training areas were behind the walls, cut off from the horizon
and any slender possibility of escape.

When the heavy mahogany gates had been pushed open
and Lilla followed the line of warriors in, he'd tried to
summon the effort needed to look, to notice the placement
of guards and memorise the route from the gate to the slave
barracks. But when the shadow of those walls had fallen
across him and the gates had rumbled shut, a piece of his
spirit had died.

They hadn't been taken to the slave barracks. They'd been led into a small plaza and to a pit dug into the ground. The ropes had been loosened – removed for the first time since their capture – and they'd been shoved down the steps and a bamboo gate dropped to lock them in. Hundreds in each pit, crammed together in humid, fetid gloom. And here they'd stayed.

For four weeks.

Tayan was going to come for him. Lilla knew it as surely as he knew how dawn looked on the first dry day after the Wet, when it bled across the grand plaza's steps, gold and gleaming. Tayan was going to come, despite the danger, despite not treading the jaguar path, because he was a fool and he loved Lilla and one of the promises on their marriage cords was that they would always find the other and bring them home. A foolish promise when Lilla was a warrior, perhaps, but the promises cut both ways, so when Lilla had pledged always to find Tayan – *because how could he not?* – the shaman had pledged it straight back, full of love and without hesitation. How Lilla regretted that promise now.

He stood in the filth and the perpetual gloom of the pit, crushed shoulder to shoulder with nearly a hundred Yaloh and Tokob, and he knew despair. The song had a resonance down here somehow, a weight and potency, though Lilla hadn't seen any pyramids built within the fortress as they'd shambled towards it.

On the other side of the pit a fight broke out, words becoming shoves becoming a scuffle and then fists were flying. Lilla and Kux and a few others broke it up, wrestling the fighters away from each other and through the press of captives, though in that moment he, too, craved the release of violence.

'Don't give them what they want,' Lilla yelled instead of

giving in. 'They're trying to break us down and break us apart. Don't let them. We are Tokob and Yaloh. We are allies and we stand together against our enemies. Calm yourselves; don't let their madness affect you. Remember your ancestors. Remember Malel.'

The man he'd been holding broke his grip and Lilla readied himself to fight, a small vicious part of him glorying in it, but the warrior just scrubbed his hand over his mouth and then spat, turned away and shoved deeper into the crowd until he was lost.

Lilla took a deep breath and rubbed at the stinging pain of the scar in his chest. The scar Dakto had cut into him and then rubbed with charcoal. A messy, unpretty triangle – a pyramid, a crude rendering of the slave mark he would soon be forced to wear on each shoulder. An extra reminder of his servitude. His shame – if he chose to see it as such. He knew that had been Dakto's intention and so Lilla did his best to wear the mark proudly.

I made him so angry he had to do this. That in itself is a victory.

And yet now he's gone. I could have used that anger. He was starting to listen, starting to see the truth, I know he was. Why else would he have told me what he did?

Despite Lilla's determination, the thought of beginning again, of trying to convince another macaw or dog warrior, filled him with weariness. Dakto's time in the Sky City had primed him, given him a taste of something he'd never had before and surely couldn't help but miss now he was back in the Empire. Lilla didn't like to think how long it would take to build up that trust with another so he could begin to turn their thoughts to freedom. Rebellion. He stiffened his spine; it didn't matter how long it took. What mattered was that he'd do it.

Kux found him and Lilla adjusted his tunic to cover the scar. 'Another fight about swearing to the Empire.'

Lilla grunted. 'They always are. After everything Dakto told me about how they control their slave warriors, about how we can control at least this one choice, and still they think swearing is the answer. Think claiming their families will ever benefit any of them . . .'

Kux's face twisted. 'You speak of choice and your faith in that Xentib bastard in the same breath,' she said in a harsh whisper. 'Why do you trust him, especially after that?' Her hand slapped the healing symbol on his chest and Lilla couldn't help the hiss of pain.

'His time with us changed him, Kux. A whole sun-year out from under the song, away from the Empire. Free. He didn't need to tell me what he did.'

Kux shook her head and the scent of old sweat rose from her tangled hair. They were all of them filthy, stinking, starving. 'Who cares? He's not here, Lilla. We've got nothing left but the promise that we'll see our families again once we're freed, yet you want us to swear to the Empire but *not* name our families, our children? You'd rather we abandon them to the Pechaqueh for the rest of their lives, never to be freed except by their own efforts, which may never be enough? At least if we work for freedom together, we can achieve it.'

'That's just what they want you to think,' Lilla said, low and urgent. If he could convince Kux, another Fang, they might have a chance.

Tayan is going to come for you, and you won't even claim him as your husband. You're going to abandon him.

Lilla forced away the thought. The guilt was enough to bring him to his knees, if he let it. He wouldn't. 'If we claim them, then when we rebel, they'll be executed. It ensures our compliance because once we've claimed them, they become another collar around our necks and another brand in our flesh.'

Kux sucked in a breath, and so did the warriors pressed so close they couldn't help but overhear. 'What did you say? You're telling me *my own fucking children* are another form of slavery?'

'Yes. No. No! I'm saying that's how they use our loved ones against us.' The pit was a rising ripple of sound as his words were passed on to others. It had been this way every day he'd spoken to them since Dakto had given him this knowledge. Lilla didn't fully understand why the man had done it, but he wasn't going to waste it. The pain in his head and the ever-present whine in his ears began to increase, as it did whenever he was frustrated or angry.

'If we don't claim them, they won't be punished for our actions, don't you see? They *can't* be punished, because no one knows who they are. We have nothing to lose but our own lives when we rise up. And once we've won, then we can look for our families and pray they still live. We do this *for* them, to help them.'

'We do it and they believe we've abandoned them.' Kux's voice was cold. 'I'll not have my girls thinking I don't love them any more. They've already lost one parent because of this fucking war – they won't lose me too.'

'They'll understand . . .' Lilla tried, but Kux's lips were pressed together against emotion strong enough to rend and the words dried up. 'It's everyone's individual choice,' he tried, but the words were slow and turgid with hopelessness. 'If we don't claim them, they aren't tainted by our so-called treason. When we win, when we see them again, we can explain.'

Kux shook her head in disbelief. 'Listen to you,' she choked. 'You talk as if we can win. We're in a fucking hole in the ground, Lilla. We're prisoners fighting over food and standing in our own shit with only the rain to clean us. And the rains are ending! There is no rebellion. There is no winning. There's only this.' Her flailing arms encompassed them all and attracted more attention as her voice rose. 'We're slaves now. We're nothing, less than nothing. The only hope we have is doing what we're told and earning our freedom and then having some semblance of a life again. Maybe we'll even get to go home, to whatever's left of home. But we only do that if we obey!'

Lilla resisted the urge to hit her. 'No! We only do that when we *win*. When we tear this fucking Empire down around their ears and take back our freedom. And we can only do that if we're able to act, if we know our loved ones are safe because they're not tainted by association. If you claim your girls, they will die when we rebel. *They will die,* Kux. If you give them up, you ensure their survival.'

'If we do as we're told, we ensure their survival!' a voice shouted from a corner.

'Do as we're told?' Lilla repeated, injecting as much mockery into his tone as he could. *Tayan won't come if you do this.* 'We are fucking Tokob! We are fucking Yaloh! The orders won't be coming from a council of elders, from our ancestors or Malel. They'll be coming from people – arrogant, cruel people, but still just people. That is their great lie – they want us to believe that they're better than us. They are not, no matter what this fucking song tells us. Would you lie down in your own shit so they can put their feet on your neck or you would stand toe to toe and spit in their faces?'

'We lie down in our shit every night!' the same voice shouted.

'You're right. But do you want to do it for the rest of your life?'

The pit was quiet but for Lilla's ragged breathing and the shuffling of warriors packed tightly together, skin rubbing on skin, forced intimacy.

'I'd lie down in fire for my family. I'd lie down in front of a fucking Drowned,' someone said and Lilla sucked in a breath to scream at them.

'Do you actually think we can win?' came a voice from his left, stealing a portion of his exasperated fury and replacing it with a single ember of hope. Fewer than half of the warriors in this pit had come around to his way of thinking; would this be one more? He turned to face them.

'Yes! And I don't think it, I believe it; I *know* it. If we rebel the day we get out of this pit, we can be back in Yalotlan a month later, helping the warriors still there to defend our homes. Come at them from behind; beat them.'

'If we were able to beat the Empire, we wouldn't be here now,' Kux yelled, as angry as Lilla. 'We are fucking losing back home, and you're whipping us up to lose here too?'

'How do you know we're losing?' Lilla demanded. 'Because those shits up there like to tell us so when they condescend to throw us some bread? Of course they're going to say that. Of course they are! But we don't know. None of us know. And that's why we have to fight, because it's the only way to be sure.'

He was sweating with passion and with hope, fists clenching and unclenching at his sides. He shifted his feet and the stench of shit and piss wafted up, almost enough to make him gag. 'Look where we are,' he began again. '*Smell* where we are. We need to—'

'*We can't win.*' Kux's voice cut over his, slicing through the rising babble again. 'We can't, Lilla, and while I love your fire and your belief and your hope, I won't sacrifice the hope of *my* children on that belief. I'll swear to serve

460

the Empire, and I'll claim them as my own. And I'll do whatever it takes to free them and see them again. To live with them, even if it is under this cursed song. You don't have children, so maybe this choice is easier for you. Maybe your Tayan will forgive you—'

Tayan will come for me and learn I've abandoned him. Tayan will never forgive me.

'—but I won't risk the lives and hearts of my girls on the promise of a rebellion that we cannot organise and cannot win. One hundred of us? One thousand could not escape this fortress without being slaughtered. No, Lilla. You make your choice and I'll make mine. And so will everyone else in here.'

Lilla looked around in the half-light, desperate. He didn't have the words, it seemed. He wasn't a talker like Tayan or the elders. He couldn't persuade.

Slowly, hating himself, he untied the faded yellow cord. Twelve knots, it had. Twelve promises he and Tayan had made each other about their lives together, their future, when they'd adopt children, how many. The whole of his life written in knotted string. Four of the knots had charms attached – things they'd achieved, promises kept. Eight more remained empty and might now remain that way forever.

Lilla kissed each of those promises and then he knelt and wrapped it twice around his left ankle, where widows wore their cords, and tied it off. He swallowed tears and pain and willed his eyes to dryness and his heart to stone.

Perhaps they'd been overheard by their keepers, because the next morning everyone in Lilla's pit was ordered out, along with those who'd been held in adjacent prisons. They were marched into an enormous plaza, with warriors training at the far end, some hundreds of them. They were slow and clumsy and Lilla watched them as Tokob and Yaloh were forced into long lines. Half a dozen warriors approached, arrogant and confident. Eagle feathers in their hair. One, a man even taller than Lilla and with a slightly crooked nose adding interest to an otherwise ordinary face, wore three more eagle feathers in a slender fan. An officer. He wandered up and down their lines with easy grace and unconcern.

'I am Feather Ekon and you are here because you fought well!' he shouted. 'You fought like the warriors you are and there is no shame in your defeat against a superior force!'

Lilla's hands tightened into fists.

'You fought and lost, but this is not the end of your warrior journey. You are in the heart of the Empire, you are under the grace and power of the song, and you can continue as warriors. Here, in the Melody. We will craft you into the finest, strongest fighting force in all Ixachipan – in all the world!'

Lilla spat on the packed earth beneath his feet. Ekon walked towards him and Lilla noted the breadth of his shoulders and his powerful, rolling gait. The Feather stopped and looked down at him. It was an unusual enough occurrence that discomfort stirred in Lilla's belly. 'The song and its glory can be yours forever,' he barked, loud enough to carry through the throng. 'The Melody will be your home now, and your loved ones will live to serve others, live together as families, live in safety, while you fight for the Empire of Songs.'

He waited to see if Lilla would do anything else; he didn't. Satisfied, or perhaps just indifferent, the man stalked away.

'Commit to the Melody, here and now,' Ekon continued, 'and accept our authority over you. You will serve for five sun-years as slave warriors – or perhaps less if you perform well. When your time as a slave warrior is complete, you will be promoted to the dog warriors. Dogs are not slaves! Dogs are paid jade and that jade can be increased in three ways: by acts of bravery; by capturing slaves; by saving lives.'

He paused and the murmur of conversation rose around the plaza, the buzz of new hope.

'Three years as a dog warrior, three at the most, and you will earn your freedom – and the freedom of your families! A Star cycle, that and no more. Perhaps even less.' He paused again, willing to let the prisoners convince each other that it was worth it. Lilla was silent, not meeting the gazes of those either side of him, not answering their excited whispers. This was not hope. This was not the gift the warrior was making it out to be.

'Upon your freedom, you will settle and build your home and your farm and you will tend your crops and fuck your lovers, make or adopt children, and live free beneath the glory of the song!'

Lilla closed his eyes and offered a prayer to the ancestors that Tayan would understand what he was about to do. '*And what of those of us who have no families?*' he shouted and the plaza fell silent. Ekon came back to him, anger tightening his mouth. He saw the Feather decide he was a troublemaker. *Oh, Feather Ekon, you have no idea.*

'What of those of us who have nothing to lose?' he asked, a little quieter.

Ekon spread his hands. 'Then you have everything to gain, do you not? Many a marriage has been made in the Melody. And if you have no family whose debts need paying to earn their freedom, why, then you will be free that much sooner. It has been done in five sun-years – slave to free. Five years. Think on that.'

Ekon stepped back and raised his arms. 'You are warriors

– prove to us your prowess, here and now, and commit to serve. Give our scribes the names and descriptions of your families and know that they will be safe under the song until your service is complete.'

Lilla was tempted to prove his prowess by crushing the man's windpipe, but again he held himself still. Again he waited.

'Groups of ten, split into pairs!' Ekon shouted. 'Show me your strength and skill; show me your footwork and your aggression. Those who fight well can join.' He didn't say what would happen to those who didn't. He let the captives' own imaginations supply answers, more varied and more horrible than whatever the truth might be, no doubt.

Lilla stepped forward with the first group and found himself facing Kux. The ancestors had a sense of humour, it seemed. The Fang's face was closed and grim and when she attacked she came in hard and fast. Lilla let her, answering strike for strike, parrying her force and holding back his own. Kux was scared and she was desperate – Lilla would not shame her or risk her chance to join the Melody if that was her destined path.

When Ekon called the halt, all of the group was cleared to join the Melody. They formed a line in front of the scribes, breathing hard and wiping away sweat.

'Name?'

'Fang Lilla of the Sky City on Malel. Toko.'

'You're a slave now, without any fancy titles. Family?'

Tayan's face flashed before his eyes, and Xessa's. His sisters and mother. 'No family.' The scribe looked up, lips pursed. 'I have no one.'

He walked away from the scribe and stood, fists clenching and unclenching as he swallowed tears. Slowly, as the day passed, he heard others give the same answer. Not many –

not nearly enough – but some. It was another sort of hurt, hearing them disavow children and parents, lovers and marriages, but a clean one. A pure hurt, *a good hurt*, and at its heart burnt the hot, endless flame of vengeance.

It made it easier to pretend he'd made the right choice.

XESSA

The marriage ritual had been both more and less than she'd expected. No Lilla, of course, and no Kime, which had cut her open all over again. But Toxte's family had come, making the trip up from their town at Malel's base, and they'd stood with Otek, Tiamoko, Lutek, and the rest of their friends to bear witness in the flesh world of the promises they made that bound their lives and spirits together for as long as they wished.

Seeing Tayan in his finery, his paint carefully applied in their honour, had reduced her to tears even before she made her promises before the gods and ancestors and spirits. The friend of her heart had teased her gently, and Toxte had pressed kisses to her hair and temples until he'd smudged the ochre painted on her brow onto his lips and she'd been sufficiently distracted by her need to kiss it from his mouth that her tears had dried.

And then Tayan had blessed their marriage cords – bare

of knots for now, because those were promises made in private – and called on Malel and Snake-sister to witness and bless their love, and Xessa and Toxte had licked their thumbs and pressed them to each other's temples – family – and then to the hollow of each other's throats – married.

Tayan and the guests drummed and played bone flutes and rattles and the couple danced the marriage completion and shared a cup of honeypot. And then it was done. No grand affair, no gathering of the whole neighbourhood to drink and dance until deep into the night. Toxte promised she'd have all that and more when the war was over, but she didn't mind. They were married, and that was all that mattered.

Now Xessa's hands went to the cord around her neck. Four knots so far. Four promises she and Toxte had made. They'd agreed, reluctantly, that it would be reckless to make more when they had no idea what would happen in the coming months and years. Xessa had wanted to anyway, had wanted to promise him children – born or adopted – and to look after him for the rest of his life, to hold his hand through every hardship and end every day with 'I love you', but she couldn't. They couldn't. She told herself to be content with what they had, and that all else would come in time.

The cord was light, barely there against her collarbones and the nape of her neck so that she kept touching it to make sure it hadn't somehow fallen off, and yet it carried a weight and a meaning she'd never really understood before. She was different now, a different woman. Not just eja, or friend, or occasional artist. Not just daughter or lover, but wife. Toxte's wife.

Ossa bounded at Xessa's side, tongue lolling, grinning, as they ran easily along the upper trail that led around the hill. It was good just to be out, breathing in the morning and the freshness of the scattered trees and plants, away from the overcrowded tension of the city.

She actually had the day to herself, and had decided to spend it foraging for medicine for the shamans to replenish their stocks. She felt guilty and yet utterly relieved at being outside the walls and away from the crushing press of humanity. The city was so overcrowded that people were sleeping in the plazas.

Not the slaves, though, she thought and that stole much of the pleasure from the day. The mood in the city was hostile and suspicious, so much so that all escaped slaves had been turned away, the gates shut against them. Most were camped around the walls, crying to be let in, pleading and begging, and Xessa would never have ventured out of the city if the Yaloh council hadn't sent a couple of Paws to drive them away. Suspicion of outsiders had grown like fungus after Ilandeh and Dakto's betrayal, even more so after the riots in Xentibec and the slaughter of the Quitob in the temple, and was now a ravening beast all of its own, and anyone with the wrong clothes or tattoos or piercings was forbidden entrance to the Sky City.

Xessa was profoundly ashamed, not just of the Yaloh, but of her own people, too. They had allowed this to happen. They had looked away and let those poor slaves be denied safety. They were going to die in the fields and orchards, be slaughtered in front of the Tokob walls, and no Toko would raise so much as voice, let alone hand, to stop it.

Including me.

Xessa slowed to a walk, chest heaving, and scruffed Ossa's ears as he pranced by her side. She had no answer for herself. The early morning was cool and windy, bright with bird life and the wild racing leaps of monkeys above their heads. The trees were thick this high up on the shady side of Malel, out of the reach of the wind-driven salt, and it was rich and green to her eyes and nose.

A shock of movement on the trail ahead stilled her: a deer, and then three more, slipping ahead of her with graceful bounding leaps, out of the jungle, along the trail, back into the jungle. The pale fur of their tails and hindquarters like flashes of wispy cloud come down to earth. The sharp black of their hooves kicking up dirt. The warm animal musk of them just gracing her nose before it was gone.

Ossa was in point, on the off chance she hadn't seen them, and she stroked his head in appreciation, stilling again when a doe paused and looked back, her long neck in a graceful curve, her eyes liquid black. And then gone. Xessa smiled and stayed still on the path a little longer, in case there were more. The balance. Malel's bounty. A welcome distraction.

She thought of Tayan – to him those deer would have been little more than blurred, bouncing shapes, species unknown. How disconcerting that would be, not to know what might be coming towards you, predator or enemy. One part of her nightly prayer was that her eyes would stay sharp until the day she died, not failing as those of some Tokob did. To never know the individual colours of a sunset or the flash of a parrot through the canopy, the delicate movement of a lover's hands as they signed their love for you. Her mouth curved.

But how big the world must be for people like Lutek and Tiamoko and Toxte, who could both see and hear clearly. How intrusive and yet how wonderful, so bright and . . . there, right there, inside your head, against your skin. Impossible to ignore even when you wanted to, maybe even especially when you wanted to.

She shook away the musing and began to walk again, Ossa ranging ahead along the path, his nose in every spoor and flower, his tail waving. Despite his ease, Xessa's gaze roved the undergrowth around her, flicking back to her feet every few paces and then on to Ossa's bliss-seeking nose and tracking ears as he trotted ahead, joy in his every line.

A sense of something, maybe the tiniest hint of a vibration through the soles of her feet or the feel of the jungle stilling. Perhaps it was just a . . . a knowledge, the warrior's awareness, but Xessa halted, toes splayed wide on the trail. Fifty paces on, a flicker of movement – Ossa jumping, landing back feet, front feet. She raised her arm so he knew she'd seen him and then held her palm out, requesting information. He pointed his nose downhill, giving the signal for predator.

Shit. Just what I need.

She had a dog and a knife and a sling, a bag for carrying any medicine she found, but no more.

Xessa took another few steps, looking where he'd indicated, but she could see nothing in the shade beneath the trees. The wind picked up and shook the undergrowth and she startled, seeing things that weren't there and, potentially, not seeing things that were. If it was a jaguar, chances were she wouldn't notice it until it moved, charged her with teeth bared and tail lashing, and opened her from screaming mouth to steaming guts.

Xessa crouched and put her right hand into the mud, peering low across the trail for eyeshine or slink of predator in the low scrub. She clicked her tongue and Ossa looked up. She held out a palm and he pointed again, gave the predator signal again. She tasted the air for the musk of cat, got nothing. Looked back at the dog. His ears flattened and then pricked again, and once more he signalled predator, without her asking this time.

Shit.

She was upwind of whatever it was, so if she could hide, it might pass her by. Xessa scrambled up off the trail into a dense stand of palm growing around one of the outcrops of sharp, black rock that sprouted from Malel's skin. She crouched and patted her knees – Ossa got his front legs onto her lap and put his head on his paws. She put her fingers between his eyes and he stilled, panting lightly. Beneath her other hand, Xessa felt his hackles rise and prayed he didn't whine because there they were, on the trail, close enough to spit at: a dozen warriors with red feathers in their hair, with sharp stone and obsidian in their hands. Empire warriors. Their hair was braided Pechaqueh style, but the patterns dyed in their kilts and the flashes of tattoo she saw spoke of different tribes. Her stomach cramped with tension and bile scalded her throat.

Another dozen emerged from the trees, and then a dozen more, these ones wearing grey-banded eagle feathers.

War had reached the Sky City.

Warn the city. Warn the city. Warn the city. The words pounded in counterpoint to her heart and her feet, the left one leaving a trail of blood from a cut that would, she prayed, be washed away by the rain that had started moments after the warriors below her had vanished back into the trees and she'd been able to slip away.

Xessa was under no illusions about her ability to move silently, so she thanked Malel for sending rain to cover the noise she made. The warriors had seemed cautious but not surprised to find the game trail. As if this was planned. She didn't waste time speculating; her only task now was to reach the city and tell them the enemy was here.

She climbed straight up through uncleared jungle until the trees and undergrowth thinned enough to run, and then began to traverse the slope towards the city. The sky was the roiling black of an angry ancestor come for vengeance and the rain was heavy for so late in the Wet, making the ground treacherous under her bare feet.

Xessa fell, the bright pain of a split knee overlaying the black pain of a bruise deep into the bone. Ossa's hot breath warmed the side of her neck as the cold wind buffeted her and she regained her feet. They ran on, Xessa's long, loping stride shortening, tightening, as her feet bruised and her breath came ragged and the way back grew longer and increasingly unfamiliar this high up the slope. Ossa limped, his hind leg held up to his belly. He'd slipped when a pile of loose stones gave way beneath him and had damaged his paw or knee.

His suffering broke her, and how he kept going regardless. There wasn't enough time for her to rest, but Ossa could, at least. Heavily, Xessa crouched down and the dog came back to her. She patted her shoulders and he gathered himself and jumped up, paws scrabbling for purchase and nails scoring the back of her neck. She grunted at his weight and then his hot body was draped around her neck, fore and hind legs dangling down over her chest.

Xessa grabbed his forelegs in one hand and a root in the other and hauled herself back to her feet, her breathing sharp and painful in her chest. The ground was shrub and sharp rock and she was probably outlined against the sky if anyone cared to look. Clinging to whatever she could find, she made her way on, slower than before. The wind strengthened further, blowing into her face and bringing a cold, stinging rain that battered at her eyes and made it hard to breathe. The clouds whipped overhead and the world was thrashing greens and hard, wet greys and spatters of sunlight there and then gone.

Xessa wound through an ancient rockfall, picking her way among slabs taller than she was and over others smaller than an infant. Her knees buckled and she caught herself just in time, forced them straight and kept walking, bouncing gently between the rocks on her cut feet, one hand holding Ossa in place until she regained her balance.

She came around the shoulder of the hill, but her sob of relief caught in her throat. The city wasn't there. Xessa blinked, confused, and then quartered the landscape and saw it, far below. Of course, she was too high, had come out onto the scree field near the Swift Water's main tributary. Deep enough for a Drowned.

Should she go back the way she'd come, and potentially run into any warriors tracking her, or risk the water and head through the scree, which would slip and roll beneath her torn feet and alert any Drowned to her presence?

Ossa butted her head with his and Xessa clung to a boulder and lowered herself onto her knees, biting her lip at the shuddering in her thighs. The dog slithered off her shoulders and looked up at her, then he sniffed the wind and gave her the predator signal from behind and downhill.

Shit. Shit shit shit.

Xessa was out of options. She took a deep breath, clicked three times, and whistled once. *Home.*

Ossa cocked his head but she cast him and he went, and Xessa sat back on her heels and watched her brave, clever dog race downhill through the scree towards the city, limping but running, running for her. One of them at least would make it back and if whoever found him had any sense, they'd realise something was amiss.

Xessa hauled herself back to her torn feet and picked her way after the dog through the scree, arms out for balance and praying the stream ahead of her was free of Drowned. Not much to eat up here. Not much to sing for. *Please be empty. Please be empty. Malel, ancestors, let it be empty.*

The ground slid from under her and then came up to meet her knees, the palms of her hands and then her forehead. Lightning exploded behind her eyes and the pain in her feet was so great the thought of standing made her want to weep. But Ossa was running, running on three legs. If he could do it, so could she. Xessa pushed herself back up and shambled downhill towards the city shining palely through wind and rain and oncoming gloom. And then someone was coming towards her, a dark blur through the downpour.

'Enemy,' she signed, the gestures big so they could be seen. 'Northern slope. Enemy.'

It had been Toxte, of course – her husband had come looking when the day had worn on and she hadn't returned. He'd slung her arm over his shoulders and raced her downhill and in through the city gate. He'd shouted for Ossa and then shouted what Xessa had told him and caused a panic. But a necessary one.

Now Xessa was in the upper healing cave, despite her protests, while Beztil swabbed at the myriad cuts and bruises decorating feet, shins, and knees, her elbows and hands and forehead. Beztil, not Tayan.

'Tayan?' She signed his name. Then: 'Pechaqueh. I saw Pechaqueh on the northern slope. Eagle feathers. And red ones.' Panic flared within her. 'Shaman, where's Tayan?'

Beztil wouldn't answer and Xessa looked at Toxte, who was bandaging Ossa's hind leg. She wanted to ask, but the dog needed healing too – even more than she did. She only had cuts and bruises. She shoved Beztil's hands away and snapped her fingers rudely in her face. 'Where is Tayan?' she repeated.

Beztil's cheeks puffed out and her shoulders slumped, but she met Xessa's gaze. 'The last anyone saw him,' she signed with obvious reluctance, 'he'd gone up to the womb to speak to that fucking monster you caught. He's become obsessed.' Beztil pressed her lips together and then softened. 'More warriors followed those you first saw, hundreds, thousands more. It wasn't a scout or a patrol – they've cut us off from the womb. We can't get to him,' she added as Xessa lunged upright.

Beztil grabbed her arm. 'No one can. He's trapped.'

The enemy had come, and not just above them on Malel's sacred skin. They'd marched out of the jungle below, too, taking up position on the city's western flank, where the slope was clear of river, orchards and fields – a wide, open space that was going to run with rain and blood and be scattered with corpses. Where all their fates would be decided.

The high elders of Tokob and Yaloh spoke from the ritual platform in the largest festival plaza not long before dusk, asking for calm and for every non-fighter proficient with bow and blowpipe to defend the walls the next morning.

Xessa, Toxte, and most of the ejab had a place near the front of the crowd as normal, and Xessa watched High Elder Apok's face for . . . she didn't know what for. A way out. Some way to rescue Tayan and the ejab guarding the Drowned in the womb. A plan that wouldn't see them all dead or captives at the end of it.

She was shaking and leaning on Toxte's hip, the sole of her left foot cut and swollen, hating the feel of the bandages and the soft doeskin boot she had to wear to protect the wound from dirt. It cut her off from the ground, left her feeling out of sorts and irritable, and it was such a little thing amid the horror of the Melody being here, but perhaps that was why she couldn't stop focusing on it. It was small, and so it was easy. Understandable. Nothing about the Pechaqueh greed and hate and arrogance was understandable.

Toxte's arm tightened around her chest as she fidgeted again, and his mouth brushed the top of her ear in a kiss. She turned her head into it.

Apok kept on speaking, Elder Rix signing his words. Xessa looked around the faces closest. Fear was the overriding emotion everywhere, closely followed by despair. They were cut off from the fields and the harvest that would be ready any day now. They were cut off from the Swift Water and now had to rely solely on rainfall – and the Wet was ending. All of the Paws who'd been fighting in Tokoban, pushed relentlessly and inevitably backwards, were now considered lost. They couldn't expect reinforcements. They were surrounded, and they were outnumbered. They had non-combatants to protect.

'Our only option is to defeat them in open combat,' Apok was saying and Xessa *felt* the ripple of disbelief go through the crowd. Toxte's arm tightened on her ribs until he short-ened her breath and she squirmed to loosen his hold. 'If we wait behind our walls, we are only ever going to be on the defensive. If we attack, we have the chance to break their spirits and overwhelm their numbers. Our warriors will march out at dawn.'

There was another ripple and Apok and Rix both paused as the crowd shifted. The high elder glanced sideways at Rix, and the eja elder's shoulders slumped before he nodded. Xessa stood straighter, one hand fisted in Toxte's tunic.

'Now that the Swift Water and the fields and orchards are cut off, the council asks the ejab to volunteer for the reserve. You would only fight if there was no other choice, but we cannot deny that it may come down to you being the last line of defence between our civilians and the Empire. We ask you to think carefully and come to the council house at dawn with your answer.'

Shit and fuck.

Being asked to fight was far, far worse than being ordered to. Xessa and Toxte stared at each other and the panic Xessa had felt the night before they'd been supposed to capture the Drowned roared back until she was dizzy with it. She held on even tighter, and Toxte tilted his head in silent query: *Will you fight?* She made herself scan the crowd, take in the non-fighters, the parents holding children tight against them, too tight, crushing.

The Sky City needed her and Xessa had always given it what it needed. She firmed her jaw against the promise of tears, of raw denial, and looked back to Toxte. She nodded, jerky and graceless, and his eyes slipped closed as anguish flickered like lightning across his face, his need to protect her weighed against their joint need to protect the city. Their duty.

'I'll be at your side for all of it,' he signed, fierce as a hawk, his eyes blazing. 'I won't leave you. I'm never leaving you.' Then he pulled her in against him and wrapped hard, warm arms around her. She let him, never wanting to move from the safe darkness against his chest. Couldn't, because the circle of his arms and the press of his body *was* safe, whereas the world had been revealed to be anything but.

She held him, because war had come, and not just to Tokoban and the Sky City. War had come to Xessa – and she wasn't ready.

ILANDEH

Sky City, Malel, Tokoban
19th day of the grand absence of the Great Star

Ilandeh stared down on the Sky City from above. The march around the base of the hill and then up the northern flank had been brutal – mudslides and flash floods had barred their route between the rolling hills, forcing them up and over each one until they were exhausted and mud-splattered to the thighs.

They'd had to get there by the tenth day, though, or risk leaving the High Feather and his Talons vulnerable, and so the mixed force of macaws, eagles, slaves, and dogs had pushed on relentlessly despite the weather and the slick mud and rock beneath their feet. They'd done it, just, reaching their position in the afternoon of the tenth day. Feather Calan had allowed a two-hour rest around the curve of the hill out of sight of the city so the warriors could regain some strength, and then they traversed the slope and filtered out to take control of the ground between the Sky City and Malel's womb.

478

It was the first time any of the warriors except Ilandeh had seen the city up close, its location and defences and walls and fields. The murmuring had been quiet and disciplined as they analysed what it was they were going to take, and then just a little lighter with relief when they spotted High Feather Pilos's Talons marching up out of the jungle below. Everything – everyone – was in place and on time.

Below the expanse of limestone walls enclosing the city were thick orchards and terraced fields green with crops and the double loop of the Swift Water that bent back on itself as it rushed downhill. Each formed a series of obstacles difficult to navigate – defences that prevented a straight uphill assault. Instead, and at Ilandeh's recommendation, Pilos would attack the western wall and curve his warriors up to meet Ilandeh's above the city. Feather Calan's forces would filter down to give battle at the eastern walls.

A three-pronged attack that would drive the defenders down through the city and into their orchards, fields and to the river – their own defences becoming a series of traps to hold them still so the Melody could round them up. Eventually.

The arrival above and around the sides of the city had caused chaos among the hundreds of refugees camped outside the walls and tall, barred gates. A trampled track leading up northwest told of many who'd already fled, while the rest screamed and begged and beat at the gates. Northwest would lead to nothing but the salt pans marking the border between Ixachipan and Barazal. They could be chased down and roped once the city fell. There was nowhere for any of them to go except into the Empire and under the song.

It seemed Ilandeh had done her work in the Sky City a little too well. Her fostering of bad blood between Tokob, Yaloh, and Xentib seemed to have blossomed into something bigger than she had anticipated, causing the Sky City to refuse entry to desperate civilians fleeing the Melody. She wondered whether any of them had come from the towns below, and whether that meant her Whispers had been discovered and executed. She breathed a swift prayer that they were safe. Either way, divisions in the defenders was work well done, as it was always easier to knap a flint that already had a crack in it.

And if there were any Whispers among those pleading for entry, she knew some at least would have scaled the walls during the night. By now they'd be ready to act, disguised as Yaloh and clad in a dead person's clothes.

The Melody had slept out on the slope, hundreds of small fires lighting the hill around the city, double watches to prevent a night attack that hadn't come. Ilandeh had been surprised by that – the Tokob and Yaloh facility with ambush and trap had convinced her they'd be fighting from the moment they emerged into sight of the city.

Still, it would be over soon. She and Calan had crept down to Pilos's position once night had fallen to co-ordinate their attack, and now they just had to wait and see how the defenders would fight – whether they'd march out to try and break the forces arrayed against them, or whether slave warriors and dog warriors would take the walls and hold them for macaws and then eagles to wash the streets with blood.

Pilos's order was to give the defenders until halfway to highsun; if they hadn't surrendered or come out to fight by then, the Talons would assault the walls. All around Ilandeh stood the rest of the macaws, fierce and bright in their war paint and their salt-cotton armour, feathers and spears and glass blades winking in the morning light.

As they watched, the gates opened and warriors flooded

out to both east and west. And then the upper gate opened too. They were making a stand of it.

Ilandeh glanced downhill and saw Calan hold her spear and small shield crossed above her head; she returned the gesture. 'Let them come!' the Flight shouted as the lines around her shifted. 'Do them that honour, for though they fight for the wrong reasons, they are brave.'

The Tokob began their war chant and the Yaloh wove theirs through it, and as it rose into the sky it sent a warning shudder down the length of her back. It wasn't full of fire and vengeance and promises of retribution; it was a quiet defiance, eerie, and hauntingly beautiful. If the sacred song of the Empire could be given human voice, it might sound something like this. She shuddered again at such blasphemy and whispered a soft, fervent prayer for forgiveness to the holy Setatmeh.

The Melody's own chant rose sporadically along the lines and grew in strength and vigour and Ilandeh added her voice to it, feeling it lift her and fill her with righteousness. Their chant too was beautiful, and it drove them all, speeding their hearts and their blood. When they reached the moment within the song that called for movement, for passion and fire, they began to flow downhill towards the enemies who would one day be happy, productive members of the Empire.

'Range,' called voices up and down the line as they ran, and the front ranks loosed their arrows. They thrummed through the morning and the Melody flowed behind them, three volleys and others coming back to meet them, and then they reached the second range and their throwers launched their big, heavy javelins.

An arrow buzzed past, close enough to make Ilandeh flinch. It punched into the macaw behind, stealing his legs from beneath him. Downhill, Calan's slave warriors and dog warriors were falling too, ragged holes opening up in the front line. The eagles would go in last.

Slingers now, almost more dangerous than the archers, for an arrow in the arm could be removed and bandaged, but a stone in the same place would shatter bone. The storm of missiles got heavier and more macaws fell. Unlike Calan's eagles, they didn't have a screen of slave warriors to take the brunt of the initial fight. The small wooden shield in Ilandeh's off hand was to bat away spear thrusts, but she angled it over her head as best she could and kept on running. The faster she got in with the enemy, the better.

The lines came together and shattered, the Tokob breaking up into their Paw formations, six groups of five fighting as a unit and supporting each other. The Yaloh split too, both tribes accustomed to fighting within the close confines of the jungle, where lines and large groups were impossible and battles were normally only a couple of hundred warriors fighting short, intense duels. It was easy to flow through the gaps they left in their own lines and so engage the rear fighters as well as those at the front. The defenders' second wave was immediately engulfed, leaving them no reinforcements.

Ilandeh ducked under the swing of a club that would have taken off her head and punched out with her spear; the woman batted it away, stepped inside Ilandeh's reach and swung again. The Flight dropped to her belly, rolled onto her back and stabbed up, raking open the woman's leg. Her opponent screamed and smashed the club down, but she rolled again, made it to one knee and punched the flint tip of her spear through her enemy's stomach.

There were still snatches of the war chant echoing across the hill, but mostly the sounds were grunts, curses, and shrieks of pain, the clack and clash of weapons, and the meaty tear of flesh and gristle.

Two Tokob came for her, one from each side, their paint bright and their faces hateful. Ilandeh took a hatchet on the small shield tied to her forearm, then wrapped her hand around one warrior's elbow and yanked hard, pulling him onto her spear and spinning them both so the second man's thrust killed him instead of her. He stopped in horror, screaming a name, and she wrenched her spear free and used it to steal his voice and the name both, punching into his neck and tearing back out.

Something hit Ilandeh in the back and she went down hard, attacker on top of her and the side of her face slapping mud. They rolled together a few strides down the slope with Ilandeh pinned inside arms and legs thick with muscle and her spear flailing as they tumbled. They came to a dizzy stop and the Whisper dragged her knife out of her belt; the fall had broken off part of the obsidian blade and the remnant was shorter than her little finger, but with two jagged, wicked points. She rammed it into the leg that was pressing on hers and *dragged* upwards towards the hip.

The scream set Ilandeh's ear ringing but he let go and she let momentum carry her over, rolling until she faced him again. There was a lot of blood but not enough to indicate she'd hit the killing place, and he had a knife too. It hit her in the chest, punching into – through – her salt-cotton so she felt it slide, hot and agonising, across her collarbone. That was a killing place too, but her knife was already in his armpit, slicing muscles and nerves and taking the strength from his hand.

It fell away and she reared up, trapped his hand under her knee and slammed her broken knife down into the side of his neck. She paused over the dying man and then pulled away the top of her armour. It was staining red already, redder than the feather in her hair, hot and throbbing and hurting to breathe. Ilandeh put the wood-and-cotton handle of her knife in her mouth and bit down; then she drew the Tokob blade out of her chest. Only the tip was red, perhaps the length of her thumb-joint; her armour had stolen most of the force. Still, the wound bled freely.

She breathed experimentally, but couldn't hear or feel any bubbling. She ripped a wad of cotton from the medicine pouch on her belt and stuffed it against the wound, tightened the strap on her armour to hold it in place, and checked her surroundings again.

More were coming.

The sun told her two hours had passed. Corpses littered the hillside, all the tribes gathered to fight for or against the Empire adding their blood and life to Malel's sides until the thin skin of soil on her flank was a red slurry and fighters slipped and skidded and fell and died.

A distant roar as Calan finally committed her eagles, reinforcing the dog warriors who'd pushed the defenders back along the eastern line. The enemy had seen them too and shouts of alarm rose up. There was a collective shuffling together, a searching for orders, longing gazes cast towards the city. She scanned her own section of the battle and found it disciplined and holding firm. Below, some of the Tokob facing the eagles ran for safety.

'Cut them off!' she shouted, gesturing to the pod around her and then whistling. Second Flight Beyt, restored to her proper place as Ilandeh's subordinate, looked up and Ilandeh pointed at herself and then downhill. The other woman nodded and waved her on.

Ilandeh ran on burning, shaking legs, the shield on her left arm long since splintered into nothing and the flesh beneath pummelled black. She'd lost her spear and found another, lost that and stolen an axe from a dying Yalotl. Her pod formed the arrow shape with her at the tip, and they plunged down through the panicking, fighting roil of defenders. *Cut them off cut them off cut them off.*

A few more Tokob broke for the city, then a knot of Yaloh. Ilandeh forced more speed into her legs, teeth gritted against pain and the uneven, slippery ground and the desire to stop. She was macaw, the half-blood warrior daughter of a Pechaqueh noble, she was Flight, *she was Whisper,* and she would not let down the Empire of Songs or the High Feather. She *would not.*

Even so, it was mostly Calan's dog warriors who got there first. Ilandeh knew they would be the ones only a few moons or a few actions away from freedom, that tantalising taste like honey on the lips that was a future armed with digging sticks and cooking pots rather than spears or knives. A future with their freed families around them, land to call their own, and the glory of the song forever in their hearts.

Perhaps a hundred of them got between those fleeing and the Sky City's eastern gate, fighting viciously to keep the Tokob and Yaloh away from safety. Ilandeh sped up some more, ignoring the fierce battles all around her, intent only on supporting those dog warriors at bay before the walls.

Calan's spear-throwers opened up on the Yaloh flank, and more of the enemy broke and ran. The dogs were badly outnumbered now and overseers were cracking whips and forcing the slave warriors forward through the enemy while the eagles followed, taking apart Paw after Paw with lethal efficiency. The slaves wouldn't be in time to save the dogs. Ilandeh might be – as long as the gates didn't open and reserves pour out to take them in the rear.

'Setatmeh!' she screamed and the dogs saw her, took heart, and pulled into one long impenetrable line in front of the gate that neither Tokob nor Yaloh knew how to counter.

Ilandeh's arrow formation punched into the biggest knot of Tokob and cleaved it in half. They spun to face the new threat and the dogs responded, curling the edges of their line inward to trap them in the scorpion's pincer. Between them, none survived. It was wasteful, but the first day's battle always was. They could begin taking slaves once the defenders' will had been broken.

Above on the walls, arrows began to flicker down and the Melody warriors pushed forward, pressing Tokob and Yaloh away from their city and towards the slave warriors and eagles. Another pincer, bigger but still lethal.

Out of arrow range, Ilandeh paused to breathe, her battered left hand pressed to her sodden salt-cotton. The blood had soaked through the stiff layers and rendered them useless. She was wearing nothing more than a padded tunic. Someone barged into her from her left, slamming her into the ground with a roar of animal rage. The back of her head hit mud hard and stars burst in her vision. When they cleared, there was a woman snarling in her face, a woman both familiar and armed.

'Lutek of the Tokob,' Ilandeh croaked and smiled a death smile as her hand scrabbled for her axe.

Lutek's lips peeled back from her teeth and the knife flashed as it began its downward arc. Ilandeh grabbed with her right hand and pushed; she jerked her left knee up and Lutek's weight shifted to the side; Ilandeh threw herself in the same direction. She lost her grip on the warrior's wrist and Lutek punched her in the face and slipped her arm free, her knife scoring through the base of Ilandeh's thumb. She stabbed again, but a warrior's sandalled foot connected with her ribs and tumbled her over. A hand dragged Ilandeh to her feet and by the time she'd found her balance in their grip, Lutek was gone, swept away by the swirl of the battle.

The Whisper fought for air. She'd known what would happen when her old friends, all those she'd betrayed, saw her, she just hadn't expected the flicker of guilt that had made her hesitate, a tiny fraction of a heartbeat only, but enough. If the dog warrior who'd dragged her to her feet hadn't intervened with a well-placed kick, she would have died. It could never – *would never* – happen again.

The Tokob had rallied once more and were again fighting a retreat towards the eastern gate while archers and darters on the walls shot over their heads, forcing the Melody back. The Yaloh streamed uphill towards the northern entrance. Splitting up, forcing the attackers to split too if they wanted to chase them down. Her macaws were still at the northern wall under Beyt's command, supposing the Second Flight was still alive, but if they had archers there, too, it would make it difficult to close with the Yaloh without being cut to pieces. More defenders appeared on the city walls with arrows, slings, and spears.

Ilandeh looked for Feather Calan, to see whether she'd order the slave warriors to storm the walls regardless, but then drums began echoing from above and behind. The retreat. Pilos must have decided they'd bled the city enough for the first day.

Ilandeh jogged away from the wall, out of arrow range, beginning to let herself feel her exhaustion, her hurts and aches. This battle was over, but she'd been tasked with one final conquest on this first day. Grim and tight-lipped, she paused to haul air into her lungs and stared north. Uphill. Towards the womb.

TAYAN

The womb, above Sky City, Malel, Tokoban
19th day of the grand absence of the Great Star

This isn't happening. This can't be happening. This isn't happening.

Eja Quin had been in with Tayan, watching over him from the cave mouth, while Eja Nallet had hold of the rope harness Tayan wore. They didn't know anything was wrong until Tayan had stepped far too close, not noticing because there was no tension on the rope. It was Quin who stopped him and discovered there was no one on the other end.

When they scrambled out of the womb, Nallet and her dog were gone and there were Melody lining the horizon. She hadn't even jerked on the rope in warning. The Empire had deployed across the hill above the city, cutting it off from the womb. Cutting them off. Quin had ventured out once night fell, but there were too many sentries and too many fires. He hadn't found a way through.

Now they crouched in the mouth of the tunnel leading into the womb, Eja Quin next to him and his dog Zal at

488

their feet. The spirit-magic Quin had taken had worn off the previous evening, leaving them trapped between the Drowned and the Melody. There was no food, no water, and only Quin's spear, knife, and net to defend themselves.

'They're pulling back. Done for the day, looks like,' Quin breathed. 'I say we wait for night and make a run for it.'

'You didn't find a way through last night,' Tayan pointed out.

'Would you prefer to stay here and be caught by the Pechaqueh with one of their gods tied up and crippled?' Quin asked and Tayan shuddered. He couldn't begin to imagine what they'd do to them if that happened. He squinted some more, but it was all just a flowing, many-coloured mass and a roar of noise occasionally punctuated by a scream higher or louder than the rest. He couldn't tell Tokob from Pechaqueh, friend from enemy. Could only distinguish the city because he knew it was there and knew its colour against the hill.

'We should have gone when they sent in the eagles,' Quin said again. He looked at Tayan. 'First opportunity I get, I'm going. If we can't get into the city, I'm heading wide around it and down into the jungle. Start looking for survivors, for somewhere to go, to hide. You can come or stay, but if you come, you do what I say when I say.'

'How did we do?' Tayan asked.

Quin sucked his teeth and then spat. 'We held,' was all he would say and so they waited, huddled down low, hungry and thirsty, as the sun peaked in the sky and began its slow slide to the Underworld.

A light rain had begun and the hill had quietened in the aftermath of slaughter when Quin put his hand on Tayan's chest and shoved him hard down onto the floor of the tunnel. 'Scouts,' he whispered and readied his spear. The shaman slid further backwards into the tunnel to give him room, his heart a sick thudding in his chest and his dry mouth even dryer. Behind them, in the womb, the holy Setat – *Drowned, it's a fucking Drowned* – began humming.

Quin yelped and spun around. 'What's that?' he hissed as Zal growled.

'It's fine, it doesn't affect you,' Tayan said hurriedly. 'I've been listening to it for days. Ignore it. Oh, shit.'

There were shouts from below on the hill in the gloom: had they seen Quin move? The eja was staring out at the rain and then back into the tunnel leading to the Drowned, indecision etched across his face.

'In,' Tayan hissed, dragging at his arm. He didn't wait to see if the man followed, just slithered further down the tunnel and then jumped up and ran. They hadn't been in the womb since the previous afternoon, too intent on what was happening below and trying to spot a safe route through to the city, and now Tayan cursed his own stupidity. There was no orange glow from the womb, just the humming of the Drowned in the dark – the last of the candles had burnt out.

'No fucking way,' Quin breathed when he realised. 'I am not going in there in the dark. No. Fucking. Way.'

The pale light at the end of the tunnel darkened abruptly as bodies moved into the entrance. They crouched, still, silent. '. . . hear that?' someone asked. A woman. Familiar.

'Didn't you say this whole place was made of songstone, Flight Ilandeh?' another voice asked.

'I did, and it is. But what was the songstone echoing?'

Tayan closed his eyes, but not in fear or recognition of Ilandeh's voice. At his own stupidity. Songstone. Fucking *songstone*. Of course that was it; of course that explained why the womb was sacred and why the prayers and chants the high shaman spoke in here had such power. He should have realised.

And that was why the holy Setat hummed. He'd thought it harmless noise, a way to comfort itself, perhaps, but nothing that creature did was harmless. The headaches and thirst, the lethargy in the ejab dogs, the fact that he could spend an hour in here and have written nothing, though when he came back out he had vivid memories of learning remarkable things, things just beyond recall.

The fact he had become so convinced it wasn't a threat. An image of Tayan's own hands on its leg, fixing its bones the way Toxte had done. How many days ago had he done that? *Had* he done it at all? Xessa rubbing her brow, confused: *I'd swear I saw it standing in front of you, but my head was pounding. I must have imagined it.*

They'd done everything it wanted short of freeing it.

The other end of the tunnel glowed brighter, a red blooming of light. Whoever was there had lit a torch. Was advancing. They could stay in the tunnel and be captured, or go into the womb and hope the sight of the Drowned would distract the Pechaqueh enough for Quin to kill them. And then they'd have to run, no matter what. But that was for after. That was for if there *was* an after.

Tayan tugged on Quin's arm and moved, slowly, on hands and toes, fumbling across the narrow tunnel into the blackness of the womb.

Gentle splashing, the humming louder in here. Louder and changing, slowly, from hum to song, and Tayan was standing, blinking into the blackness, shuffling forwards until cold water seeped over his sandals. He could hear Quin's harsh breath, tiny whimpers, Zal's growl increasing in the back of her throat.

Alarmed voices from behind and the faintest tinge of

orange light that gave shape and form and substance to the blackness. And there it was, the holy Setat, the rope and collar torn from its neck, standing before them and singing.

A sudden cacophony of barking, deafening in the small space, echoing and re-echoing from the songstone, enough to break the grip of the song, at least a little. Quin gripped Tayan's shirt and threw him back against the cave wall so hard his skull bounced off it and lights exploded in his eyes. Dazed, he sank to the floor, blood a hot trickle down the back of his neck.

The torch was blinding and dancing all over the place as the Pecha lunging into the womb swung it, trying to see everything at once.

Glints of orange and gold reflecting from the crystals in the walls and the polished gems and stones lining the shelves. Twin flames reflected in the holy Setatmeh black eyes as it sank onto its haunches, limbs spidering around it, head swaying on its long neck. Zal, at the edge of the water and barking; Quin, lunging at and stabbing the warrior in the leg with a shout.

The holy Setat leaping forward and clamping its claws around the dog's skull and wrenching it off her body with a single tearing twist. Quin screaming, the wounded warrior screaming, the last of the dog's barks echoing, the holy Setat singing.

Noise. Movement. Flickering light and dancing shadows. Tayan, unable to focus. Quin, backing from Ilandeh as she advanced on him. The shaman trying to croak a warning. The holy Setat rising up behind him like one of the lords of the Underworld and snatching Quin so fast the spear tumbled from his grip. The eja didn't even have time to shriek before its mouth had torn through his throat.

Sudden silence, but for the rush and patter of blood into

the shallow pool. Sudden stillness, but for the flicker of the torch. The holy Setat ripped at Quin's throat some more, swallowing mouthfuls of hot flesh and blood, and then let his corpse fall. It held out a hand and trilled. *Come.*

Tayan struggled to his feet, wobbling, his vision wrong somehow.

Come.

Smiling, Tayan stepped into its arms.

Pain. Red and amorphous, pulsating thickly behind his eyes and inside his head so that his hearing faded in and out with his pulse and his vision blurred, cleared, blurred again. Cool rain on his face and wind over his body. Outside, then. And not dead. Not . . . eaten.

Tayan cracked an eyelid. Firelight at several distant points and one close by, bright enough to make him turn away. Movement caused more pain, and also a murmur of interest from someone on his right.

A sandalled foot in the ribs kicked him onto his back, stealing his breath. Tayan curled up on instinct, trying to breathe, but a second figure crouched at his side and yanked his head back by his hair. A woman. A face he knew.

Ilandeh.

'Enough,' she snapped at whoever had kicked him. Then she met his eyes and hers were very, very cold.

'Bitch,' he breathed. Then: 'How did I get here?'

Her fist slammed into his mouth. 'Shut up,' she said raggedly and he saw bandages peek from the neck of her tunic. 'You, the cave, the god . . .' She trailed off, unable to speak, mouth contorted with desolation. 'You really are fucking savages, aren't you?' she asked in the end, quietly, as if she didn't want an answer.

'Why didn't it kill me?'

'How did you do it?'

'I didn't,' he said, and then snapped his mouth shut.

Ilandeh's lips peeled back from her teeth. 'Xessa. That snake-fucking little bitch,' she breathed. 'I should have killed her when I had the chance.'

Tayan lunged for her, didn't even know he was going to until his fingers were hooked and curving for her eyes. Ilandeh swatted them aside and then reared up over him and punched him. His nose broke, mashed across his face, and blood burst from it and from his mouth. He wailed and rolled onto his side. It was as if she'd ripped his face off his skull and no matter how hard he tried, he couldn't will his eyes open against the pain.

I'm still conscious, though, he thought muzzily and even managed a bubbling, wheezing little laugh. *Lilla would be proud of me. Maybe I am a warrior after all. Maybe this is my jaguar path. Tayan the warrior. Fear me.*

He made another noise – half-laugh, half-sob – and lay in the dark and the hurt, concentrating on the rain on his arms and the horrific pain in his face. Everything else was distant.

'Shall I put him with the other prisoners, Flight?'

'No, not yet. Keep him close by but secure. Once the Sky City is ours, High Feather Pilos will want to speak to him, I'm sure. And the holy Setat may demand him as its offering for the atrocities he has committed against it. Do we have a way to transport it to the river yet?'

'We're working on it, Flight. I swear.'

'Work fucking faster.'

Ilandeh stood and nudged Tayan with her foot. 'Don't die on me, little shaman,' she said in a voice like the dry rustle of death. 'You don't get away from your crimes that easily.'

ENET

The source, Singing City, Pechacan, Empire of Songs
22nd day of the grand absence of the Great Star

'Enet! What have you brought me?'

Always the same question, the same eager, desperate, begging tone that filled her with contempt, even as his appearance filled her with dread. Courtesans, slaves, and Chorus warriors were the only people who saw Xac, and Xac was no longer pretty.

One of the blessings of the magic which filled him from the moment he became Singer to the moment he ascended was that he was big, powerful, almost swollen with the song, and that when the magic moved most strongly within him, his skin flushed gold, as if lit from within by his divinity. But these last moons, as together they had explored the depths of his need and depravity, as his power had swelled even more with the use of the stone knife on offering after offering, his body had begun to change even more.

Lustrous black hair had thinned and fallen out in clumps and his skin had paled from a healthy brown to a sickly,

495

brittle grey. When the power moved within him now, of course all that could be seen was the holy lord, mighty in body and in magic, but the rest of the time . . .

The rate of offerings had escalated, fuelled by the Singer's raging need, by the ever more elaborate threats of violence if Enet did not acquiesce. One of his body slaves had been found dead in the source two days before. She'd . . . had her throat eaten out. The Chorus had discovered her near the offering pool and the official story was that a holy Setat had done it. Enet had examined that body. She knew those teeth marks; the Singer had left them in her own flesh more than once during their bed-play.

Every day administrators and overseers requested an audience with her; every day they spoke of concerns. The Singer's appetites. The Singer's habits. The Singer's prowling presence through the source in the middle of the night. And, from the courtesans, the Singer's lack of desire.

She put discreet plans in place that prevented anyone leaving the source except the councillors after each meeting. Chorus warriors at the exits, and some of her own slave guards keeping a covert watch on the pyramid from outside. The courtesans had always played with each other when the Singer was otherwise occupied; Enet encouraged them to continue that practice.

But the city was sour with speculation, and not even the mark of the Chosen on Enet's throat stopped the whispering that followed her everywhere, through every market and plaza, in every temple and at the latest new moon offering.

At her request, two courtesans were in the gardens now, visible through the colonnade and vocal enough to provide the Singer with a diversion.

'Answer,' the Singer demanded, anger suffusing his face. Perhaps two were not enough. Perhaps all of them . . .

'It is not the chosen day, holy lord,' Enet said, not having to force the fear into her voice. And it wasn't, though really there was no chosen day any more. There was nothing but his wants and how long she could delay them. No matter the books she read and the folktales and legends and shamans' stories she consulted, no matter her divinations with dice and card and star charts. No matter *what she did*, the Singer's hunger grew.

Enet thought back to Pikte's death – her diamond boy – and how she had thought then that she could control this, that their son's death would be enough for him, would sate him for months. Her heart spasmed in her chest and the void of her grief ate away a little more of her spirit. Pikte had died for less than nothing; he had died for a lie and a broken dream and a man driven mad. Not all of the offerings had been accepted at the last new moon ritual, something that had never happened in all their long history, and after that the mood of the city moved from suspicious to panicked.

Pechaqueh and free watched her with open hostility. Only the mark of the Chosen kept them from doing more than stare, she was sure of it.

'The song is hungry,' the Singer said, the special phrase he'd devised to hide his true meaning. It was Xac who was hungry, Xac who yearned for blood as some people did for the dreams brought on by a certain frog-venom or fungus. This was the creature Enet had created, and now that she had done so, she dared not look away lest it take her distraction for weakness and make her its next meal, Chosen or not.

'Holy lord, today is not the day for that,' she tried. 'Why not watch the entertainment in the garden? If you have desires, great Singer, let me satisfy them.' None of her revulsion showed in voice or face or manner as she slid one palm against his knee. 'Listen to the men in the garden, holy lord. Are they not pleasing?'

The Singer's mouth was partly open in dull incomprehension, but then a glint lit his eyes and Enet's guts writhed within her. 'Fetch them in here,' he said.

'Holy lord, that's not what—'

'Fetch them in here,' he repeated and though he did not raise his voice, gold flashed beneath his skin and the song swelled.

'It is not the day,' she tried one last time, her voice faint. Seven days. Seven since the last. Never had the intervals been so short. *One every third month at most,* her mind supplied over and over, a litany that had become meaningless through repetition. A mockery.

The Singer bared his teeth at her and she knew he was quite, quite mad.

'Would the Singer like to practise his archery?' Chorus Leader Nara asked from behind her and Enet breathed a sigh of relief. Even this was a risk, though: the Singer had shot one of the children who sang for him in the evenings. The girl lived, but still . . .

'The Singer,' Xac said in tones more frightening for being so even and without inflection, 'would like to be obeyed. The Singer has no fucking qualms about finding a new Chorus Leader or a new Great Cunt if it comes to it. Now bring them in here – or take their place.'

He wasn't even pretending to speak in riddles any more, and Nara moved to the gardens and summoned the lovers inside, as incapable of resistance as she was. They arrived quickly, flushed with their need and honoured to serve the holy lord, as they had not done for so long. He was radiant with magic and the strength of the song in the source was such that they saw only his majesty.

The Singer's desire was rising steadily and it thrummed

like fingertips across Enet's nerve endings, speeding her heart despite her disgust and her worry. The tonic she'd drunk thrummed with it too, a little stronger each day, a little more perfect, gracing her with everything she would eventually need. Strength. Will. Rightness.

Eventually? It should have already happened, she thought as she watched the courtesans begin their work on the Singer. They had no idea what was coming for them.

The holy lord lunged forward and slapped Enet, hard. Her head snapped to the side and she tasted blood. For a moment of utter, adrenaline-filled terror, she thought he had read her designs through the song. 'You offer me two.'

She chanced a glance at the courtesans, who were shocked and still, hands on each other, hands on him. Nara shifted his weight but didn't speak. *Offered him two? I haven't offered him any. I tried to stop him.*

'Holy lord?' she said carefully.

'Where are the rest?'

'L-lord?' What rest? Two was the limit. He'd never had more than two.

'*The rest,*' he roared.

The courtesans yelped and then giggled, shocked, at the Great Octave's humiliation. They thought they'd have a story to tell the others in the morning. They thought they'd still be alive.

'More,' Xac bellowed as he put a hand around each man's neck and dragged them to him as if to suckle. 'Bring me more. More, you fucking bitch, *more!*'

Enet fell to her face in worship to let his ire wash over her, but he ripped off her headdress and hauled her upright by her hair. 'As the great Singer commands,' she gasped, clinging to his arm for balance. The courtesans weren't giggling any more; the courtesans were afraid.

He tossed her down as if she were a corn doll and pulled one of the youths into his lap. His hand disappeared around his back for the stone knife hidden in his belt. Enet centred herself and returned to kneeling, ignoring her ruined hair, the stinging in her scalp. She put her hands in her lap and waited to be summoned into blood and death and orgasm.

'*I. Said. More,*' the Singer growled and she finally understood. He wanted more and he wanted them now. Seven days, and more than two. The Singer's bloodlust was a starving jaguar and it had claws and teeth firmly fixed in his spirit.

The song pulsed and raged and the courtesan in the Singer's lap was chasing the gold sparkles in his skin with his lips and tongue, moaning artfully. The Singer brought hand and knife from behind his back and met Enet's eyes. He pointed the blade at her. 'More.'

Enet bowed and rose, because there was no other choice, and walked from the source with her mind whirling. Despite everything, she looked back with concern. The first man would die, surprised, too late to struggle, but the other . . . The second one was always the most dangerous for the Singer, half-sated with death as he was. Enet herself had been forced to step in a time or two to stop a slave with nothing to lose from attempting to kill his lord. Nara met her eyes and hefted his club; despite everything, he would do his duty.

Enet turned into the corridor that would take her to the courtesans' rooms and found herself face to face with Councillor Yana. The old eagle stood straight and proud and very, very cold. Shame flushed her and she forced it away. 'Councillor,' she murmured, 'watch over him while I am gone.'

Yana caught her around the throat and slammed her into the wall. 'I always watch over him. It is I who deals with

500

all of this when you have had your way, when you have poisoned him and the song and the whole world with your sickness. You should leave, yes, but don't come back. Don't bring any more poor souls to be torn apart in there. Don't ruin him any more than you have already. Take your fortune and go and I will personally ensure that you live out your days unknown and in luxury.'

'The Singer—' she wheezed.

Yana squeezed harder and the edges of Enet's vision began to bleed blackness. 'I will look after the Singer. I will wean him off this sickness and restore him to health. Whatever your plan was, *Enet*, it has failed. The Singer will be confined for his own good until this heresy has burnt from him. *I* will ensure he is happy and content and that the Empire is stable and prosperous under his hand. *You* will not be here.' He let her go and took a step back.

Enet leant against the wall and coughed, rubbing her throat and trying to think. 'How dare you speak to a Chosen so,' she began, and then squeaked as Yana drew back his fist. She slid along the wall.

'I will go,' she croaked, 'because my Singer has ordered me to. I will do as he commands and return with more offerings. Wait! Listen to me, Yana. Can you not see how strong we are? We are winning in the north. The blood feeds the song and the song blares across the sky and all who hear it are commanded by it. I have made him stronger.'

'You are killing him,' Yana said and took a threatening pace forward. 'And I will kill you if I see you in here again. Chosen or not, I no longer care. Get out.'

This was no youthful bravado or empty words, for Yana was neither young nor given to boasts. Enet knew without doubt he would put a blade into her if she returned to the source. And if she did not? If she left all this behind instead?

Could she, after having come so far? After giving *Pikte* to the song?

The world spirit's time approaches. Its awakening is near and he cannot manage it. He could not even before the blooding that was supposed to strengthen him.

This was a mistake, but I did it for him and I did it in good faith. For the world spirit and the holy Setatmeh. For us all.

Always Enet had been here to do what was needful. Always she had put herself last, had sacrificed everything for the good of the Empire and the good of all the world. She would not stop now, and if Yana thought to halt her, she would have to do what was needful there, too.

She inclined her head to the old councillor and walked away. Behind her, the source rang with sudden screams.

It was almost dusk when Enet returned. She would have gone back sooner, after seizing a couple of beggars from the street and scrubbing them down in the nearest bath house, because by then the Singer wouldn't have known any different. But she hadn't gone back, because the song had changed, had risen and risen in disharmonious clangour, wave upon wave of hideous dissonance until it . . . broke, shattered into discrete, clanging shards that grated and roared against each other in a cacophony that spurred fear and madness in those who heard it. And everyone fucking heard it.

Across the Singing City, Pechaqueh, free, and slaves had stopped, hands over their ears, and turned to face the great pyramid rising at the centre of the city. Fear had grown wings and spread street to street, suffocating. She'd seen people packing up and slaves struggling under laden baskets and chests. Many of those fleeing were Pechaqueh.

Enet retreated to her own estate as the day lengthened

and the song wailed and pulsed and wept. Smoke lingered on the breeze and beneath the song's madness rang screams and shouts and destruction. It was broken, the Singer was broken, both perhaps irreparably. And despite herself, she had to know why. She had to know if her time had come, even though it was too early. The tonic hadn't had long enough to work its magic in her flesh and her other preparations were still not complete.

Yet she would do what she must. For the Empire and the world. As ever.

Enet picked two of her nearest pleasure slaves and set out again for the source, moving against the flow of traffic with her guards forcing a path until she came to the plazas surrounding the great pyramid and found them empty.

The pyramid itself was unnaturally silent and very still. She saw no one as she traversed the winding corridors flanked by her guards, trailed by her slaves. It seemed empty, no slaves or courtesans or administrators, not even Chorus.

They were still three corridors from the source when they found the first corpse. A slave boy, small and delicate as her Pikte had once been. A long trail of blood down the corridor. 'Hurry,' she snapped. 'The Singer may be in danger.'

Enet allowed two of her guards to move ahead of her and they followed the blood trail back to the source. Two more bodies, Chorus warriors – one dying, and one very dead – and then they arrived at the vast oval chamber.

Enet halted so fast that the slaves and warriors behind bumped into her. She ignored them, ignored everything but the crimson splashes and pools, the destroyed furniture and artwork, and the bodies. All the bodies.

Draped across the low tables, piled in heaps among the pillows, scattered across the mats, tumbled in the shattered, torn gardens, and even floating in the offering pool, lay the dead. Courtesans, slaves, stewards, and Chorus. Even the councillors, piled and draped and tumbled like kindling, like wet washing. Like massacre. Everyone. Every. One.

In its midst the Singer, red from head to heels. He sat against a wall, arms limp at his sides, legs splayed before him. Expression empty. As she watched, he lifted a hand and licked blood from his fingertips.

He'd killed the pair of courtesans and craved more. He hadn't waited for Enet's return, it seemed. He must have sent runners for the council and then summoned his courtesans and then the stewards and administrators and slaves, and here in the source, where the song was at its most irresistible, he'd held them in its grip and slaughtered them all. Slaughtered them as they begged, slaughtered them as they fucked, as the song drove them and rode them and broke upon them. And then drowned in their blood.

But not Enet. He hadn't sent for Enet.

The Great Octave's legs gave way; she knelt with a thump and little grace. 'Holy lord?' she ventured. The Singer's head moved with ponderous slowness at her words.

The slaves and guards she'd brought with her were on their faces in obeisance. She could hear a steady, low stream of curses from one, sobbing from another. Fear had them all in its scarlet claw.

The Singer held out a red hand and beckoned. Enet summoned every shred of nerve and rose to her feet; she crossed the space between them without flinching, blood oozing around her toes out of the saturated mats. She knelt before him, hands on her thighs, eyes downcast.

'I needed more,' he whispered, his tone slurred and yet almost childlike. 'Do you understand?'

'Of course, holy lord,' she murmured. 'You are the Singer; you are divine. Nothing you do is wrong.'

He gestured and she flinched, then followed his pointing finger to one of the courtesans, young and beautiful – before. He was naked and his ribs had been shattered and ripped from his chest, exposing the smashed remains of his heart and lungs. 'Is that wrong?'

The finger moved to others, dead as they took their song-driven pleasure from each other. 'Was that?'

Enet licked her lips. 'It was not wrong, holy lord. But it was, perhaps, a little hasty. It may be you will feel better if you rest now, while I . . . tidy up. And . . . perhaps such levels of indulgence should not be repeated.'

'But I needed it. I only had the two and you were gone. You left me.' Bewilderment leached through the haze in his face. 'Don't ever leave me again. I command it.'

'I will never do so, my love. Never again.'

'You are my Chosen,' he said. 'Enet, Great Octave, Spear of the City, and Chosen of Xac. Never leave me.'

'I promise, holy lord,' Enet murmured, packing the screams down inside, into the void left by her dead child. Her murdered child, who had died so that his mother might create . . . this.

'I will arrange for a new council to be assembled in the coming days. When you have rested.' She put her hand on Xac's knee. 'You have done mighty work here today, holy lord, and now it is time to rest, to absorb the power that you loosed and weave it into a song that none of us will ever forget. Come, my love. Let me bathe you.'

'Don't go,' he begged as she stood and Enet bit her lip to stop it curling. Disgust mingled with a heady fear. She walked the edge of a precipice. She helped him to his feet and planted a kiss on his gore-streaked forehead.

'Never.'

THE SINGER

The source, Singing City, Pechacan, Empire of Songs

I am the song. Song. I am the . . . I am the song and the song is good. The song is glory and war. I am war. I am the song. All will kneel, will kneel, will kneel before the song. Beneath the song. Under the song.

I am the . . .

I am . . .

Am I the song? Am I the song, Enet?

The song requires blood. Enet says. Blood. Bloodsong. Songblood. I am the song and the blood.

My song, my blood. Enet says.

I am the song. I am the blood. I am . . .

Enet says.

Enet.

I am the song and the song is blood.

Song. I am the song.

I am the . . . I am . . .

Am I?

I am the blood.

The Stone Knife

I am the blood and the blood is Enet.
Enet says.
Enet is the song.

XESSA

She didn't understand this type of warfare. She didn't understand any of it: the tactics, the strategies, the retreats that became attacks or counter-manoeuvres. And she didn't know how to fight people, either, not hand to hand when they had knives and spears, when they didn't move like her enemies usually did.

Xessa's opponents came at her from beneath. They were animals with claws and teeth, and while one had tried to pull her spear from her hands, she'd never learnt – or had to learn – to do the same. You couldn't disarm a Drowned. You didn't need to block high because their nature wasn't to slash overhand. You knew the fight against a Drowned, even if you didn't always come out of it unscathed. Xessa didn't understand anything about this. The Tokob who'd had basic training in spear and bow work knew even less, and they were dying in droves, their presence barely slowing the Melody in each day's battle.

Each battle that ended that much closer to the city walls as warriors died and were replaced, first with ejab, and then with anyone who could – and would – wield a weapon. There were children on the walls now, throwing stones from slings and struggling with bows. *Children.*

And the womb had been breached. Tayan was taken. 'Then he's one step closer to rescuing Lilla, isn't he?' Toxte had tried, but it had fallen flat, because they'd both – all – known the truth of how that would go from the start. Tayan was no warrior. If he'd made it out of the womb alive – if he reached the Empire of Songs alive – he wouldn't be sold to the Melody. If Malel watched over him, he'd become a scribe or record-keeper, perhaps even a healing shaman – as long as he could chant the right prayers over his patients. What he wouldn't do was find his way back to Lilla. *Supposing Lilla is even still alive.*

Ten days of battle, ten nights of mourning and raging and the desperate shouts from shamans for bandages, medicine, someone to *please help me hold him*, and through it all the final, terminal disintegration of the alliance between Tokob and Yaloh. For the last two days, the tribes had split completely, Tokob fighting on the western side of the city, Yaloh on the east.

They sent the barely trained civilians against the slave warriors, the ejab and farmers against the dog warriors, and the Paws against the eagles. Still it wasn't enough. They knew it; Xessa knew it. She was going to fight anyway, because there was no other choice.

Gourds, jugs, bowls, and shallow platters were left on every roof and below every eave. They littered every open space, every plaza – a desperate attempt to gather enough water to live another day.

So much water that people slept in the plazas next to the

platters and bowls to guard it from theft. So much that if the Drowned smelt it, they might climb the heavy mahogany gates and enter the city. Tayan would have been able to tell them otherwise from his time in Pechacan, but most people believed the Pechaqueh were somehow immune, and that the Drowned would come for the city, not the Melody. People were was so panicked by the rumour, on top of everything else, that a dozen old ejab, the spirit-magic having broken them years before, patrolled the streets. Ravaged by the magic they'd never thought to need again, slowed by it instead of strengthened, their limbs shaking as they held net and spear, still they did what they could, when they could. Otek was among them: Xessa's surviving father, shambling through the northern quarter, plagued by spirits and perhaps soon by enemy warriors. Two had already died, their hearts unable to take the strain.

Xessa had never known anything like it, and the nobility of their sacrifice – the sheer fucking heartbreak of it – was enough to steal her breath.

It also strengthened her will. Ejab fought the Melody now, and so would she. She'd fight and die, or she'd fight and be taken captive, but she'd never give up. Because despite the losses and the hopelessness and the death stalking them, they were holding. And with every day that they held, they dealt more death to their enemies. They could still win this. They had to win this.

Xessa stretched and twisted, trying to get a sense of her body and the limits imposed on it by fatigue and injury. She ate and drank and pulled on her repaired armour. Ossa lay on a mat, his ears twitching but the rest of him unmoving. An arrow had skewered his shoulder the day before and he could barely walk. He'd endured so much in the last days, his flesh torn and muscles strained. He had to rest. She spent a few moments hand-feeding him and stroking his ears, shaking away fear at the thought of fighting without him at her side. None of the warriors had dogs and they managed well enough.

Xessa took a deep breath, sheathed her knife and collected the spear and blowpipe. She stepped over Ossa and left without a goodbye. She told herself it was because she didn't want to disturb him, but really she couldn't face the thought of it being the last time she ever kissed her dog.

Xessa found Lutek, Eja Esna and High Elder Apok standing on the council house's gently sloping roof with Toxte and a few others. She climbed the external staircase and then looked down over the city. Her husband and his dog greeted her with kisses, but the sight of Ekka just made her stomach tighten again. The sky was boiling with clouds – the eja part of her cringed, but the rest of her, the Xessa who was thirsty, stared at them with hope.

The roads and buildings and plazas were milky-white, wet limestone and puddles and containers reflecting the stone-grey air, but Xessa didn't concentrate on those. They weren't the Sky City, not really. The city was retired ejab, tense and failing and doing their duty. It was children crying for dead family, crying for thirst, for fear. It was wounded warriors stumbling towards the healing caves, and shamans with sacks of medicine walking the walls and waiting at gates and scrabbling for plants and bandages that were running low. It was fear and panic and the whiff of defeat.

On both sides of the city the Melody were a dark mass, slashed with bright feathers and kilts and decorated shields, stark against the black stone and trampled shrubs. Archers kept them out of range while the first wave of warriors and armed civilians poured out of the gates to meet them.

To east and west, it was as if the Underworld had climbed up onto Malel's skin and unleashed its horrors upon them.

In the west, Melody and Tokob came together. She imagined the shock through the ground and air as the two forces met, the impacts of spears and clubs on armour, through flesh, the stamps and falls and screams shivering the sky, splitting the earth, enough to make Malel weep for her children. Or perhaps hide her face in shame.

'. . . lost the goddess's protection,' Eja Esna was saying when she could drag her gaze back to the group. The ejab chest heaved ragged breaths and her words were garbled, hard to read. 'Vaqix died in the womb and then she' – a finger jabbed in Xessa's direction – 'put that abomination in there and now Malel has taken her blessing from us. We've lost everything. Better to open our own throats, or throw ourselves at the Pechaqueh and let them kill us, than to live on without the goddess.'

What frightened Xessa most was that no one contradicted her. For long seconds no one signed, no one spoke. Heat chased cold through her limbs.

'We have not lost her blessing,' Apok said eventually. 'We have not. It is Malel for whom we fight. There will be no quiet surrender or despairing suicide. There will be no wild charge into the enemy ranks with the sole aim of dying. We are warriors and the lives and freedoms of every Toko, every Yalotl, depend on us. Will you let them down, Esna? Will you allow your brother's children to be slaughtered without doing all you can to spare them? Are they worth so little?'

Esna stumbled back as though the words were knives. Her lip wobbled but she shook her head.

'Then go with Lutek and fight. All of you, with Malel's blessings, fight and win.'

Lutek slung her arm around Esna's shoulders and steered

her down the steps and Toxte took Xessa's hand, pressing a kiss to her lips and hair, avoiding the paint on her brow and cheeks so he didn't smear it. She kissed him back hungrily and recited her new daily prayer. *I am eja. I will defend my people against all their enemies. Whether they bleed green or red, they will not beat me.*

But save this man, Malel. Spare my husband.

What were they hearing as they jogged uphill? Aside from breath and blood and feet pounding the paths, what else could they hear? And did those sounds – of life and the deaths that ended it, of screams and the clash of weapons – provide strength or steal it? Xessa was glad not to know.

Ekka ran between her and Toxte. The dogs had never been trained for this, but they were protective of their owners and aggressive with strangers, and they had taken to the fight as though born to it.

Xessa wore the ejab symbols of courage and protection on her hands and face, but Lutek had taken a moment to draw the warrior's bands on her biceps and wrists, and around her knees and ankles too. Xessa called on her ancestors and the spirits to guide her, her gaze travelling down to the side every few strides to look for Ossa. Each time he wasn't there, her chest got a little tighter, her palms a little clammier.

Another incoherent prayer babbled in her head as they closed in on the rear of the Tokob line and wriggled through to the front. Instantly, they were in the battle, not allowed even a breath to adjust to the chaos all around them.

A warrior wearing a string of dog teeth around his neck lunged at her and she jabbed; he got a hand on her spear and nearly wrenched it from her grip, punching his own towards her as she stumbled. Desperately, Xessa let go with her right hand and twisted side-on to evade the flint point. She tried for a grab of her own and missed as he pulled back. He still had control of her spear, but the ball of her foot slammed into his chest hard enough to force him backwards and he finally let go. Xessa rammed her spear at his face, cutting the cheek and ripping through an ear. He screamed and she paused to let Ossa leap in and tear flesh from her enemy. He wasn't there. The hesitation nearly killed her.

A second warrior stepped forward as the first fell back and swung a club, studded with obsidian shards, across Xessa's chest, peeling open bamboo scales and salt-cotton like the petals of a dying flower. Clumsily, she batted it away with the shaft of her spear, the impact shuddering through her hands. One of the shards snagged on the wood and the weapons locked together. Xessa twisted the spear, taking the club out of the woman's grip so unexpectedly that she didn't know what to do next. The spear was still impaled on the club, useless.

The woman came for her with a knife and Xessa surrendered to her training, flinging the net hanging from the back of her belt. It snarled her enemy's head and Xessa wrenched the club free and slammed it into the woman's shoulder, smashing her collarbone, the obsidian opening her face and neck and chest. She fell to her knees and Xessa ripped it back out, dropped it and reeled in the net, coiling it in her hand. Net and spear. Just like a Drowned. Familiar.

But it was red blood spouting from her enemy. Red blood, not green. Nausea surged in Xessa's dry throat; she tried to swallow and managed a look to her left and right to see who fought with her – Toxte left, a warrior right to take those threats she couldn't hear coming, putting themselves at risk by doing so, for there was no one they could scream at for help. If Xessa didn't see them in trouble, they were dead. A risk they took because the defenders needed every last warrior who could stand in line and wield a weapon. Because they were losing.

The next woman to step forward was taller than Xessa, heavier than her too, with a longer reach and front upper teeth filed to points – a Tlalox. Xessa bellowed at her and parried the axe off to her right and whipped her spear in a wide arc to club the woman in the head. She missed, not sure how, and the axe was slicing for her leg. Xessa leapt high, tried for another smack with her spear shaft, caught the warrior on the elbow as she landed, stumbled, and then she was on one knee and the axe this time would take her face off.

Ossa would leap in and tear out the woman's belly, but Ossa wasn't here, and Xessa's reliance on him, on how they worked together, was going to get her killed. She shoved her spear at the Tlalox, a wild strike that just spoilt the woman's aim. The obsidian axe blade missed Xessa's head and shaved a chunk of flesh from the side of her left shoulder so that it hung down like a lolling tongue, salivating blood. She screamed in shock and hurt, and went for the knife, not the net, and lunged, stabbing wildly, avoiding the axe only by Malel's grace, no skill involved. The blade went into the Tlaloxqueh arm, out and then back into her shoulder and her lead thigh and if the woman said anything, if she begged or cursed or prayed, it was beyond Xessa, who was lost in terror, knife hand pumping until the woman fell backwards and was dragged away so another warrior of the Empire could take her place. And then another. And another. And another. Would it ever end?

Someone wrapped an arm around her waist and dragged her backwards: Toxte, pulling her into the protection of the line. He pointed to the grotesque hanging flesh on her arm.

'Shaman!' he shouted in Xessa's face and pushed her through the warriors clustered behind. Bloody knife in one bloody hand, bloody spear shaking in the other, she squeezed through the throng, chewing her tongue to stop from screaming every time someone pressed against her arm.

She reached the rear of the battle and a shaman was there with a queue of wounded waiting for him. He flicked a glance at her and indicated she join the back of the line. Dotted across the hillside were other shamans and other wounded. Above, sporadic flights of arrows flew from the city wall into the Melody, which retreated out of range. The Tokob facing them, sensing an advantage, gave chase.

Despair washed through Xessa when she understood the ruse. Her people were now more vulnerable, with further to run to get back to safety, while the Melody was out of arrowshot. In the chaos of battle, the Tokob probably had no idea what had happened; they'd sensed an advantage and taken it, and the Melody had turned it against them. How easily manipulated they were, like children playing at war. Warriors waiting for treatment, who had also seen and recognised the ploy, began sprinting towards the rear Paws, screaming at them to pull back under the protection of the walls, but Xessa had seen enough retreats become routs that she didn't expect this one to be any different. She was simply, selfishly, glad that it wasn't Toxte's section that had fallen into the trap.

We're going to lose. We're running out of water and running out of warriors. There's no winning this. We're going to lose.

But we can make them fucking bleed.

She stood at the back of the line and resolutely didn't pay attention to the agony pulsing down to her fingertips and up to the side of her head with every liquid thud of her heart. A boy and a girl dragging a trellis loaded with gourds passed, and one handed a container up to her. Water. Xessa tried to make it last, but four gulps and it was gone, not nearly enough to take the furry, insistent edge from her thirst. She stared after the children, but then the shaman was ready for her.

He tugged the bone needle and thread through Xessa's wound, sealing up the hanging flesh, and then requested the bandage in her medicine pouch: he'd run out. Already. When it was done he took her chin in a bloody hand and stared into her eyes. He gave her a brisk nod and pointed – back at the battle.

A manic laugh burst from her, but the shaman was implacable. The day wasn't over yet and Xessa had promised to make them bleed.

It turned out killing people, even enemies trying to steal your land and home and freedom, was very different from killing the Drowned.

The latter filled her with savage joy, the former with a roiling, churning sickness that shamed her and that she knew none of the warriors were feeling. How could they? This was *their* purpose, *their* duty. They walked the jaguar path for this very reason, and she did not. The knowledge didn't stop her sobbing like a lost child.

She sat on her doorstep in the last of the light, too weary to move any further. Toxte was checking on his family, trapped here now to await the final outcome of the war, but Ossa was with her. During her endless day he'd eaten a little of the meat she'd left him and drunk a lot of their precious water, and he seemed to be improving. He lay by her side with his head in her lap. His eyes were dull and his nose was dry, but his tail beat a gentle rhythm on the stone.

The faces of the dead rose in her mind and Xessa squeezed her eyes shut and leant forward to press against Ossa. His tongue found her chin.

We're fighting for our lives. Every one of those warriors wanted to – tried to – kill me. They'll kill us all if they can. They deserved it, deserved the deaths I gave them. They're trying to steal us.

But they're slaves. They're just people like us. Forced to fight because otherwise the Pechaqueh will kill them.

No. No! They deserved it.

Xessa kissed away the tears that beaded Ossa's skull like a crown of tiny polished diamonds. She'd fought hard and fought well. She'd protected her city and her people. She'd done what she had to – what they all had to. No one doubted that except her.

Ossa's tail thumped again as Lutek and Tiamoko came to stand before her. Xessa blinked and scrubbed her hand over her cheeks. Of course she was crying over Ossa; there was no reason for them to think anything else.

'I pissed myself the first time I killed someone,' Lutek signed when she looked at her. Stark, without preamble. 'Right there, in the middle of the fight, my first fight. Straight out of me like a flood, enough you could float a Drowned in it. While fighting. Never been so scared in my life as I was that first time.' She smiled, half-embarrassed, and shrugged. 'Second time I puked up my guts. Pretty much as soon as the fight was over, on my knees hacking up what felt like every meal I'd ever eaten. It happens.'

Tiamoko pushed his hair back off his forehead and his massive shoulders rose and fell in a sigh. He was too young for the hardness in his eyes. 'I cried. Sobbed like a little one the first time they get pierced.' He touched the bamboo stud in his lower lip. 'On my knees in the blood. Sobbing because

I'd killed someone. Because I'd lived, maybe, I don't know. Just . . . cried, for hours.'

Xessa stared at them in turn. Lutek, sarcastic and fast and deadly, like a viper. Unafraid of anything. Tiamoko, the patient intensity of the jaguar, but always quick to laugh.

'So what we're saying is, if you want to puke, or piss yourself, or cry, just go ahead and do it,' Lutek said. 'We all have, that and more. You've taken human life. How different that is to killing a Drowned none of us can know, but we do know it's not easy. Even for us, it's not easy. So do what you need to do, but then get some rest. And be ready again at dawn.'

Xessa swallowed hard, unable to sign her fingers were wound so tightly together. Lutek gave her a wink and Tiamoko ruffled her hair. 'Love you, eja,' he said, to her surprise. 'If you ever want to tell me about it, or about how you're feeling or anything like that, you can.' He patted Ossa gently and stepped back.

'It's hard,' he signed when she looked up. 'Really hard. And I hope it stays hard for you. That way you won't learn that actually, as time passes, it gets easier. Because it shouldn't. Killing should never be easy and we should suffer for it. It should haunt us. Only these days . . .' He trailed off, rubbing his palms over his upper arms. 'Never mind,' he said and turned away before she could respond.

Frowning, Xessa watched others shambling past towards their own homes. Heads down, subdued, exhausted. Some stared without blinking, or performed repetitive, automatic actions. But there were one or two, like Tiamoko, who shook it off even as she watched. Dismissed what had happened, what they'd done. Those were the true killers, she thought, the ones so scarred they didn't even see the marks any more.

That's what Tiamoko is, despite his youth. That's what they've made him.

She shivered and pressed her face to Ossa's head again, hoping Toxte would get back soon. She'd already checked on Otek and made sure he'd eaten and had enough water. Now she wanted her husband.

I don't ever want to be like that, she thought suddenly. *I don't want to have killed so many that it means nothing. I don't want to be dead behind the eyes or in the heart.*

She felt guilty thinking it about fellow Tokob, about the people who killed to keep her and those she loved safe, but the idea wouldn't leave her. Something indefinable had changed, and she didn't think it would ever go back to the way it was again.

PILOS

They were running out of time. Every report that that Elaq sent to Listener Citla in Yalotlan, that she forwarded via runner, told him so.

The Sky City should not still be resisting: they'd cut off their water supply and they outnumbered the defenders. There was no relief coming. There was no way out. And yet still they fought, Tokob and Yaloh still allied, just, against them, marching out each dawn in their bright paint and hair charms, their brighter righteousness.

Pilos offered up a prayer to Singer and Setatmeh alike that they would surrender before dusk. They'd taken the Tokob holy cave on the first day of the attack and the city had to know that. People had been seen fleeing through a small gate in the upper western wall, so he'd stationed three pods out of sight around the flank of the hill; they'd captured the runners and dragged them back in ropes, paraded them within sight of the city. If the defenders could see that their

521

efforts weren't buying anyone time to get away – if they could see their own loved ones among the captives – surely that would break their resolve.

But still – thirsty, exhausted, with no hope and no re-inforcements – they'd marched out at dawn to offer battle once more. Pilos had no choice but to accept it and to respect them for it. He wiped sweat from his face and knew, deep in his belly and balls, that they'd fight until they died, until there was no one left who could stand or lift a spear. It would be red slaughter before it was over and the number of slaves they'd reap for the Empire would be pitiful. Another failure for Enet to condemn.

'The song will provide,' he muttered to himself and, as if in answer, he noticed a figure waving its arms as it slogged uphill, wide of the battle, towards him.

Pilos frowned and then swore. It was Citla and two guards. But the Listener shouldn't have come herself – she should have sent a message. Pilos jogged down the hill towards them, Feather Detta following.

'The song, High Feather,' Citla gasped, clutching her chest. She swayed on her feet and Pilos steadied her. She was clearly exhausted from the journey, but also from being away from the song. A Listener's life was attuned deeply, almost entwined with, the song's magic and the sustenance it provided. To be out from under it would be an exquisite agony, as if she'd had her heart torn out while still alive.

It meant that whatever news Citla had to impart must be of the utmost importance. 'Tell me,' Pilos said, and his voice was heavy with dread.

'The song is broken, High Feather. Shattered, defiled. Not just its harmony but its meaning. The song is dying.'

* * *

It had taken hours for the runner to skirt the city and bring back Ilandeh after the Listener's awful, horrifying news. Fortunately, as soon as Citla told the Whisper what had happened – how the song had shattered eleven days before and hadn't recovered before she'd left its bounds – Ilandeh had cut to the heart of the matter.

'What do you need, High Feather?'

'Get back to the Singing City as fast as you can. And I mean fast. Find out what the fuck is going on. Use Councillor Yana and Elaq. I suspect Enet, but be thorough. Cast your net wide and find out what's happening, then get word to me through the song if you can. And if you can manage it, keep the Singer safe.'

'As the High Feather commands.'

'Perhaps the Singer's ascension is approaching,' Feather Detta ventured and Pilos shivered.

'Perhaps. Though what Citla described bears no resemblance to any ascension I've ever lived through.' He looked to the Listener, who was slumped and grey.

'No,' she murmured. 'Not ascension.'

'And if it was, with Enet being Chosen, that would make her the most likely candidate to become the new Singer. And that fills me with even more fear.' Eagle and macaw were uneasy at his admission, but it served to emphasise the seriousness of what had gone wrong.

'I'll find out what's happening and then come back if we can't speak through the song,' Ilandeh promised. 'You'll have finished here by then – they can't last much longer without water – so I'll meet you on the road. As for Enet: want me to kill her?'

'A bold offer, Flight, and I appreciate it. While it may come to that, for now just find out what she's up to. Stay at my estate, not the barracks. You'll be safer.' He flicked a finger at the feather in her hair. 'You'll have to take the scarlet out. I'm sorry.'

Ilandeh's face was neutral; she shrugged. 'As the High Feather commands.'

He hesitated, knowing it was scandalous, but then untied one of the eagle feathers from the fan in his hair. 'Wear this. It'll guarantee you access in the Singing City.'

Detta's mouth dropped open and Ilandeh's cheeks reddened as she took it; her fingers trembled against his.

'High Feather, my blood is—'

He cut her off with a gesture. 'Gather your supplies and go. Now. All haste,' he emphasised.

Ilandeh snapped out of her reverie, meeting his eyes. 'Yes, High Feather. I won't let you down. Under the song.' She touched belly and throat, stared at him one last time, awed and afraid at the status she held between her fingers, and then she was gone.

'Detta, this ends now. We'll disengage at dusk as usual, wait for them to settle, and then throw everything we've got at those walls through the night until we're in. Rotate the warriors at the walls for as long as you have to, but do not stop. I'd wanted to maximise the number of slaves we'd take, but that's a secondary concern now. Just get them beaten.'

'Yes, High Feather.' Detta was shocked at what he'd heard, but he was an eagle and an officer. He touched belly and throat and raced away, calling Feathers and Coyotes to his side and issuing orders with crisp authority.

'Citla, rest as long as you need to and then get yourself back into the song. It's doing you no good being out here.'

The Listener nodded, weary and haunted, but she didn't move and he let her be. It was halfway between highsun and dusk. Pilos sucked his teeth, tapping the club gently against his calf as he watched the sway and crimp of battle below. The Tokob had begun to understand the Melody's tactics and replicate them on this side of the city. Reports said the Yaloh were learning to do the same in the east. Where before they'd fought in supported groups of thirty or so, now they strung out in lines three deep, like the Melody's. It had made the fighting more intense. It had forced his warriors into a bloody, long-drawn affair that they had no time for.

Pilos swapped his club for a spear and shield. The slope was slippery and he picked his way down with care until he reached a flatter section where the lines strained and shoved at each other and the din of battle beat against his eardrums. A man peeled out of the rear rank with blood turning his face into a crimson mask. He staggered past Pilos without recognition, heading for the shamans. The High Feather took his place, rolling his shoulders and his neck, circling his wrists and breathing deep to prepare for the rotation into the front line.

He stepped into a gap between two warriors, slid beneath the strike of a spear and batted it upwards with his own. It shivered in the Tokob hands and Pilos followed up with a kick that sent his opponent staggering back into the warriors behind. The enemy's lines were ragged, their instinct to break into small groups warring with the knowledge they'd be cut down if they did. This close up, they were neither one formation nor the other, and Pilos's line exacted a terrible toll for their hesitation.

Only the sheer number of two tribes allied against him – and the fact that half his Melody was with Feather Atu securing Yalotlan – had held defeat at arm's length this long. But they were fighting farmers and potters as often as warriors these days, and the lack of quality was beginning to tell.

Pilos jerked sideways as another spear came for his face then lanced his own back along its trajectory. This warrior was faster and sidestepped, her spear jabbing again, and then once more. Pilos slipped the first but the second caught him high up on the chest, juddering over the wooden plates and into the salt-cotton of his armour.

He twisted sideways so it slid on past, tearing through armour but not flesh, and then struck over the top, a downward blow that went into the top of her shoulder, not enough to reach the lung or even a big vessel, but it weakened her arm and she squawked and he used the opening to rush her, ramming his spear up under her armour into her hip. He was lucky, the blade missing the pelvic bone and sinking deep into meat instead. There was no squawk or scream this time; she grunted, guttural and low, animal-like, and Pilos ripped it back out. She fell. Another took her place.

Pilos grinned as his spear tip blocked the swings of an axe, too short to make ground against him. This one fought defensively, knowing he was outmatched and hoping the warriors to either side would come to his aid. They didn't, too busy keeping themselves alive, and it wasn't long before his shrill scream was added to the rest, splitting the air, an offering to glory.

Melody warriors could fight in line and individually, in small packs, in arrowhead shapes, in ambush and at night. The right formation for the right ground and the right enemy. Thousands of hours of practice made them the best killers the world had ever seen and they proved it now.

Word had spread that High Feather Pilos battled with them, and a chant started far down at one end of the line. A chant of praise, of might and majesty, glory and triumph. A chant to lift the heart while *the* song, the true song, was absent.

The ground underfoot was treacherous with blood and

corpses, and Pilos slipped and went to one knee, pausing there for five heartbeats to suck in hot air before lurching back upright and engaging the next. Fighting for his rage and his honour and for the Empire. For the song, shattered though it might be.

But not gone. I will return to the Singing City and fix the song. I will do all that is necessary to restore the Singer to his glory and the song to peace. But first, we will claim this land, and when we build the pyramids and cap them with songstone, then will the Tokob goddess know true harmony. Then will she see glory and weep to be a part of it, reunited with the incandescence of the world spirit of which she is but a dull splinter.

Sucking in more air, Pilos joined his voice to that of his warriors, a bloody grin staining his face along with the slanting, late-day light.

XESSA

Sky City, Malel, Tokoban
33rd day of the grand absence of the Great Star

Heaps of dead littered Malel's skin: Tokob and Yaloh, Pechaqueh, Axib, Tlaloxqueh, Quitob, Xentib, Chitenecah . . . piles upon piles of dead.

Xessa thought the stones of the city might shiver apart under the vibrations of voice and drum and stamping feet as survivors danced the death rites for as many as they could, mass rituals to sing the departed to rebirth.

She'd slept from dusk to midnight, wrapped in Toxte against the terrors of the day, doing her best to climb inside his skin and hide, until a sentry had woken them. It was their turn to relieve the watchers on the walls.

The thought of it gripped her insides with fear – in the darkness and the flickering, jumping light of torches, it was even harder to read hands or lips, to know what was happening or what she was being told. But with so many warriors dead or in the healing caves, even children were taking their turns as sentries. She would, too.

Thirst crawled into her throat as she limped through the city, Ossa limping at her side. It hadn't rained today, and their water supplies were desperately low. The dog had refused to be left behind this time, and he'd slept better and drunk more than she had, for she'd given him his water ration and then shared her own. She licked dry lips and watched him pad at her side. Worth it.

Toxte left her for his own assignment further downhill and she stood and watched his broad back and the sway of his hair begin to vanish. Her chest tightened when he glanced back, just once, his hand raised. Xessa waved and nodded and turned away and tried not to feel the clawed hands of the lords of the Underworld dragging them apart.

I'll see him at dawn.

Tiamoko was waiting for her beneath a sputtering torch. His smile was weary but genuine. 'You found your shadow, I see,' he signed and pointed at Ossa. Xessa nodded, her mind still occupied with thoughts of her husband being swallowed by the night. They walked to their position and Tiamoko wedged the torch in place in the top of the wall and they stared out into the dark. Ossa lay down, resting his head on her bare foot. To either side, other sentries were arriving to take over from those who had finished their shift.

'You should go,' she signed after tapping his arm. He blinked slowly and she huffed. 'Go on, go and rest. You're exhausted.'

Tiamoko blinked again, staring over her shoulder. So tired he was practically asleep on his feet. Xessa slapped his bare arm, but instead of flinching he just narrowed his eyes and rose onto his toes. Cocked his head.

A cold shiver went down Xessa's back and she felt the tiniest hint of a vibration through the stone pathway. Ossa's head lifted.

She began to turn, but Tiamoko grabbed her shoulders and she squawked in pain as her injury roared at the contact.

'They're at the walls,' he said, panic distorting his mouth. *'They're in the city.'*

Xessa tried to make sense of it, but a dark figure slid over the wall behind him and she grunted a warning and shoved him out of the way, tried to bring her spear to bear but the attacker was already on her, a short man, thick with muscle, one side of his head shaved and tattooed. A Quitob dog warrior. Xessa could see the inked patterns clearly because the man had her in an embrace, her arms pinned to her sides, and he was hammering a knife into her back.

Bamboo and salt-cotton absorbed the first blow, and Ossa disrupted the second. The dog leapt at the warrior and tore his hamstring out and was gone before the man could turn on him. His leg buckled and he slid down Xessa's front until she leapt back, spun her spear in her hands and punched it down between his shoulder blades with all her strength. There was no guilt or shock at this death – she didn't have time for either.

A great flood of adrenaline dumped into her bloodstream and dulled all but the sharpest of her hurts. Tiamoko was fighting only steps from her, but more and more of the Melody were pouring over the wall like ants. A black tide that she didn't know how to stop.

A Pechaqueh head appeared over the wall next to her and Xessa smashed its face with the butt of her spear, sending them backwards into the dark, but to her right another had climbed up and over onto the walkway. She blocked his spear and thrust back, but slowly enough for her opponent to duck on instinct. In the tiny gap his flinch gave her, she stabbed at yet another man, this one closing with Tiamoko. She sliced his leg, and then jumped sideways, deflecting a

jab from the man facing her and following up with a blow
to his temple with the haft of the spear. He fell to one knee
and Ossa tore his throat out.

Xessa went to Tiamoko's aid again, now being pushed
back by three opponents. She ripped her spear down the
flank of the nearest, parting his salt-cotton and the flesh
beneath and Tiamoko was able to slide out into space. He
forced a woman back, bleeding from leg and shoulder, as
Xessa batted away at the other, defending desperately. She
feinted, slid her spear over a clumsy parry and into the
shoulder. Tiamoko took him in the back, his hatchet chopping
into the man's spine. In the seconds of stillness, surrounded
by corpses, they looked both ways along the wall and saw
it was lost, defenders being overwhelmed and falling like
trees succumbing to the sheer weight of strangler vines. Xessa
met Tiamoko's eyes. He pointed down into the city. 'Run.'

There were no non-combatants any more. In the intermittent
light of torches and cook fires, the sudden blazing of houses
burning, Xessa saw greyhairs and youngsters, pregnant
women and spirit-haunted ejab take up weapons and fight
for their families and themselves. Fight for their city and
way of life. Fight and die.

The Melody was methodical: those who offered battle
were engaged and cut down without mercy; those who
surrendered were roped, forced onto their knees, and put
under guard.

It was carnage. It was death on a scale Xessa couldn't
comprehend, even seeing only slivers through the flame-
flecked night.

The inside of the Sky City wasn't built for defence.
Hundreds retreated into one of the healing caves, holding
the entrance against their enemies, but there was no other

way out. Perhaps they simply wished to die a little closer to Malel; perhaps they were praying for rescue. Others climbed the stairs onto the few buildings big enough to have stone roofs and held there, but again, they had nowhere to go.

The Melody pushed them back from three sides and then somehow, without warning, from below, too. Surrounded. Warriors trying to make a stand got caught up in the crush, and once they were moving, they couldn't stop. Somehow, Toxte had found her, and with him were a dozen ejab. They were pushed deeper into the avenues and plazas at the centre of the city by wave after wave of Melody warriors: desperate fights in the half-light among houses splashed with blood and screams, where the young and old were dragged from hiding and butchered if they wouldn't surrender.

Now dawn was coming, and madness rode its wings.

Eventually Xessa and Toxte burst from the streets into the grand plaza below the council house where hundreds, thousands, of Tokob and Yaloh had pressed together. Each avenue leading in was cordoned off by a double row of defenders – the ejab slipped in and were directed to the east. Scores of torches burnt all around the plaza, lighting its edges and leaving its centre in pulsing, milling darkness.

They wriggled through the frantic crowd and stood with thirty warriors, mostly ejab, at the eastern entrance. They were to hold it no matter what. Xessa had her spear and knife but her lungs were tight, her thirst shards of obsidian in her throat with every breath. Toxte was haggard, his mouth a slash more bitter than any wound.

Her eyes settled on Ossa – his lithe black form as he lay on his side at her feet, his broad head and elegant muzzle, those huge ears that were her ears, his unwagging tail. Exhausted and hurt, only his fierce loyalty had carried him this far. Lilla and Tayan were gone: dead, captive – she didn't know. Lutek and Tiamoko were on the western side of the plaza, she thought, out of reach, distant as the sun. Otek was missing and her fear for him was a bird trapped high in her chest, wings frantically beating. Here and now, Toxte, Ossa, and Ekka were all she had left in the world: her husband and their dogs, her ancestors and Malel.

Protect Ossa. Protect Toxte. Protect the city. Eja. Warrior. Life-bringer.

Life-taker.

A ripple of movement, of gestures, down the line told her the enemy was coming, and in force. Demons. Monsters that looked human. Denizens of the Underworld. The few warriors mingled among the ejab shouted directions, organising them into a Paw to face the threat.

A black shape in the corner of her eye and Xessa spun to it, the recall whistle already on her lips, but Ossa was still at her feet. The figure was a little boy, running, mouth wide and square with screams, a long-haired, black-painted warrior wearing a grey-and-white banded eagle feather chasing him down, spearing him in the back and leaving him to fall. Killing him. Killing a child.

The plaza erupted into motion and then someone wrenched her around to face the eastern road again: the road that was suddenly full of the enemy. Xessa and her makeshift Paw lunged to meet them. Their line shattered under the impact and the first Melody warriors were shoving through, into the plaza, into the mass of civilians, the mass of innocents.

'—*stay in formation or we're*—' Toxte was shouting, trying to pull them back together, to prevent them scattering, but it was too late. Small, fierce battles erupted as the second line of the enemy engaged the broken Paw. They were overwhelmed with the ease of a Drowned cutting through water lilies. Lethal and against the current, killing everything they touched.

Xessa's spear shivered as it deflected a club that arced towards her. She stumbled sideways under the impact, and Ossa leapt in and caught the enemy's free hand in his jaws, tearing, holding on and shaking. The woman's mouth opened in pain and Xessa got her spear in the way of the club again so she couldn't smash in Ossa's head. The dog let go and backed off, flanks heaving, paw curled up. He was nearly done. She had to get him to safety.

The woman facing her had somehow lost her weapon; she punched Xessa in the side of the head and the eja reeled backwards, stars bursting in her eyes. She hit her again, and again, until Xessa's head was ringing, vision blurring, her spear flailing blindly. She blocked the next punch with it and punched back, fist crashing into the warrior's jaw, and in the split second it gave her Ossa leapt in again.

The dog buried his muzzle in anything soft he could find and tore. Tore through material and tore through flesh, wrenching away great gobbets of meat. Blood sprayed, thick and bright, coating them all, and the woman tried to twist away. Ossa followed her, his muzzle deep in her belly.

Xessa stabbed her in the chest. Ossa tore at her some more and then leapt away, his black coat ruby red under the first bars of dawn, the stench of blood and shit clinging in Xessa's nostrils, making her gag. She wiped at her face, realised her hand was red, her face already sticky, blood in her eyelashes, running down her forehead and cheeks, insinuating its way into her mouth. She gagged again, coughed a stream of black bile, and made herself check for danger.

She wasn't in the road mouth any more. Somehow she'd been pushed back and now the Melody was flooding in through the entrance she was supposed to have held. Toxte – where was Toxte? She spun in a circle. Fighting everywhere, the Melody in lines and formations, impenetrable groups of warriors for the defenders to splash and break against. Everywhere, Tokob and Yaloh were dying or surrendering. None of them were her husband.

We've lost.

Xessa began weaving through the battle, looking desperately for Toxte, blackness threatening at the edges of her eyes like a second night falling even though the sun, finally, was rising.

Two men came for her, hefting clubs. The eja drew her knife and flung it, underhand, the way she cast the net to tangle a Drowned, and it took the man on her right in the belly. He dropped to his knees. Xessa grunted, leapt over a corpse and parried the club of the other. She slammed the butt of her spear into his exposed ribs and forced him back, then pivoted and sliced downwards into the kneeling man's stomach, opening him up from chest to groin. Xessa spun the spear and punched the butt into his face, sending him back in a spray of blood and teeth.

The club thudded into the side of Xessa's left knee with a sickening crunch. Her leg buckled, the sheer size of the hurt stealing her breath and strength. She collapsed. The warrior swung again and Ossa tore into his arm, the dog arriving out of nowhere. In the moment Ossa's intervention won her, Xessa spun on her knees, pain exploding through the left, and stabbed the man in the chest, the belly, the shoulder, a frenzy of panicked stabbing until he fell, twitched and died.

The white-hot fire pulsing through Xessa's left knee convinced her it was smashed to pulp, but when she made herself stand and test her weight on it, she could move. It felt as if there were shards of broken pottery inside the joint, but if it came to it, she could fight. If it came to it, she could run.

Within a few dozen steps, she had to do both. These were

eagle warriors – free and elite Pechaqueh – the first she'd seen up close. She didn't have time to study them, instead parrying with a speed born of panic, not practice. The impact shivered through the spear improperly set in her hands and she stumbled back, managed a second wild block, and somehow managed to slice her opponent's arm.

The breath of his pain against her face and she whipped the spear in a vertical arc, driving the butt up between his legs. She missed his balls, the shaft slamming into his thigh, but it staggered him, giving her time to pull back and thrust. It went high and the flint tip raked through his cheek, missed his eye and laid open his nose. As he bellowed, she thrust again and speared his throat.

Something slammed into her shoulder and sent her sprawling. She kept hold of the spear, just, as her hip slammed into the stone and she rolled away from the direction of impact. Footsteps thudded around her – whoever had hit her had kept their footing and run on, heedless. The woman chasing them, however, did not. She had a scarlet feather in her hair, bloody in the orange light like the edge of the glass axe that arced for Xessa's face.

Xessa rolled again, twice. Glass chips sprayed her back and the side of her neck as the axe head splintered on the stone. She lashed out with her good foot and caught the side of the warrior's knee, collapsing it. The woman fell towards Xessa and turned it into another attack. The eja grabbed at her axe hand and missed again, forearm slamming against forearm instead. The woman landed hard on her, crushing her lungs, but Xessa got her other hand up and around her throat and twisted, shoving her away, scrambled to her feet and snatched up her spear and stabbed her, three quick thrusts in and out of the belly. Enough.

Stepped back into shattered obsidian and yowled, even

the toughness of her sole no match for that sharpness. Looked for Toxte or her father. Started moving again, beginning to shake.

More enemies sprinting across a plaza stained dark with blood in sweeps and swathes, piles of bodies twitching, others still, yet more crawling, dragging, limping. She passed a group of Tokob throwing down weapons and dropping to their knees before the enemy.

Xessa looked around at the carnage, now lit up by a golden-edged dawn, and sucked in a breath. There'd be no more running today; there was nowhere left to go. Fight, then. Fight or die.

Probably fight *and* die. No one was giving orders; no one could tell her what to do. Toxte had vanished, despite his promise before all this madness started: *I will never leave you.*

But you did, she thought, adrenaline burning away the tears that filled her eyes. *You have.* She wondered if it would be better or worse to die next to her husband and knew she'd never find out. She set out again, hobbling, only the mad swirl of battle screening her from the enemy. Ossa, red with gore and slower even than her, limped at her side. She knew he wouldn't be left behind, no matter how badly hurt he was. They needed each other. No destination in mind, nothing but the imperative to find someone, anyone, that she loved and stand over them, protect them for as long as she could.

Fight, Xessa. There's nothing left but the fight. Make your ancestors proud.

A hand grabbed her shoulder and she spun, spear coming up too slowly, but it was Otek. Her father. The old ejab eyes were wild, but not with spirit-haunting. He was afraid. Ossa was circling them slowly, performing his duty as best he could and if Xessa had had the time or the peace to do it, she would have broken her heart for him.

Two exits out of the plaza were still being contested, but the defenders were outnumbered and they were being cut to pieces even as she watched. The other two avenues were already in Melody hands. Everyone in the plaza was trapped. Xessa was trapped.

'Run,' Otek signed. 'Go, now.' He shoved at her but then they were under attack again, half a dozen stalking them, Tlaloxqueh and Quitob in their distinctive paint, and there was nowhere to run to anyway.

'Eja,' she saw one say, perhaps recognising the bamboo snake-scale over her salt-cotton, and something like ugly triumph blossomed in their faces.

Ossa was bristling and stiff-legged and Otek was wild. *Fight or die.*

A Quito danced in, holding his hatchet up high: too high. Ossa responded as he'd been trained – as Xessa had trained him – leaping for the lower belly to tear him open. Xessa began the command to recall him when a second warrior spun, graceful as a shaman in celebration, and brought his club down towards the dog's back.

Everything stopped. Xessa's breath, lips pursed. The blood in her veins, still. The spear in her hand, motionless.

And then Otek threw himself in the way and the club caved in his skull in a single blow.

Xessa could move again. She threw her spear, punching the warrior off his feet as Otek landed face down with a thud she felt all the way into her heart. She pulled out her knife and tore at the warriors crowding towards them, Ossa slow but snarling, his jet-black coat stiff with blood.

Someone shoved her and Xessa fell to her knees, heedless

of the pain and the blood and the danger. The knife fell from her hand and she pulled Otek into her arms.

The impact of falling bodies shivered through the stone and she ignored it. Someone grabbed her shoulder, but she shrugged it off. There were feet and legs in her periphery, encircling her. She ignored them. Otek's eyes weren't spirit-haunted. They weren't empty. They were cenotes of agony. Of love.

Xessa broke. Broke into pieces so sharp that breathing cut her, that thinking flayed her. She kissed his gaping mouth and Ossa, who had always sat so calmly in her father's lap, licked his unresponsive cheek.

And Otek died.

Someone fell over her. Xessa didn't care. Something shifted in her heart then, an ember of anger that nothing could quench. They had taken the friend of her heart. They had taken her husband and her father. *They had hurt her dog.*

Xessa laid Otek's body gently on the stone and picked up the knife again. She slashed it through the leg nearest her, and then again up into the groin of another and then hands, filthy fucking *slave hands*, were on her arms and there were ropes around Ossa's muzzle and a big fist in the scruff of his neck and more ropes around his paws and she wanted to tell them about his wounded shoulder, but they were hauling her back, away from Otek, away from Ossa, a sticky hand wrapped around her jaw and her head wrenched back and up until she had to stand, arms tight behind her.

A man faced her, older than her, forties, a little silver in his hair, lots of eagle feathers standing proud at the back of his head. He had a war club and wooden squares sewn onto his salt-cotton that reminded her of a Drowned's back and belly armour.

He pointed the club at Otek. 'Brave,' he said and then he

nodded and the hands let her go. Xessa tightened her fingers on the knife they hadn't taken from her and saw the warrior's face become still, ready, the rest of him relaxed. *Hate. Feel nothing but hate, eja.*

Nothing but hate.

Xessa rammed the blade at his throat. The point nicked skin before his empty hand shot out and punched her unconscious.

PILOS

He had them. While thousands were no doubt hiding in houses and buildings elsewhere, Pilos had most of the defenders contained in one huge ceremonial plaza.

Scores began to surrender, those civilians trapped with their offspring among the fighters giving up first. And once it began, it spread faster than fever. *Control the children; control the council.*

The warriors began to drop their weapons and plead for clemency and the Melody switched smoothly from fighting to capture, disarming and herding together Tokob and Yaloh, forcing them to give up their armour and their sandals. A barefoot, unarmoured, frightened captive was less likely to run.

There was still fierce fighting in the western part of the city, but the dogs had it under control. By dusk tonight – tomorrow night at the latest – the Sky City would be theirs. But what would be the cost to his beloved Melody? The

541

dead were everywhere, and everywhere eagle feathers stirred in hair, twisting on bodies that would never move again.

This might have felt like the decisive battle, and likely was, but there were thousands of sticks of jungle still to comb. The Melody would be desperately under-strength by the time Tokoban and Yalotlan were fully subdued.

Under-strength but with no enemies left to fight. The whole of Ixachipan will live beneath the song and all its people will know its glory.

If it still has any.

Pilos pushed away the thought and watched the eja. Her hands were tied before her and she sat on the stone with her head bowed. Her dog was trussed by her side and he wriggled occasionally, straining against his ropes, and then the woman put her bound hands on him and he was still. She made no other move, gave no indication she was aware of anyone around her. She was staring at the spot where the old man had died. Pilos had ordered the corpse to be dragged away. Warriors staring at their dead were angry warriors. Better to have them on their knees with nothing to look at but others like them – and the Melody standing tall on guard.

'Feather Calan.'

The woman was hoarse from shouting orders and rusty with dried blood, her salt-cotton stained. 'High Feather?'

'Get the prisoners moving. I want them into the jungle before dark. Send them along the most secure trails through Yalotlan – where our pyramid-builders are numerous and well guarded – and get them into Xentiban. They're to hold at the border with the heartland and wait for us; we should be no more than a few days behind. We'll enter Pechacan and the Singing City together.'

Calan swelled with pride at being in charge of such an operation. 'As the High Feather commands.'

Pilos found a smile for her and punched her shoulder. 'You fought well and commanded well, Feather. I am pleased.'

Some of Calan's fatigue vanished in the heat of her delight. 'You honour me,' she croaked.

'You honour yourself, Feather. Be about your business now. Under the song.'

Pilos squatted opposite the still, coiled presence of the eja. She didn't move, didn't meet his eyes, didn't so much as twitch. He was impressed.

'Can you hear me?' he asked. Nothing. He tapped the top of her head. More nothing. Was she the one Ilandeh had told him of? Pilos had never met a deaf person – the inability to hear was not tolerated in the Empire, where the song was everything. Such children were offered to the holy Setatmeh with respect. It was a kindness; no one should be without the glory of the song.

Pilos forced her face up to his; she looked down. If she didn't look at him, she wouldn't know he was speaking. He let go, frustrated, and then reached out and poked the dog's flank. The woman's bound hands came up and clubbed him in the chest. She threw herself off her knees and at him, so that he fell back onto his arse. The dog was snarling through its muzzle and the eja was growling and grunting. Pilos winded her with a punch to take her strength and then kicked at her wounded leg so she shrieked and fell away.

The dog was frantic and Pilos leant over her. 'Calm the dog or we kill it.'

She spat at him, but didn't have much saliva to make a proper job at it. Then she licked her lips and put her fingertips between the dog's eyes and it quietened.

'You understand me, then,' he said. 'You are one they call eja? A hunter and killer of the holy Setatmeh – the Drowned?'

A flicker of nameless emotion in her eyes but she didn't even shrug. 'You can write?' he asked. 'Or shall I bring someone over here to translate your hand-speech?'

Her eyes cut to his weapons and then the kneeling, captive warriors, back to him. All of them were bound, but that didn't seem to matter to her. This one wanted blood. 'Not a good idea,' he told her softly. 'The Singer wants to meet you and so we have to ensure your compliance. I will do that by killing your people, one by one, in slow and inventive ways, if you do anything to jeopardise my life or your own. But I will start with your dog.'

She definitely understood that, her breathing ragged. She shook her head.

'You'll be good?' A nod this time. 'Don't test me on this, Eja.'

Pilos stood up and strode to the nearest group of captives. 'I need a Toko who can translate for the eja.'

There was a long silence and then a man began to rise, but another, far older, stilled him and used his shoulder to push himself upright. 'I am Eja Elder Rix. Eja Xessa is young and inexperienced. I will answer all your questions if you let her sit with the rest of our people. She is of little use compared with me. My knowledge is greater.'

Pilos beckoned and when the old man approached, he stared him out. 'You are in no position to bargain with me,' he murmured and snapped his fingers. One of the dog warriors guarding the group stabbed the nearest Toko in the heart. Rix bellowed and struggled as the captives erupted, screams of fear mingling with threats. Pilos held him back, despite his wiry strength.

'But thank you – I need as many ejab as I can find; you have done me the favour of identifying yourself. Now come and translate for . . . Xessa, did you say? Come and translate for her, Elder. And know this now,' he added as Rix ceased his struggles and began instead to pray for the woman dying at their feet. 'Hush, and listen,' Pilos commanded, slapping his face. 'You will not lie or conspire with her; you will translate only what she says and you will not communicate with her yourself in any way. The moment you do, more will die, children included. You will watch her hands and tell me what she says. Nothing more.'

'Why are you doing this?' Rix demanded.

'You will understand when you are brought under the song and into glory,' Pilos said, the treacherous voice in his head wondering if he lied. He shook it away and checked Rix's bonds, then dragged him over to where Xessa sat, not listening to any more babbling protests.

The plaza was secure, but Pilos was still glad for the eagle honour guard that ringed him and the ejab, half facing in, half facing out. He'd fought too many wars and had too much respect for even defeated enemies to believe for one moment that he was safe. He snorted; there wasn't anywhere within or without the Empire that High Feather Pilos was safe. Still, no point in taking needless risks. He cut the woman's bonds and one of the eagles stood behind her with knife and hatchet. Another crouched over the dog.

'Why kill the holy Setatmeh?' he asked without preamble.

'The Drowned—' Rix began.

'I am not asking you,' Pilos said. 'I am asking her.'

'I am elder,' Rix tried.

'Second Flight Beyt,' Pilos said. 'Kill another. Rix here needs to understand I am a man of my word.' He glared at Rix, pinning him in place when the other man would have protested some more. 'I hope you understand now,' he murmured when another Toko was dying. There were still screams and shouts, but it settled much faster this time, the captives huddling low and avoiding eye contact, only quiet sobbing and muttered prayers and the stink of fear drifting from them. 'One word that is not related to the questions I ask this woman and one of your people dies.'

It was wasteful, but the Melody needed to establish dominance – it was the only way to safely transport large numbers of prisoners with minimal guards. Once the captives understood the cost of defiance, they'd fall into line. They always did, no matter how much they blustered beforehand about how they wouldn't surrender.

'Why do you kill the holy Setatmeh?' he asked Xessa again. He watched the incomprehensible gestures and expressions.

'Because they are predators who kill us,' Rix said in a monotone. 'They take young and old, shamans and farmers, warriors and artisans. They are monsters who must be destroyed.'

'They are gods,' Pilos said. Neither responded. 'Do you understand that?'

'I understand you believe that,' Rix translated. 'You revere them because you are afraid of them. That does not make them gods. They destroy the balance, taking more than they need, just as you do.' Rix paused and looked hard at Xessa. 'They kill for fun as you do. You are all cursed.'

Unease stroked cold fingers down Pilos's back. 'What do you know of curses?'

Xessa smiled and it had nothing of warmth in it. 'I know our lives are bound together,' Rix said as she signed. 'I know my life has been preserved so that I might end yours. I know I will laugh when I do so.'

Pilos didn't let himself react. He held his hands still, away from his charms and amulets, and he donned a mask of polite amusement. 'I look forward to the attempt,' he said lightly and saw only cool acknowledgement in the ejab face. 'She toys with your life as well as her own, Elder,' he said.

'She is young and she is angry,' Rix said. 'She thinks she still has some power here. Some sort of control.'

Pilos gnawed at his lip and then nodded. 'I see you, at least, understand better. You are to meet with the great Singer himself at the heart of our Empire,' he added abruptly, looking back at the woman. 'He will decide your fate. It is his will.'

'No. My death is at my will, not yours,' Rix said for her. 'You cannot prevent that, no matter what you do. I do not submit myself to your authority.'

'You already have,' Pilos said. By the song, she overflowed with misplaced confidence. If she displayed such in front of the Singer, the holy lord would likely tear her apart with his bare hands. *It's his favourite pastime these days, after all . . .*

But the High Feather found himself grinning nonetheless. 'You would make a fine warrior in the Melody were it not for your limitations.'

'I have no limitations,' Rix said and there was a hint of pride in his tone that matched Xessa's expression. Pilos waved away the comment. 'It is easy to die, High Feather Pilos, and when I do, Malel will accept my spirit for rebirth. But I will not die before I have tasted your life on my tongue.'

'And if I cut off your hands so you can neither fight nor die nor speak?' Pilos asked; her certainty pricked at him. 'How will you kill me then?'

'Why do you want me alive?' she asked instead.

Pilos had no wish to debate with her, but what was the harm? 'I don't, particularly, though every slave is valuable. The Singer wants to meet the frog-lickers. He wants to understand where such ignorance could come from. Everything I do is in his name, for the glory of the Empire. You will understand one day, though I grieve to think that you will never hear the majesty of the song. You will never truly understand what it is your people have been given.'

In the end it was Rix who broke. Perhaps Xessa took the threat against her dog's life too seriously; perhaps the elder didn't take the threat against his people seriously enough. Either way, Pilos had known it would happen eventually. The elder lunged for him, hands slamming into his chest and sending him over onto his back, then hooking into claws to take out his eyes. The eagle guarding Xessa wrapped his arm around her throat and hauled backwards, readying a knife to plunge into her stomach. The eagle guarding the woman's dog threw himself at the elder and knocked him off Pilos, then dropped his knee between the old man's shoulder blades and jammed him into the stone.

'Stop!' Pilos ordered with a wheeze. He got up and retrieved his club, studied Xessa for a long moment, and then slammed it into the knee that was swollen against her leggings. She screamed and curled into herself, hands clutching the limb. She wouldn't understand why he'd done it, but Rix did. Oh yes.

Pilos bent close to him. 'And now more of your people die,' he said with genuine regret. 'And you go to the Singer anyway.'

ILANDEH

Outskirts of Singing City, Pechacan, Empire of Songs
62nd day of the grand absence of the Great Star

Ilandeh had removed the scarlet feather and sewn it back into
the seam of her tunic beneath her arm, where it had lived for
a year while she played the part of a merchant in Tokoban.

She couldn't part with it. While it marked her as a half-
blood, proclaiming to all Pechaqueh that she was lower than
they, it was also a source of fierce pride. The macaws, and
the secretive Whispers within their ranks, gave her an identity and a purpose, a steady platform in the chaos of an
Empire dedicated to the glory of one half of her blood and
the denigration of the other. And yet Pilos had ordered her
to thread an eagle feather into her hair – not just any eagle
feather, but one from his own fan – and pretend instead to
be something she could never be. Something she should never
even think about being.

They would know she was a fraud the second she set
foot on the processional way. It would be obvious. Ilandeh
was no eagle. But none of her inner turmoil showed on

549

her smooth, sweat-beaded face as she ran the last few sticks to the city. She was a Whisper and deception was her greatest strength. Macaw in her heart, she would be an eagle in her skin.

Weeks back beneath the song as she raced to the capital at Pilos's bidding, and she still couldn't get used to it. As Listener Citla had said, it was . . . wrong. Poisoned. Broken. A clanging dissonance that rubbed against her nerve endings and put a sharpness into her mood. Like that before her blood came, but all the time.

She saw evidence of it everywhere. When she'd stopped to demand food and water she had witnessed slaves punished more harshly than they deserved. She saw the defiance in the eyes of many Pechaqueh whose duty was to provide food for warriors – defiance even though she wore an eagle feather. They resented the rations that were her due, as though she were demanding enough to feed a Talon. There were bodies on the path most days, merchants and farmers, slaves and half-bloods, even full Pechaqueh sometimes. The waterlogged fields and mud-slick trails were sullen, the sky angry, and the song sharp as obsidian.

Elaq had nearly gutted Ilandeh on sight when she arrived wearing an eagle feather, and only respect for Pilos had allowed her entry to the estate to explain herself.

'I swear by the song the idea was his, eagle,' Ilandeh said for the second time. 'A sun-year in the Sky City was easier than the last month with this in my hair, but the High Feather gave me my orders and my life is his to command.'

Elaq stalked back and forth and Ilandeh stood with her hands behind her back, trying not to yawn. She had run and walked every single day from Tokoban to here and she was exhausted. Now she couldn't sit until Elaq did, and the old eagle seemed determined to remind her that no matter what colour feather she wore, she'd never be his equal.

As if I need reminding of that.

'What do you know of the song?' he demanded in the end, sitting and gesturing. They were in a small room far less ornate than any she would expect the High Feather to occupy; she thought it might be Elaq's own.

'Listener Citla travelled from her post in Yalotlan to the Sky City to bring us news of its shattering, but she didn't know what had caused it. I have heard some gossip on my travels, but it is wild. I do not know the truth.'

'I doubt any of us do,' Elaq said. 'All I can say for sure is that the council has vanished, and so have the courtesans and the Chorus. Every one of them, as far as I can tell. I'm pretty sure the councillors are all dead, though not Enet of course. That would be too much to hope for.'

'But why? She is Great Octave. She is Chosen. What could she gain by killing the entire council?'

Elaq's mouth twisted. 'She's not the one that killed them, though, is she? Or it's not likely. As for what she gains? Autonomy. Control, now, before the Singer's ascension. You can hear as well as me – what state do you expect the holy lord is in?'

It was so close to heresy that Ilandeh just shook her head, her mouth open. Elaq's bitterness was unexpected, but shouldn't have been. Of course Pilos would employ only the most loyal, most dedicated of eagles to run his home and estate and businesses.

'Did Councillor Yana manage to discover anything that may be useful to my investigations? The High Feather wants to know what happened. He needs to know his enemies, and—'

'Enet is his enemy.'

'Honoured eagle, I am a Whisper. I go where full bloods cannot and I do what they will not. For Empire, song and the holy Setatmeh. For High Feather Pilos. If there is anything I need to know to protect him or the holy lord, I ask that you tell me.'

He examined her and then sighed. 'I have a guest here. We have been awaiting the High Feather's return, but . . . well, he's one of yours.'

Ilandeh raised an eyebrow. 'One of mine, high one?'

Elaq grimaced. 'Eagle will do . . . eagle,' he said, though he nearly choked on it. 'I had word some weeks ago there was a macaw wandering the Singing City. A macaw who was seen – you don't need to know by who – visiting the Great Octave's estate on several occasions. He couldn't very well refuse when I extended my hospitality and the High Feather's to him.'

Ilandeh's chest was tight, as if the wound she'd sustained in Tokoban had suddenly reopened. 'I suspect I know who you mean. And you think . . .'

'I think he had no need to be visiting the Great Octave once, let alone four times in a month.'

'You think he's a spy for Enet.' It wasn't a question, but Elaq nodded anyway. 'He was with me in Tokoban for a year. What would she gain from that?'

'You told the High Feather there is songstone in Tokoban. You will have relayed to him how best to bring the tribes under the song – that includes an estimate of how many days and how many deaths, yes?' Ilandeh nodded, feeling slightly sick. 'I imagine your fellow Whisper will have told Enet the same. Plus whatever information he gathered from the dogs leading the captives here – all the latest Melody gossip for a brave Whisper who'd been out of the Empire for a year.'

Ilandeh grimaced and felt anger begin to build in her gut. 'Meaning Enet knows approximately how long she has to act before the High Feather and the Melody return victorious, and how battered and reduced in number they might be when they do arrive.'

Elaq was pensive, but he nodded again. 'You are quick,' he said approvingly. 'I should have expected it if Pilos trusts you. What I don't know is what she intends to do with that knowledge – if whether the breaking of the song' – she saw him wince in remembrance – 'had anything to do with it. Her survival indicates it did, but then she wasn't seen in public for two weeks after it happened. At first, I thought she'd died too. You can't imagine how fucking upset I was when I heard she was reaching out to nobles to join the new council.'

Ilandeh stood and smoothed her kilt and then removed the eagle feather from her hair. 'Would you be so kind as to hold this for me?' she asked. He took it and nodded. She breathed deep. 'Show him in.'

A boy went to fetch him, and moments later Dakto entered; his gaze was clear and his features composed, like any good Whisper who'd been trained to give away nothing. It was so good to see him – and so bad.

'Second Flight Dakto, it has been some time. You look well – and have been missed.'

'Flight Ilandeh, you have seen some action since last we met, I'd say,' he replied with an easy casualness that was new and unpleasant. 'You have the look of battle still in your eye.' He stretched onto his toes. 'No feather, though. Working?'

Ilandeh shrugged. 'You, on the other hand, have neither seen battle nor appear to be working. I am curious as to why you decided to ignore your standing orders and escort captives here instead of waiting for me at the Neck.'

'It is a good thing I did, considering you shattered the illusion of our life in Tokoban. Did you think of that before going on a killing spree? Did you think what might happen to me?'

'And how would you know what I did in Tokoban?' she asked quietly and he flinched. 'But yes. We did, after all, stand and watch the sacrifice of the Coyote Aez to the false goddess Malel. Of course I wondered what would happen to you. And yet we are Whispers. It is what we do.'

'A year, Flight. A year we were there, living with them, eating and hunting with them. Laughing and watching the ejab kill your gods—'

'*Your* gods?' Elaq said sharply.

Ilandeh grabbed Dakto's wrist and twisted, shoving him down, tightening the lock on his arm. His free hand hit the mat and a yell burst from behind clenched teeth as she increased the pressure on the back of his elbow.

'The holy Setatmeh are gods to us all, Second Flight Dakto,' she grated. 'Would you forsake the Empire and all you have accomplished? All the glories of the song that grant you peace and wealth? Would you shame yourself and your Pechaqueh blood in front of an eagle?' She twisted a little more and spit strung down from Dakto's teeth as his mouth opened in pain. 'Would you lose this arm in defiance of all you have been given?'

Dakto groaned, a long drawn-out sound. 'No,' he gasped. 'No, Flight. Forgive me. Eagle Elaq, I beg you, forgive me. My words were ill conceived. Song and Empire and glory.' She let him go and he stood, clutching his shoulder, mouth a thin line of anger.

'You stand here in the High Feather's own house and you utter blasphemy? You dishonour yourself, Dakto. You dishonour the Melody and you dishonour your Pechaqueh heritage.' *You dishonour me,* she wanted to add, but didn't.

The Whisper laughed, a ragged, ugly sound. 'And what of my Xentib blood? Why am I not to honour that? Why is the father who raped my mother when she was a servant more important than she was? Why should I honour that animal or the animals who bred him? The song has lived inside them for generations, warping who they are, what they think. *If* they think. They're as docile and arrogant as a glutted Setat and are good for nothing other than beating slaves and clawing for status. I spit on all of them.'

'Including Enet? How long have your been her spy in the Melody?'

Dakto's answer was to rip a tiny, wicked glass blade from inside his tunic and swipe for her throat. Ilandeh ducked, but not fast enough: the obsidian opened her face beneath the eye and across the bridge of her nose.

She pulled a knife of her own and Dakto leapt, empty hand chopping down onto the wrist of her knife hand, swiping again with the little weapon. Ilandeh parried it and twisted sideways, inside his guard, to elbow him in the chest. Not hard – too close for that – but enough to elicit a grunt. She drove through her legs and stabbed, a gutting strike.

Dakto's hand slapped down on her wrist again, but not enough, too focused on his own overhead attack, which she deflected with her left forearm, pushing hand and blade up above her head and sinking down to free her knife hand. The point entered his thigh and she ripped it down towards the main artery.

Dakto was bigger than her, stronger by far, and a talented fighter. It was a shame he hadn't thought through the consequences of his insubordination or ever imagined fighting Ilandeh. How she'd move; how fast she was. How her fierce loyalty to the Melody would outweigh anything she'd ever felt for him. She couldn't get a lock on the arm above her head but the sudden spurting wetness over her right hand told her she didn't need it. She ripped the knife out of his leg, danced back and kicked him in the chest.

Dakto scored a final cut on the top of her shoulder as he staggered backwards and only then, it seemed, did he realise that he was dead. He looked down as his leg collapsed into the pool of scarlet soaking into the mats beneath his feet. He met her eyes, surprised, horrified, and weakly amused.

'Flight,' he said.

'Under the song,' Ilandeh panted and his features creased with disgust.

'No,' he grunted. 'May my ancestors guide me.' He toppled sideways and bled to death. No one moved until it was done.

'Well,' Elaq said, advancing with a medicine chest he'd procured from somewhere. 'Now I definitely understand why High Feather Pilos likes you. Though you'll be the one explaining to him the cost of purchasing the new mats. Let me see your face.'

Ilandeh stood still, breathing through the pain and the adrenaline, rubbing together fingers sticky with the blood of a man she'd once considered a friend. Occasionally more than a friend, and one of shared heritage. 'Forgive me for bringing disharmony to this house,' she said. 'If I had suspected, I never would have chosen him to live in the Sky City.'

'Sometimes the rotten blood proves the stronger,' Elaq said mildly.

Ilandeh winced as he poked at the cut. 'I accept full responsibility. And I will see to the purchase of the matting and anything else the household needs to re-establish order. Again, I apologise.'

Elaq laughed. He took a needle and thread from the chest and gestured her to sit on mats not saturated with blood. He knelt at her side. 'This is the house of the Empire's greatest warrior. We are not unused to combat here, although it usually takes place in the training yard and doesn't often end quite so terminally. Still, Dakto needed to die. His dangerous ideas had the possibility of infecting others.' He paused and eyed her for an uncomfortably long time; Ilandeh's Xentib blood yammered in her veins and leaked down her face.

'I do the Singer's will and the High Feather's,' she said in a low voice. 'If you would put me to the test, I will walk into the Blessed River with this blood running into the water and let the holy Setatmeh decide my worth. As the eagle commands.'

The first stitch went into her face and she hissed hurt before Elaq spoke again. 'Of all Pilos's macaws, yours is the loyalty I would not doubt.'

'Thank you, eagle. That means a lot,' she said, and submitted to the needle.

'Flight Ilandeh, if you're well, there's someone I'd like you to meet.'

The swelling across Ilandeh's face was monstrous and she could barely see out of her left eye. Sleep had been elusive, images of Dakto spinning across the insides of her eyelids in stuttering counterpoint to the song, which itself juddered and veered in unexpected, irregular bursts.

The visitor was huge with muscle in the shoulders and arms, narrow in the waist and powerful in the thigh. A made warrior. Anxiety tickled the back of Ilandeh's throat and she squinted at Elaq, who gave her a reassuring nod.

'This is Chorus Leader Nara. He arrived at dawn; he's been hiding since the . . . Well, I'll let him tell you.'

'Chorus Leader? Hiding?' Ilandeh asked, her voice nasal from the blood and swelling clogging her nostrils.

'What Eagle Elaq suspected is true, Eagle. The Singer massacred them all – every one of the Chorus, all the courtesans and children, the stewards, the councillors, the slaves. One giant . . . orgy of violence that broke something in his mind and broke the song. He killed everyone except Enet and me, held them helpless within the power of the song and slaughtered them.'

Ilandeh stared at him in silence, sickened. 'Why not you?' she managed in the end.

Nara lifted his tunic and pulled at bandages – the cut seamed him from below his left nipple all the way to the top of his right thigh. 'I was very nearly dead. Enet wasn't even there. Her slaves and guards tossed me out with the other corpses, too unnerved to check for life in any of us. Probably there were others who died in the gardens, taken by the holy Setatmeh. I managed to crawl away and find shelter, got myself stitched up. I've been hiding and recovering ever since. The High Feather has always put Empire above all else, so this seemed like the only place to come.'

'Setatmeh preserve us,' Ilandeh murmured. 'Is there anything we can do to save the Singer – from her, from himself? Where has this bloodlust come from?'

'From the Great Octave. That I can promise you is true. She has done this. She said we were wrong about the consequences of blooding the song.' He laughed, a harsh bark of noise. 'She might even have been right, if only she could have persuaded the holy lord to retain control of the desire. Instead, here we are.'

'But why?' Ilandeh asked, frustrated. 'Is she trying to kill us all? Does she want the Empire to crumble and Ixachipan to be bereft of the world spirit's song? *Why* is she doing this?'

'That I cannot tell you, Eagle,' Nara said softly. 'I expect no one but the Great Octave herself can answer that.'

Elaq was watching her, waiting. Judging. Ilandeh licked her lips. 'Chorus Leader, you mistake me,' she began and Nara narrowed his eyes in alarm. She held up her empty hands. 'I am loyal, unto death. But I am no eagle. I am a Whisper of the macaws. The High Feather himself decorated me as subterfuge, knowing it would make it easier for me to infiltrate the Singing City and learn Enet's plans. But you should not do me the honour of naming me eagle; it is not my place, nor my blood.'

The shock and dawning horror on Nara's face made Ilandeh's wound throb as blood rushed into her cheeks. Shame followed it. She looked away, swallowing thickly. These men were both full bloods; they outranked her militarily, socially, and in status. And here she sat among them wearing their pride in her hair.

'You knew about this?' Nara spluttered. Elaq shifted, uncomfortable, but nodded. 'I thought I could trust the High Feather. I thought I had found allies to help me save the Singer from the Great Octave. To allow such, such sacrilege towards our blood . . . I cannot believe it.'

'And yet it is done,' Elaq said. 'Just yesterday, Flight Ilandeh killed one of her Whisper subordinates who showed signs of treachery. She did it without hesitation. I believe her loyalty is without question.'

'Her loyalty, perhaps, but her blood is tainted. That weakness will show through eventually.'

Ilandeh breathed.

'And yet hers is the only face Enet doesn't know. I cannot go; none of the High Feather's household can. But Ilandeh can.'

'Could you put me into the source as a steward, even a slave?' she asked, steering the conversation to firmer ground.

Nara sucked his teeth and glanced at Elaq. 'You'd willingly become a slave for this cause?' he asked.

'I am a Whisper, Chorus Leader,' Ilandeh said calmly. 'I will be and can be whatever my High Feather and the Empire needs me to be.'

'And the slave marks?' Elaq pressed.

The flesh on Ilandeh's back crawled at the thought of that brand being pressed to her shoulders to mark her for eternity as property. She licked dry lips. 'When it is over, the brands will be amended to show I am a free woman. As I already am,' she added with a hint of fire. 'I am a Whisper. We know our duty.'

'Even an eagle would balk at such a task,' Nara admitted after an uncomfortable pause. 'And yet a half-blood will do what we fear to.'

Ilandeh kept a neutral expression with only a little effort.

'The High Feather has already marked her as an eagle. Another choice would be to make her one of the Chorus – their numbers are still too few and Enet is supplementing them with her own guards.'

'Impossible,' Nara snapped, outraged, and Ilandeh was tempted to agree with him. 'The Chorus are the highest of eagles, those with greatest honour, outstanding warriors and leaders. She is a macaw. Tainted!'

'My loyalty is without question, Chorus Leader,' Ilandeh grated and heard the danger in her voice at the repetition of her inferior blood. Elaq heard it too and shot her a warning glance. 'True Pechaqueh will not stoop to assassination or infiltration, and that is why the Whispers were developed, so please, with respect, allow me to fulfil my orders. I assure you that whatever feather I wear in my hair will not change who I am – only who I seem to be. Believe me, no one is more aware of my *taint* than I am.'

She rose to her feet before either of them could reply. 'Get me into the Singer's inner sanctum, high ones, and I beg you do it fast. I will not allow the holy lord to languish in pain or danger when my heart and my High Feather both command otherwise. Now, if you would excuse me, my wound pains me and I would rest.'

Ilandeh touched belly and throat and strode from the room before either could call her back or do more than stare in open-mouthed astonishment. She was shaking, but it had nothing to do with the hurt.

PILOS

Singing City, Pechacan, Empire of Songs
72nd day of the grand absence of the Great Star

The Street of Fighters and the Way of Prayer were not lined with cheering Pechaqueh, free, and slaves, as they had been the last time the Melody returned from war. Atu and his three Talons were still in the north, sweeping through the last sticks of jungle, but Pilos had not waited for them. Not with everything he knew. In the end, he was only ten days behind Ilandeh, but he didn't regret his decision to send her on ahead.

A few noble youngsters with their slave guards stood wide-eyed along the avenue. A few adults looked with interest; a few more looked away with what appeared to be fear as Pilos marched at the head of his warriors and the long, long lines of slaves. The song now sounded throughout most of Yalotlan and the architects and engineers were already mapping out sites in Tokoban for pyramids. Within a few moons, the song would be supreme.

The song.

It grated at Pilos's nerves, provoking rather than soothing, clawing instead of cradling. It scratched around inside his head and made him short-tempered, aggressive. And not just him. Bickering and insubordination was rife among the Melody – his exhausted, once-proud Melody, who had fought a brutal, merciless war to fulfil the Singer's will and had then had to march back here not in triumph but in haste to . . . what? Save the Singer? How exactly did Pilos plan on doing that? Would he besiege the source, perhaps, and demand Enet's head on a stick? Would he lock the Singer away to break him of this terrible addiction, now whispered about quite openly on the streets of the Singing City? Whispered about, but accepted, it seemed. Because although it was broken and although it was almost painful, the new song was in its way strong. It screeched of Pechaqueh supremacy; it wailed of the Empire's might; it whispered of vengeance and violence and greed. And, as ever, the Empire's citizens could do no more than respond.

Pilos didn't know what he could do other than be here, as his Singer's loyal follower and worshipful disciple. For the Empire that he loved above all else, he would do whatever was necessary. He just didn't know what that was. Yet.

Everyone who had been in the source that day was dead, Councillor Yana included. Enet had avoided the catastrophe, of course, and Pilos knew from the list of new councillors that at least a third of them were her creatures. He suspected the rest would be too – or soon enough. That the Singer had allowed this, allowed Enet to order and appoint his council for him, spoke volumes about how far he was lost in the grip of whatever blood-madness had him.

The mood of the Melody soured as they made their way to the great plaza before the palace, anticipating the joy and adulation of the city and receiving indifference instead.

Indifference despite the conquest of two tribes and hundreds of sticks of land through the worst Wet of the last Star cycle, despite the thousands of slaves, despite the confirmation of a rich vein of songstone within the Tokob hills that would see old pyramids restored and new ones built, the song heard in new jungle and new ears . . .

The sickened song.

Hello, Pilos.

Pilos halted mid-step, Feathers Detta and Calan stopping as well. Detta signalled for the Melody to pass them by and assemble in the plaza for the Singer or council to review them. 'High Feather?'

You're back. And you're thinking . . . so many things.

'Enet?' Pilos's voice was hoarse to his own ears. 'How?'

How can I reach you through the song? Think a little and I'm sure you'll work it out.

'Because you are Chosen,' he acknowledged. 'I had not expected you to master the Listening so soon, though. My congratulations.' Very carefully, he pictured himself as a boy at worship in front of the Singer's great pyramid, the sun-hot stone stinging his bare knees and the sun itself beating the back of his head. He reconstructed the awe and wonder he'd felt, the press of adult bodies around him smelling of spices and chillies and sweat, the murmur of thousands of voices raised in praise.

Amusement. *Very good, Pilos. And yet not good enough. Too little too late, some would say. I might say. Your thoughts have been very troubled of late, have they not? You worry for our great Singer, and that does you credit. But there is no need . . .* Her voice drifted on the jangling currents and was gone, then back . . . *need to see me.*

'The Melody is presenting itself before the palace as we speak. When I have discharged my duty to them I will request an audience with the great Singer as is required. Afterwards, if there is time before nightfall, I will visit your estate. I have a gift for you.'

He heard the beginnings of a question from Calan, quickly cut off, and frowned, slashing his hand through the air and straining to maintain the image in his mind that would be a wall between Enet and his deeper thoughts.

You grow bold.

'I follow protocol, Great Octave, nothing more.' Around him, his Feathers began a marching chant that praised the Singer and glorified the Empire and had the additional benefit of a strong beat that was easy to follow. Pilos held the picture of himself in his head and let the words and rhythm wash into his ears until soon, and yet not soon enough, the tickle in the back of his head that was Enet was gone.

He opened his eyes, gasping at the effort and the drain on his will and mind, and Detta gestured the Feathers to keep chanting as they hurried to the head of the Melody and there prostrated themselves before the palace of the Singer. The thousands of warriors who'd won the ballot to be present in the plaza picked up the chant, and soon enough it swelled, louder and louder, until it echoed back from the walls of the buildings edging the open space and even the songstone capping the great pyramid seemed to resonate with it, taking their words and their rhythm and adding harmonics and layers until the entire city seemed to shake with their victory.

A shiver ran through Pilos and he heard Calan's voice come strangled as the young Feather's emotions got the better of her.

People came to see them then, oh yes: scores and then hundreds and then thousands cramming into the buildings and along the narrow paths, climbing onto roofs and leaning out of windows on upper floors. Pilos felt a vague unease that the chant might be seen as a challenge to the Singer's authority, and it sharpened into panic when there was movement in the mouth of the entrance halfway up the pyramid's side, as the council and Chorus made their way out in response to the driving noise.

Not the council he was familiar with. Not the councillors he knew and had sparred with over points of law and order for the last three sun-years. Strangers, all. Enet's toys.

Pilos nearly swallowed his tongue when the Chorus began marching down the pyramid's steps to either side of the councillors: one of them was Ilandeh! Or was it? The woman had a cut across her face that made it hard to identify her, but there was something familiar about that loping gait.

'High Feather?' Calan asked under cover of the chant and he knew she'd seen her, too. So it was Ilandeh.

'I see her,' he muttered. 'A bold move, but a good one.' Detta scowled at that but held his tongue. Calan just shook her head. He put Ilandeh out of his mind, glad that a Whisper's identity was rarely even revealed within the Melody.

Pilos rose and raised both arms; the chant came to a halt and the plaza seemed to ring bright and clean with echoes. The song was cleaner too, as though it had responded to their voices and stabilised a little. Adjusting the cloak of feathers around his shoulders, Pilos stepped forward and inclined his head, touching belly and throat. 'Honoured council to the great Singer, devout children of the holy Setatmeh, you give the Melody great status in receiving us here. We return in victory, councillors, and with great spoils. Farmland. Slaves. Songstone. All Ixachipan is now part of the Empire of Songs and rich in its glory.'

He snapped his fingers and eight eagles advanced, a long line of captives bound between them. 'And, as the great

Singer himself ordered, I bring him ejab – the warriors dedicated to the slaughter of the holy Setatmeh themselves. There are more; these are but a sample. And I have brought this man, in addition, for the Great Octave's amusement.'

There was a murmur among the council and one stepped forward. 'Ejab, you say? The Great Octave and the Singer would like to meet these creatures. You are not needed.'

'I would be uncomfortable at the thought of such abominations being in the Singer's presence without adequate restraint,' Pilos cut in. 'Even with the exceptional Chorus guarding him, I fear for our holy lord. They are talented and vicious warriors.' Aside from Ilandeh, this Chorus wasn't exceptional, and every warrior staring up at them could see it. Pilos crushed that thought to dust.

The councillor was outmanoeuvred and knew it. He turned with an angry click of his tongue and stalked back up the steps. Pilos didn't look at Ilandeh as he and Feather Detta followed. He didn't dare.

They shuffled their way into the source, the respect they offered lessened by the scuffle of eagles forcing the captives to show humility. He let the councillors pull ahead of him, knowing they'd do more to announce his presence than he could and, as expected, every eye was fixed on him when he came into the council chamber. The elaborate hanging hiding the Singer was in place, though his bulk was visible as a dark smudge behind it. Next to him, and in full view, sat Enet. The long line of her neck was turned to the chamber and, although he had expected it, still the dark feather tattooed from her clavicle up the side of her throat made his arse clench.

But only one feather. She has not received the other that would mark her his successor. So far she is destined to ascend rather than be Singer. So far.

567

It was a relief, but not much of one.

Pilos pushed all such thoughts aside and indicated his eagles should bring the prisoners forward. 'Great Singer, holy lord, councillors.' A tiny pause. 'Great Octave. The Melody returns in triumph. The Yaloh and the Tokob have surrendered and now join us in the Empire. Pyramids advance across the jungle and the glory of the song will soon be ascendant. There is songstone in the hill called Malel, holy lord, great lodes and veins of it. As much songstone as we could possibly need.' He didn't look at Enet as he said this.

There were murmurs of appreciation, a scattering of applause.

'And you have brought slaves here, into the source?' Enet asked.

The hypocrisy curdled Pilos's stomach but he replied with serenity. 'I have brought ejab as the Singer commanded.'

'That one is no eja,' Enet said and pointed.

'No, Great Octave. I had thought the shaman might amuse you. He is my gift to you to celebrate being Chosen of the Singer.'

The peace-weaver Tayan had gone pale at the pronouncement, but Enet laughed. 'So generous, High Feather. I do hope you have the paperwork for him. For now, tell us more about these ejab.'

Pilos didn't need to fake his disgust or his rage. 'This is their elder, Rix. When it comes time to slaughter the holy Setatmeh, Tokob shamans like that one give them a mix of herbs and frog secretions that make them hear things that they believe to be spirits. These sounds cover the holy Setatmeh song. Over the years this spirit-magic, as they call it, affects them. They become . . . unreliable, skittish. Moon-mad, some might say.'

Enet startled and glanced at the Singer. 'How interesting.

We will need to know what this mixture of herbs is, of course. But an elder, you say? One of the leaders of his people and yet now, here, in ropes. How tragic.'

Rix had been composed all the way here, and Pilos admired and respected him for it. He did not think Enet would be the one to break this man's dignity with a few weak jibes.

'The woman at the end is deaf, so has no need for frog-licking. All ejab, in fact all Tokob, from what I can tell, have a type of hand-speech that they use to communicate without voice. That is how she talks.'

Enet's face twisted. 'Deaf? A pity she will never hear the glory of the song. It would be kinder to kill her.' Her eyes bored into his, daring him to contradict her on the song's beauty.

'Indeed.'

Enet leant behind the hanging and whispered. 'The Singer in his wisdom finds her amusing and wishes to see this hand-speech. The elder can be her translator.'

'As the holy lord commands.' Pilos gestured and his eagles unbound their wrists and then pressed knives against their spines. He wondered whether this signed conversation would end in violence as the last one had and he checked to make sure the rest were securely bound.

'Eja Xessa, tell the Singer and the council why you slaughter the holy Setatmeh.'

'You said she was deaf,' Enet snapped. 'Why bother talking to her?'

'Because she can read your lips,' Rix answered before Pilos could. Xessa's hands moved. 'And your hostility would be clear even if I could not. I am not a trained monkey; I am a person and I am a killer.' The corner of Rix's mouth twitched in appreciation.

Pilos grabbed Xessa's arm, not as amused as Rix. 'Don't antagonise your betters, slave,' he growled. 'Your good behaviour, and yours, elder, are all that stand between some of your people and death. You should know this by now.'

Xessa wrenched her arm free; then she hawked and spat phlegm onto the mats. Pilos slapped her face and she leapt for him, but Feather Detta wrestled her backwards and others restrained Rix as the council erupted with outrage and frightened squeaks. A few councillors scrambled away towards the gardens.

'She's an animal,' Enet said dismissively. 'Clearly all ejab are. The High Feather is wasting our time. Offer them all to the Setatmeh; it is only fitting that the gods take their lives.'

Rix waved, gaining Xessa's attention, and then translated Enet's words – or Pilos assumed he did. They could be saying anything.

'Watch her,' he murmured to Detta.

Xessa showed no emotion, but Pilos heard a faint snort of derision. She locked gazes with the Great Octave, her own flat and dead, and began to sign.

'Ejab kill the Drowned because they are killers who take our people, because they are unnatural creatures who kill for entertainment and not just food. They kill for fun, take our children and elderly and rip them apart, leave them scattered across the riverbank. The Drowned are the animals here, not Tokob.' Rix paused and sucked in a breath, signed a question and received an answer, and then continued, slower than before.

'You keep slaves and pride yourselves on being civilised; you think you are better than the rest of us. You are not. You are the slaves, slaves to these monsters you keep glutted with human flesh in the hope they won't lure you in next. You tell yourselves you are too good to be eaten by your gods, but the truth is your gods are too gorged and lazy to hunt you. Your lives are lived in terror masquerading as worship. While you cower and give them defenceless people to be consumed, we are true warriors who take the fight to the Drowned. We will not stop until every last one is dead. Every last Drowned and every last Pecha. Only then will there be peace.'

The silence was profound and Pilos knew Rix understood he was a dead man breathing. That they all were. Perhaps it had been their plan from the start, a way to avoid slavery and maybe take some of the council – even the Singer – with them. Pilos had an intense urge to offer them his respect, even as he acknowledged the utter waste of life that was to come.

'Words with as little thought behind them as the imitations of a parrot,' Enet scoffed, surprising him. 'Animals jerking against the ropes that bind them. Savages who bark of honour but gave up their homes, their gods, and their offspring to save their own skins. They can tell us nothing, teach us less. Have them killed and be done with it.'

'Is this the will of the Singer?' Pilos asked.

Enet's gaze was undiluted malice. 'Of course it is.' Pilos waited her out until, with a tiny huff of irritation, she leant behind the hanging and whispered a question.

It was Xessa who moved first, as soon as Enet looked away, Pilos was sure of it, but it was Rix who took the punishment on himself. The woman's foot lifted, her face twisting with rage, and Rix shoved her hard into Pilos and they both went down in a sprawl. The eja elder screamed a war cry and went for Enet, leaping through the kneeling councillors who shrieked and scattered, hampering the Chorus and Detta. Rix was within a stride of the Great Octave when Ilandeh leapt at him from where she'd been concealed from any Toko who might recognise her. The elder tore down the hanging as he was borne to the ground.

571

Pilos fought his way clear of Xessa and planted his sandal between her shoulder blades, forcing her into the mats where she thrashed, roaring. The other Tokob, still roped, were struggling with the Chorus and the eagles and the source descended into chaos.

Pilos paid it no attention. He stared at Enet and the Singer. He stared at the monster crouched at the heart of all he held dear. 'Sweet Setatmeh, what have you done?' he murmured.

Hulking and huge, the Singer was bloated and puffy in the face and belly, but not, he thought, with food or beer. His limbs had grown thin and Pilos had never seen skin so pale. Hair that had once been lustrous and waist-length had thinned until it hung in tufts from his scalp. He was no longer a man. His eyes were black and empty and his mouth worked constantly, chewing on air.

If not for the movement of his jaw, Pilos might have thought he was already dead and had been propped up in order to deceive the council. Instead of prostrating himself as he should, he stood and stared, grinding the eja into the mats, pressing down with the force of his rage and the weight of his disgust. His spirit quailed within him.

Rix had recoiled when he first saw the Singer, but now he struggled again in Ilandeh's grip, thrashing. Detta lent his strength to the Whisper's and they wrestled him backwards. 'We are the first children,' Rix was screaming, 'born from Malel's womb at the very heart of creation. What you see as surrender we know is patience. You'll fall, all of you, and that fucking monster there, too. We—'

Ilandeh put him in a lock, choking him, and Xessa made a noise of recognition and began to thrash harder. A broken whistle shuddered from her lungs as she tried to attract attention and Pilos dropped his knee into her back. If anyone else recognised Ilandeh, if they denounced her as the spy in the Sky City, Enet would have all the justification she needed to kill her, him, and probably the whole of the Melody's high command.

Detta clubbed Rix in the face and, as the man sagged, took control of him from Ilandeh. With a brief nod, she stepped back and then vanished into the garden.

'Great Singer? Shall I take the ejab to the offering pool?' Pilos asked, trying to keep any tension other than concern for the Singer from his voice. He considered letting Xessa get up, letting her tear Enet apart for him, but he couldn't risk it – she was more likely to go for the Singer, and, no matter what had happened, what he had become, Pilos could not allow that to happen.

'Great Singer?' Pilos asked again as he wrenched Xessa's arms behind her back. He kept his face averted from his lord. *Lord of the Underworld,* a small, hysterical voice supplied. He quashed it with savage speed.

'No,' the Singer rumbled. 'Leave them all with me and get out.'

Pilos went cold, both at the proclamation and the Singer's voice. Where were those rich harmonics that fluttered through his words, that bent the song to his will? Why did he sound so weary and yet so, so hungry?

'Holy lord?' he managed. 'The danger—'

'*I will deal with this.*' And now there were harmonics and more. The song reeled and blared out of control, rising to a pitch that set Pilos's teeth on edge and could not be denied. All the stability the Melody's chant had provided it was gone in a heartbeat. Everyone standing, slave or eagle, fell to their knees.

'All of you out, now,' Enet said. 'The holy lord will see the Tokob are punished according to their crimes and the Chorus will ensure his safety here in the source.'

'You cannot mean this, Great Octave,' Pilos tried, desperate. 'Enet, please.'

Enet's face was blank, as though she was staring at an insect. 'You have brought violence into the holy lord's presence and allowed unrestrained god-killers within steps of his person and the holy Setatmeh who swim in the offering pool. You have placed his life in danger with your reckless actions. You are hereby stripped of your status as High Feather and as Spear of the Singer. You are ejected from this council and the Singer's presence. Yet the holy lord is merciful, and so you may keep the deaf god-killer to punish yourself. Now leave.'

Pilos gaped for less than a heartbeat, and then he hauled Xessa to her feet and threw her into the arms of one of his eagles. 'Shut her up. Get her out of here.'

'High Feather Pilos, Great Octave,' the Toko peace-weaver began. 'Please, my people are—' An eagle uncoiled a short whip and lashed him across the shoulders. He fell, howling, and Pilos saw how the Singer twitched – not at the sound, but at the line of blood on Tayan's back.

'Stop!' he shouted. 'No violence in the source.' The eagle flushed and stepped quickly away. Pilos stared from Enet to the yelling Rix, Detta handing him off to another Chorus warrior now, then to the Singer himself. No one contradicted Enet's proclamation – not even Xac.

Pilos took a deep breath and commended his spirit to the song. 'My fate is irrelevant, but the holy lord must not sully his hands with blood. It is our sacred, eternal law. Great Singer, please do not do this. Allow us to execute them on your behalf, or offer them to the holy Setatmeh. Please.'

'You have no voice in this council, eagle warrior,' Enet said with a lift of her chin. 'And be grateful you are still that. The Singer is divine; he knows more than you will ever comprehend and everything he does is sacred. Now *get out.*'

'Holy lord, you must not blood the song,' Pilos tried in a final, desperate attempt. 'Not again. It is killing you!'

'*I said out, or join the Tokob in their punishment.*'

Pilos matched wills with Enet for a moment that lasted an eternity and roasted the air between them. Then more Chorus warriors appeared and began advancing on the former High Feather and his eagles. The song soared higher into a roaring imperative that battered at him, rejecting him and his proposals. That screamed with bloodlust and madness. The council were already scattering, almost running from the source after only the briefest of obeisances. The peace-weaver was kneeling on the mats, staring in utter horror at the Singer. Pilos thought he might be crying.

'Under the song,' Pilos said, marvelling at the steadiness of his voice. 'Chorus, see that the Singer is protected at all times. From *all* threats.' He bowed and left, Detta and his eagles forming up behind him. Protecting his back.

You have taken everything from me, Enet, but it is as nothing compared with what you have done to him. You have made him little more than your drooling puppet.

And I am going to kill you for it.

TAYAN

The source, Singing City, Pechacan, Empire of Songs
72nd day of the grand absence of the Great Star

The Empire of Songs was ruled by a monster. It was all Tayan could think as he knelt amid the swirl of men and women fighting and screaming. The rope they were all tied to jerked him this way and that as they struggled, but he stayed on his knees, the fiery bite from the lash set deep in the muscles of his back.

He stared at the thing that had been revealed when Rix tore down the curtain and tried to convince himself it was a person. Next to it sat Enet, watching the Chorus quell the prisoners with a curl to her lip that was part disgust and part . . . concern, though she hadn't seemed particularly worried when she'd sent Pilos and his warriors away. With Xessa.

Tayan sobbed. He hadn't been able to tear his attention from the Singer until it was too late, until the friend of his heart was gone and he hadn't even signed that he loved her.

Around him, the last few ejab that were still fighting were clubbed onto their knees and three Chorus warriors now

576

held Elder Rix. They forced him onto the mats, hauling on the collar to cut off his breath, the easier to tie his hands behind him. It had been a good plan, the only plan they had, and it had failed. Everyone there knew what would happen next and as stillness fell in the room, the Tokob began muttering prayers.

Tayan took a deep breath and added his voice to theirs. He was shaman; he would call the ancestors to witness and beg Malel to take them to the spiral path to rebirth.

'Holy lord, these insects are beneath you. Do not tax your strength on them. I will bring you fine gifts tomorrow, great Singer. Tomorrow is the appointed day. Tomorrow. Shut them up,' Enet hissed and the warriors hit Tayan and the ejab some more. The prayers faltered, stuttered, stopped.

Death was coming, one way or another, and the shaman wanted nothing more than to delay its arrival for a few heartbeats more.

'I know how this works,' he blurted, too loud. 'The flesh-traders took our names, homes, and families when we crossed into Pechacan. My husband was captured; he will have been sent to the Melody. He will work – as I will work – so that we may be free. His name is Lilla, he is a Fang warrior of the Sky City. He is tall and broad and he has a tattoo of—'

Enet waved a hand, though she seemed a little relieved. 'Yes, yes. I remembered the husband you spoke of at such boring length the last time you were here, little peace-weaver, so I did keep an eye on the slave records as they came in. So far we have captured seven men named Lilla from Tokoban, and two from the Sky City' – Tayan gasped – 'but neither claimed you as kin when they swore their life and spirit to the Melody.'

Enet's smile was as beautiful as a death rite. She took a small clay jar from a table and mixed the contents with a cup of water and drank it down. A tiny grimace twisted her lovely mouth. 'No one claimed you, peace-weaver. Not a husband, not a friend, not a family member. But I promised you we would meet again, didn't I? And now here you are. Mine, even if you were gifted me by a traitor.'

'No,' Tayan breathed. And then again, louder: 'No. No, that's not true. I don't believe you. Lilla wouldn't do that – he'd never abandon me, he wouldn't. It's a mistake. *You've made a mistake.*'

The song lurched crazily and drool ran from the Singer's mouth. He jerked, as if Tayan's shout had awoken him – or, as with some magics, the shock had jolted his spirit's connection to his flesh. The Singer pressed a trembling hand to his chest. 'I need one,' he rumbled. 'I need one now.'

'Not today, holy lord, Xac my love. Tomorrow is the appointed day.' There was a sliver of desperation in Enet's voice, a hint of pleading. She was trying to regulate the Singer's consumption of whatever medicine he was taking, but why? It was . . . He looked spirit-haunted.

Blood thumping in his head, Tayan eased himself to his feet and raised his bound palms in a gesture of peace. The rope connecting him to the other slaves tightened, forcing the next in line to half-stand, almost choking. Tayan ignored her. 'You are sick, great Singer, I can see it. I have travelled many sticks to meet you.' A warrior grabbed him; he ignored them.

'If you would tell me of your illness, then I can cure it. I'm sure of it. I am a shaman and a skilled healer. I will cure your body, great Singer, and then you will fix the song.'

'How dare you,' Enet began, scrambling to her feet. 'Chorus, take him to the offering pool. I will not have—'

'You can fix me?' the Singer asked, his voice childlike. Enet spun to face him, gaping.

'I can, holy lord,' Tayan promised, faint with adrenaline at a ruse that couldn't possibly work.

'I only feel well when I have them, you see,' the Singer continued. 'And I need them, all the time. More and more of them.'

'More and more of what, Singer?' Tayan asked gently, as though he was trying to tame a wild dog.

'People. I need people.'

'I am sure the Empire's people love you,' Tayan began; then he knelt as the Singer stood and shambled towards him. He reached the eja next to Tayan and fell to the mats in front of her. Tayan put his hand on the Singer's clammy shoulder and Enet choked on outrage. The warrior behind him grabbed a fistful of his hair and pressed something sharp to the side of his neck.

The Singer blinked at Tayan. 'I need them all the time,' he repeated, and then he pulled a beautiful, pale-bladed knife from his belt and rammed it into the ejab torso, out and back in, again and again, his arm pumping up and down with sickening regularity. The warrior behind him fell back and Tayan scrambled away as far as the rope would let him. The song spun out of control, growing in power until it seemed the individual stones of the pyramid were in danger of vibrating apart. With the song came emotions, pouring through them all like a storm: need and desire and lust combining until Tayan shook with the force of it, until he wanted nothing more than to feel Enet or the Singer or both of them writhing beneath him.

There was blood everywhere and the Singer shoved his face into the gushing red font. His jaw moved, but he wasn't speaking. He was chewing his way into the woman's belly, enlarging the knife wounds, his sharp nails digging through cotton and flesh and muscle to soft, stinking innards, hot and pulsing. His skin burst with golden light.

Gasping with need, fists clenched against it, Tayan shuffled back towards him as the other ejab shuddered and hunched in place, overwhelmed with sensation and distant horror. The shaman groaned and then swallowed hard and knelt at the Singer's side in the blood, willing himself not to vomit at the warm sticky stench of it all, at the sight of the slobbering, chewing monstrosity. Willing himself not to lean forward and bury his face as the Singer was doing.

Tayan put his hands on the man's back, the shock of contact sending a thrill throbbing into his belly and balls that nearly undid him. The Singer sat back on his heels, red from nose to waist, panting.

'I can fix this,' Tayan lied. 'Wouldn't it be better if you didn't need . . . people? Because you have all this power, don't you, lord, but in this you are powerless. You are in its grip. I can break that grip. I will do anything for you.' *If you will take me in your arms.* He clenched his jaw, trapping the words behind his teeth.

The Singer's eyes were a strange, light amber colour and Tayan wanted to drown in them. He was foul and terrifying and quite, quite insane, and in the hurricane of desires moving through the room, Tayan put his hand on the Singer's cheek, leant in and kissed his bloody mouth.

'Yes,' the Singer whispered against his lips. 'Yes, I want that. I want – I need – my power back.' He put his hand in the neck of Tayan's tunic and twisted. 'Everyone out.'

The warrior cut the rope attaching Tayan to the rest of the prisoners and dragged them out. Enet spoke over the thud of hurrying feet. 'He lies, holy lord. He is a Tokob shaman. Tokob, great Singer. A god-killer.'

Tayan inhaled saliva and coughed, pulling away from the Singer's suddenly tightening grip. 'Not I, holy lord,' he said quickly. 'I am a shaman; I have never killed a holy Setat.'

Enet appeared in his periphery, vicious with triumph. 'No, you just tortured one instead. We know the reports. We know exactly who you are.'

'No! It was already captive. I did nothing to hurt it. I spoke to it, learnt from it and learnt about it—' He cut himself off. 'I didn't hurt it,' he repeated. 'I couldn't.'

'The Tokob kill our gods!' Enet repeated with desperate spite. 'You cannot trust him.'

'Why don't you want me to help the Singer?' Tayan's voice was low, and he didn't dare look at either of them, but even within his madness and depravity, the Singer heard. And understood. For good or ill, Tayan had cast the bones and now he had no choice other than to live out the fate they decreed. Perhaps he really could save the man. He didn't know. He didn't think Enet knew.

'Your holy kin, great Singer,' Enet hissed, not responding to his question but seeking to deflect it. 'This man tortured one of your kin. Who is to say he will not torture *you*?'

It wasn't clear whether the Singer had heard that, but Tayan had. He looked up sharply as something fell into place. 'Kin? How can the holy Setatmeh be kin?'

'Have you still not worked it out, little peace-weaver?' Enet demanded, suddenly sure of herself again. She knelt on the Singer's other side and caressed his shoulder. 'You want to know why the holy Setatmeh are gods. You should be asking who they were before they became gods. Before they *ascended*.'

She laughed at the expression on his face. 'Now do you see who it is you've just promised to cure?'

XESSA

The prison on Pilos's estate was small and Xessa was its only inhabitant. She didn't know why. She hadn't understood anything after their plan to kill the Singer had failed. All she knew was that she'd left and the others hadn't.

Toxte. Tayan. Lilla. Lutek. Tiamoko. Tika.

Her fathers, Kime and Otek.

Her dog, Ossa.

Toxte. Toxte. *Toxte.*

The names were a litany of pain, each one a wound that wouldn't stop bleeding. For most of them, she had no way of knowing if they were dead or slaves. She could promise them vengeance, but she already knew she couldn't keep that promise. She was a prisoner – a *thing*. If nothing else, the brands on her shoulders, which had cut their way through the tattoos there, were reminder enough.

And Ilandeh! Xessa ground her teeth together and thought

582

of all the ways she'd hurt the woman when next they met. That was one promise she was making, because it didn't bind the spirits of the dead to the flesh world until it was fulfilled. She'd kill Ilandeh, slowly and inventively. For Toxte, vanished in the dawn and the battle. For Tayan and Lilla, captives. For the betrayal of the Sky City and the deaths of thousands. Ilandeh was responsible for it all and Ilandeh would pay in ways she couldn't even imagine. Ways Xessa couldn't yet imagine.

The fantasy was all that kept her going through the days of her incarceration. The slaves or servants or whatever they were who brought her food and took away her waste had quickly learnt to put their hands over their mouths when they spoke. Only the slanting light through the cracks in the heavy wood door told the passage of days. She'd spent the first three lying still, refusing food and waiting for her dead to come and prise her loose from her skin. She picked at the threads stitching her spirit to her flesh, seeking death, drumming the death rite with her hands on the packed dirt floor. She didn't die.

On the fourth she woke crying, reaching for the soft warmth of Ossa and not finding him. They'd tied him like a turkey for slaughter and that's probably what had happened; she didn't know. She hadn't seen a single dog since the city fell and his absence was a missing limb. Half her heart. In the deep, animal corner of Xessa's spirit, it hurt more than losing her home, her people, or her liberty.

On the fifth day she woke from a dream of Toxte. He was angry with her and she couldn't bear it, couldn't bear to think of his spirit on the spiral path raging at her. She gave in to him and to living and began to eat, to move around the small empty room where she was kept, practising her fighting forms until her skin beaded with sweat and she stank. More days passed and she became used to her own smell and that of the pail where she pissed and shitted.

Xessa whistled and clicked commands and orders, seeing how much it annoyed the guards and slaves who passed the prison. When they told her to stop, she pretended she couldn't understand them, gesturing at her ears and shrugging. Their frustration was delicious – and dangerous. She had the broken nose to prove it. She drummed more death rhythms on the wall to farewell those who had returned to Malel and she danced the sacred steps in the confined space.

Eventually, she decided to live – not just gave in to it. Chose it. No one would take Xessa's spirit but the goddess and not even she could break it. Not now, not ever.

The door opened in the middle of the eleventh day when Xessa was lying on the dirt floor, staring up at the dust dancing in the cracks of sunlight. The door never opened in the middle of the day and so she scrambled to her feet, the sudden movement after so much stillness sending a rush of blood to her head. She blinked and backed away, falling into a fighting crouch.

The man in charge of the estate, whose name she thought was Lock, entered. He was armed but held his hands away from his weapons.

'You are to be bathed and dressed in fresh clothes. High Feather Pilos wishes to see you. You will not be harmed if you comply. Do you understand me?'

She debated the wisdom of pretending she didn't, then shrugged and nodded.

'Can you write?' Lock asked. Another nod. 'Good.'

Xessa told him he was a monkey's mangy, shitting arse and infested with maggots and he watched her hands with blank incomprehension. 'Finished?' He didn't wait for an answer. Xessa followed almost at a run and was through the door before she noticed the four warriors guarding it and him. Two reached out and slowed her rush as the other pair slid behind, boxing her in.

The shove in the back was part of the universal language and she stalked between her captors, noting their wrinkled noses at her stench. Their discomfort made her feel disproportionately better, but that lasted only until she glanced down to her right and Ossa wasn't there.

Xessa balked at the entrance to a small building set in the gardens. She could smell the cold dankness of water. Lock faced her. 'You go in and wash,' he said, miming. He held his nose and pointed at her.

She shook her head. 'Weapon. For Drowned,' she signed. Lock shrugged. She made stabbing motions and the warriors guarding her tensed. She pointed at the water and repeated the gesture.

Lock scowled. 'There are no holy Setatmeh in the bath. Not that we'd give you a weapon if there were. You are not in danger.' Xessa shook her head again; there was no way she was going in there unarmed. 'It's safe,' he added, but she backed up against the warriors, turned and tried to push her way free.

They grabbed her by the arms and wrestled her through the low door. The room was small and cool, the pool malevolent in its centre and surrounded by benches holding cloths and soap. Lock reached the edge, grabbed Xessa beneath her arm as the others released her and twisted his hips and somehow she was sailing upside down through the air. She landed arse-first in the water hard enough to sink to the bottom.

Bright, all-consuming terror filled her and Xessa came up out of the pool faster than a jaguar's pounce and flailed for the edge, screaming. One of the warriors began to laugh and

Lock was saying something but she couldn't see through the mass of wet hair. She reached the edge and pulled herself up; the laughing warrior shoved her back with his foot and she sank her teeth into his calf until he wrenched away, kicking. And then Lock was in the water with her, wrestling her against his chest, pinning her there with her arms trapped against him. In the water.

In the water.

Xessa threw up on his shoulder and he grimaced, bent his knees and brought them both down until they were neck-deep to wash it off. She was sobbing, rigid with a fear stronger than any she'd ever felt. They were going to hold her here until a Drowned came and ate her. She had no weapon. *She had no weapon.*

Lock's chest rumbled as he spoke to her. He held her still, one hand caressing the back of her head, arms tight to hold her but the rest of him relaxed as if there was nothing to be scared of. Xessa counted his heartbeats against her cheek, slow and strong, not racing with fear. When she reached thirty and nothing had torn her apart she leant back slightly.

Lock looked down at her, let go of her skull and raised a palmful of water to his mouth. He sipped and pulled a face. 'Salt. Do you understand? Salt water.'

She licked the water from her upper lip to confirm that he spoke the truth. The Drowned thrived in fresh water but sickened in any that was poisoned with salt or rot or wood ashes. There could be no Drowned in this pool, or at least not one that could survive for long.

Xessa shuddered, head to toe, but she nodded and Lock let her go and hoisted himself out of the pool. She stood in the water, alone and small and, despite his words, still afraid. Shaking.

'Bathe and put on those clothes there. Be fast and do not

try to escape. There is no way out. And there is nothing to fear if you obey.' He picked up a spare kilt from a shelf and gestured to the warriors to leave the bathhouse. He changed into the dry kilt and then squeezed water from his tunic and hair. He wandered out.

How readily he'd tried to soothe her, though he wore the feather of a full-blood Pecha that made her his enemy and killer of his gods. She didn't understand, but she pulled herself out of the bath, shuddering, and checked the room – no other exits, nothing lurking in the shadows or beneath the benches. The clothes he'd indicated were cut in the Pecha style but plain, woven from undyed maguey. Slave clothes.

Xessa ripped off her leggings and shirt and knelt, dipping a cloth into the water and scrubbing her skin. Too many memories – Ossa dragging her away from the bank, venom in them both; Kime in the Swift Water surrounded by Drowned, screaming, his fingers bitten off; Toxte in the womb, fixing the Drowned's leg; Tayan, calling it a 'holy Setat'.

As the dirt and old sweat was scrubbed away, she revealed the dark, jagged, unlovely lines on her flesh. Slave brands and Drowned scars and knife scars, the marks of both – of all – her enemies. Eternal reminders imprinted into her flesh that she was not safe and she was not loved. But tied around her neck, filthy and faded, was her marriage cord.

There was a small jug next to the soap and she used it to wash her hair, hissing as she dragged the wooden comb through tangles of blood and dust and sweat and grime.

Lock had said be fast, but now that the fear was gone, or at least banked down, Xessa took her time. Like the whistles, the pretended incomprehension, the drumming, this too was a test to see what she could get away with, and what they would punish. Lock came back and beckoned, but there was no real anger in his face at the delay. He was a strange one, much like Pilos himself, who had such a tight grip on his anger she wasn't sure he even felt the emotion.

Xessa slipped into the new clothes – they'd even provided a length of material as a breast binding – ignored the sandals and approached the exit, clapping her hands so she didn't surprise a warrior and take a spear in the gut.

Lock examined her, frowned at her bare feet, shrugged and beckoned, and the small procession returned through the gardens, past the prison to the large house with two floors and a small pyramid perched at the centre of its roof. The High Feather's house. The jaguar's den.

They sat her at a low table opposite Pilos. A warrior stood either side of her and Lock sat next to his master. It was a lot of protection between Pilos and one little, unarmed, hopeless eja. It made Xessa feel better. Stronger. More in control. Paper and charcoal sat before her on the table, and one of the warriors twitched as she reached for it. She'd need to move slowly to avoid getting stabbed by mistake.

'Where are my people?' she wrote and held it up.

'High Feather Pilos is not here to answer your questions,' Lock began. 'You answer his. You are his property – and you are lucky to be so. After your actions in the source—'

'Enough, Elaq,' Pilos said, 'and I am just an eagle these days. High Feather no longer. And what happened in the source is of no concern to the eja.'

'It is of great concern,' she wrote. 'You are my enemies and you left my kin there to die.'

'Stop,' Lock – Elaq – said, waving his hands. 'Your behaviour in the source has stripped the High Fe— has stripped Eagle Pilos of his status and his roles within both the Melody and the government of the Empire. You will help him reclaim some of that lost status by being one of the attractions in his fighting pit. You will entertain the nobility of the Singing City.'

Xessa shook her head.

'You will do this,' Elaq said, his face twisting with anger. The change was sudden after his actions in the bathing room, as if he regretted being gentle with her. Pilos was calm, watching her.

Xessa shook her head and then wrote: 'I am eja. I fight Drowned. I kill Drowned. Not people.'

'You fought and killed warriors of the Melody,' Pilos said. 'Badly, it is true, but still. Now you will fight for my pleasure and that of the nobles and perhaps even the Singer himself in time.'

Xessa slashed her finger in front of her face in vehement refusal.

'Kill some of her people, High Feather. Every time she refuses to fight, kill one,' Elaq said, facing her so she was sure to understand. A wave of heat washed through Xessa and she twitched; hands clamped down on her shoulders, holding her still.

'It is wasteful,' Pilos said, 'but I see no other option. Bring one in.'

Warriors wrestled a figure in through an archway. Tiamoko. Brave, beautiful Tiamoko, more boy than man despite the death he wore in his eyes, who had fought with such courage and honour. Who had helped Lutek bring Tayan back to her, however briefly. They forced him to his knees at the end of the table. He was battered and exhausted, filthy. The brightness of those eyes was gone, their calm, patient lethality dulled. The health had faded from beneath his skin, but he knew her. And he knew she held his life in her hands.

The warriors holding him forced one of his arms flat on

the table and one of them raised a hatchet, watching Pilos for the order.

Pilos watched her. 'We will start with his hands.'

Tiamoko watched her. The warriors restraining her watched her; she could feel it. Xessa wanted to scream. She wanted to snatch up a weapon and kill them all, rail against her captivity and that of her people. She wanted to make them see they were wrong, that their lives, their city, their whole Empire was a lie, a deceit built on suffering.

She did none of those things, because she understood some of how they'd become so powerful. They threatened the people you loved and then they stripped away what made you who you were. They turned you into an animal and then slowly they built you back up in their own image, until their beliefs were yours. And one day, if you were very obedient and very lucky, they'd free you and the first thing you'd do would be to buy slaves of your own. And so it went, rolling endlessly like the cycle of the seasons, like the rise and fall of the Great Star at morning and the Great Star at evening. Until you wanted to be Pecha by name the way you were in your heart and you abandoned the traditions of your people and came to hate the hiss of blood in your veins.

They were all waiting for her answer. Xessa raised her hands, and then stopped, picking up the charcoal instead. 'I will fight,' she wrote shakily, and the words on the paper writhed and mocked her, taking on a malevolent life that wormed inside her and made her their slave. Their property. Their entertainment. 'And I wish to claim my family.'

Elaq spoke to the warriors and they dragged Tiamoko away before either Toko could sign anything. Tears blurred Xessa's vision and her breathing was ragged.

'Write their names and descriptions down,' Elaq told her

and she did so. Toxte. Tayan. Lilla. Tiamoko. Lutek. At the bottom, she added a question: *What happened to my dog?*

Elaq took the paper and read it, nodded. He pointed something out to Pilos, who shook his head and gestured. Xessa was lifted to her feet. Elaq led them out of the room and through cool corridors painted with lush murals and back out into the heat of the gardens and along the path to the high gate.

They left the estate, merging into the crowds on a wide limestone road and then veering off between tall buildings that grew shorter and shabbier the further they walked. Xessa craned her neck to take in the sights, memorising their route. Three or four sticks, about an hour's walk, and the smells of war began to tickle at her nostrils – blood, sweat, shit, fear. The eja faltered and the warriors closed in around her, hustling her along.

They reached a tall, unplastered building with no windows and the smell of battle became stronger, overpowering. Xessa gagged and put her hand over her nose. Around and down they moved: a slope carved into the earth that led beneath the building and into gloom. A bamboo gate across the passageway, the tops of the poles sharpened into spear tips to prevent anyone climbing in – or out.

'Special one from the High Feather – Eagle Pilos – himself,' Elaq said and Xessa noted how he positioned himself so she could see his mouth. 'She's a fighter but to be trained in Melody style. Some important people want to watch her, so make sure she's good. And she's deaf.'

The scarred woman he was talking to cocked her head at Xessa. 'Can't fight when you're deaf.'

'This one can,' Elaq said. 'As long as she can see your lips, she understands. Won't respond to anything else.' The woman turned away and fiddled with the gate – it swung back and she stepped through, beckoning. Xessa looked at Elaq. 'Pay attention. Fight well. Make your owner proud.'

Xessa wanted to spit in his face. She wanted to tear it off with her teeth and fingernails. Instead she carved her own into a mask and put her back to him, and strode through the gate into darkness. They wanted to take her and sharpen her and hone her until she could kill all she came across. Until she was lethal and unsurpassed.

In the gloom, Xessa smiled like a lord of the Underworld. Like a fucking Drowned, all teeth and malice and hunger. They wanted to make her a weapon? Then that's exactly what she'd become.

EPILOGUE

The source, Singing City, Pechacan, Empire of Songs

I am the Great Octave, Chosen of Xac. I am the future and the future song. I am the Empire that will be.

I will be. The song, the Singer, the hope of all faithful. Through me will the world spirit awaken. Through me will Ixachipan be free of strife and hunger and disease. Through me will power and wealth and beauty be manifest.

I am the glory of the Pechaqueh restored. I am the glory of power reborn.

I am Enet and I am – I will be – the song.

And my song is good.

ACKNOWLEDGMENTS

So, 2020, eh? Bit of a year. And with that in mind, first and deepest heartfelt thanks go to the medical community the world over, and to all those who work behind the scenes to co-ordinate the global and governmental responses to the pandemic.

Songs of the Drowned is a project that started life as a rambling, slightly tipsy pitch to my husband in a quiet little pub in London in 2018. His enthusiastic response gave me the courage to work up a proper, this time sober, pitch to send off to my agent, and from there, well, it snowballed.

As always, I tried to jam in as many of my favourite things as possible, and as always, my agent, beta readers and editors forced me to relax my death grip and cut out the bits that didn't serve the story. So, thanks, in turn, to Harry Illingworth of DHH Literary Agency, for the endless encouragement and insightful commentary; to Mike Brooks and Stewart Hotston for extraordinary beta reading and to Sam Hawke, who helped me rework the opening chapters (also, they all write awesome books you should definitely read); and to Jack Renninson and Natasha Bardon at HarperVoyager for taking on another series and doing such an amazing job at teasing out what exactly I was trying to say with this book.

Thanks to Richenda Todd, copy editor extraordinaire, who deserves all the cake for doing such an incredible job under very tight time constraints and saving me from terrible calendrical errors on three separate occasions – including pointing out that I'd miscalculated a historical reference by more than 1,200 years . . .

And thanks to Stephen Mulcahey and Nicolette Caven for the beautiful and evocative cover and map, which really tie the book together and bring it to life.

Thanks also to all the staff and alumni at Writing the Other; you're doing great work and helping to deliver authentic and realistic diverse worlds and characters through your lectures and courses.

Special thanks to David Bowles – lecturer, translator, author and historian – who helped me ground my fantasy world in reality and add depth and truth to my characters. It was a privilege to work with and learn from you.

As always, to the Five – JP, Kareem, Laura, Mike, Sadir – for just being awesome and always supportive, even if we can't meet up right now. And to the rogues' gallery of everyone I've played RPGs with this year – you've been a source of endless fun and supreme frustration. My DM skills are not the best, but, to be fair, look who it is I'm working with. I love you all.

And to the authors of the Bunker – it's a privilege to know you and share the worries and weirdnesses of this very peculiar industry with you. A special thankyou to the ANZ contingent, who first brought up the subject of writing your id, which has had a profound effect on how I approach my work now. Honestly, it's a game-changer and I can't thank you enough.

And, of course, my family and friends, for your endless love and support, and Mark, for giving me space and time when I need it, and distractions when I need those. There's no way I'd be able to do this without you. I'm the luckiest idiot ever. I love you.

Black Lives Matter.